A ROSE BY ANY OTHER NAME...
IS AN ALIEN

A yellow rose floated in the high-sided glass bowl, its petals the color of translucent amber. The blossom was easily as large as Semana's cupped hands.

"Ahh, pretty," she cooed. "But where's the scent?"

Immediately her nostrils tickled with the spicy fresh scent of roses.

"Thank you, lovey." She chuckled. "Remember those details."

Semana offered the rose a chunk of raw meat on the end of a wooden skewer.

Four gray claws sprang up and snatched at the piece of meat, tearing it neatly apart. The image of the rose faded to reveal a small armored creature with no obvious head. It had twelve legs, each ending in a tiny set of pincer claws and the four arms, each armed with massive examples of the same. It was a mottled gray in appearance, resembling a mutant crab. The little beast was busy stuffing meat into its two mouths.

"I wonder what pretty thing you'll be for our mark," she murmured. Then she turned to her desk and began to make out the invitations to InterGalactic Assurance's unveiling.

I think I'll ask Captain Sheridan to do the honors, she thought.

Look for

in your local bookstore

BABYLON 5:

BETRAYALS

by
S. M. Stirling

Based on the series by
J. Michael Straczynski

BXTREE

First published in the USA 1996 by Dell Publishing, New York

First published in Great Britain 1996 by Boxtree Ltd, London

This edition published 1998 by Boxtree
an imprint of Macmillan Publishers Ltd
25 Eccleston Place London SW1W 9NF
and Basingstoke

Associated companies throughout the world

ISBN 0 7522 0163 8

9 8 7 6 5 4 3 2

A CIP catalogue record for this book is available from
the British Library.

Printed and bound in Great Britain by Mackays of Chatham plc,
Chatham, Kent.

To Jan Stirling, with love.
And to Harlan, for being a great guy and
good friend.

Historian's Note: The year is 2259, during the Narn-Centauri War.

CHAPTER 1

SECURITY Chief Garibaldi turned to gaze out the great window in Captain Sheridan's office, to the view beyond. Gardens and parks stretched away as far as the eye could see, curving upward on either side of the vast cylinder that enclosed them. Thin clouds floated gently "above" them—everything towards the notional center of the giant cylinder was above—occasionally blessing the crops below with a genuine rain. The air had an aliveness to it that was totally unlike the neutral filtered taste of shipboard, full of growing things and damp earth, with an underlying tang of ozone and synthetics. Like many other things on Babylon 5 it was unique, a mixture whose proportions were matched nowhere else in the area humans had explored.

Odd, he thought, as he watched a small shower curve downward, the light turning the drops coppery-gold in color. *When you get caught in a shower here, you really resent it. Somebody* is *to blame.*

Behind him Susan Ivanova and Captain John Sheridan leaned towards each other, earnestly discussing the delicate timing of the docking procedure to be used when the Narn and Centauri delegations arrived for their peace conference.

Pellucidar, Garibaldi thought gazing idly outward, *must have looked something like this.*

He turned back to the group clustered around the big black desk and wondered if any of them had ever read anything so frivolous as Edgar Rice Burroughs when they were kids. *Actually, sometimes I wonder if they ever were kids.*

Sheridan glanced up. His piercing blue gaze was like the Platonic ideal of Absolute Duty. It would have been inhuman if Garibaldi hadn't known that while Captain Sheridan would let nothing stand between him and his duty, he would also always reserve the right to define what that duty ultimately *was.* The Earthforce General Staff tended to think of its officers as weapons they could trigger at will. He wondered what would happen when they found out that Sheridan wasn't that type of man at all.

"I've had some complaints from merchants that a number of sales have been interrupted by your security drills. With the result that their clients have changed their minds." The Captain leaned back in his chair and studied his Security Chief with a neutral expression.

Garibaldi pursed his lips and looked down at his folded hands. *Just when I'm sure he trusts me,* he thought with a purely imaginary sigh. *Now, what does the good Captain want to hear?* At times he was just probing for a reaction, building his database on you.

The heads of staff had met in the Captain's luxurious—with its inlaid floor and comfortable couch—and spacious—an unimaginable seven by five meters—office to discuss preparations for the upcoming peace conference. Right now, to Garibaldi the place felt about as spacious as a closet. Ivanova was focused, as usual; Franklin's dark face held a certain professional interest as he watched the interactions.

"Well, Sir, we have been laying the training on a little thick, but if anything happened during the conference, the complaints would be a *lot* worse. It's like any other form of readiness training: a pain in the butt until it's needed." *A little stiff,* Garibaldi thought. "Um, was it my people who backed out of those sales?"

"In several cases, yes," Sheridan said, fiddling with a data crystal. "In others it was simply the disruption that was the problem. They complained particularly about the hull breach drills."

Garibaldi winced. "I was pretty upset about those myself." He leaned his chin on one fist and looked the Captain in the eye. "When the citizens bothered to show up at their evacuation stations at all, they arrived up to a half an hour late. So I think we'll need to keep the pressure on in that area until we get people up to the necessary speed. That's basic lifesaving stuff, after all. About the other drills, well"—he shrugged—"I can appreciate their frustration, but it *is* a temporary situation. And we can't very well force our people to make purchases they don't want." He pursed his lips thoughtfully. "I can write a memo and have it sent to the offended parties, apologizing for the inconvenience . . ."

Sheridan considered Garibaldi without speaking.

Susan Ivanova wrinkled her brow in puzzlement. *What brought this on?* she wondered. She'd thought that Sheridan and Garibaldi were finally getting comfortable with each other.

When he'd first arrived and read Garibaldi's rather ugly personnel records, Sheridan had wanted the Security Chief replaced ASAP . . . but that was then.

And yet, she thought, *Michael has an unfortunate record for failing under stress, and this conference is* very *important.*

Their natures were so visibly opposite. Sheridan was turned out in military perfection, his blond hair precisely combed, buttons polished, badges aligned just so. Garibaldi's brown brush cut managed to look slightly disheveled, and in company with his present wide-eyed expression he resembled a frowsy chipmunk. While his uniform was no less pressed than the Captain's, he managed to make it look like a rumpled leisure suit.

Still, watching the Captain trying to play Psi cop with the Security Chief was enough to make her hackles rise. What was it he'd said to her? *A good commander is popular, but because he's good, not because he tries to be liked.*

Garibaldi shrugged again. "That might placate 'em," he went on. "But I'm not about to cut back on security just to satisfy a few disgruntled merchants." He paused. "Unless you make that a direct order. Sir."

Sheridan grinned; the expression transformed his face, turning the cold military bearing boyish for a moment. "No, that won't be necessary. Just wanted you to know what was going on. That memo's a good idea, though."

Sheridan's link chittered and he answered with a frown, "Yes."

"Captain," his assistant said, "I'm sorry to interrupt, but the Centauri Ambassador would like to speak to you. I told him you were in conference, but he was very insistent."

"It's all right, Sergeant; tell him I'll be with him in a moment. And put the Narn ambassador through when he calls."

"As I'm sure he will," Susan said.

The three Earthforce officers stifled groans of agreement. Anything that involved Narn and Centauri in the same room had been difficult enough before the war. Since the outbreak of open hostilities, it had been nearly impossible.

"I don't blame the Narn for being touchy," Susan said thoughtfully. "Granted, they can be a little difficult at times—"

This time Garibaldi *did* snort aloud.

"—but they certainly didn't push the Centauri hard enough to justify a declaration of war."

"And," Sheridan added, "the Centauri have been *winning.* Rather more quickly than anyone thought likely." His voice changed timbre. "Put the Ambassador through."

"Captain Sheridan," Ambassador Londo Mollari's accented voice came through the link tinged with regret. "I am sorry to interrupt your conference. But I have a complaint to make about the quarters assigned to the Centauri delegates to the peace conference."

All of the Earthforce personnel leaned forward. Were the Centauri looking for an excuse to cancel? They *were* pushing the Narn back . . . but the nonaligned systems would be offended by too blatant a show of disregard for interstellar public opinion.

"What seems to be the problem, Ambassador?" Sheridan asked calmly.

"The amount of space we have been assigned . . ." Londo said, his voice strained, "is quite inadequate. The rooms are so small, and so sparely furnished. We Centauri require a certain degree of style and spaciousness, as I'm sure you know. I must request that, at the very least, we be assigned several more rooms. Otherwise, I fear we may insult the delegates. Which, of course, would get things off to a very bad start; as I'm sure you'll agree."

"Ambassador Mollari," Sheridan said patiently, "your delegates have been assigned the largest quarters we could find. You did request that they be housed as close to the ambassadorial wing as possible for reasons of security and convenience. Consequently, since that's the most popular residential area on the station, there was limited space available. But they are exactly the same size as those offered to the Narn. And the Narn have expressed no dissatisfaction whatsoever."

"The Narn idea of decorating is rocks and steam," Mollari sneered. "Centauri sensibilities require something more . . . gracious."

"The Centauri government is welcome to decorate the suites in any way that pleases your delegates," Sheridan said. "At Centauri expense, naturally. Provided you restore the rooms to their original condition." He was smiling now. "Will that be sufficient, Ambassador?"

"It will have to be," Londo said with asperity. "Thank you for your time, Captain." He signed off.

"Do you think it's likely to be a problem?" Ivanova asked. "The rooms, I mean."

"Nah," Sheridan said with a dismissive wave of his hand.

"He just wanted to be sure we hadn't given the Narn more space than the Centauri."

"Subtle," Franklin observed with a half smile, his dark eyes twinkling.

"And who am I to deny the Centauri an opportunity to be subtle?" Sheridan asked, smiling comfortably, clasping his hands behind his head. "What's more, who do you think will come out ahead when that redecorating job is done?"

"Mollari . . ."

"Right in one—damn, what is it this time?" His link chirruped again.

"The Narn embassy, Sir."

"Like clockwork," he muttered. Then: "Sheridan here."

"Captain Sheridan," G'Kar purred. "I have just finished inspecting the quarters assigned to the Narn delegation. At present they are barely adequate."

"You're welcome to effect any changes you feel necessary to make your people comfortable, Ambassador. At your government's expense, and with the provision that you return the rooms to their present condition when the delegation has departed." *Déjà vu,* he thought.

Garibaldi wrote a note and held it up where Franklin and Ivanova could see it.

DIDN'T WE HAVE THIS CONVERSATION ALREADY? Ivanova's full lips twitched.

"I would like to assume, Captain, that our quarters will be duplicates of the . . ."—G'Kar paused delicately—"opposing representative's." The tone of warning was unmistakable.

"Absolutely, G'Kar. You have my word on it."

"I certainly hope so," the Narn growled. "Good day, Captain."

"And who are you to deny the Narn an opportunity to make veiled threats?" Garibaldi quipped.

"Why spoil the fun?" Franklin agreed.

"Those were pretty thin veils over those threats," Ivanova remarked with a grin.

"Aren't they always?" asked Garibaldi. *Trouble is,* he thought, *the Narn are an impulsive bunch and all too likely to carry 'em out.*

"I think maybe I'm finally getting the hang of this diplomatic nonsense," Sheridan said smugly. "If everybody stays this predictable things should work out just fine."

"Don't tempt fate," Ivanova warned. "Let's hold our congratulations for after the conference."

Londo Mollari rubbed his hands with glee and turned to smile benignly on his assistant, Vir.

"Exxcccellent," he pronounced, looking speculatively around his small but sumptuous quarters. Normally the hangings, mosaics, and rugs gave him a small warm glow of pleasure every time he looked at them. Today they did not; the pleasure of anticipation was far greater.

He held his hands up at arm's length, palms out, thumbs extended, making a frame with them, as though measuring by eye. "Yyyesss," he murmured, pointing at the wall and nodding. "Um hm."

"Londo," Vir asked, "what are you doing?"

"Well, not all of the decorations we'll need to order for the delegates' quarters will be returnable."

Londo whirled his hand. "Wall coverings, draperies, and such like. It would be a crime to waste that which can be reused." His eyes still tracked speculatively across his quarters. "Don't you agree?"

"Shouldn't we just rent?" Vir asked timidly.

"Vir! *Rent?* You would have me furnish the delegates' quarters with the shopworn pickings of some low-class rental agent? Think of the impression it would make upon visitors. What would they say? Hah?"

Vir opened his mouth to speak.

"I will tell you what they would say. They would say, 'Look!' " Londo gestured dramatically, setting the upswept crest of his dark, silver-shot hair quivering. " 'Look how the mighty Centauri have fallen in pride. Their representatives

sit on stained couches with frayed cushions and display
cheap paintings in chipped frames.' *That's* what they would
say!"

Vir looked at him patiently with large liquid eyes, then
opened his mouth to speak again.

"And it would be *my* fault for having listened to *you*!"
Londo raged. "Would you have me represent the Centauri
people as bankrupt?" He glared, then turned away from his
assistant, the skirts of his elegant brocaded jacket swirling
about him. Londo posed, one hand to his brow, in an attitude
of injured dignity.

"I'm sorry," Vir said humbly. "I hadn't thought of it that
way."

"Well, you should learn to think before you speak. Especially with this conference coming up." Londo turned and
shook a finger at Vir. "What you think should stay behind
your lips. Unless *I* tell you what to say you're thinking. Is
that understood?"

Vir's face showed that he was still working his way
through that last bit. "Um . . ."

"Good. And besides," Londo said, flinging a fatherly arm
around Vir's shoulders. "Why should doing our best for the
Centauri people mean that we do less for ourselves? Eh?"
He gave Vir a little shake. "My quarters haven't been re-
decorated since I came to Babylon 5.

"I've made requests for funds"—his eyes flashed with
outrage—"but some mean-spirited little petty-bureaucrat
somewhere is holding it up." Londo squeezed Vir's shoulder
'til he squeaked. "Sorry. But when you consider my new
status within the government such delay is unconscionable.
And, you see, this way," he leaned confidentially close, "I
am being frugal, yet I get what I want. The government has
given me permission to spend whatever is necessary on the
delegation's comfort. So . . ." Londo waved an arm and
smiled.

"It's . . . not . . . completely honest, though," Vir commented daringly.

Londo sighed and slumped in resignation. "I can see that I am not quite getting through to you, Vir. These," he gestured around him, "are not my quarters. Don't you understand that?"

Vir looked around, moving just his eyes. Then he shook his head, just a little. It looked more like a tremor. "No, Londo, I don't." He patted the air, palms downward. "These *are* your quarters," he said gently, as though he thought the ambassador might be slipping into lunacy.

"No. They belong to the ambassador. Which means that they belong to the Centauri government. *I* merely occupy them during my tenure. And isn't it my duty to look after government property to the best of my ability? Hah? You can't argue with that, now can you?"

Vir shook his head helplessly. Somehow, no matter how wrong something seemed at first, Londo could usually talk his way around it.

"When you present it that way," he conceded, "redecorating your quarters does seem like a good idea."

"A good idea!" Londo flung up his hands in exasperation, gazing ceilingward for guidance and strength. "It is essential. I represent the permanent Centauri presence on Babylon 5. I want our delegation to see that I project an image they can be proud of." He glared at a thoroughly cowed Vir. "Now, make a list. Here's what I want. . . ."

G'Kar leaned back in his chair, a contemplative look on his mottled face. The shadows in his dimly lit office sculpted it into a dramatic work of planes and hollows, as hard as the crags of Homeworld. The air was sharp with the scent of heated rock.

"Well," Na'Toth said briskly, leaning forward to place her hands on the warm rough stone of G'Kar's desk. "That's satisfactory. I'll begin ordering what we need, bloodstone to line the walls and so forth. I'll also contact environmental control to have the atmosphere adjusted."

G'Kar seemed not to have heard her. His gaze was solemn and far away.

"Ambassador?"

He waved a hand as though flicking away an annoying insect.

"Yes, fine," G'Kar muttered.

"Is something wrong?" Na'Toth asked, her red eyes concerned. Had she missed some nuance in the ambassador's brief conversation with the Earthforce Captain? Sometimes she found humans completely opaque when it was apparent that they thought they were being overwhelmingly obvious. *Does that mean I'm more subtle than they are, or just the opposite?* Not to mention their revoltingly mobile faces. Some Narn found humans aesthetically pleasing—ethereal, elfin. Na'Toth considered them skinny and rubbery. Not to mention cunning and tricky.

Paranoia was an occupational hazard in diplomatic work. When you threw in clandestine intelligence, it was virtually a job requirement.

"No, no. It's just . . . I'm wondering how we can make this conference work for us. Peace is absolutely essential," G'Kar said.

Na'Toth blinked. "I hadn't realized that you were so enthusiastic about peace with the Centauri." Her voice was wary. *In fact, I thought you wanted to be personally responsible for the agonizing death of every Centauri in existence.*

G'Kar snorted. "Oh, I want peace," he said almost meditatively. "The kind of peace one finds on a planet scoured of life, its atmosphere blown off into space."

His eyes were dreamy. Then he smiled and glanced at his assistant. Not a friendly expression at all; it was more like something perched on a crag, watching its next meal staggering towards death. "You can imagine which planet I picture so devastated. It's a daydream I've enjoyed since my boyhood. Perhaps you have a similar pleasant vision?"

Na'Toth merely smiled, a smile that showed they were enjoying a rare moment of perfect communication.

Then G'Kar sighed and sat up, leaning forward and clasping his hands in front of him on his desk.

"Actually, though, I would very much like to see peace come of this conference."

Na'Toth's eyes widened with disbelief.

"That's not going to happen, Ambassador," she said emphatically. "The Centauri are only coming here for the sake of appearances. And they'll do anything imaginable to scuttle this conference."

G'Kar waved his hand and shook his head dismissively.

"I know that." His voice was laden with exasperation. "War with the Centauri is, and always has been, inevitable. But I would like that war to take place at a time of *our* choosing. The Centauri caught us shamefully flat-footed and we have yet to regain our balance, let alone any advantage."

He curled his hand into a fist and growled, "We need *time*." His eyes met Na'Toth's. "So. Let us make every effort to secure peace at this conference. Before my pleasant little daydream becomes a nightmare vision of Narn."

Deep in the bowels of Down Below—the unfinished sections of the station—where climate control was fitful at best, a group of shivering T'llin, wrapped from head to foot in ragged blankets, huddled together. They grouped away from the chill metal of the walls, beneath the single glowstrip that left shadows and rime-frost in the corners of the chamber.

T'll was a planet of great heat and little water, grilling under its F5 sun, and its mark was clear in the hawklike features of race that had evolved there. They were a handsome people, with large almond-shaped eyes, disconcertingly black from rim to rim. Those eyes were possessed of two sets of nictitating membranes. A clear one, usually deployed due to the dryness of the air in Down Below, and a gray one that flicked rapidly down and away, displaying the agitation the group was feeling.

Their aristocratically aquiline noses were blade-thin, their lips merely a subtle roundness about the slit of their mouths, hinting at the strong muscle beneath the skin. The skin itself was an exquisitely pale shade of blue, so finely scaled that it was only apparent in bright light and utterly hairless on head or face or body. Their bodies had the coiled tensile quickness of a snake about to strike, stripped down to an eerie minimum of bone and sinew and flat hard muscle.

"What word?" Haelstrac whispered urgently. "When will they come?"

Miczyn held his hands up and looked politely away from her distress. "I don't know exactly when," he admitted. "Their route, of necessity, will be roundabout. But they *are* coming. They are traveling here now. This I do know."

"Does the Prime Phina have any orders for us?"

Miczyn looked at the burly male who had spoken.

"The Prime Phina said only 'be ready.' But the Prime Olorasin said: 'Do nothing rash, this is not the time for boldness.' She wishes us to contain ourselves in patience until she has spoken to the other representatives on Babylon 5." Miczyn could almost feel the anger that greeted the Prime Olorasin's message. Translucent nictitating membranes slid over eyes, hiding the red glint of rage.

"It was agreed," he reminded them, "to try a diplomatic approach. First."

"It was agreed," Haelstrac conceded bitterly. "As for myself, I shall obey the Prime Phina's stricture and make ready for them. We will need a secure and comfortable place for the Primes to rest and work."

"Such will not be easily obtained," the big male named Segrea rumbled.

"Tsssh! In Down Below anything can be obtained for credits," Haelstrac said. "All we need is a good supply of them."

Segrea smiled and bunched his big fists.

Miczyn's hand flashed out. "Do nothing rash," he reminded them, his voice alarmed.

Segrea's smile widened, revealing narrow, pointed teeth that gleamed whitely in the shadow of his blanket. He gifted the younger T'llin with a comradely thump between the shoulders that surprised an "Oof!" from him.

"Oh, never rash," Segrea assured him. "We're very calm and professional."

A whispering chuckle ran among some of his friends; the more squeamish shuttered their eyes and looked away.

It was people who wandered into the wrong sections of Down Below who were rash.

CHAPTER 2

SERGEANT Midori Kobayashi and Corporal David Griffiths knelt side by side on the uncarpeted floor, bent forward over their knees, their hands bound behind their backs.

Their captor strode back and forth behind them shouting out a sermon on God, the government, aliens, Psi cops, and the iniquities of his employer, who had unjustifiably fired him.

"So I was late for work. So what? I told him why. You think he listened?" He leaned suddenly over Kobayashi and shouted in her ear.

"He didn't care! He said that. *I don't care,* he says." The man thrust his PPG against her cheek. "Bet he cares now."

"Bet you're right," Kobayashi agreed, licking dry lips. The floor was hard enough to hurt her knees, despite this being the same posture she could take for hours at the dojo. "I hate bosses like that, they think they're God."

"Shut up!" the man screamed and kicked her in the butt. "You don't talk. Only *I* get to talk." He started to giggle. "I'm the boss. Y'hear that?"

He nudged the Corporal with his foot. "I'm in charge here, hee hee hee." His face clouded. "An' if I fire you two from Earthforce it's gonna be *permanent!*" he shouted. He started to walk back and forth more rapidly. "So where is he, huh? Where's that little Drazi git?" He looked wildly around the crowded storeroom, as though expecting to find him lurking on one of the floor-to-ceiling shelves.

He tapped Kobayashi's link, which he'd transferred to the back of his hand. "Where's that Drazi I axed for? Don't try to fool me, man, I ain't stupid." His eyes glowed with fury and he was panting. "I'm tired a people treatin' me like this."

"We're trying to find him," a soothing male voice replied. "No one's seen him. How are Midori and David? Are they okay?"

"Don't lie to me!" The man fired his PPG into the air and Kobayashi's and Griffiths jumped. "I know where he is, he's in his store. He's always in his store. You get him and you bring him here or I'm gonna kill one of these people."

"I think he's heard we're looking for him and he's gone into hiding. You know how these people are. Do you have any idea where we should look?"

The man paused, silent while he thought about it, then his face contorted in rage and he screamed, "Twenty minutes! Twenty minutes and then I kill 'em! You hear me? Get the Drazi." He tapped the link off. "Get the Drazi," he muttered over and over as he paced.

Outside the locked door of the storeroom where Kobayashi and Griffiths were being held hostage, four Earthforce personnel in body armor and riot helmets crept forward. One dropped a bulky key-card into the slot on the door. The computer built into the card began to work its way through thousands of combinations while the Security Force people waited nervously.

The light turned green and the door swung aside. A man and a woman burst through and took up a stance on either side of the door, pressed against the wall. Another man threw himself on his stomach, while the fourth waited outside as backup.

The startled face of the hostage-taker could be seen through gaps in the loaded shelves.

"Freeze!" the man on the floor yelled, his PPG leveled on the man standing.

"Yeah? Freeze this!" he screamed and shot Sergeant Kobayashi in the head. She fell onto her side and lay still, while all three Earthforce Security people fired on her murderer.

He dropped his PPG and fell slowly, almost carefully, with a loud groan, to lie half covering Midori's body.

The woman rushed forward, pushing back the visor on her helmet. "Sarge, are you all right?"

"I'm dead," Kobayashi said through clenched teeth. "He shot me in the head, for cryin' out loud." She tried to sit up, but was weighed down by the limp bulk of the man lying half on top of her. "Hartkopf, get off of me!"

Her former captor rolled away and brushed his hair off his face with a rueful grin.

"How'd I do, Sarge?" he asked cheerfully.

She glared at him.

"How you did was, you kicked my ass, Hartkopf."

His smile wavered and fell.

"I guess I kinda got into the role, Sarge. Y'know?"

"This isn't community theater, Corporal! You're not supposed to get so far into your 'role' that you start slapping your captives around." She narrowed her eyes. "Maybe next time *you* should be tied up on the floor while somebody else gets to chew the scenery."

"Sorry, Sarge," Hartkopf looked sheepish, and his voice was a sorrowful mumble.

Sure, you're real sorry you got to kick the Sergeant in the butt. And I am Marie of Rumania....

"Well, folks," Garibaldi said, striding into the room with his hands in his pockets. "Let's critique this fiasco."

Behind him eight other newly assigned security people, sent to assist at the Narn-Centauri Conference, began to slide into the small room, their faces solemn.

"Sekou Toure', would you like to tell us where your team went wrong?" Garibaldi's eyes evaluated the young man before him. *Very young,* he thought. *Was I ever that green?*

It had been a while since he personally ran new people through a training exercise, but he didn't entirely trust the

Earthforce basic on something like this. Certainly not when he needed to know exactly how his people would react under emergency stress. Better to spend the time now with the newly assigned squad than have the tool they represented buckle in his hand when the bovine by-products hit the air-recirculation device later.

Sekou Toure' swept the helmet from his dark head and brushed a nervous hand through crisp, black hair.

"I . . . should have shot him right away?" His nervousness thickened his Senegalese accent.

"You?" Garibaldi indicated the young woman member of the team, who opened her mouth and then closed it again, shaking her head. He held his hands out in invitation. "Anyone?" he asked.

"Um, Barzan didn't keep him on the link talking?"

"That is a problem, but it's also realistic. Sometimes the perp will avoid being talked out of his hostages by simply refusing to talk. Barzan, you didn't do that badly. Your main flaw was that at times you were a little timid. Never, never, *never* show weakness to one of these guys. They will note it, they will exploit it."

He met their eyes, one by one. "C'mon people, the Sarge here is dead, we've been stepping all over her brains!" There was nervous laughter. "And so's the perp. Hasn't anyone got an opinion about what could have been done differently?"

"Gas!" Midori snapped impatiently.

"You're dead," Garibaldi said, shaking an admonishing finger at her, and the class laughed again.

He looked them over with his tongue in his cheek. "It's a sad day, folks, when the dead have better ideas than the living. Gas." He raised his brows and spread his hands expressively. "A nice, quiet knockout gas sent in through the air duct and it's over.

"Not dramatic, I grant you," he went on to the sheepish faces of the armored and helmeted rescue squad. He held up one finger. "There's an old saying I want you all to mem-

orize: work smarter, not harder. Or to put it another way—
don't kill flies with a PPG." He cocked his head. "Okay,
class dismissed. Write it up. I want your reports on this mission on my desk tomorrow."

Midori Kobayashi walked up to him, surreptitiously rubbing her bottom.

Garibaldi leaned towards her confidentially. "Did I hear
you say Hartkopf kicked you?" he asked.

"You did. Sir."

"Leave it to me," Garibaldi said. "I've got a much more
evil mind than you have. Besides, right now I need an outlet
for my frustrations."

Midori smiled happily, and bestowed an almost fond
glance on the young corporal as he shuffled out behind the
others.

"Please tell me about it when you're through, Sir. I keep
a diary of my most pleasant memories. I think it might be
something I'd like to add."

"Oooohh!" he said with a mock shudder. "You're a mean
one, Kobayashi. I like that in a Sergeant." He grimaced. "Or
maybe the added fun of turning twelve raw recruits into a
crack security team in less than two weeks is affecting my
sense of humor."

"Drazi ship *Eimen*, adjust your course seven point five by
three. You are straying into an occupied lane. Earth ship
Destiny, hold your position."

Susan Ivanova frowned at the board before her, then
glanced up and through the observation dome. "Centauri
ship *Voira*, you are in the wrong lane! Hold your present
position, instructions follow." Her long, competent fingers
flew over the board and transmitted the corrected instructions
to the Centauri ship.

"Commander, I protest!" the Centauri Captain objected.
His lip curled in a grimace of impatient disdain. "This docking bay is on the other side of the station. It will be another
half an hour before I am properly docked. Since the error is

yours, why can I not use the docking bay before me and save the time and effort?''

"Captain, if you insist, I will of course allow you to dock there," Ivanova conceded graciously. "But I must advise you that the warehouse facilities you've contracted for are on the opposite side of the station, well over a mile from where you'd be docked.''

"Oh." Embarrassment and chagrin flickered over his face almost too fast to register. So did a quick calculation of extra costs for breaking bulk twice on his cargo. "Then I will, of course, accept the correction.''

"Thank you, Captain.''

Just once, I'd like to have an interaction with a civilian where they say, "Why yes, of course, Commander Ivanova, and thank you," she thought sourly. *Which is as likely as my being elected Queen of the May.*

The Narn-Centauri war had shifted a *lot* of neutral shipping through Babylon 5, and both sides were chartering everything they could as commerce raiders picked off their merchantmen and raided convoys. Every docking bay was stacked up; she supposed it looked good on the credit reports back Earthside, but it just meant more work and aggravation here. Ivanova went to work correcting the other errors she'd spotted. When she looked up there was yet another crisis in the making.

"Larkin!" she snapped. "Are you asleep over there? This is the fourth major error you've pulled on those boards in fifteen minutes!''

Ivanova frowned. *No one gets to have a bad day at this job. Especially not on* my *watch.*

"Kamal," she said, "give Larkin a hand." Her heart was beating faster than she liked . . . *Damn! that was three possible collisions in a row.*

Larkin was a presentable fellow, and he had an excellent record. But for the life of her she couldn't see how he'd earned it. In the three days he'd worked traffic control he was obviously not making the grade. A tendency to forehead sweat and shifty eyes didn't help either; she told herself not to judge by appearances.

Not making the grade, hah!, that's *putting it mildly. I knew when I saw how often he'd been transferred that there must be some problem,* she thought dismally. But there'd been neither sign nor hint of it in his written records. And in any case you took what you were sent in Earthforce. *Maybe I should contact his former superior. If there's no trace of a problem elsewhere, I'll send him to Medlab for Franklin to check out.* And if there was nothing physically wrong with him?

Then Larkin and I will have to have a little talk, she promised herself. *I am not passing a problem like this on to someone else.* In this job it was only a matter of time before he got someone killed.

As soon as he could take his eyes off his screen Larkin threw a look at Ivanova, where she stood on the platform above him. A look that should have made her uniform burst into flame and burn her to bones.

Bitch! he thought ferociously. *Bitch, bitch, bitch!* The lack of imagination in his swearing was made up for by sheer venom. "I've only been here three days," he muttered to Kamal. "You'd think she could cut me some slack."

"In traffic control?" Kamal asked incredulously. "Not bloody likely."

He glanced up at Ivanova. "The iron lady'll cut you just as much slack as she does the rest of us, and especially herself. Namely, zero. B5 is not a soft assignment. Take my advice, buddy, if you can't take the heat *ask* to leave the kitchen, before they throw you out. It'll look better on your record, believe me."

"I didn't say I couldn't take it," Larkin snapped. "But the systems are different here. I don't appreciate being logged onto the busiest board in the place before I've had a chance to get used to the changes."

Kamal's dark brows came together. Larkin was on what

they called the "baby board," the training board they'd all occupied until moved up to more difficult assignments.

"If you need additional training, Larkin, you should say something."

"Shut up!" Larkin snarled. Kamal glared at him for a second, then went back to work.

They were always like this, Larkin thought. Everything came so easily to *them*; they didn't know what it was like to struggle, to fall behind no matter how hard you tried. *It's going to be like all the other times,* he thought, self-pityingly.

And he began laying his plans.

"But don't you feel, Captain Sheridan, that as the injured party it is only right that the Narn delegation be allowed to enter the station first?"

The Narn Ambassador smiled; humans liked that. He also stood, the better to tower over the seated Captain.

Sheridan looked up at G'Kar from behind his desk and tried to school his features to patience and sympathy. This was the fourth meeting of this type that he'd had with the Ambassador. Each one more specific, as though the only problem must be that the stupid human couldn't understand the subtle Narn.

"No, Ambassador. I don't. Because it might be construed as a show of preference. Which might make the Centauri feel that Babylon 5 is not so very neutral after all."

The Captain watched G'Kar display a carefully gauged look of pained frustration. Before the Ambassador could speak Sheridan added: "In fact, I don't see how even the Narn delegation could avoid feeling somewhat favored." He leaned back in his chair and looked up at G'Kar with narrowed eyes. "No, I think it best that an aura of strict neutrality be maintained. That way no one's expectations for the conference will be tainted by the least sign of slighting or preferring one delegation over the other."

Maybe I should mention the word neutral *a few more times,* Sheridan thought. *See if by sheer repetition I can force the concept into that thick skull of yours.* In fact, the Narn *were* the injured party, but G'Kar knew as well as anyone else that the Earth's government couldn't say so.

G'Kar looked over the Captain's head and flicked his fingers as though gathering his thoughts with his hands.

"I knew you'd agree," Sheridan said, rising and offering his hand.

Startled, G'Kar shook it.

The Captain came around his desk and, placing his hand on the other's shoulder, walked him to the door.

"Thank you for coming, Ambassador." *Get out of here before Mollari arrives,* he thought, smiling insincerely.

"But . . ." G'Kar began.

"Good day, G'Kar," he said firmly, leaving the Narn little choice but to decamp.

"We'll talk again when you have more time," G'Kar assured him smoothly.

"That will be sometime after the conference," Sheridan said. "I'll look forward to it."

He closed the door, virtually in G'Kar's face. Then turned and leaned against it, blowing out a relieved breath.

Suddenly Sheridan chuckled. *My body language is trying to tell me something.* He shoved himself away from the door, wishing he could barricade it, and returned to his desk. *But if I want to be scrupulously fair, if I want to avoid any semblance of . . .* He dropped into his chair, sighed, and rubbed his eyes tiredly.

"I'm even talking to *myself* in officialese," he muttered. "God, I'll be glad when this is over."

"Excellent!" Londo Mollari exclaimed. "I have been hoping that you would take that attitude."

Sheridan *felt* as if he was goggling at the Centauri. He knew he wasn't, but he wasn't far from it.

Of the two of them it's Londo who's most likely to catch me off guard, he thought. He always felt more capable of handling G'Kar. Maybe because the Narn was so direct and comparatively straightforward—straightforward like a tank.

Or maybe it's because Londo looks so much like my aunt Jane's good-for-nothing ex-husband Frank. The two of them were equally devious; Londo could have made quite a career selling real estate in the Martian habitats.

Sheridan sat forward, folded his hands on his desk, and leaned towards Londo. "Let me get this straight. You were hoping that I would deny your request to allow the Centauri delegation to debark first?"

"Absolutely." Londo's face was as open and honest as a choirboy's.

Then he smiled deprecatingly. "I hope you will forgive me for testing your resolve. But if this conference is to have even a ghost of a chance, there must not be even the slightest hint that Babylon 5's neutrality has been compromised." He folded his hands in his lap and looked thoughtfully down. One of his favorite elder statesman poses. "I am aware of how . . . moving . . . a case the Narn can make of this situation." He looked up and pointed at Sheridan. "You humans are inclined to feel the attraction of an emotional appeal. Which is not a flaw," he insisted, leaning forward and wiping away the thought with his hand. "That you should have heart could never be thought a flaw. But"—he laughed, one sophisticated man of affairs confiding in another—"it is my responsibility to ascertain your position in this matter. Any hint of an inclination, one way or the other, might have an incalculable effect."

Sheridan looked at the Centauri in something like awe. *Bald-faced effrontery* didn't quite cover it, not when slipped in so smoothly. Deviousness raised to the level of an art, perhaps. The Centauri were an old people.

"Well, thank you for your thoughts, Ambassador. But I assure you—on my honor—that our neutrality will be guarded diligently."

"How well said," Londo complimented him and rose, offering his hand in farewell. "I'll leave you now, I'm sure you have a great deal to do. As have I," he said with a friendly smile and departed.

Sheridan stared at the door. *Londo just offered me a bribe,* he thought. *I heard him offer it. But somehow, I feel like I owe him an apology.* The Captain shook his head. *God! I'll be glad when this is over.*

"Lady, we don't bargain here. That's the price. Take it or leave it."

Haelstrac blinked large black eyes at the merchant, then looked down at the blanket she'd been trying to purchase. Her long, four-fingered, blue-tinged hand stroked the soft material regretfully. Passersby jostled her from behind; the air smelled of alien flesh and alien spices, reminding her how far she was from home.

She sighed impatiently. "Have you something similar, at a lesser price?"

"This is actually a very good buy," the merchant said, launching into his spiel. "The fabric will keep its new appearance for years, and it actually rejects dirt and stains!"

"Save yourself the trouble," Haelstrac said, waving a discouraging hand. "I have the will to buy, but not the funds. Have you something similar," she said slowly, as though the merchant might not speak Interlac with any proficiency, "that is not as expensive?"

I shouldn't be here, she thought, looking nervously around the shop, and through its front window out to the mall proper. But she hadn't thought the Primes would approve of being furnished with black-market—that is, stolen—goods. *I ought to be able to shop here in peace,* she grumbled mentally. *The same as anyone else with sufficient credit.*

Unfortunately, the Narn, who considered Haelstrac's people Narn property, wouldn't agree. And equally unfortunately, there were an astonishing number of Narn on the station lately. For that matter, the Narn shouldn't have been able to crush her planet and people simply because they wanted to and had the superior technology. The whole line of thinking was unproductive . . .

She tugged her cowl forward a bit more and glared at the blankets the merchant placed before her. They were of far lesser quality, but they were also much lower in price. She nodded curtly and passed him her credit chit with a sour twist to her thin lips.

It is shameful, she thought bitterly, *that the best we can offer the Primes are cheap blankets in some dank, dark hole in Down Below.* Their presence would be such an honor, her opportunity to be of aid to them a memory to be prized for all the generations of her family. *And I can offer so little.*

As she left the shop clutching her parcels, Segrea loomed suddenly beside her.

"Oh!" she said sharply and jumped. "What are you doing here?" she whispered.

"Why, risking imprisonment and deportation, Haelstrac," he muttered laconically. "The same as you are." He took the bulky packages from his small friend, opened the bags and looked within. "Would you care to explain *why* we're risking so much for so little reason?"

Haelstrac hissed impatiently and huddled into herself, refusing to look at him.

Segrea looked down at her expectantly, but she hurried away without speaking.

"This way," he said, easily catching up to her. "It's shorter."

"It's also more crowded," she pointed out, balking.

"All the better," Segrea said cheerfully. "It's hard to get lost in the crowd when walking down an empty corridor." His eyes studied the main corridor efficiently. Off this little cul-de-sac the mall was crowded. Carts festooned with merchandise were surrounded by shoppers. Men and women of several species bought and sold as far as the eye could see. *Not a Narn in sight,* he thought with relief.

Segrea adjusted his cowl, cutting his line of sight to straight ahead. "Let's go," he muttered, and he and Haelstrac moved briskly forward.

They were nearing the gloomy corridor that beckoned them home to Down Below, when a roar cut through the usual white-noise surf-sound of the area. A Drazi shoved a human who lurched into a Centauri. Furious, the Centauri turned and struck the human in the face. Enraged, the man shoved the Centauri, who staggered into Haelstrac, knocking her to the floor with such violence that her cowl fell back and she slid several feet.

Haelstrac looked up into the shocked, red eyes of a Narn woman in military garb.

"T'llin!" Na'Toth hissed. She lunged for Haelstrac, who lay frozen on the floor.

A mighty kick to her hip sent Na'Toth flying. Segrea gathered a handful of Haelstrac's robe and ran, dragging her until she got her feet under her.

Even then Haelstrac's feet barely touched the floor and she ran on tiptoe, tripping and being dragged for meters by her huge friend. Her lungs were burning and her hearts were beating fit to leap out of her skin.

"Let me go!" she gasped. "I can keep up." He released her and she immediately overbalanced and fell heavily.

Segrea turned back for her and stopped.

Haelstrac caught his astonished expression and looked behind in terror.

The corridor was empty, and there was no sound of pursuit. She began to laugh breathlessly, but choked it off suddenly at his severe look.

"There's going to be trouble from this," he rumbled, glaring at her.

And you're going to lay the responsibility for it all on me, she thought, and was ashamed.

G'Kar watched Na'Toth pace back and forth furiously, noting the hitch in her walk. Somebody must have hit her *very* hard; his aide did not show pain easily. She glared at the rock walls of his office as if to track down T'llin saboteurs through sheer force of will.

Understandable, G'Kar thought. Na'Toth had been stationed with the occupation forces on T'll for over a year. From what he had heard—through the military grapevine, the official reports spoke only of happy intraspecies cooperation—garrison duty there was enough to give you eyes in the back of the head, built-in sensor systems, and a permanent state of bad nerves.

"I've complained of this to you before, G'Kar," she said breathlessly, and not for the first time. "They're like vermin, they multiply. More and more and more of them are coming here. And what do you think they're coming for?" Na'Toth put her hands on his desk, leaned toward him, and glared.

G'Kar looked back, waiting her out.

"I was attacked, I was humiliated and not *one* person tried to stop them!"

"What do you want me to do?" he asked reasonably. "Make your complaints to Station Security, not to me. *My* job is to prepare for this conference and to watch the Centauri and to improve our relations with the other races." He shook his head distastefully. "It is not to hunt down whatever is hiding in Down Below. Talk to Garibaldi, give *him* something more to do."

Na'Toth was silent, fairly choking on her rage. Her eyes said things she would never dare to put into words. She closed them slowly and, trembling, took a deep breath.

"Ambassador," Na'Toth said, with her eyes still closed. "If there is a large contingent of T'llin on Babylon 5, it seems to me that their presence here might pose a threat to the conference." Opening her eyes, she shrugged, elaborately casual. "I mean, their presence here at this particular time can hardly be sheer coincidence. You must admit, Ambassador, that they couldn't be described as our friends."

Na'Toth studied G'Kar's impassive face. It was plain that she wasn't getting through to him. She leaned forward again, placing her hands on his desk. "Of course, I could call Garibaldi and make my little complaint. And I don't doubt that he'd sympathize and make all the right noises and then forget all about it as soon as I was out of sight.

"But if *you* complain, Ambassador, it will carry a great deal more weight." She straightened and looked down her nose at the seated Ambassador. "Particularly if you complain to Sheridan." Na'Toth crossed her arms and waited.

G'Kar had to admit they'd sent him a very clever woman to be his assistant. She never seemed at a loss when it came to finding him things to do.

"Na'Toth," he said with exaggerated patience, "you caught a fleeting glimpse of one T'llin. I hardly think that calls for emergency measures." Her nostrils flared with outrage. "But," G'Kar said, forestalling her, "I think it does bear further investigation. And, since we want to be sure that investigation actually takes place, I'm assigning it to you. I want you to report the incident to Station Security, so that it is a matter of record. Then when you come to me with your findings we'll be able to confront Garibaldi on his terms." G'Kar spread his hands. "Am I being so unreasonable?"

"No, Ambassador."

"Then go do it," he said quietly, "and let me get back to work."

She turned to go. "And Na'toth."

"Yes, Ambassador?"

"We derive a good deal of diplomatic and political advantage from our position of *moral superiority* over the Centauri." He used the human tongue for emphasis on the phrase. "It really would be unfortunate if our relations with the T'llin were unduly publicized. I'm relying on you to see that they aren't. One way or another. I'm sure you understand me."

"I understand you perfectly, Ambassador," Na'toth said, smiling unpleasantly.

The Narn had learned a good deal from their long struggle with the Centauri occupiers.

CHAPTER 3

"**Y**OU could say that when you're working in customs, you're on the front lines," Garibaldi explained.

His twelve students stared wordlessly back at him, every one of them with their arms crossed over their chests, while colorful crowds of humans and aliens eddied around them. The harsh lighting in the customs area made the youngsters look jaded and grim, while literally alien scents tickled the nostrils.

"Everyone on this station had to be passed through here."

Well, Garibaldi admitted to himself, *everyone lacking a death wish.* He'd opened too many boxes containing the frozen or smothered corpses of people too desperate or too dumb to go the forged documents route, to believe that many got through the net that way.

Why confuse 'em with nonissues? They'll learn in time.

A creeping depression nudged him as he looked at the earnest young faces before him.

What I should say is, leave now, boys and girls, if you value your peace of mind. Because you're going to see people at their very worst in this job, Garibaldi thought. *Every day, over and over again. And absolutely everything has to be learned the hard way.*

Of course, the Security Chief reminded himself, *that's because the truth is so damned hard to believe. Which means warning 'em would be a waste of breath.* He sighed in imagination. *Back to work.*

"And what should your attitude be when you're on the front lines? Chang?"

Chang, who'd been watching a party of attractive Centauri women sidle past them, nearly swallowed his tongue. "Uhhh . . ."

"How does 'alert' sound?" the Security Chief suggested. Everyone laughed and the young Chinese man grinned sheepishly.

I could be standing here barking like a basset hound, Garibaldi thought hopelessly. *I should just pass them on to Kobayashi or someone and give them some out-of-the-way jobs that would allow me to forget about them for the next few weeks.* It wasn't as if he didn't have enough work right now.

But he couldn't do that. No one knew better than he the power of the written record. And the last thing Garibaldi wanted was for someone to be able to hold it against these youngsters that they'd passed through his training.

So he took time he could ill spare and talked 'til he was sick of the sound of his own voice, hoping that *someone*, contrary to the visible evidence, was paying attention. Garibaldi shook his head sadly.

"Obviously, when you're in charge of processing a huge number of people, you're going to have to use your own discretion a lot of the time. There's nothing cut and dried about this job," he warned them.

Then he started taking them around, introducing them to their senior partners.

"This is not a day off," the Security Chief warned one of his people, whose pleasure at the arrival of a young trainee who could be handed all the donkey-work made it apparent that a little downtime was being contemplated. "These kids might have to be well enough trained to take over your job at a moment's notice. I will be very upset," he said with heavy emphasis, "if they can't take over in an emergency."

Then Garibaldi turned and led his dwindling flock of acolytes off to the next docking bay.

* * *

The first thing they noticed as they approached was several enormous packing crates towering over the knot of people surrounding them. It was apparent, even from this distance, that things had reached the shouting stage.

"Ma'am, you have two options," the harassed customs officer was explaining loudly. "You may either step aside until we've processed the rest of the *Destiny's* passengers . . ."

"But that will take *ages*!" a lush female voice complained. "I have an *appointment*."

The combatants were still invisible behind a wall of people and boxes as Garibaldi worked his way towards them.

"Then, you may leave your . . . belongings here and return for them later."

"I can't do that!" the woman's shocked voice replied. "These are very valuable." The voice implied that valuable might be a foreign concept to the security person.

Garibaldi finally broke through to them in time to watch an astounded Cristobel Santos indicate the enormous boxes with both hands and ask, "*Who* is going to steal *those*?"

"What's going on?" the Security Chief asked Santos.

"Are you in charge?" the civilian demanded.

He turned to her with exaggerated patience, then stopped. And stared.

The woman was gorgeous, everything her lush voice had promised. Her smooth, clear skin was the color of cinnamon and her thick black hair was arranged in heavy curls tumbling over a colorful scarf and brushing her slim shoulders. The woman's sherry-brown eyes were amused at his no doubt dumbfounded expression. Her full lips softened into a smile, revealing small, even, white teeth. She moved just a shade closer to him.

Whoa, now! Down boy, he warned himself. *Watch out for this one. Here's a lady who enjoys the power of being beautiful just a little too much.*

Mantrap, a corner of his mind confirmed. Whenever he'd met someone like this in the past, he'd ended up sincerely regretting the acquaintance.

"Could you wait just one moment, ma'am, while I talk to the officer, please?"

The woman cast him a wounded look and pouted.

With those lips I suppose it would be a shame not to, Garibaldi observed, forcing himself to turn back to Santos.

"The lady wants to bring those boxes through this gate . . ."

"Well, I don't see why I can't. My documents are in order . . ."

"Please," Garibaldi said to the woman, holding up both hands for silence.

"I explained to her that it was a time-consuming process and that the boxes, or at least one of them, would have to be opened." Santos hurried on, as though certain of being interrupted. Visual inspection was standard procedure, to back up the scans. "And that we didn't have the facilities for that here."

Translation from officialese, Garibaldi thought, *I don't have a crowbar.*

"I suggested that we take them down to the freight customs area and she wouldn't let me through!" the woman protested.

He held up his hand again and the woman subsided, her eyes glittering with fury. Then he held his hand out to Santos.

"Her documents?"

Santos slapped the data crystals into his palm as if she wanted to smash them.

"I'll escort the lady and her boxes to the freight customs area," he said. Then he pointed to one of the newbies in his train. "This is Chang, Santos. He's your new trainee." Garibaldi almost winced at the pain of betrayal in Santos's eyes. "Everybody's getting one," he offered by way of excuse.

He turned to the beauty beside him.

"If you and your party would come this way," he said and started off.

"Thank you," the woman said, in a voice like nuts and cream. She turned to the porters attending her and instructed them to follow. Then she turned her attention back to Garibaldi.

"My name is Semana MacBride."

She held out her hand and he shook it—briefly. Semana raised her elegant brows.

"Is that because I haven't passed customs yet?"

He smiled down at her. "It always pays to be cautious."

Garibaldi looked her over. Her costume was eccentric. He could swear that Semana's dress was Minbari. It had the demure, silken look of the robes worn by Ambassador Delenn. But this one was accented by an array of extravagant jewelry and gypsy-bright scarves.

That's pretty bold of her, he thought. *There aren't many human women would care to run around in Minbari clothing.* There was an element of contempt for the opinions of others in an attitude like that. It implied a personality that enjoyed creating discord. *I sure hope she isn't staying long.*

"What's in the boxes?" he asked.

"The elements of a statue that I'm to set up in one of the parks." She gave him an arch look. "TransGalactic Assurance wants to make a grand gesture."

He glanced over his shoulder at the crates, his expression dubious.

"I don't know where you're going to put it. It must be huge."

"Ugh!" Semana said with a dismissive wave of her hand. "It's the worst piece of kitsch you ever saw. But it is on a smaller scale than the wrappings indicate."

"Why weren't they in the freight section?" Garibaldi asked. "It would have saved you a lot of trouble." *Us too,* he added mentally.

"Well," Semana explained, "as art it stinks. But as a

commission . . ."—she gave a dainty shrug—"it's golden. This is my first major break and I didn't want to risk any damage to the statue. There are some pretty delicate electronic components, for example. And if anything happened en route, well, I couldn't be sure I'd be able to get it repaired."

She looked at him from under her lashes. "I wanted to ship them freight. It would have saved me a lot of credits. But the Captain refused to allow me to supervise the loading, something about insurance." She grinned. "That's ironic, isn't it? So I took an extra cabin and stored them there. That way, I could be sure that nothing would crush them, that they hadn't been dropped, and that the temperature would be constant. Artists aren't always the best at electronics," she said to his inquiring look. "I didn't dare risk fractures of any kind."

"So you're, what, an artist?"

"Oh no," she said. "More's the pity. I'm a dealer. And that's another reason I'm here." Her face took on a faraway look. "I'm sure there's a new art form taking root here. There has to be! A new expression for a new experience." She turned to him, eagerly, her face alight. "Don't you agree?"

"I really couldn't say," Garibaldi answered with a deprecating smile. "I don't hang out with the art crowd. Assuming we have one."

Semana grinned impishly, took his arm and hugged it close.

"Well, it's time you found out. I'll send you an invitation to the unveiling. What's your name?"

"I'm Michael Garibaldi, the Security Chief."

"Ooooohhh! No wonder you handled that little nuisance at the gate so expeditiously." She hugged his arm a little tighter and leaned close. "Could you do the same for me in freight customs? I really do have an appointment." She looked up at him hopefully.

I'm being vamped, Garibaldi thought, amused and suspicious. *Of course*, he warned himself, *she's an artsie, maybe they all gush like this*. At that, it was refreshing to be vamped for something as simple and straightforward as a minor bureaucratic snafu. A nice change from spooks and subversion . . .

They arrived just as one set of freight had been cleared and the customs officer was about to begin another. Floater pads and people with hand-terminals bustled about, scanners beeped, and somewhere near was the throbbing of heavy magneto pumps as a freighter loaded volatiles directly into a stationside pipeline. The air smelled of ozone and metal; Semana looked even more wildly out of place among the utilitarian coveralls, color-coded conduits, and bare surfaces.

"Hold it," Garibaldi said. "I want to process these first."

The agent turned and displayed three degrees of surprise. One that it was the Security Chief beside him, two that he'd begun to process *freight* himself, and three that he and his freight had apparently just come in from the passenger lounge, accompanied by an absolute goddess.

Garibaldi inserted Semana's data crystals and started to record them. Then he picked up a "crowbar" and slapped it onto its receiving plate on one of the smaller crates. In seconds a green light flashed, showing that the seals had been released.

"Be careful!" Semana snapped, as workmen began to lift the cover. "I mean," she said, flustered, "it's fragile."

"What's it made of, glass?" Garibaldi asked.

She grinned at him. "Of course not. But if you hit a statue in the right place it will shatter all to bits. I've heard of it happening," she said to his raised eyebrow. "Happens to diamonds too."

A layer of packing had been removed to reveal a humanoid figure of indeterminate gender. It was carved from a pale blue stone. Hooded head looking upward, arms upraised, the figure wore some sort of medieval robe. The face was only hinted at with wide, pupil-less eyes, a narrow nose, and a slit for a mouth.

"You sure know art," Garibaldi commented by way of agreeing with her assessment of the statue's merits.

Semana laughed. "Hideous, isn't it?"

"It looks like it's melted."

"Well, it's been molded rather than sculpted," she explained. "It's constructed of a claylike . . . stuff. Dentists invented it over two hundred years ago."

"The whole thing's like this?"

"It's worse," she said.

The Security Chief shuddered. "That's one park I'm going to be avoiding."

He looked down at a readout of the manifest. *Organically based hydrocarbon compounds with trace amounts of salts, calcium, and stabilizing rare earths.*

"Well, what do the sensors say?" he asked.

The tech at the consol touched the screen. "Yessir. Carbon, hydrogen, calcium, and salts—fair amount of water too. Sort of gloopy."

"That's an appropriate word," Garibaldi said. No signs of life in any of the crates, nor of any contraband. "Okay." He handed her the data crystals. "Enjoy your stay on Babylon 5."

"Thank you." Semana smiled warmly as she took them. "I intend to."

I do indeed, Semana thought. She'd have to watch out for that one, though. Experience had shown that any man who didn't respond to "the rub," as she called her technique of taking a man's arm, was immune to her charm. And anyone who was immune to her charm was likely to get in her way.

She gave a mental shrug.

Actually it's a stroke of luck that I met the Security Chief right away. Count it as a good omen, then.

Semana followed the porters with the lifter full of art—

so-called—down the access corridor and then into an industrial-strength lift, to the storage she'd arranged.

"No! Do not stack them." *Whence comes this antlike urge porters have to pile things up? Is it genetic or what?* There was plenty of room in the module to put the figures side by side.

Satisfied at last, Semana dismissed the disgruntled crew, locked the palmplate of the space behind her, and followed them down the row of numbered doors.

She soon found herself alone in the echoing corridors. Lifting up her hatbox-shaped handbag, Semana peeked inside.

"Hello, precious," she whispered. Then laughed. "Just be patient a little longer and Mommy will get you something to eat."

"Semana MacBride," Garibaldi murmured to himself as he studied the documents he'd had copied. She'd been a freelance planetary surveyor until recently, when for unspecified reasons, she'd begun a second career as an art dealer. Odd. Why should someone go from flying a one-person survey ship into uncharted systems to dealing in lousy art? About the only things the professions had in common was that a few members of each made a great deal of money and most barely got by.

I wish they made people give reasons for career changes, he thought. *Most people love to gab about stuff like that.*

That was sheer frustration talking. He wouldn't want to give his own reasons for changing jobs on some official document. *But people like MacBride . . . even their lies tell you something.* And he was sure she was a liar, probably an operator of some kind.

"No point in wasting time," he said, and tapped the screen on his desk.

"Memo to EarthDome, Central Records. MacBride, Semana, ident—"

He went through the string of identifiers, including the

gene scan from customs. At the end he paused for a second: "Priority One, Security Clearance."

In a few days he should know everything there was to know about her. After all, he'd accessed Captain Sheridan's own personnel file, back when the CO had been new here.

"I'm sorry, Susan, but there's nothing wrong with him."

Dr. Franklin frowned and looked down as his slender brown fingers turned a hypo. It was seldom he felt obliged to apologize for a patient's good health. *In fact, I think this is the first time.* "I hate to see you taking it so hard."

She gave a half smile and waved her hand.

"Sorry, I didn't mean to be so intense." Susan gave the doctor a worried look. "There's no trace of drugs?"

"No, Susan, no drugs, no disease." He was silent a moment. "And if it's a psychological thing, he's hiding it pretty well."

Ivanova grimaced. While there was "something not quite right" about Larkin, that was a long way from being "something blatantly wrong." "I don't really have any excuse for ordering a psychological exam." *Nor do I want to.* In a sensitive job like Larkin's such an exam included a Psi-scan. *I don't want to force someone to go through that.* Because force is what it would amount to.

Oh, he could refuse the scan. But then he'd be removed from his current job and most likely put in some boring, dead-end office, like . . . tourism or something. Circumstances that would oblige anyone with ambition to resign from Earthforce.

Ivanova didn't want to be responsible for cutting short someone's career, either. She wouldn't agree to a Psi-scan herself, come to that.

Susan shrugged hopelessly.

"I don't understand it," she said in exasperation. "He's been doing the same job for four years. He should be an expert. I've never had anyone come to Babylon 5 with that much experience. But," she turned to Franklin, palms turned up, "he cannot do the job. I have a first-year controller on the boards who can work rings around him. Everyone has had to pitch in and help him at one time or another. If we get really busy I shudder to think what will happen."

"Maybe he's burned out," Franklin suggested. "And he's blocking it. Have you talked to him yet?"

She shook her head. "No, things have been so hectic." She sighed. "I've tried to get in touch with his last two senior officers, but they haven't gotten back to me yet."

And I wonder if they intend to, she thought suspiciously. If Larkin was a loser—and he gave every indication of being one—they'd hardly extend themselves to admit that they'd passed the problem on rather than solving it.

"I'll have to speak to him, now though. I was really hoping it was something that could be cured with a hypo or something."

Franklin smiled understandingly. "Not this time." He patted Susan's shoulder. "Have that talk, maybe you can convince him that he'll be happier in another job."

"Yeah," Ivanova growled.

But Larkin didn't seem the type that was willing to be convinced.

Larkin had accepted Ivanova's order to report to Medlab with extreme good grace.

"Yes, Sir," he'd said, with a faintly puzzled smile.

But he was building up to a fine rage now.

Hours! he thought. *Hours of prodding and poking and stupid questions.*

How had she dared? And she'd sent him off in front of everybody. *So they could all know that she thinks there's something wrong with me. Bitch!*

It was always the same. For some reason the commander took a dislike to him and before he knew it the others were sending out those subtle little signals that said "keep your distance."

Why me? What is it about me that makes them hate me?

His mother had always said it was jealousy. "They're afraid of you, dear," she'd said.

But that didn't make sense. Sometimes he could barely keep up. Especially here on B5. *Why is that?* Larkin chewed his lip. *Drugs? Could someone be drugging me?*

No, that was ridiculous.

Then why send me to Medlab? Were they supposed to find something out? His head came up in horror. *What if . . . what if it's true and someone is trying to get me?*

Then they'd been after him for years. *It must be a misunderstanding,* he thought desperately. *They think I'm someone else.*

But his ability to stay one step ahead of them—in total ignorance of this conspiracy—had, in some weird way, confirmed their belief that he was the one they wanted.

My God! he thought. Rushing into his quarters he sealed and locked the door behind him, programming it for privacy. Larkin turned and looked around the room, wondering if they'd been in here.

"No," he said aloud. "This is insane. You have no proof, it's all conjecture." Conjecture that fits the facts, his mind argued.

Irrelevant! Keep your eyes open, Larkin, he admonished himself. *What's most important is that you deal with the situation.*

He'd done it before when he'd found himself being persecuted. A tight little smile curved his lips and he sat himself down at his personal comp.

I've got a bitch to bring to heel, he thought comfortably, and grinned. *An iron lady to melt down to size.*

CHAPTER 4

N A'TOTH glared at Garibaldi, who stared back at her from the screen with a mild, unreadable expression.

"We have the altercation on record," he was saying, "but I'd no idea you were mixed up in it. Why didn't you report it to the Security personnel on the scene?"

Tamping down her temper with an effort, Na'Toth said, "I felt that I should inform the Ambassador first, Mr. Garibaldi. The T'llin are regarded as an enemy race, and I was shocked to see them here." She leaned forward. "They are pirates, of a particularly dangerous variety. As far as we can tell, based upon their actions, the T'llin regard thieving and murdering as praiseworthy behavior. Just off the top of my head I could cite you at least ten cases of unprovoked violence against Narn."

"I've heard of T'llin before," Garibaldi said dryly. "Though not in those terms. But we have none on record as residents."

"You surprise me," Na'Toth sneered. "Because they comprise a growing population in Down Below. I've grown accustomed to the idea that you know everything that happens on this station." She blinked and asked sweetly, "Does this mean that I should lower my estimate of your abilities?"

"You should do whatever you think appropriate, Na'Toth. I'll add your complaint to the report and I'll have my people keep an eye out for anyone matching your description."

"Why, thank you," she said, her voice ripe with disgust.

Garibaldi leaned forward confidentially. "But I feel I should advise you that from your statement, all I can charge this T'llin with is falling at your feet."

"Her companion attacked me," Na'Toth said with clenched teeth.

"You said that you never saw your attacker's face."

"Well, who else would it have been?" she exploded. "Why would anyone else kick me away from her?"

"You were in the middle of a brawl," Garibaldi pointed out. "And there were Centauri involved. Isn't it just as likely that one of them decided to strike a blow for Centauri Prime?"

"That is feasible, but it is not what happened. This must be investigated, Garibaldi. My government insists upon it!"

"I'll act on that," the Security Chief said carefully, "when I hear it from G'Kar." He sat and stared at her.

Humiliated, Na'Toth broke contact. She flung herself back in her chair, staring furiously into space.

How could she have forgotten herself so far as to allow a human the opportunity to put her in her place?

Perhaps G'Kar has a better understanding of me than I'd realized, she thought.

He'd played her nicely if that was true.

Well, she thought briskly, *no use repining. I've made my useless complaint. Now to accomplish the second part of my orders.*

Garibaldi lounged back in his chair, chin cupped in his hand, contemplating the blank screen before him.

The Narn were a passionate people, given to outbursts and exclamations of all sorts. But the Security Chief had learned—more or less—when they were just blowing off steam and when they meant business.

I've never seen Na'Toth so close to losing it, he thought. *"My government insists on it" is the kind of phrase that should only come out of G'Kar's mouth. Her circuits must really be fried for her to make a slip like that.*

He leaned forward and keyed up the computer.

"Commence a search for T'llin refugees registered in Babylon 5 immigration logs for the last twelve months," he ordered.

While the computer processed his request, the Security Chief cast his mind back over the last few months. He admitted to himself that he had noticed a quiet, unobtrusive upsurge in the population of a heretofore rarely observed alien. Many of them had children with them.

Pirates, hmm. Well, Na'Toth, they don't act like any pirates I've ever dealt with. Pirates steal, and murder, and break up bars. Come to think of it, he'd never even seen one of these people in bars. *And they travel with kids. Of course,* he thought fair-mindedly, *so do gypsies.* Who stole nonstop, it was part of their cultural heritage. But they didn't murder, at least not often, and then it was usually among themselves. *Pirates.* He grimaced and shook his head.

The computer beeped politely to announce the completion of its search and announced, "No persons of T'llin registry have come aboard the station in the last twelve months."

Uh-oh.

Whatever else they might be, the T'llin were uncommonly clever. People had been known to skip B5 without being detected, but getting aboard anonymously was another matter.

I think I'd better look into this. He sighed.

Na'Toth would be pleasantly surprised.

A yellow rose floated in the high-sided glass bowl, its petals the color of translucent amber. The blossom was easily as large as Semana's cupped hands, folds within folds of intricate beauty.

"Ahh, pretty," she cooed. "But where's the scent?"

Immediately her nostrils tickled with the spicy, fresh scent of roses.

"Thank you, lovey." She chuckled. "Remember those details."

Semana offered the rose a chunk of raw meat on the end of a wooden skewer.

Four gray claws sprang up and snatched at the piece of meat, tearing it neatly apart. The image of the rose faded to reveal a small armored creature with no obvious head. It had twelve legs, each ending with a tiny set of pincer claws and four arms, each armed with massive examples of the same. It was a mottled gray in appearance, resembling a mutant crab. The little beast was busy stuffing meat into its two mouths.

"Want some more, Tiko?" Semana asked, waving another gobbet of meat.

The little monster metamorphosed into an enormous orchid, complete with a fresh, nonspecific flower scent and a touch of velvet at the flower's throat.

"Uh-uh. Something harder," Semana insisted. The orchid stubbornly remained in the dish. "Come on, Tiko," she coaxed, "make Mummy an artificial object."

A tangle of jewelry appeared—pearls and diamonds intertwined with gold and silver chains.

Semana smiled, almost wishing she could pet her little monster. But the loss of a finger wasn't worth the dubious pleasure of stroking its hard shell.

"I wonder what pretty thing you're going to end up faking for our mark," she murmured. Then she turned to her desk and began to make out the invitations to InterGalactic Assurance's unveiling.

I think I'll ask Captain Sheridan to do the honors, she thought.

Na'Toth slumped sullenly at a corner table in a dark and sleazy bar on the borders of Down Below. The place reeked of stale beer and stale bodies and the table before her was sticky with something she was just as happy not to be able to see.

Usually it took no time at all for her to spot one of the station's professional informers and to beckon them over.

She was known for being generous with credits, so they came readily.

But this evening they were apparently busy elsewhere. She'd been here two hours and not a one was to be seen.

Perhaps they've changed bars, she thought. Like the fickle rich, moving on to something new and more interesting. *Or safer.* She glanced around. One or two other customers had, like her, been sitting alone, nursing a drink for a couple of hours or more. She raised her arm to attract the waitress.

"Where's Graze?" Na'Toth demanded.

"How should I know, I'm not his keeper. You want a drink?"

The Narn glared at the human woman, who stared back at her with dumb insolence. Na'Toth slapped a credit chit down on the dirty table. The waitress picked it up disinterestedly and slipped it into a reader. Her small eyes narrowed.

"This just covers the bill," she said, her voice offended.

"Your tip is on this one," Na'Toth purred, holding up another. "Uh-uh," she said, pulling it back when the human reached for it. "I'd like some answers."

The waitress sighed and adjusted her hip-shot stance. "Yeah?"

"I want to know where Graze is."

"He's probably at the fight," the waitress said. "Everybody else is who could get the night off." This was tossed over her shoulder at the bartender, who took no notice.

"Where is this fight?"

The woman looked over her shoulder and then back at the Narn, her tongue in her cheek. "I'll tell you what," she said. "I'll take you there. I've got a break coming up in a few minutes."

"Your boss won't mind?" Na'Toth asked suspiciously.

The woman laughed. "Yeah, like he needs me here tonight."

Half an hour later, Na'Toth followed the woman through the labyrinth corridors of Down Below. There were fewer lurkers about than usual, only the real crazies and dopers remained, jittering and mumbling in corners or lying comatose on the floor. But off in the distance she could hear the sound of voices raised in excitement.

"Stop." A cowled figure had stepped out of the darkness to bar their way.

"Brought you a customer," the waitress said, nervous and excited.

Nothing could be seen of the face within the shadowy recesses of the hood. It was impossible to even determine the species, since the being's hands were hidden in its sleeves.

The figure contemplated Na'Toth for a minute.

"It's almost over," it said at last.

"Then let us in for nothing," the waitress urged. "We're only looking for Graze anyhow."

After another pause the cowled figure shrugged and turned away.

With a squeal of excitement the waitress grabbed Na-'Toth's arm and instantly released it under the Narn's red glare.

"Tsk! See ya around, then," she muttered, offended. Then she rushed after the receding figure.

Na'Toth followed them at a distance, as the sound of cheering voices grew louder. At last they passed through a curtained doorway, turned a corner, and those she'd been following plunged into the crowd, to be lost to sight in seconds.

Na'Toth stopped and stared around in astonishment. *I'd no idea there was anything like this down here.* The crowd had formed in a huge open area, a truncated version of the main mall far above. Voices echoed from the bare walls, and the packed bodies made the room both hot and steamy. Na-'Toth choked from the gamey smell of the audience as much as from lack of oxygen. Spotlights had been rigged up on the overhead beams to provide lighting, but most of the room was in near darkness.

The fight was apparently taking place in the center of the enormous hall, but was invisible from where she was standing, and inaudible as well.

Narn were few in Down Below, and there were none to be seen in this crowd. Men and women, mostly Drazi and human with a few Centauri mixed in, bellowed at the top of their lungs. The sound reverberated around the huge room until it was almost unbearable.

Na'Toth frowned in disgust and discomfort. *I couldn't find my mother in here.* She began to sidle around the edges of the crowd, looking for a familiar face.

Suddenly there was a wild roaring that lifted the noise level from painful to agonizing. She flinched and covered her ears as the crowd went wild. People were leaping about, hugging, dancing, fighting among themselves, apparently unaffected by the racket they were making.

Na'Toth was swept along against her will as the crowd surged suddenly in her direction. A blanket was thrown over her head. She lashed out with skilled violence, and felt something crunch under the edge of her hand. There was a wail of pain. The surge of satisfaction was drowned when a heavy blunt object bounced off the top of her head . . . quite hard. In the darkness under the smothering blanket, stars and streaks of light painted themselves over her vision. Doggedly she jerked her arms free and tried for a break-hold on the hands bunching the cloth at the back of her neck. That left her torso open, and someone—several someones—began hammering at it. Breath wheezed out of her in an involuntary grunt. She kicked and felt the blow go home, but whoever it was grappled with the leg, using two thin but steel-strong arms.

The flesh in contact with hers was dry, satin-rough skin with tiny scales, fever-hot. T'llin. The nightmare tension of memory filled her mouth with the taste of desert grit, memory of patrols ambushed in the blazing nights. She jackknifed her whole body off the ground, ramming two of the beings who held her into the bulkhead, and tore herself half-free of their grip. Na'Toth felt one of them stumble and fall when she brought her foot down hard on what felt like an instep.

A hard something struck her. This time the impact rang through her bones like the touch of lightning, leaching away her strength.

Shock stick, she thought blearily. "Help!" she croaked. "I know who you are," she heard herself mumbling. *Shut up!* she thought—was struck again. This time the shock stick must have been turned to maximum; unconsciousness took her like quicksand, a soft helpless floating into nothingness.

"Be careful with that!" Londo snapped. He rushed forward to examine the article for damage. "Do you know what this cost?" he demanded.

The Drazi workman ignored him and moved off.

The ambassador turned to Vir, who had just entered the room and was looking around in a combination of admiration and horror.

"They pretend they don't understand me," Londo said temperamentally. "But I know they can understand every word. And I'll tell you this," he said, striding up to the crew foreman, "if there is so much as a scratch on anything you deliver, it goes back. Do you hear me? And not one credit shall you get from the Centauri government. Hmm?" He nodded dismissively and stalked off.

After a moment he motioned to Vir.

"How do you like my new bed?" he asked, patting a vast construction of gilt and gossamer. "Beautiful, isn't it?"

"It's enormous," Vir said in awe. "Huge."

They looked at each other.

"Don't think I didn't take that into consideration when I chose it," Londo said out of the side of his mouth. "And this," he said, drawing Vir over to where two workmen were removing a painting from its case, "will go in my reception room."

After a speechless moment, Vir said, "It's beautiful, Ambassador, but . . ."

"What?"

"It's rather . . ." Vir's hands circled indecisively. He glanced at Londo, who was looking impatient.

"Rather *what*?" Londo asked.

It's rather prurient, Vir thought. *Not that I can say so.*

"It's more of a bedroom painting," he said diplomatically. "And," he turned towards the bed, "it complements *this* so nicely. I'd think you'd want to keep them together."

Londo's eyes lit up.

"You know, I hadn't thought of that. Actually, there was another painting I liked almost as much . . ." The ambassador put one hand on his hip and thoughtfully cupped his chin with the other. "I hadn't wanted to be too extravagant. But"—he clapped his hands together and rubbed them, looking fondly down at Vir—"now that you've pointed this out"—he shrugged expansively—"I can see that I'm doomed to have them both."

"I thought you were going to reclaim some of the furnishings from the delegates' quarters," Vir reminded him.

"We-elll. I was, but then I thought, people tend to be careless with things that don't belong to them. Between you and me," Londo said, leaning close, "they also tend to appropriate such things. I'm going to distribute my old furnishings among the delegates' suites and tell them I did so to give their rooms a 'homey' touch. Eh?" He nudged Vir, grinning at his own cleverness. "Besides, as I said before, they'll be spending a great deal of their time here."

In your bed? Vir thought in astonishment. Then he remembered Londo's weaknesses. *Well, maybe.* Though he personally thought the ambassador was doomed to disappointment. *The women who attend this conference will probably be dragons, all business.* Which meant no pleasure for poor Londo in his huge, lonely new bed.

"How much have you spent, Ambassador?" Vir asked tentatively.

"Not more than has been allowed, less than I'm going to, and enough to choke those maggots in accounting." He gave Vir a look that said "killjoy" as plain as words and marched out of the room.

Segrea's fist flashed out and flattened the human's nose. To his astonishment he felt it break and blood poured from it in an alarming gush.

Mercilessly, he followed up with another blow to the man's face, this time striking at his cheek. The human ducked his head and the blow took him just above the eye. The bone below the thin skin hurt Segrea's hand, but the human was hurt more. A cut opened, and again blood poured.

These humans wouldn't last a week on T'll, Segrea thought. *They lose fluids so easily.* It wasn't just the blood that made him think so. The human's naked sides were pouring with sweat, and when Segrea struck him drops flew into the crowd.

Segrea had taken a lot of punishment from his adversary, luring him, and the bettors, on to overconfidence, while the room heated up and the oxygen grew thin. Blood trickled from the corner of his mouth, where the inside of his cheek had been cut when the human had struck him with a powerful left, crushing the tender flesh against his sharp teeth.

Now he pounded his opponent with his fists, three-fingered fists that had looked so small and ineffectual at the beginning of the fight. Blow after blow after blow. Beating the hapless and gasping human around the ring as though they were engaged in some hostile dance.

Meanwhile, throughout the crowd, other T'llin put their carefully hoarded credits on Segrea at odds of six to one.

The human shook his head and skipped backwards, trying to gain some space to catch his breath.

But there's no air, Segrea thought, almost pitying. The man was a good fighter.

The air of Babylon 5 was somewhat richer in oxygen than

that of T'll. So here, in the rapidly depleting air of this barely ventilated room, he had the advantage of the human. He stayed fresh while his opponent staggered from more than Segrea's continual pounding.

The man slipped in his own blood and went to one knee, then he scrambled up, his eyes shocked.

"Finish it!" Haelstrac shouted from the sidelines.

Segrea nodded. Yes, it was time to put an end to it. Sooner or later Environmental Control would notice the incredibly high levels of carbon dioxide down here and send Security to investigate.

Besides, the crowd had been given their show. He pulled his fist back and threw all his weight behind it, striking the human on the point of his chin. The man's eyes crossed and he went over backwards like a falling tree. The slap of his bare back against the metal floor was loud in the sudden silence.

Segrea raised his arms above his head and the crowd let loose a wild approving roar.

As aliens of all types patted him in congratulations, Segrea watched Haelstrac grab the collar of the man who'd taken her bet. She gave him a shake and held out her hand. Then Miczyn was beside him.

"You have to come with me," he said urgently. "There's trouble."

CHAPTER 5

Susan Ivanova brushed the lush brown waves of her hair back and fastened it tightly, then began to braid it into the simple, businesslike style she wore while working. It hardened her face, and her gentle mother would have complained of that.

"You're so pretty," she would have said. "You should make more of yourself."

But it definitely commands respect, Ivanova thought. *And that, after all, is the name of the game.* It was also *how* you made more of yourself, in ways that really counted. *Mother would have come to understand that.*

Ivanova stared at her face in the mirror, seeing her mother's eyes and lips, her father's strong jaw and slightly squared chin.

No she wouldn't, Susan admitted. *She would have been nagging me about grandchildren for ten years now.* Ivanova sighed, and smiled sadly. *How I wish you'd had the chance to nag me, Mother.*

The three-note summons of the door chime broke her reverie.

"Just a minute," she called, buttoning her cuff.

She strode across her living room to the door. A room that, despite her years on Babylon 5, didn't seem to bear the imprint of her personality. Or perhaps revealed it all too well, efficient, attractive, functional—its beauty muted by severe lines and cold colors.

"Open," she said, and fastened the other sleeve.

No one was there.

Ivanova looked out the door and up and down the hallway. No one. But precisely centered in front of the door was a plain white plate. On it was a data crystal, standing on its larger end.

Susan automatically stooped to pick it up, then froze. To say the least, this was unusual. She straightened, frowning in thought. Then, sighing in exasperation, tapped her link.

"Garibaldi?"

"Ye-esss," he answered.

She grinned. "This is Ivanova. Someone's left me a little . . . offering, I guess, outside my door."

"Don't touch it," Garibaldi cautioned her.

"My thoughts exactly."

"I'll be right over," he said.

"Well?" she asked him, half an hour later, as she leaned against her door frame.

Garibaldi scanned it one more time to be sure.

"It's a data crystal on a plate."

"I'm missing breakfast for a data crystal?"

"On a plate," the Security Chief said, offering it to her.

"Shouldn't you be checking it for fingerprints or skin oils or poison, or whatever?" she asked, not taking it.

"I already did. It's clean."

"Why doesn't that make me feel better?" she asked glumly. Taking the plate, she walked over to her computer. "Care to join me?" she asked.

"I thought you'd never ask," he said, drawing up a chair. "Um." He put his hand over hers, before she could insert the crystal into its slot. Susan looked at him curiously.

"It's possible that whoever left this has recorded something that you might find embarrassing. So, if you'd like, I can wait outside until you've reviewed it."

She smiled, pleased at his discretion. *Every now and*

again, the guy succeeds in showing an appropriate degree of sensitivity, she thought. *There's hope for you yet, Michael.*

"Fortunately, I haven't done anything embarrassing," Ivanova said.

"What, never?" Garibaldi asked.

"Well, not on camera."

"That you're aware of."

She looked at him out of the corner of her eye. *Then again, not a whole lot of hope.*

"Thank you, Garibaldi. But I've already had the creeps once this morning. I don't need a second helping."

"Is that a subconscious hint that you're hungry?" he teased.

Ivanova inserted the crystal.

"I want some coffee too," she groused.

The screen showed a picture obviously taken by a camera hidden on someone's collar button. It had the shaky, bouncy quality of movement that a "worn" camera has, and that no amount of technology can completely eliminate.

The camera wearer turned in a slow circle, as though trying to establish the location beyond a doubt.

"That's Io Base," Ivanova said. "I recognize that fountain. It's right out in front of headquarters."

"You were assigned there?" Garibaldi asked, watching the screen intently.

"No, my brother was. An image of the fountain preceded all his recordings. I think it was an emblem the censors used to show that it had been passed, no state secrets included."

On the screen, a young man in an Earthforce uniform exited the headquarters building and headed towards the camera.

He had smooth brown hair, brushed back from his high forehead, level blue eyes, a full, almost feminine mouth, and a firm jaw with a squarish chin.

"He looks a lot like you," Garibaldi observed.

"He should," Susan said in wary astonishment. "That's my brother Vanya."

On the screen the young Earthforce soldier had come into conversational range.

"You have it?" Susan's brother asked.

"Right here," answered an accented voice. A hand appeared holding a credit chit. Vanya Ivanova reached for it and the hand dropped from sight. "Do *you* have it?"

Vanya held up a crystal.

"This has a list of the passwords and the order in which they must be given in order to get you into the armory." He held up a key card. "This will open the armory door. And this one will get you into the secure area." He licked his lips. "Listen, wouldn't it be easier all 'round if you just let me give you the specs on these weapons?"

"Easier, perhaps. But not as accurate. We have no guarantee that you have access to the complete plans. This way we use our scanners, nothing's left out by accident."

The chit changed hands.

"You'd better not be holding out on me," Vanya warned.

"It's all there," the voice said soothingly. "A little trust, if you please. *I'm* sure you know better than to try to palm me off with the key to the enlisted men's washroom."

Susan's brother narrowed his eyes.

"My information's good," he said. "If you don't trust me you can always find another source."

"Then give it back," a hand appeared, "and I'll go elsewhere."

The young man clenched his hand around the credit chit.

"No." He looked around, a muscle in his jaw jumping as he thought. "After tonight, though, we're finished."

"We're finished when I say we're finished, Vanya Ivanova. Yeeesss. I know your real name, and your rank, and your serial number. I've got you good and hooked, little fish, and the harder you fight it, the more you'll hurt yourself."

Vanya glared, and the skin around his nostrils whitened.

"Ivanova, Ivanova, calm yourself. You can only be a virgin once. From now on it won't hurt so much, I promise you. Now, when I call you and ask to buy information from you, you will sell it to me. Won't you?''

"Or what?"

"Or I will have to inform your superiors that you are the troubling leak they've sprung. And, my friend, I can prove it.''

Vanya blanched and rubbed a hand through his hair, mussing it.

"Don't take it so hard, boy. We'll have a profitable relationship, I promise you. When you leave the service you'll be rich, and no one need ever know. Come,'' there was laughter, "we're partners, eh?"

"Not exactly,'' Vanya said bitterly. Then, with a final defiant glare, he turned on his heel, walked back to the building, and went inside.

Garibaldi looked at Ivanova. A muscle was jumping in her jaw. She kept her eyes on the screen.

The camera wearer had apparently decided not to film anything else, for the screen went blank.

"It doesn't prove a thing,'' Garibaldi said. "A recording like this, delivered anonymously . . . doesn't mean a thing.''

"It's not true,'' Susan said as though she hadn't heard. "He would never, *never* do that.''

"I believe you,'' he agreed. "And these things are so easily, and so seamlessly faked that they're not even admissible as evidence in kangaroo courts.''

"I know it isn't evidence,'' she said in a choked voice. She pressed her lips together so tightly they disappeared, and turned her face away. "How could they *do* that to him?'' she asked, hoarse with outrage and pain.

"They're doing this to you, Susan, not to him. But it can't touch you unless you let it.''

She covered her eyes with one hand and visibly struggled to regain her composure.

"Okay,'' Garibaldi said, hoping to distract her, "you've made someone mad. Who?''

"I make someone, somewhere, mad five times a day, Garibaldi. So if that's your only criteria for a suspect we'll have to round up a quarter of the people on the station."

"Don't flatter yourself Ivanova, you're not *that* irritating."

She snorted a moist little laugh.

"Now that I have your attention, I'd like to point out, again, that this crystal doesn't mean a thing in real terms." She froze and he hurried on, "It was a rotten way to start your day and a low blow besides, but it doesn't count for anything."

"I know that it shouldn't matter, but it will." She turned to him, her eyes full of fury and bright with the hint of tears. "My brother's dead. He can't defend himself."

"He wouldn't have to!" Garibaldi exclaimed.

"Oh, wake up, Garibaldi! Even alleged mud sticks! If this becomes a matter of public record, then every time I come up for promotion it will be a factor. It shouldn't be, but it will." She slumped miserably in her chair. "You know that as well as I do."

Garibaldi raised his brows and puffed out his cheeks.

"I dunno, I kinda like to think of the folks on the review board as a reasonably fair-minded bunch. Not perfect, mind you, but fair."

"Yeah, well, fair is a playground word, Garibaldi."

He stood up. "You need your coffee."

She raised her hands and snapped, "*This* is not going to be solved by coffee!"

"Not even real coffee," he agreed. "Look, Susan, you are not obligated to turn this thing in. And I recommend that you don't. But I should warn you that this looks like step one in a blackmailing campaign. So be prepared for things to get ugly."

Susan glared up at him.

"Uglier," he amended. He tapped her shoulder. "C'mon, let's go eat."

She chewed her lip for a moment, then stood and slipped into her jacket.

"Y'know," she said as they headed out the door, "if you were any kind of a friend you'd offer to pay."

"Oh, all right," he grumbled.

"Well, not if you're going to take that attitude."

"I said all right."

"Real coffee?"

"Don't push it."

Na'Toth woke, lying on her side, an ache in all her muscles from the spasms brought on by the shock stick. Her mouth was as dry as the blanket that still covered her head, and she felt somewhat smothered. Her hands and feet were bound, not excruciatingly tight, but it wouldn't be easy to free herself. She was queasy and the back of her throat burned. Through the pain that pounded in her temples she heard voices.

"How could you?" a male voice whispered, hissing in his rage. "Do nothing rash! Do-nothing-rash."

"If you say that one more time, Miczyn, I may be driven to do something very rash indeed," a deeper voice rumbled.

"He's right, though," a woman said in a harsh whisper. "This was very foolish, very ill planned."

"Unless we intend to punish them," the deep voice remarked, "I suggest we dismiss these overeager youngsters. The fewer who know our councils, the better."

"Go!" the voice named Miczyn said. "But remember the Prime Olorasin's stricture." There was a thoughtful pause. "This is not the time for boldness."

Na'Toth moved cautiously, and turning her head managed to move the blanket slightly. Blessedly cool air flowed in, sweet and welcome despite its metallic tang, refreshing her somewhat. From the cover of a fold she could see feet in worn boots and the ragged hems of their garments. She wished for the boldness to move just a little more, to see their faces.

They must be T'llin, she thought. *Prime is a T'llin office. And Olorasin, I know that name.* Though how or in what connotation she couldn't remember. A thrill of terror stabbed through her. *If they are T'llin, these people will kill me without a qualm.* In fact she couldn't understand why she wasn't already dead.

Carefully she tested her bonds. Her hands and feet were somewhat numb, but they would at least allow her to run, if not to ably defend herself. *Assuming I can free myself in time.*

A large pair of battered boots approached her and gave her a nudge. Na'Toth was amazed by its gentleness. She'd expected to be kicked. *By the size of the feet,* she thought, *I doubt I could have faked unconsciousness if he'd put any effort behind it.*

The deep voice, sounding tired, said, "Stuff her out an air lock. There's nothing to connect her to us." He gave a nasty snicker. "Not if she's too dead to talk."

"I saw her face," the woman said. "She's the one you saved me from, Segrea."

"Then . . ." Miczyn said, in a slow stunned voice, "she's the Narn ambassador's attaché."

There was an inarticulate sound and a muffled boom as someone slammed the bulkhead. Na'Toth's heart sped up again and she held her breath.

"Are you *sure*?" the deep voice demanded.

Na'Toth forced herself to lie still, though her glands told her to fight, to flee, and she almost strangled trying not to pant.

"I asked around. That's what I heard. 'The Narn's assistant fetch-it got her ass kicked,' is how my Centauri source put it."

"Oh, wonderful!" the woman snapped. "By all means let us push her out an air lock. No one will ever miss *her.*"

"What are we going to do?" Miczyn asked, his voice quivering on the edge of hysteria.

Big boots came back into view, headed for Na'Toth.

"She didn't see any faces when the youngsters took her, did she?" he asked.

"N-no," Miczyn said. "They said they had the blanket over her head before she had any idea they were there."

"Then we're going to take all her credits and leave her here. When she wakes up she can take care of herself. Everybody knows the risks they're taking when they come to Down Below. And that's just what security will tell her if she's fool enough to make a complaint."

Segrea threw back the blanket and studied the Narn female carefully. He hated their faces, the bony chins, the wrinkled flesh around their red eyes, the loathsome black spots on their foreheads that always reminded him of the rotting of some tender skinned fruit. He made a sound of disgust and began to ransack her clothing, handing his prizes off to Miczyn and Haelstrac.

They stripped her of anything that had a remote chance of being valuable, including her honor-knife, which they took from its sheath in her boot. Na'Toth almost moved then, her eyelids fluttered, but she managed to keep them closed. The T'llin searching her felt her tense and froze. She decided to allow herself a little groan.

"She's coming to," Miczyn gasped, his voice shrill.

"Yes," Segrea murmured, considering. He stood. "Let's go."

"And no more of this," Miczyn insisted. "Do noth—"

"Shut up," Haelstrac snarled.

"Captain Sheridan, there's a gold level communication from Admiral Wilson."

"Put him through," Sheridan said, entering his security clearance code.

He'd been expecting some sort of communiqué from the Joint Chiefs. Since it was unlikely that they'd allow this Narn-Centauri conference to take place without putting their mark on it in some way. Sheridan tried to prepare himself for whatever unnecessary and no doubt time-consuming business they'd thought up for him.

Wilson's dour face filled the screen, wearing the expression of a man who'd heard the last trump sounding.

"Captain," Wilson said gravely.

"Hello, Admiral," Sheridan said, keeping it short, but smiling pleasantly. *I have nothing better to do than to cater to your every whim, Sir,* he thought.

Maybe that was a little unfair. Wilson was a brisk man who stated his business and went away. There were several who would happily niggle you to death with questions about details that were frankly the province of lower ranks than Sheridan's.

Wilson stared silently out of the screen for a moment. Then he cleared his throat.

Almost nervously, Sheridan thought, growing a bit uneasy himself.

"I've been asked to inquire what arrangements you've made for the reporters," the Admiral asked.

"The reporters!" *Of all things!* Sheridan thought in astonishment. "We're housing them in Section Blue sixteen, Sir. It's recently been remodeled, so they'll be seeing our best side. And we're providing them with office space and conference rooms in the business park on Green twelve. Which is also far enough away from the actual Narn-Centauri conference site that there should be a notable reduction in security problems."

He'd been proud of that. "We're arranging for daily press conferences with Narn and Centauri representatives, simultaneously, in different rooms. The reporters will be assigned by lot to a different conference each day. And we're having someone from the Public Information Office, a woman named Jeri Freedman, do a summing-up after the Narn and Centauri news conferences."

Wilson looked pained, almost ashamed.

Uh oh.

"Um. The, uh, President's niece will be attending as a reporter for her college news-pad. She has requested an opportunity to interview both delegations.'' The Admiral hadn't lifted his eyes from the desk before him during this speech.

"Of course, Sir. I'll put her name on the list. Quite a number of reporters have asked for interviews.'' *And quite a number of them are going to be bitterly disappointed.* Sheridan wondered how the President's niece handled frustration.

This time Wilson's eyes bored into his. "It would be a good idea to put her name at the top of the list,'' he said.

"Uh, yes, Sir. That is an order, Sir?''

The Admiral colored slightly. "Yes,'' he said in a choked voice.

Sheridan felt a sinking feeling. It was shocking for someone on the Joint Chiefs of Staff to end up carrying water for a politician this way. Some genuinely heavy pressure would have had to be applied to get Wilson to do it. *And I now have a recorded order,* Sheridan thought. *The great military game of cover-your-butt is in full swing.*

"Did I understand you, Sir, to say that the young lady wished to speak to the entire delegation?''

"You did. There are also several celebrity reporters on their way, making similar requests. I suggest that you ensure that they also receive an opportunity to . . . you know. Do the in-depth thing.''

"Yes, Sir.'' *I suppose I should be grateful it isn't worse,* Sheridan thought. Then, *How could it be worse?* He was being ordered to do something totally out of his control. *They might as well order me to make it rain on Mars.*

"I think,'' Wilson said, slowly, "that perhaps President Clark's niece should be segregated from the general run of reporters.''

"I agree, Sir. But the young lady''—*Doesn't this girl have a name?*—"might be looking forward to hobnobbing with future colleagues.''

"Yes.'' The Admiral stared lugubriously from the screen. "Have her accompanied by a Security person, then. Don't let her do anything crazy.''

"Yes, Sir." *Crazy?* He wondered what was on file about this young woman.

"Everything else under control?"

"Yes, Sir."

"Good. Wilson out." The Admiral's face was replaced by the Babylon 5 logo.

"Yes, Sir." Sheridan sank down in his chair. This was a very tall order. *On second thought, both G'Kar and Londo will be happy to accommodate President Clark's niece. I know they will. They'll be thrilled! But there'll be a price.* And that price worried him.

It was one thing to become indebted for a good solid reason. Satisfying the egotistical whim of a spoiled kid just didn't qualify in Sheridan's estimation.

Larkin sat at his boards in a state of barely contained excitement. Ivanova was late to her post and he knew it was his doing. Major Atembe kept glancing at the door, obviously impatient to turn control of C and C over to his superior. Gleeful laughter bubbled within Larkin, barely contained. It made him giddy, and that amused his coworkers.

"What, did you get laid last night?" Kamal muttered with a knowing smile.

"A gentleman never tells," Larkin replied primly. But his smile was bright enough to imply that Kamal was right.

A lot you know, Larkin thought, feeling superior. *There are any number of reasons for me to be feeling good. It says something pretty pathetic about you that sex is the only one you can think of.*

He wondered what Ivanova's reaction had been to the data crystal. *I wish I could have been there when she played it. C'mon! I want to see your face,* he thought impatiently. *Get your ass to work, Iron Lady. I'm looking forward to seeing you rust.*

They all crumbled in the end. Because everybody had a weak spot and if you so much as touched them there, the toughest mother in Earthforce crumpled like a crushed rose.

Ivanova might be the toughest nut I've ever tried to crack, Larkin thought speculatively. For a moment he felt like an artist evaluating a portrait subject. Then impatience overwhelmed him again. *C'mon, bitch, I want to see your face!*

Just then Susan Ivanova entered Command and Control, moving briskly to her station.

"Major Atembe," she said with a smile, "my apologies for being so late."

"Not at all," the Major replied and began to relay his report.

Larkin's spirits sank. She was perfectly calm; to all appearances she had not a trouble in the world. *Maybe she hasn't played it yet,* he thought. *That must be it.* She couldn't possibly be this controlled if she had.

"Larkin!" Kamal hoarsely whispered. "Get your eyes back on your board. Things are going to hell out there!"

Turning back, Larkin was shocked to see how chaotic things had gotten in just the few minutes he'd been distracted. With a sick feeling in his stomach he dove into the task of straightening his neglected traffic patterns. It seemed as though everyone out there had seized the chance to run helter-skelter round the station. By sheer good luck, and an unusual amount of concentration on his part, everyone was back in their proper approach in just a few minutes. *And no one the wiser.*

He looked up and caught Ivanova's eye. She raised one brow meaningfully and Larkin's insides turned to water.

She knows, he thought in terror. *What am I going to do? She knows it was me!*

CHAPTER 6

Garibaldi stroked the smooth surface of a leaf as he idly looked out Captain Sheridan's office window. The planter beside him was filled with a variety of plants, most of them from Earth; miniature palms, dwarf rosebushes, a spray of bougainvillea, a cluster of pale pink geraniums.

Plants were everywhere on B5, marvelous little air machines that they were. And according to the shrinks they provided an enormous psychological advantage, offering the illusion that B5 was an actual world, instead of a giant tin can in space. But the Chief's eyes were on a party of workmen just off to the right.

"Oh no," he said.

Sheridan looked up for a moment from the security report he'd been reading, his face a study in broken concentration.

"What?" he asked vaguely.

"They're setting up that damned InterGalactic Assurance statue practically in front of your window. If I were you I'd invest in some shades, pronto."

Sheridan's eyebrows went up in inquiry.

"I only saw a part of it," Garibaldi admitted, "but it was uuuug-ly!" He shuddered. "There ought to be a law against setting up stuff like that in public. Aesthetic pollution."

The Captain shrugged. "If it were up to me, I'd tell 'em to set up their statues on Earth where there's room for them. And I'd ask your advice before granting permission for one to be put up. But it isn't up to me and they didn't even ask *my* advice, so I guess we'll just have to live with it."

"I dunno," Garibaldi muttered, "I think this thing may be a menace to public health. It's that awful."

Sheridan folded his hands before him on his desk. "I'm doing the unveiling."

The Chief stared at him, his jaw dropping. "You? You're kidding!" *That's way outside your preferred duties,* Garibaldi thought in astonishment. Then realized how familiar he'd been. "Sir," he added belatedly.

Sheridan had to smile at the Chief's startled reaction. *I hadn't realized I was that transparent.*

"I figure it's good practice at public speaking of the insincere and politically innocuous style," Sheridan said. "Besides, it would take a tougher man than I am to say no to Semana MacBride."

"She's a stunner," the Chief conceded, taking a seat before the Captain's desk. "But she dings my 'watch-it' button. I'll be glad when she's gone."

The Captain's brows went up. "Just because she brought us an ugly statue?" Sheridan asked. "Or is there something else?"

Garibaldi waggled his hand, scowling. "Just a gut feeling. I've sent to Earth Central to see if she's got a record, but I don't expect to hear back 'til tomorrow at the earliest. I dunno." He shrugged. "Maybe all art dealers feel like con men."

"Well, then, I'll definitely expect you to show up for the ceremony," the Captain said. "It'll give you a chance to observe her in her element."

"You know I wouldn't miss one of your speeches, Captain."

"Don't lie to me, Garibaldi. I know it's the hors d'oeuvres you're after.

Garibaldi entered his office in Security with a sigh of relief. *Now, to call Susan.* That was a nasty little problem she was having, a real low blow. He sat behind his desk and reached for the caller. But a tone indicated an incoming message.

G'Kar's angry face filled the screen as though he were inside it pressing his nose against the glass.

"Chief Garibaldi," he growled, almost frothing, "I want to see you in my quarters immediately!" Then his image was gone.

The Chief stared at the screen in astonishment.

"Well, G'Kar, I'm kinda busy right now," he said to the BabCom logo. "Would you care to tell me a little about your problem?"

Irritably pushing himself to his feet, he set off for the Narn Ambassador's quarters. "No rest for the wicked—or those of us who have to deal with 'em.'' *This better be good. I'm not fond of being sent for like this.*

He'd barely gone twenty paces before his temper began to cool, and he reminded himself that the Narn were under a lot of pressure, a situation they often dealt with by throwing a tantrum.

No, Garibaldi told himself, *G'Kar was sincerely angry, so it wasn't just letting off steam. He probably does have a legitimate complaint.* Or it could be some sort of ploy to make the Centauri look bad. *Nah! Not this close to the conference.* Unless it was something the Centauri themselves had done to be annoying. They were growing more obnoxious by the hour. *Or by the victory.* They'd been much more agreeable as washed-up has-beens.

He entered the lift and leaned against the wall.

"Don't go imagining things," his grandmother had once told him when he was obsessively worrying about something. "It's like looking for trouble. And if you go looking for trouble, you'll always find more than your share."

Which was certainly true enough.

Unfortunately, looking for trouble was in his job description.

* * *

"I will not tolerate assaults on my staff, Garibaldi," G'Kar raged. "How could this happen? She was assaulted, she was robbed"—the Ambassador lowered his voice dramatically and pointed at Na'Toth—"it's a wonder she wasn't killed."

Stretching to his full height, G'Kar crossed his arms over his chest and allowed his face to assume its most regal expression. "I wait to hear your explanation."

Garibaldi looked at the Ambassador for a long moment, long enough to establish that he wasn't about to jump through hoops just because somebody was yelling.

"Before I attempt any explanations," he said, "I'd like to ask a few questions."

He turned to Na'Toth, who had bandages around her wrists, startlingly white against her dark skin, and a sullen, guilty expression on her face.

"Where did the attack take place?" he asked.

She shifted painfully in her seat and lowered her eyes.

"I was in Down Below . . ."

"The attack took place in Down Below?"

"Yes."

"Were you alone?"

She took a deep breath, as though holding on to her temper with difficulty. "Yes."

Garibaldi thrust his hands into his pockets and turned to the Ambassador.

"That explains it, G'Kar. Going into Down Below by yourself is asking to get mugged. I don't like it any more than you do, but it's a fact of life."

"Is that all you have to say?" G'Kar hissed, his red eyes focused like laser beams on the Security Chief's face.

"No. You asked for an explanation of how this could have happened, now you've got it." He turned back to Na'Toth, who was also boring holes in him with her eyes. "What were you doing down there?"

"*I* was minding my business," she said aggressively. "Since you wouldn't mind yours. I was trying to obtain information about the T'llin hiding on the station. They saw me and attacked me with a shock wand.''

''And robbed you,'' Garibaldi added thoughtfully.

Na'Toth stood and drew herself up to her full height.

''They took my honor-knife,'' she said as though her honor had gone with it. ''They discussed killing me, but were afraid of reprisals.''

The Chief felt sorry for her. Na'Toth was a proud woman, and a very capable warrior; it was surprising that anyone had gotten the drop on her. To be helpless to protect something she obviously valued had hit her hard. And she still quivered from the effects of the shock wand.

''You should report to Medlab,'' he told her.

''I want your assurance that *this* time you'll do something!'' she insisted.

''This is the second time my attaché has been attacked by these T'llin, Garibaldi,'' G'Kar said, moving to stand uncomfortably close beside him, ''and I, too, want to know what you're going to do about it.''

With the reminder of the earlier incident Garibaldi narrowed his eyes and looked at Na'Toth.

''Did you see their faces?'' he asked her.

Her very immobility was as good as a flinch.

''You didn't, did you?''

Na'Toth lowered her eyes.

''No,'' she said reluctantly. ''But,'' and her eyes came up again, ''they spoke of the Prime Olorasin.''

''Prime is a T'llin political office,'' G'Kar informed him. ''And Olorasin is the name of a T'llin renegade.'' He walked around his desk and sat down. ''I don't imagine the average mugger in Down Below would take much interest in T'llin politics. Do you, Chief Garibaldi?''

''No,'' the Chief agreed. ''But my point was that Na'Toth can't describe or identify the particular T'llin that attacked her, because she didn't see them. Therefore, though I will do my best, you have to admit it's going to be hard to apprehend these people.''

"If there are any T'llin on Babylon 5 at all," G'Kar said with certainty, "they shouldn't be here. Because I know that they don't have legal travel documents. I know that, because the Narn Regime has restricted them to their homeworld as being too dangerous to let loose on an unsuspecting universe. Therefore, I suggest, Chief Garibaldi, that you round them all up and ship them back to T'll before they *do* kill somebody. If they haven't already." G'Kar favored him with a contemptuous smile. "That should simplify your task somewhat. Shouldn't it?"

"I'll look into it," Garibaldi assured them. "And I'll keep you up to date on my findings. In the meantime, I'd like your assurance that there'll be no more vigilante spy excursions to Down Below." He looked steadily at G'Kar, ignoring the small, outraged sound Na'Toth made in her throat.

"I assure you," G'Kar said after a moment, placing his hands carefully before him on the desk, "that I consider my assistant far too valuable to put in harm's way. And we have much to do in the coming weeks. But I want your assurance," he said, pointing at the Security Chief, "that you will be doing your utmost to find and expel these people."

"I will-do-my-job," Garibaldi said firmly. "Go to Medlab," he said to Na'Toth. He nodded at both of them. "Good day."

And with that he left the two Narn glaring uncertainly at each other in the gloom of G'Kar's office.

Garibaldi got off the lift on the Mall level and leaned on the railing of one of the overhead walkways to look at the people below. His professional eye picked out half a dozen suspicious occurrences before the pickpockets and the hustlers noticed him. He watched while the corridor below bled shady characters until it was clean.

Then he turned his mind to the interview he'd just had with the Narns.

G'Kar hasn't tried to bull his way over me like that since he first came here. Over time, the Narn had learned that

humans would only give in to his obnoxiousness occasionally, that the Minbari didn't have to and the Centauri were
only amused by it. He'd adjusted his behavior accordingly.
So why is he trying this now?

*At a guess, it's the T'llin. They're living evidence of Narn
misbehavior.* On site at a time when the Narn were trying to
represent themselves as an innocent, civilized society crim-
inally attacked by the black-hearted Centauri.

*Things could get really awkward if the T'llin decide to
crawl out of Down Below in their rags and stare hollow-
eyed into the* Universe Today *cameras discussing the Narn
situation as they see it.* And G'Kar knew it, too.

Hence all this talk about pirates and murderers. Suddenly
he wondered if Na'Toth had ever been attacked at all. He
also knew that it was only a matter of time before G'Kar
moved to outflank him by complaining to Sheridan that he'd
been dragging his feet.

*Whereupon the Captain will naturally ask, "Why haven't
I heard of this before, Garibaldi?" And I get another black
mark. So . . . okay, two things,* he thought as he strode towards the lift. *First, get to Down Below and find out what
the deal is with these people. Second, get the Captain up to
speed on this.* He was getting the feeling that things were
going to blow up very fast on this one.

"You're going to be fine," Dr. Franklin said, and turned to
put his instrument away.

Na'Toth swung herself into a sitting position and then
swayed as though dizzy.

"Whoa," Franklin said, putting a steadying hand on her
shoulder. "I said you're *going* to be fine. First you have to
go back to your quarters and sleep for at least twelve hours.
I'll give you a sedative to help you rest."

"Nonsense, Doctor. We Narn are more hardy than you
humans. And I have work to do."

"If you don't rest now, you'll be impaired for a week,
Na'Toth. I know what I'm talking about."

She slid off the examining table and stood leaning against it, blinking rapidly before taking her full weight on her feet.

"I simply cannot spare the time. I'll remain seated at my desk for twelve hours. It's my body that needs rest, not my mind. As I said, we Narn are a strong people." She gave him a kind but condescending smile.

Franklin cocked his dark head and crossed his arms over his chest.

"Lady, I know more about Narn physiology than you ever will. Because, unlike you, I've not only taken Narn bodies apart," he raised his brows and leaned towards her, "I've put them back together again."

Na'Toth blinked.

He lifted her hand and slapped a packet of pills into her palm. "Now go back to your quarters, take these, and go-to-sleep."

She still looked mulish, in a way that only the Narn can. So he said, "I'll call G'Kar and have him look in on you later."

"No!" Na'Toth said quickly, closing her hand over the pills. "I'll take them." She turned and struggled to the door.

"Should I send someone with you?" Franklin asked, his brow furrowed with concern.

"Of course not," she said proudly. "I got here by myself, didn't I?" But she had to admit, lying down on the doctor's examining table seemed to have taken something out of her. "I'll be fine."

Franklin watched her leave with a frown on his face. Then he turned to his viewer. In a moment, G'Kar answered his call.

"Ah, Doctor. How is Na'Toth?"

"Very stressed, G'Kar, but otherwise not significantly hurt. What she needs right now is bed rest. But I'm concerned that she'll stop off at her office to straighten things out a little and get carried away. You're much the same way, I've noticed. Incredibly hardworking."

The Ambassador smiled and nodded, his expression that of a cat being stroked.

"I appreciate your concern, Dr. Franklin. I'll make certain Na'Toth takes your advice. Thank you. G'Kar out."

Franklin smiled privately. *Well, his attitude has sure improved.* He could remember when G'Kar always signed off with a sneer.

Haelstrac and Miczyn watched the rental office with growing anxiety. Through the large office window across the corridor they could see the cheery, middle-aged woman who'd been serving their human shill, insistently dragging him to her Minbari superior's office.

"Why are they doing that?" Miczyn asked. His cheeks were pale with anxiety. "They haven't made anyone else go in there."

Haelstrac shrugged irritably.

"Because they don't know him, because the deposit was of a certain size, because they're impressed with him, or not. How should I know?" she snarled, taking her own anxiety out on her companion.

The Minbari looked their representative over with a cold eye and said a few words.

The human nodded and smiled and said a few words back, while the female rental agent remained stubbornly cheerful. Though her eyes watched her superior warily.

There was a tense moment as the Minbari apparently considered the human's remarks. Then the Minbari nodded and offered a tiny, polite smile. The woman rental agent appeared to laugh aloud as she escorted her client out of the office.

Across the corridor, Miczyn and Haelstrac released their pent breath at the same time. Then they retreated to the place where they were to meet their go-between.

"It's got eight toilets and eight sinks and a reception area in front that completely hides the space in back. There's a delivery door that opens out onto the back corridor." The man handed over two sets of keys. "For a, uh, slight fee I'll be happy to act as a front for you."

Miczyn stared at him mystified, while Haelstrac glared.

"We're not wealthy," she said firmly.

"Oh, I come cheap," the man assured them.

"And if we accept your proposal," Haelstrac said cautiously, "will you agree not to abuse our trust by, for example, using the office for some illegal activity?"

"How illegal?" the human asked.

Miczyn's eyes flashed. "Our principals will allow *nothing* illegal," he said haughtily.

The man moved closer until he towered over the young T'llin.

"Then they shouldn't be told that what I've just done on your behalf is against the law." He snaked his head close to Miczyn's. "Should they?"

Haelstrac thrust her arm between them. "Let me put it another way. We do not want the difficulty of dealing with Station Security. While we might not object to helping a friend"—she paused and gave him the full benefit of her sharp-toothed smile—"if our friend were to help himself at our expense . . . Well. There would be unpleasant consequences." She bowed formally to the human. "I will discuss your proposal with my friends. Make no plans until you have heard from us."

They withdrew and hastened to Down Below where they met with their confederates.

"It's done," Haelstrac said, holding up the keys. "Gather everyone up and send them to our new address in the business park on Green twelve."

"There's a problem," Miczyn said. He was gratified by the stillness this announcement caused to settle over the group. "Our go-between wants to front for us. I think he also wants to use the address for some illegal purpose."

"Yes," Haelstrac agreed. "What shall we do about him?"

"We shall hire him," Segrea murmured. "And keep him too busy to get into mischief. If we offer fair compensation and guarantee his safety I think you'll find him reasonable." He gave a little chuckle, and the others smiled and nodded. Segrea had a way with the unreasonable.

CHAPTER 7

HE *should* have tapped one of the covert operatives they'd stuck down here. Or at most availed himself of the numerous paid informers that hung out in the bars just outside of Down Below. Because there was no justifiable reason for the head of Station Security to be slouching around the most dangerous part of B5 dressed like a bum.

Except that after days of dealing with the ambassadors and the upper echelon and the endless bureaucratic make-work I need to do something real.

Besides, Garibaldi had lived in places that made Down Below look genteel, and survived. Not happily, but at least efficiently. *Well,* he sighed, *every day's an education and every place has a lesson to teach.* He just hoped he'd learn what he came to find out and not some lesson he'd already received too often. *Like how easy it is to get your ribs broken.*

He rubbed his face and mumbled, looking around vaguely, then stumbled on.

Garibaldi wore a grimy kerchief tied around his head pirate style, and a torn parka two sizes too big for him. His pants were ripped up one leg and held together with duct tape, and his T-shirt was so filthy he'd barely been able to bring himself to put it on.

The only decent things he wore, besides his underwear, were his shoes. On the theory that he might need to run at some point.

When your feet are your getaway, put 'em in a limousine,

he'd told himself. They'd stood out a mile until he'd found a pair of pants long enough to flop over them. The toes still stuck out, which bothered him like a hole in the pants at a fancy reception.

Aw, c'mon, he chided himself, *give yourself a break; it's dark down here, it barely shows.*

The Chief leaned against the wall at the juncture of two corridors, to all appearances exhausted, and looked surreptitiously around. People were pretty thin on the ground around here and he was beginning to worry that he'd strayed into uncharted gang territory.

Garibaldi strained his ears. *Oh, great,* he thought, *there it is again.* Someone was definitely following him. *It's the shoes. The damn shoes!* He'd known they'd be trouble and had refused, *as usual,* to listen to his own best advice. He was either too far out of practice for his own good, or he was getting old. *Nah, just getting more stupid the higher up the chain of command I go.* Like a lot of other people he could name.

That solved a mystery that had puzzled him as a young recruit. How could *all* the Echelons Beyond Reality be so dumb? An old—and strictly nonregulation—drill song went through his head, and he muttered it under his breath:

"I used to be an officer,
'till they found I was too smart;
They stripped away my rank tabs
When they found I could walk and fart..."

For a moment he contemplated leaving his shoes behind, placed in the middle of the corridor so they couldn't be missed. He smiled to contemplate the fight that would follow. There was another tiny sound and his head came up. *They're closing in.*

No more time for little games; it was time to use the shoes for the purpose he'd worn them. To get him out of here in one piece. As quietly as he could, Garibaldi bolted.

He tore down the corridor, cursing himself for getting caught in an area where there were few cross corridors. *Did they herd me into this?* he wondered. Perhaps he'd been subliminally aware of them and had reacted by trying to move out of their way. *Right where they wanted me to go.*

There was still nobody around. Not that he expected *help*, but it would have been nice to have a crowd to hide in.

Up ahead he saw the dark openings of a cross corridor and he put on a burst of speed. Behind him his followers weren't even trying to hide their pursuit anymore. The hard slap of feet on the bare metal of the corridor echoed and their harsh breathing was loud and spiked with irritated grunts.

Two? Garibaldi thought as he ran, not bothering to turn and look. *I coulda sworn there were more than that.*

He swung into the dark of the left-hand corridor, hoping to get back to the peopled sections of Down Below.

It was more the motion of air bearing a whiff of warm body odor that warned him than any visual clue.

He turned his body away from the attack and caught the blow of the sap on his shoulder blade. "Ah!" he cried involuntarily as the shot-filled sack struck him hard enough to make lights dance in front of his eyes. He swung back, putting his weight behind his fist, and hit his opponent while the man's arm was pulled back for another strike.

He couldn't see the guy and hit him clumsily, somewhere in the middle of his chest, but hard enough to win a grunt from him. *This guy must be enormous!* Garibaldi thought. He turned to run. The other two were catching up fast. A hand flashed out and caught his sleeve and the Chief skinned out of his jacket and kept going.

Up ahead, light spilled out of a corridor. *Lights and people,* Garibaldi thought in relief. *Shoes, do your thing.*

Behind, an incoherent roar of rage was followed by two smaller echoes.

Just as he reached the light, the sap, thrown like a baseball, slapped into the back of his skull with the force of a well-swung bat, and he went down bonelessly.

As his vision faded out he watched three people flee the corridor as the sound of his assailants' feet came closer.

Thanks, he thought sardonically.

"You're a lucky man," Dr. Franklin said cheerfully, after running one of his diagnostic devices over the Security Chief. "You've got nothing worse than a bone bruise."

"I thought I had a concussion," Garibaldi mumbled. He was seated on the examining table, holding his aching head in his hands while Franklin took a look at him.

"Oh you do," the doctor agreed, happily. "Less of one than you deserve, in fact. I was referring to your shoulder."

Garibaldi sat up straight and looked at him from the corner of his eye. "Have I ever told you how much I hate you?" he asked.

"Oh, that's just your headache talking. I'll give you something for that."

The Chief grinned painfully. "Thanks," he said. "Y'know, I don't remember much, but I could have sworn that somebody sat on my shoulders hitting me with my shoes."

Franklin went over to the counter, put down his instrument, and handed Garibaldi a mirror.

"Oh, geeze!" Garibaldi put it down disgustedly and looked away from Franklin, who stood watching with a carefully blank face.

The Chief looked in the mirror again. Suddenly, as though if he caught the mirror off guard he'd see something different. On the left side of his face was the perfect imprint, in lurid purple, of the sole of one of his running shoes.

"Don't say it," he warned Franklin.

"Say what?" the doctor asked, all innocence. "That you were an idiot for going down there alone? That you might at least have told someone where you were going? That it's a miracle they didn't recognize you and smash your skull? What don't you want me to say? Tell me and I won't say it."

Garibaldi grimaced and rolled his eyes. "Thanks. Only a real friend could restrain himself like that. What am I going to do?" he asked, gingerly touching his cheek. "I can't go around looking like this."

"You'd do better to ask Ivanova," Franklin told him. "Women have this gunk they put on to even out their skin tones. She'd probably know what you should get."

"Maybe I could get a little blush while I'm at it," the Chief said with a sneer. "Soften my features a little."

"Mmmm. Might work," Franklin agreed. "But don't soften them too much or they'll move you into social services." His face grew serious and concerned. "Michael, would you mind telling me what were you doing down there?" he asked. "Was it personal? Is there something that I . . . ?" He spread his hands helplessly, his expression offering aid if any were needed that he could give.

The chief gave him a quick grin. "I was trolling for T'llin."

"For what?"

"Pirates, according to Na'Toth and G'Kar. They want 'em off the station. Yesterday. And I wanted to see what I could find out about them. The T'llin I've observed seem to be families mostly, with a sprinkling of single people. Refugees." He shook his head and then groaned. "I just don't see them as cutthroats. The description doesn't match their behavior. Not that I've really studied the matter, that's just a casual observation." He shrugged. "The only complaints I've had are from the NARN."

Franklin looked doubtful. He cocked his head after a moment. "These are the people who attacked Na'Toth?" He leaned against the counter and crossed his arms over his chest. "They sure did a job on her. And as far as you know they're the same people who nearly broke your head."

"Yeah, they could be. But like Na'Toth, I didn't see them, and unlike her, I have to be positive about people I accuse."

"The timing fits," the doctor pointed out. "You go down

looking for these people and someone nearly cracks your skull open.''

"No.'' Garibaldi shook his head and winced. "The T'llin are gone. There are absolutely no sign of them. Kids and grampas and all. Gone. And no,'' he said, holding up a finger to forestall the doctor's next comment, "they didn't know I was looking for them, because I didn't tell anyone I was. So there was no leak.''

"Mmm,'' the doctor conceded. "But they knew the attack on Na'Toth might bring the station authorities down on them.'' He shrugged. "So they've gone to ground.''

"But where?'' Garibaldi demanded. "If they had credits they wouldn't have been in Down Below in the first place. And they are not there now! I'd stake my career on that.''

"I notice you didn't say your life,'' Sheridan said, coming up behind him.

"Nooo,'' Franklin agreed. "He's already done that.''

"Can I go?'' Garibaldi asked, picking up his shirt.

Franklin handed him a packet. "For your head.''

"Thanks.'' The Chief stuffed it into his pocket.

"We need to talk,'' Sheridan said as the Security Chief hopped off the table.

"Yes, Sir. We do.'' Garibaldi looked into Sheridan's puzzled blue eyes as he spoke. "If this would be a convenient time, Sir, perhaps we could go to one of our offices?''

"Mine,'' Sheridan said. Turning, he led the way out of Medlab.

Susan Ivanova smiled reassuringly as Ilias Larkin took a seat opposite her. She hated these interviews and the little cubby of an office they took place in gave her claustrophobia.

Or maybe it's just that I don't like telling people they don't measure up. That was true enough. She couldn't understand repeated failure. In Larkin's case it seemed almost willful. He was, so the tests said, intelligent enough for the work he was doing. There wasn't, so the tests said, any physical reason for his rotten performance. *Which leads to discussions like this,* Susan thought sourly, *where I get to be mom.* Sometimes a really overbearing mom, but at this stage things were still relatively friendly.

"You may be wondering what this is all about," she said, trying to look and sound positive.

Why can't I just say, "straighten up soldier or you'll end up working in the kitchen"? she wondered plaintively. *Then I could go back to work.* But no, studies had shown that sometimes a quiet talk could take care of problems like Larkin the first time out.

He just looked at her, angular features unreadable, straight brown hair falling boyishly over his forehead. But his Adam's apple bobbed as he swallowed nervously and his hands writhed in his lap like a nest of snakes.

"There's no need to be nervous," she continued. "I just wondered how you're fitting in here." She looked at him expectantly, still smiling.

He cleared his throat and looked down.

"That's really for you to tell me, Commander," he said quietly. He looked up at her with the wary eyes of a trapped rabbit.

"Well, to be honest," she said, folding her hands on the desk and leaning slightly forward, "you don't seem too happy."

"No, I'm fine," Larkin assured her, looking down and squeezing his thighs until his knuckles turned white.

Ivanova quietly took a deep breath and considered her strategy.

"Well," she said, going for broke, "although you came here with an excellent record your work is dangerously below standard and it's getting worse." He actually turned white. *Nice going, Ivanova, hit him with the soft soap, that'll win him over.* "So either you're not settling in, and incidently, not everyone does adapt to the station, or you're no good at your job. Since you've worked in traffic control for over four years and have a good record, that can't be the problem. Or maybe you're burnt out. Traffic's a stressful job and people do come to hate it . . ." She put on her best "talk to me" expression, but he didn't look up.

Okay, plan B, she thought.

"Why did you move into traffic control in the first place? Your aptitude tests don't show any particular . . . natural inclination for it," she said delicately.

He looked up and this time his eyes were burning. "It looked like a fast track to promotion, Sir."

Susan felt a sinking feeling. *Oh great,* she thought, *ambition without the willingness to work.*

"Well," she said patiently, "the fast track to promotion, if there is one, comes from doing the best work you can. Frankly, I think if you were working in one of the jobs you're best suited for you'd do much better. I *know* you'd be happier."

"Please don't transfer me, Commander," he pleaded. His expression became desperate, almost terrified. "I'll do better, I swear I will. I'll be the best controller in C and C. Just give me another chance." He looked at her with his eyes swimming in tears. *"Please".*

Good grief! This guy was ready to fall apart. *At the very least I've got to get him to talk to a psych counselor. And out of traffic. He's just not temperamentally suited to it.*

"Ilias," she said aloud, "you're miserable at this job. Why do you want to torture yourself like this?"

Now his lips were trembling. *He's going to cry,* she thought in disbelief.

"All right," she said, raising her hands. "But I want you to talk to a counselor. And I'm going to look into finding you work that will be more rewarding for you. Just look," she said, forestalling his protest. "But I'd like that to be one of the things you discuss with your counselor. And you have got to work on your inattentiveness, Larkin. Someone could get killed if you make a mistake." She stared at him, her expression serious. "We will not be having another of these discussions," Ivanova warned him. "If you don't attend counseling sessions and if your work doesn't improve immediately and stay improved, I'm moving you. Is that understood?''

He swallowed convulsively and nodded.

"Good." She stood up. "Stay here awhile to compose yourself. I'll expect you back at your post in fifteen minutes." Then she fled the office.

Good grief! Susan thought. *How has he managed to keep this job for four years?* She hoped she wasn't making a fatal mistake by keeping him on. *I'll just have to keep my eyes on him,* she thought. After all, it might be a temporary problem. *The counselor should sort it out,* she thought as she returned to her post.

How dare she? How dare she talk to him like that? *As if I was deformed or stupid or something,* Larkin thought, wild with rage. He stood and paced the tiny office, panting with emotion. *I'll fix you, bitch! I'm gonna put you in the hot seat!* How he didn't know, but she was gonna bleed. *Oh yeah,* he thought. *I'm gonna kick your ass.*

"So what possessed you," Sheridan asked as he took his place behind his desk, "to do something so incredibly"—he checked himself—"unwise?"

Garibaldi rubbed the side of his nose. *I deserved that,* he observed. *I deserved worse than that,* he admitted more honestly. "There's . . . been a situation brewing up that I wanted to check out personally."

"A situation?" Sheridan asked.

"A diplomatic kind of thing. See," the Chief adjusted his stance, "there are these people called the T'llin. No doubt you've heard of them." Sheridan nodded. "Well, G'kar says they're desperate, violent criminals and have to be deported back to Narn space. But most of them are families and they have never, not once, caused any trouble on the station except of course their illegal entry." He took a deep breath and burrowed his hands into his pockets. "Until they ran into Na'Toth."

Sheridan leaned back in his chair. "Ahn ha. And when did G'kar demand that they be deported?"

"After Na'Toth was attacked the second time."

"Do you mean to tell me that a diplomatic attaché was physically attacked twice by the same people and this is the first I'm hearing of it?" Sheridan was on his feet now and coming round the desk. "What were you waiting for? Murder?"

The Chief lowered his head and looked up at Sheridan.

"The first time Na'Toth was 'attacked' was in the middle of a brawl. She admitted that she didn't see her attacker and there were a number of Centauri involved. The T'llin she did see was a woman who fell at her feet just before Na'Toth got kicked." He shrugged. "I have to admit I didn't take the complaint all that seriously given the circumstances. But I really didn't have time to check it out."

"Oh?" Sheridan asked. He was still seething; Garibaldi should have informed him immediately. *Even if it was a Centauri and not a T'llin. It was still an alien diplomat that was attacked.*

"Apparently Na'Toth went to Down Below to see what she could find out," Garibaldi continued. "She went alone, and she was attacked and robbed."

Sheridan threw up his hands in disgust.

"So you decided to imitate her."

"I'm not sure I was mugged. I think I may have gotten too close to what I was looking for, and they stopped me . . . but made it *look* like a mugging."

Sheridan walked around his desk and sat down again. He stared at Garibaldi for a moment, considering what he'd been told. "What, if anything, did you find out?"

"They're gone." The Chief waved his arms in frustration. "Vanished like smoke. I did not see *one* T'llin in Down Below, and I was there long enough that I should have. And, by the way, Na'Toth didn't see her attackers the second time either."

"But G'Kar—" Sheridan began.

"—wants them hunted down and turned over to Narn authorities," Garibaldi finished for him.

Sheridan leaned his elbows on the desk and thought. "Do you think they've left the station?" he asked.

"Officially, they were never here," Garibaldi said with a wince. "We have no record of *any* T'llin ever coming to Babylon 5."

The Captain flopped back in his chair in shock and stared at the Security Chief. "Just how many T'llin are we talking about?"

The Chief grimaced. "Close to a hundred."

Sheridan's jaw actually dropped. "That's supposed to be impossible," he said. "I know that we've had the occasional individual creep on or off the station . . . But a group that size? How did it happen?" The Captain's eyes coldly demanded an explanation. "Just what was Security doing while that many people slipped onto the station undocumented?"

Garibaldi frowned and shifted position uncomfortably. "I don't know what you've heard about the Narn-T'llin situation, Sir."

"I've heard enough," Sheridan growled.

"Well, we've probably heard more. You do, in Security." The Chief probed his cheek with his tongue. "Knowing what we did, I guess there was a sort of unspoken conspiracy of silence about the matter."

"You *guess?*" Sheridan leaned forward. "Do you actually have any doubt that you were wrong to ignore this?"

The Chief pursed his lips. "No, Sir."

The Captain glared at the Security Chief for a moment more, then he remembered his meeting with the Primes and he gripped the armrests of his chair. *I'm not completely innocent myself,* he thought. *I let my sympathies get the better of me too.*

"I understand your feelings, Chief. But our primary duty

is to this station. Maybe your instincts are correct and these
are just innocent people fleeing for their lives. But we can't
be sure until we've at least questioned them. Find these people, if they're still on the station. Find out what they're up
to. If G'Kar is worried about them maybe we should be too.''

"Yes, Sir.'' Taking the Captain's remark as dismissal, the
Chief moved towards the door.

"And Garibaldi,'' Sheridan said levelly, ''keep me informed.''

"Yes, Sir.''

CHAPTER 8

SEMANA smiled at the crowd. *They're sure chowing down on the goodies,* she thought with amusement. Particularly welcome to the humans in the crowd were the exotic confections and cheeses of Earth that she'd imported. *Amazing how rare decent chocolates are out here.*

She watched Dr. Franklin study a tiny tomato stuffed with feta cheese as though he thought it too rare a thing to put into his mouth. He popped it in anyway and chewed, an expression of bliss descending on his handsome dark features. Then he looked around almost guiltily. Semana caught his eye. She smiled and nodded, saluting him with her champagne glass.

This is really pleasant, Semana thought. And all at InterGalactic Assurance's expense. *They'll never miss the little bit I kept for my trouble,* she reasoned. Besides, she was constitutionally unable to spend all those lovely credits without getting something for herself.

They'd spread a tarp over the grass around the statue, both to protect the delicate greenery and the guests' shoes. Long tables covered in white cloths flanked the lumpy, veiled form of the sculpture and waiters with trays of champagne and Centauri wines moved gracefully among the glittering throng. The air here in the green spaces was very fresh, and when a passing shower sprinkled the guests, everybody, aliens and humans alike, laughed delightedly.

Almost everyone had accepted her invitation to the unveiling, including Ambassador Kosh, and they'd all assured her he wouldn't come.

She'd welcomed him as graciously as she had the rest of her guests, but hadn't understood the few words he'd said.

Maybe he has a glitch in his translation program, she thought, gazing at the enigmatic alien. He stood off to one side, curtained like the main event of the evening. Her lips quirked. *Very like,* she thought.

And the Minbari ambassador. *What did she do to herself?* Semana wondered. *She's got* hair, *for heaven's sake!* And her figure seemed different too. Semana cocked her head, *I wonder whose idea that was.* It didn't seem a very Minbari thing to do.

The Centauri ambassador had been among the first to arrive.

"I know I should be fashionably late," he'd said after gallantly kissing her hand, "but I could not resist your charm, dear lady."

And how I managed not to puke... Semana thought sourly.

As yet her mark hadn't shown and she was getting anxious. As anxious as Captain Sheridan looked. You'd have thought he was going to have major surgery instead of merely mouthing a few platitudes to people he saw every day. She almost felt sorry enough for him to go over and say a few soothing words. But she didn't want to get roped into anything. *It wouldn't do to have the good Captain following me around like a puppy while I'm trying to put the whammy on G'Kar.*

"I'm sorry to be late," a deep voice said at her elbow.

She turned and gifted the Narn Ambassador with a dazzling smile.

"I'm delighted you could make it, Ambassador," she said warmly. "I know you must have a thousand things to do with the conference coming up." Semana gazed raptly into his red eyes. "May I offer you ... something?" she asked, making a disarmingly helpless little gesture.

"Ahem."

"Ah!" G'Kar said, slightly startled. "This is my aide, Na'Toth."

"Charmed," Semana said, dismissing her. "I've only recently discovered the pleasures of Narn art, Ambassador. Do you have a favorite artist?"

Na'Toth glared as Semana slipped her arm into G'Kar's and walked away with him, gazing worshipfully up at his delighted face.

Across the room she spied Londo Mollari actually pouting at the couple as they walked on together. *Well*, Na'Toth thought with sour amusement, *she's been a busy lady.*

Vir was enormously relieved to see their hostess link arms with the Narn ambassador and show him such singular attention. Londo had been very taken with the lady and had dressed most carefully with an eye to impressing her.

In the rich, royal blue brocade coat with its deep satin cuffs, Londo certainly cut a dashing figure, and the Centauri ladies present had taken notice. But he brushed them off like so many annoying insects, his eyes only for their hostess.

Vir sighed. Nothing could be more intriguing to a Centauri woman than a man who ignored her. *I suppose it's how the conquering instinct manifests itself in women.* Any other time Londo would be thrilled with this attention.

It's not that I begrudge him his various seductions, Vir thought primly. *It's just that . . . Well, maybe I do resent his success with women. But he should be concentrating on other things at the moment besides his love life.*

Yes, he was definitely jealous. It had been ages since anyone had looked at him the way Semana MacBride had looked at Londo. If anyone ever had.

He smirked a bit. *Of course, it's been a while since anyone looked at Londo the way she's looking at G'Kar.*

For a moment, his eyes met Na'Toth's and he knew that she wished the human's attentions on Londo with all her heart. Feeling rash, Vir bowed to her and watched her eyes flash.

How strange, he thought. *This is the first moment of perfect understanding between Narn and Centauri since I came to Babylon 5. And it concerns how we both wish this human temptress would go away.* Vir shrugged slightly at the vagaries of fate. *I wonder if it's anything that we can build on.*

Garibaldi watched Semana take G'Kar's arm and walk away, leaving Na'Toth staring daggers at the human's naked back.

He could certainly see why G'Kar was so captivated. Semana was wearing a glittering black catsuit, cut low in front and lower in back, the outline of her perfect body softened by a sort of gossamer black robe that sparkled from a light sprinkling of sequins. Her dark hair was arranged so that a glossy length of it hung over her shoulder almost to her waist.

Women like her should be forced to wear a sign, Garibaldi thought, *warning: contents dangerous to your mental health.* Of course, if MacBride did anything to really hurt G'Kar, from the look of things Na'Toth would cheerfully rend her limb from limb. *Now* that *would be a diplomatic slipup I could really get behind.*

As he walked over to them, Semana and G'Kar had their heads together like two teenagers in the first throes of romance. She took G'Kar's big hand in her two small ones and stroked her thumbs across his fingers and wrist.

"Excuse me, Ambassador, Ms. MacBride. I was wondering if I could have a word with you, ma'am?" Garibaldi jerked his head in a come-along gesture.

"What's this about, Garibaldi?" G'Kar demanded, making a great display of his readiness to put the Security Chief in his place.

"It's . . . private," the Chief said.

"It's all right, Ambassador," Semana said, offering him a look of melting gratitude. "I think I know what it's about."

She smiled slyly at Garibaldi and led him off to an unpopulated corner.

Turning to face him, she laid one finger delicately on the shoe imprint on his cheek. "This is a new look for you, Chief Garibaldi. Very avant-garde." She kissed her fingertip and touched it briefly to his face. "Better?"

Garibaldi could feel his face getting hot, and chose not to think about whether it was from annoyance or for some less convenient reason.

"Cute," he said, putting his hands on his hips. "I have some questions for you."

Crossing her arms over her chest in a way that attractively framed her bosom, she arched a brow and asked, "Well?"

"I've been doing a little research. And I've turned up an interesting episode relating to your business activities." He watched her expression carefully.

"I know exactly what you're talking about," Semana said with quiet dignity. "You must also have found out that I was declared innocent of fraud." She looked him straight in the eye, defying him to deny it.

"True, but the case is still in the civil courts."

"It's being worked out by our lawyers. I expect the case to be dropped." She pursed her lips, and cocked her head one way and the other. "I didn't commit a crime," she said, "I committed an indiscretion."

"Excuse me?" Garibaldi's voice, face and posture indicated his extreme skepticism. "You sold your client two paintings worth *maybe* forty thousand credits altogether for five hundred thousand and you call that an indiscretion?"

"Yes." She stared back at him boldly. "I broke a rule. My mentor warned me, 'Never, never, never sell a client art strictly for investment. If he or she wants to make money, send 'em to the stock market.' " Semana shrugged. "But this guy kept pressuring me, and asking for advice. I knew someone, somewhere was going to get him to buy. So I figured, why not me? And when I sold him those paintings, that artist was *hot*. By rights their value by now should be double what I sold them for. But"—she shrugged again and smiled ruefully—"that's the way it goes. I gave him the best advice I could at the time." Semana ran a long finger down the leather facing of his uniform jacket. "I'm not lady luck, you know."

"You sure weren't for him," Garibaldi agreed. "And you're not going to try that on Babylon 5. Are you?" His eyes spoke of consequences. He watched a calculating look flicker in hers. Leaning closer, he said, "I would take it very *personally* if one of the Ambassadors was to be embarrassed."

"I'm here to deal art, if I can," she said through clenched teeth. "You have no right to warn me away from doing legitimate business."

"It's that legitimate part that concerns me," Garibaldi said, stuffing his hands in his pockets. "I'm not sure you know exactly what it means."

Semana gave an exasperated "tsk!", rolled her eyes, and looked away.

"Look. I've already explained that. It was a fluke. An overeager customer talked me into making a mistake." She looked back at him. "Believe me, I've learned my lesson. It's a mistake I'm not likely to repeat if I want to survive in this business. Now, if we're through with this discussion, do I have your"—she cocked her head, searching for a word—"*permission* to return to my guests?"

He nodded curtly and she started to leave. "But I'll be watching you," he said over his shoulder.

Semana pursed her lips for a moment. "Well," she said quietly, "I'll have to try to make that interesting for you."

Garibaldi turned to watch her sway off to rejoin G'Kar, who gave him a look that would sour milk. He just managed to suppress a smile. *Keep walking around like that, Mac-Bride,* he thought, *and you'll make following your activities a pleasure.*

* * *

"What was that all about?" G'Kar asked confidentially.

"Nothing at all, really," Semana said with a knowing smile. She slipped her arm into G'Kar's and snuggled against him. "I think he likes me." She smiled up at the Narn, inviting him into the joke. "But he doesn't seem to know how to go about letting me know without implying an arrest might be involved."

G'Kar joined in her laughter, but his eye followed the Security Chief's progress through the crowd with budding hostility.

" 'Bout that time, isn't it?" Garibaldi asked Sheridan.

The Captain was visibly nervous, and he took a sip of champagne before answering.

"I'm letting the audience wine and dine themselves into a forgiving mood," he said.

"You're putting off the inevitable, Sir." Garibaldi shrugged. "Look at it this way, it's better than combat. At least they can't shoot back."

"Why doesn't it feel that way?" Sheridan wondered.

"Don't you have any confidence in your speech?" Franklin asked, joining them.

"Yes, actually." The Captain handed the doctor a notepad.

Franklin keyed it on and scrolled the contents.

"Hmmp," he said, the corners of his mouth turned down. He shrugged and handed it back.

"What?" Sheridan demanded.

"It's short," Franklin said. "I like that."

"Can I see?" Garibaldi asked. He read it and handed it back, then shoved his hands into his pockets, his expression neutral.

"What?" The Captain's voice was taking on an irritated edge. "If there's a problem I think the least you could do is tell me."

"Tell you what?" Ivanova asked, balancing a loaded plate.

"My speech," Sheridan said, thrusting the notepad at her.

She fumbled for a moment, then Garibaldi gallantly relieved her of her plate and fork. As Ivanova began reading, he began eating.

"It's a good speech," she said, returning it to him. "I certainly don't see anything wrong with it. Hey!" She snatched her plate back. "Fork!"

Sheepishly, the Chief gave it back. "They're a lot alike," he murmured to Franklin. "That probably explains it."

"What?" Captain and Commander asked in unison.

"Okay," Sheridan said, "in your opinion, what's wrong with this speech?"

Franklin and Garibaldi exchanged a glance.

"Well," Franklin said cautiously. "It could use a little punching up."

"A joke or two to get the audience on your side," the Chief concurred.

"A joke?" Sheridan said.

"Or two." Garibaldi shrugged and looked at Franklin, who nodded.

"Terrific!" Sheridan snarled. "This is a *great* time to tell me."

"You didn't show it to us before," Franklin said reasonably.

"You'll think of something," Garibaldi assured him. "And if you don't, there's really nothing wrong with the speech."

"It just would be a little better with humor," Franklin said.

"Great!" the Captain muttered and stalked off.

"What are friends for?" Garibaldi asked.

Sheridan stood at the podium and looked out at the sea of faces. *Not really a sea,* he told himself. *There's only about*

fifty people here, more of a pond of faces. He grinned and
the audience stared back at him, most wearing a c'mon-get-
on-with-it expression. His senior staff looked on encouragingly, leading the applause and smiling.

A joke, he thought. Then he remembered one.

"Good evening, gentlefolk. Welcome to the unveiling of
TransGalactic Assurance's gift to Babylon 5." He paused for
the polite applause. "Y'know, unveiling a statue always re-
minds me of a joke I once heard when I was a youngster. In
ancient Earth mythology there were two lovers named Daph-
nis and Chloe. And they were so happily in love that the
jealous gods decided to punish them. So one day they were
running towards each other and they were turned into trees,
just out of reach of each other. Now ever since then they've
been portrayed in statues as two people yearning towards
each other, but never able to touch. Well"—the audience
was beginning to shift on their feet and look bored—"eventually the gods felt sorry for what they'd done so they turned
a statue of the lovers into living people. And the first thing
they did was to catch a pigeon and scurry off into the bushes
crying 'Me first! Me first!' "

The humans chuckled politely and, after a long moment,
the puzzled aliens graciously followed suit.

*Well, I guess that proves that humor isn't a universal lan-
guage,* Sheridan thought. He glared at Franklin and Garibaldi, who widened their eyes and shrugged. Then he hurried
on with the rest of his speech. As written.

Semana and G'Kar stood right beside the veiled form of
the statue, her arm linked with his. His face was close to
hers as she whispered. Suddenly he laughed loud and long,
just as Sheridan said, ". . . peace in our time."

Heads turned, but the Captain kept gamely on.

Na'Toth, who was standing nearby, gazed at G'Kar with
wide, shocked eyes.

"Semana has just finished explaining the Captain's joke
to me," the Ambassador told her. "It's really very funny."

Na'Toth, switched her glance to Semana.

"Perhaps, *after* the ceremony, you will explain it to me," she said pointedly.

G'Kar patted Semana's hand with affection.

"Spoilsport," he said cheerfully, and Semana giggled.

Na'Toth stiffened, then turned and walked away.

At that moment, the Captain yanked the cord and the covering over the statue fell away. Revealed were four figures, two holding up a globe that turned and as it turned became the image of different planets, now Earth, now the Narn Homeworld, now Centauri Prime. Two other figures seemed to be reaching for the globe. All four were dressed in loose robes that left gender indeterminate, with hoods pulled up over their heads, leaving only the faces showing, thereby eliminating questions about placement of ears, shape of skull, or the presence of hair or crest. The two reaching for the globe were smaller, slighter, their long-fingered hands carved with a delicacy different from the rather stylized treatment of the ones supporting the globe. A few of the more aesthetically inclined guests could be heard remarking on the greater realism and sense of life in the smaller figures; one Drazi muttered that they must be from the hand of a different artist.

"The name of the statue," Sheridan was saying over the applause, "is Peace and Unity."

After a moment, Semana realized that G'Kar wasn't applauding with the rest of the guests. She glanced at him and found him glaring at the statue with absolute horror.

"What is it?" she whispered.

"They're T'llin," he said weakly.

"What?" She furrowed her brow in apparent confusion.

"The figures . . . They're T'llin." His voice grew tinged with outrage.

"I thought they were supposed to be a sort of vague, generic humanoid." Semana shrugged. "You mean there's really a people who look like that? How . . . interesting." She grinned. "And how unfortunate for them. They're not awfully attractive."

She turned to smile at the Ambassador, but he disengaged from her arm and turned his glare from the statue to her.

"You're offended!" she exclaimed. She reached tentatively out to him. "My word on it, Ambassador, I would never willingly cause you offense. I honestly know nothing of these Tell, Till . . ."

"T'llin!" G'Kar snapped.

Semana looked at the statue and then at G'Kar. She straightened her shoulders and raised her chin.

"Which ones are they? I'll have them removed."

"You would do that?" the Ambassador asked in astonishment.

She turned to look into his eyes.

"Of course." Then she shrugged. "How easy that will be depends on which they are.

G'Kar indicated the two outside figures and Semana slumped in relief.

"Easily done, Ambassador . . ."

"G'Kar," he said.

"G'Kar," she murmured, smiling up at him. "They're not the ones holding the globe, as you can see. I promise you, by tomorrow they'll be gone.

Sergeant Midori Kobayashi had been stalking the Minbari Ambassador for some time, approaching her as cautiously as if Delenn were some rare bird that might fly away if the Sergeant were more direct.

Finally, Delenn took pity on her and turned to look Midori full in the face.

"Did you wish to speak to me?" she asked gently.

"Ah. Yes, Ambassador." Now that she found herself actually talking to the Minbari, Kobayashi was more nervous than ever.

"There's no need to be afraid of me," Delenn assured her. "I really don't bite."

Midori laughed and blushed, and, reverting to her childhood on Nipon, bobbed a slight bow.

"I was wondering," she said, her hands placed palm to palm, "if you would permit me the honor of preparing a tea ceremony for you. And for your assistant," Midori added quickly.

Delenn was a bit taken aback. Humans usually didn't invite her for refreshment. And when they did, they didn't refer to it as an honor; it was usually more of a diplomatic convenience.

"A tea ceremony," she repeated. *Ceremony?* she wondered. Humans generally had a disappointingly unaesthetic approach to such things.

"Please, Ambassador," Midori said earnestly. "It would mean a great deal to me."

Delenn bowed gracefully.

"I would be pleased to attend."

"Thank you," the Sergeant said simply, bowing in return. "Perhaps you would be so kind as to consult your schedule and inform me when would be convenient," she suggested. "It will take at least two hours, possibly more."

"Of course. Lennier will contact you. Is there anything that I should do?"

"No, no. You don't need to bring anything or do anything. I shall try very hard to make this a special occasion for you." The Sergeant bowed again and, looking as though the world had been given to her, walked back to her curious friends.

Delenn and Lennier exchanged glances.

"I shall make inquiries," Lennier said, and Delenn nodded.

CHAPTER 9

After the party Semana had ordered Drazi workmen to cover the statue again. Now, subsequent to a long and flirtatious chat with the Narn Ambassador that had won her a dinner invitation, and a brief rest, she'd returned to the site.

It was just after midday in the second watch, a time when the green areas should be empty and workers just returned from their lunch would be concentrating on their tasks instead of looking out windows or wandering around.

She'd arrived carrying a small suitcase. Semana lifted up the weighted edge of the statue's shroud and ducked beneath. She put the suitcase down and hoisted herself up onto the pedestal.

Light passed dimly through the concealing tarp and she studied the immobile faces of the statue, then shook her head in wonder.

Standing on tiptoe, she whispered a word into the ear of the figure next to her.

For a moment nothing happened and a slight frown marred the smooth surface of her brow. Then a delicate shiver passed over the statue, a movement less anxious eyes would have missed. Semana let out her breath in relief.

"Unh!" the statue said.

"Shhhh," Semana soothed. "It's all right. Just be very quiet." Then she slid between the two figures holding up the globe and spoke softly into the ear of the other reaching statue.

She returned to the first she'd wakened and began to peel makeup from the face, the smooth opaque eye shields and the plastic that had given the features a melted appearance. Then she began to cut away the plastic "robe" that had disguised his body.

"MacBride," the smaller figure, still trapped in its makeup, groaned, "I can't see!"

"Quiet!" Semana snapped, sotto voce. "I'll be right there. Everything is gonna be all right. Just keep your voice down!"

"Help my sister," the male muttered. "I can take care of the rest of this myself.

Semana studied his sleepy face and decided he knew what he was talking about. So she slipped between the other figures again and started work on the female. After a few moments, when both were free, she helped them down from the statue and left them sitting on the ground recuperating from their hibernation.

The light plastic robes Semana had sculpted around the two T'llin to support them and make them seem a part of the statue broke away easily in her hands, leaving no evidence of their ever having been part of it. She gathered up the pieces carefully, putting them together in a pile. Then she turned to the two T'llin.

"Are you all right?" she asked seriously.

Both nodded, apparently exhausted.

"Good."

Semana opened her suitcase and tossed them both a pile of silky clothing.

"I'm going to disguise you as Minbari," she said, lifting a plastic crest from her box. "I've got a map of the station here that will show you the way to Down Below, and two credit chits worth a thousand credits each."

"A *thousand* credits!" the female said incredulously. "Is that all?"

Semana arched a brow.

"T'llin currency is somewhat depressed against Babylon 5's," she said coldly.

"Apologies," said the male. "We do not mean to impugn your honor."

The female closed her eyes and then opened them slowly.

"However, if a mistake has been made"—there was decided emphasis on the word 'mistake'—"we will make contact with you so that we may discuss it," she said, then revealed her white, pointed teeth in a smile utterly lacking in warmth.

Why do I always *have this effect on women?* Semana wondered.

"Olorasin, my sister," the male said, "our friend has brought us safely through many dangers. It is ungracious now to question her integrity."

"Phina, my brother," she answered, "I do not believe integrity is integral to a smuggler's character." She smiled at Semana, this time with amusement warming her black eyes. "I believe that is why she is so very good at her profession."

Semana sniffed and then bowed slightly. She picked up a pot of pale pink stage makeup.

"Who wants to be first?" she asked.

Forty-five minutes later, two tall, slender Minbari and Semana slipped out from under the tarp.

"Well, this is where we end our association," Semana said. "I wish you the best of good fortune in your endeavors," she told them sincerely. After all, sincerity cost nothing and the Narn *were* vicious bastards. Her own experiences with them had told her that.

"Thank you," Olorasin said, obviously surprised. "And may the best of good fortune be yours."

"That is my wish as well," murmured Phina.

"Thank you," said Semana, and then she walked away without looking back. *Nice people,* she thought, *too bad they're gonna get their butts kicked.*

But that was the inevitable fate of nice people. Which was why she wasn't interested in becoming one of them.

Lennier picked up his pace a bit, without seeming to hurry, in order to catch up to Garibaldi, who was striding towards the lift at the end of the corridor.

"Good morning," he said.

Garibaldi turned at the sound of the quiet voice and smiled at the Minbari.

"Hi," he said cheerfully, waiting for Lennier to catch up. "What did you think of the ceremony last night?"

"Most intriguing," Lennier said politely, falling into place beside the Security Chief. Then more daringly, he continued, "As was the lovely lady who hosted it." He glanced at Garibaldi from the corner of his eye.

The Chief pursed his lips and looked at Lennier appraisingly. "That's true," he agreed cautiously.

"It seemed to me that though the lady charmed him, the statue offended the Narn Ambassador," Lennier said with perfect disinterest.

"Not surprising," Garibaldi said casually, "considering that two of the figures were of T'llin."

"They're gone, you know."

"Who?" Garibaldi looked sideways at the young Minbari. *G'Kar and Semana MacBride?* he wondered. *If she's kidnapped him would he even* want *to be rescued?*

"The two T'llin."

Garibaldi halted in surprise.

"You mean she broke up the statue to keep from offending G'Kar?" he asked. If there was one character trait he would never have attributed to Semana MacBride it was the impulse to be accommodating.

Lennier stopped to look at him. "I think it's more likely they simply walked away," he said.

"What's that supposed to mean?" the Chief demanded, his face a knot of puzzlement.

Lennier merely smiled enigmatically.

"Have you been talking to Ambassador Kosh?" Garibaldi asked suspiciously.

"You may wish to extend your acquaintance with the lady," the Minbari advised. "One can learn all manner of interesting things from a person like that."

"Interesting," Garibaldi said and shook his head, smiling. "That's one way of putting it." He started to walk on and Lennier once again fell into place beside him.

"I was wondering," the Minbari said, and halted. The Chief stopped and looked inquiringly at him. "Sergeant Kobayashi extended an invitation to the Ambassador and myself for a tea ceremony," he said, watching the human for his reaction. "She seemed to regard it as an important function, but we know nothing about it. Nor do I know where to begin researching. When I asked the computer about it, it gave me an incredible amount of information on tea. Rather too much to wade through for the specific information that I want."

Garibaldi's brows had shot up when Lennier had mentioned the Sergeant's invitation, but there was no trace of disapproval in his expression. Lennier relaxed somewhat.

"I know more about the Sergeant than I do about the Japanese tea ceremony," he said dubiously. "*She* is absolutely trustworthy. I'd stake my life on that. As to this tea thing . . ." He rubbed his chin in thought. "It's very formal, a really treasured part of Japanese culture. There's a lot of meditation and stuff, and symbolism . . ." Garibaldi shook his head and shrugged. "It's not something I understand, but it is a great honor," he assured Lennier.

"Thank you," Lennier said, quite pleased. "The Ambassador will be delighted to hear that."

Well, keeping you at arm's length is going to be a job and a half, I can see that, Semana thought. She shook a slender finger admonishingly at the Narn Ambassador and leaned back in her chair. *It's a darn good thing we're having dinner in a restaurant. If we were in your quarters I'd be flat on the floor right now.* Which might be an interesting experience, but on the whole, one she'd rather contemplate than undergo. Interspecies relations were all very well . . .

The restaurant was the best that B5 had to offer, an oasis of elegance in the machine city. The high ceiling gave the narrow room an aura of spaciousness, while the lush plant life and the soft lighting lent a feeling of intimacy. And the prices were more impressive than the cuisine.

"How do you feel about . . . Centauri art?" Semana asked carefully.

The suave smile disappeared from G'Kar's face.

"There is nothing Centauri that I like," he said grimly. Then he smiled again. "Let us change the subject to a more pleasant topic," he suggested, reaching for her hand again.

"Forgive me," she said with an apologetic smile. She lowered her head, then looked up at him through her lashes. "But it occurs to me that if the Narn Ambassador possessed some rare and valued Centauri artifact . . ." Her voice trailed off.

"Yes," G'Kar urged her, his brow furrowed, "go on."

"Well, it might have considerable psychological impact on them. You know how ridiculously proud they are."

For a split second, he looked as if he'd been illuminated from within, then he turned his head and looked at her suspiciously.

"Do you have such a thing?"

Semana shrugged with her eyebrows and took a sip of wine, smiling coyly. "Perhaps. I just wondered what you thought of the idea." She leaned forward, crossing her arms on the table. "So, tell me, what do you think?"

"I think it's an intriguing idea," G'Kar said seriously. "But it would have to be something very special." He lowered his voice. "I ask you again, do you have such an item?"

Semana studied her finger as it traced a pattern from a circle of moisture on the table. *Gotcha!* She looked up at him and leaned a little closer.

"Yes," she whispered.

They stared into each other's eyes for a few moments, then G'Kar licked his lips.

"I'd like to see it," he said, his eyes alight with eagerness.

Semana leaned back in her chair and looked at him over her glass, her eyes narrowed.

"I don't really know you," she said. Then she shook her head. "But I don't think you could afford it."

"Could I just see it?" he asked, greed igniting like a bomb now that she threatened to thwart him.

She pursed her lips and glanced about the elegant room, then subtly shook her head so that her earrings glittered as they swung.

"It was unfair of me to mention it," she said, looking at him sympathetically. "It really would be beyond your means."

G'Kar sat back and studied her appraisingly.

"If this . . . item were politically important . . ." he began cautiously.

"Oh, it is," Semana quickly assured him. "That's why I brought it up." She caught her lower lip in her teeth and looked sympathetically at the Ambassador. "I thought you might like to know."

"Perhaps I might be able to persuade my government to contribute to its purchase," he said eagerly. "I could contact them tonight. But I need to see it."

She pretended to stretch her neck in order to look around them. Then she faced him, her expression serious.

"G'Kar," she said, "we've discussed this more than we should in such a public place."

"*What* is it?" he demanded.

"I can't tell you that," she said between her teeth, allowing her body to go tense.

"Give me a hint." G'Kar leaned towards her, a predator with its quarry at bay, determination in every line of him.

She shifted nervously in her chair, looking sulky. At last with an exasperated sigh she held her hands about eight inches apart.

"It's about this big, about this high." She held her hand an equal distance above the table, then continued reluctantly, "It's gold . . ."

"Does it have a pale blue stone?" the Narn demanded.

"About so big," Semana confirmed, holding her thumb and forefinger up in a circle. "Along with many smaller ones."

G'Kar's breath came fast with excitement. "Do you mean to tell me that you have the Centauri Eye—"

"Shut up!" she snapped, her eyes flaring. "How did you ever get to be an ambassador?" she demanded in disgust. "Have you no discretion?"

"How did you acquire the . . . item?" he asked suspiciously.

"I didn't *acquire* it," she said disparagingly. "I bought it. How it lost its home I've no idea. I got it thirdhand."

"Then how do you know it's genuine?" G'Kar asked reasonably. He laughed softly and, shaking his head, leaned back in his chair. "You must realize that you've probably been sold a fake," he said. "Such a theft would be impossible to hide. Poor Semana, you've lost your money."

"First, I know and trust the people I got it from, and they would never be fooled. Neither would they cheat me. They have a reputation to uphold. Second . . . the stone can't be faked," she said.

"Anything can be faked," G'Kar said quickly, his voice dismissive.

Semana looked wise and amused.

"Well, you would know, Ambassador," she said.

"And I repeat, nothing's been said of any such loss to the Centauri—"

"Shush!" she said. "Do you think they'd announce a thing like that in the middle of a war? Would you?"

"How could they possibly suppress it?" G'Kar asked.

"By being just a little more ruthless than usual," Semana said simply. She looked as though she was holding back laughter. "You, of all people, should know what they're like."

"I want to see it," G'Kar demanded, unconsciously closing his fist.

She watched him for a moment, as though assessing his interest. Semana rubbed her wineglass against her bottom lip, then she put it down.

"Not tonight," she said. Then looked up and directly into his eyes. "I can't. I brought it here to show another buyer."

He frowned.

"Who?" he whispered.

Semana looked around desperately and her eye fell on Londo Mollari, seated at the far end of the restaurant and watching them with great interest. He raised his glass to her and sipped suggestively. She smiled in return and raised her glass, but didn't drink.

G'Kar's face became a mask. "Mollari?" he wheezed. "Please," he begged, "you must give me a chance to match his price. The Narn will make of your name a legend in our gratitude." He reached out to her. "Give me a chance!"

"All right," she said reluctantly. "A chance. And now, let us change the subject."

G'Kar burst into his office in a blaze of excitement, startling Na'Toth so that she dropped the message crystals she'd been sorting.

"What are you doing here?" he demanded, highly irritated by her unwanted presence.

"I'm working," Na'Toth said reasonably. *How do you think your desk gets straightened overnight? Perhaps the spirit of tidy desks pays you a daily visit?* She noted his attitude of extreme excitement. "How was your evening, Ambassador?" Her voice dripped disapproval like venom.

G'Kar opened his mouth to tell her, then closed it. He knew that whatever he said, she was likely to warn him to be cautious. *Still, if I don't tell someone I'll burst.*

He leaned towards his aide over his desk.

"There is a possibility that I may be able to acquire an item so valuable, its loss to its owners so devastating, that news of its being in our hands could have the impact of a major battle won by the Narn." He was trembling in excitement and he watched greedily to see the awe enter Na'Toth's eyes.

She dropped her head down onto the the stone surface of the desk and rested it there a moment, then pounded it three or four times before looking up at him.

"How can you be so gullible?" Na'Toth demanded sharply. "I knew she was up to no good. How many credits does she want from you?"

G'Kar was taken aback. "She docsn't want any. In fact, it was only with difficulty that I persuaded her to show it to me."

Na'Toth's face looked pinched as she strove not to call the Ambassador a fool to his face.

"And what is this . . . thing that is so valuable?" she demanded.

"The Centauri Eye of Empire," G'Kar said. "The oldest symbol of Centauri nobility." He stood back to admire the effect of those words.

"Are you insane?" Na'Toth flashed to her feet and leaned over the desk towards him, all discretion gone. "That's impossible! How would *she*, a mere nobody, ever acquire such an object? The Centauri are not the fools we've thought they were, Ambassador. The lives they've cost us have shown us that. They only regained the Eye a year ago. Trust them to at least be able to protect their most valuable treasures on their own planet!"

The moment she finished speaking, Na'Toth wished she'd choked on her own tongue. G'Kar's face was closed, his manner withdrawn.

"Ambassador," she said, her voice belatedly deferential.

"She came here to sell it to Mollari," he said. "He obviously believes it is authentic. And though it may be a fraud I don't think we can take that chance. Because if what she has told me is true . . ." His lips writhed, as though striving to form the right words to convince her of the necessity of acting.

"It isn't," Na'Toth said firmly. "It's too good to be true."

G'Kar closed his eyes, then smiled weakly, tapping one finger on the desk.

"I'm aware of the risk," he assured her. "But I am unable to let this opportunity pass me by. If it is a lie, I will deal with it. But I *cannot* allow this to slip away. Or I will regret it for the rest of my life."

Na'Toth opened her mouth.

"Don't speak." G'Kar raised a forbidding hand, his eyes turned away from her. "I think we should say good night. And I think that we should not speak of this again."

Na'Toth looked at him helplessly, then reluctantly left the office.

She stood outside the closed door for a moment, her brow furrowed in thought, her mind a whirl of conflicting emotions. Pity for G'Kar, desire to believe as he did, worry over what the Ambassador might do. But the predominant thought and emotion was fury at the human woman who played with the Narn Ambassador this way.

If she had a heart I'd rip it out, Na'Toth thought. And despised herself for the niggling doubt that said Semana MacBride might be telling the truth.

CHAPTER 10

SUSAN was running late; she'd bargained with herself for ten extra minutes of sleep and had gotten fifteen. *I hate days that begin like this,* she thought grumpily, jamming her foot into a boot. *Nothing ever seems to go right when I've overslept.* She whisked her hair back into a ponytail, fingers flying through the familiar task.

The door chime chirruped and with an exasperated sound Ivanova threw down the fastener and rushed to the door, still holding her hair bunched on top of her head.

She barked, "Open," and the door slid aside.

No one was there.

With a sinking feeling Susan stood in the doorway and looked up and down the hall. Then, with an effort of will, she looked down at her feet.

In front of the doorway, on a plain white plate, a data crystal stood on its larger end.

She snapped, "Close," and spun round, walking swiftly to her bedside table where she'd left her link. Snatching it up, she keyed it on and snarled, "Garibaldi," much too loudly, as though angry with him.

"What?" The Chief's voice was fuzzy with sleep. "Ivanova?" he asked, sounding puzzled but more alert. "What's the problem?"

"There's a data crystal outside my door again."

"On my way."

* * *

This time when Garibaldi arrived at Susan's door it was closed, with just the two incongruous items on the floor to greet him. He examined them cautiously, by instrument and by eye before disturbing them. Then, straightening from his crouch, he knocked on Ivanova's door.

"Susan?" he said.

For a moment there was no response and he wondered if she'd gone to her post. Then the door slid aside and she stood before him looking very tired and grim.

"I don't want to see this one," she said, avoiding his eyes. "I'm sure it's more of the same, and I don't want to know."

"Okay," he agreed, slapping the plate on his palm. Then he offered it to her. "If it keeps happening you might get a place setting for twelve out of this."

She stared at him blankly for a moment, then her face played a tug-of-war between outrage and amusement. Humor won. Smiling weakly, she took the plate and turned it over.

"Well, it's not exactly French porcelain, but beggars can't be choosers." She shook her head and her face began to look solemn. "Does having plates for twelve mean that I have to cook?" she asked, fighting the sadness, struggling to keep her voice light.

"Not at all," Garibaldi said, giving her shoulder a pat. "It just means you loan them to your friends who do." He studied her for a moment, as though evaluating her mood. "Can I come in for a second? I have some questions."

"Sure." Ivanova stepped back. "But I can't tell you anything. By the time I got to the door there wasn't anyone there."

"Has anyone contacted you about these crystals?" he asked. "Any odd remarks, or funny looks, or . . ." He looked as though he were dealing cards as he mentioned possibilities.

"No." She shook her head. "Nothing like that. Whoever it is, is keeping a low profile." Then she shrugged suddenly, as though shaking off something. "But what would I look for?" she asked. "And how? If people notice I'm watching them then they're going to be looking back at me, with weird expressions on their faces as they wonder what's wrong and what have they done. Which will doubtless look very suspicious to me. I don't want to turn C and C into a hotbed of paranoia."

She paced back and forth a few times, with her hands clasped behind her back. At the far end of the room she turned to look at him. Her eyes were full of challenge. "I refuse to let this joker run my life."

"Good!" Garibaldi said and nodded emphatically. "As long as that doesn't mean you won't help me."

"How can I help you?" she demanded, throwing her arms up in exasperation. "I haven't seen anybody, no one has approached me, I haven't even had so much as an anonymous note. What can I tell you?"

Her voice had been rising, and Garibaldi raised his hand in a calming gesture.

"I just meant that I'm going to have questions and I'd like to be able to ask them. Is that a problem?"

Susan looked a bit sulky, as though embarrassed by her outburst and wishing she could blame it on him.

"Of course not," she said gruffly. "I'm sorry. I have no business making you the target of my temper just because that . . . coward"—she tightened her lips—"isn't around."

"Maybe we should put a security cam on your door," he suggested.

She grimaced, then nodded.

"Good idea."

"I'll have this evaluated," he said. "And I'll talk to you later."

"Good," she said.

The Chief nodded his good-bye, keyed open the door, and left.

"Close," Ivanova said and hung her head. Her loose hair tumbled around her face and she groaned.

"I've got to get to work."

* * *

"Ah, Vir!" Londo said as his assistant entered the Ambassador's quarters. "I'm glad you're here. Take this," he said, handing Vir a notepad. "I need for you to go over these figures with Madame Sakza."

"The decorator?" Vir asked, in astonishment.

"Yes, of course. I'm going to be tied up talking to the caterer this afternoon, so I need you to stand in for me."

"The decorator?" Vir's voice was a few octaves higher.

"Yes, yes. The decorator? What is the matter with you, Vir?" Londo studied his young assistant with puzzlement.

"Londo, it's less than two weeks to the peace conference and all you have me doing is picking up material swatches and going to the art shop and discussing figures with the decorator. When are we going to get to work on the conference?" Vir's round, young face was very earnest, his expression only slightly touched with panic.

Londo closed his eyes slowly. "Ah," he said.

"Ah? What does 'ah' mean? You look like you were expecting me to ask this." Vir began to get a little annoyed. He felt he'd been played for a fool. Again. "Does 'ah' mean, I thought he'd never ask me, or does it mean, I was hoping he wouldn't ask that? Which is it, Ambassador? Have I asked too soon or too late?"

"There's no need to get belligerent, my boy," Londo snapped. "Sit down." He looked at Vir, not unkindly, until the younger Centauri complied. "I suspected that you might ask that question eventually, because you are an idealist and because I know that you hate this conflict. But I hoped that you would not ask, because that would indicate a greater understanding of the diplomatic process."

"We're not going to prepare for the peace conference?" Vir tried to keep his face blank.

"Of course not," Londo said with mild exasperation.

"But why not?" Vir leaned forward, hands on his knees; his expression showed him desperate to understand. "They'll be prepared. They'll be prepared to recite figures and statistics right out of their heads. And we'll have nothing to say. Londo, we're going to look like fools.''

"Impossible," Londo said, his voice mild. He sat down on a gilt and satin chair opposite his young assistant. "Don't you understand? We're winning. We don't have to answer to their accusations, we don't need to recite facts and figures. We're winning." He shook his head. "We can do what we want."

"Then why did we agree to a peace conference?" Vir's face was a little pale.

"We found there would be advantage in a temporary respite. And we didn't feel that giving one to the enemy would be a particular disadvantage." He shrugged. "Besides, going through the motions of talking about peace will please the antiwar factions among our alien allies and the nonaligned worlds. But even they know that this conference means nothing."

"That seems . . . very cynical," Vir said weakly.

Londo leaned back in his chair and made a dismissive gesture.

"Cynicism is an essential attitude in our profession, my boy. If you cannot develop it you will be miserable and you will never achieve anything." He studied the crestfallen look on Vir's face and sighed. "I don't like disappointing you, Vir. But the truth is, the only thing this conference is going to change is my decor. You must accept that, because it is the truth." He stood up. "Now, go. Madam Sakza awaits you."

"These just came in our diplomatic pouch," Na'Toth said with grim excitement. The door to G'Kar's office hissed closed behind her as she handed him two data crystals. "I can't wait to see the expression on Mollari's face when we show them these."

G'Kar took one of them and pushed it into its slot in the reader. Then he keyed up the contents.

Suddenly they were looking at a scene of unbelievable mayhem. Buildings were shattered like eggs, some lay on their sides, looking as if they'd been uprooted in fury and cast aside. Fires raged, and the air was full of settling dust and smoke. Screams could be heard and here and there lay a broken body.

Suddenly a woman holding a baby lurched into view. There were two little girls, of perhaps six and seven years, accompanying her, silently clutching either side of the woman's robe. The woman sobbed as she ran, looking around her frantically. As she came closer, it was obvious that she'd been wounded; a great burn scarred her skirt and she left bloody footprints behind her.

There was a sound from behind them and the woman turned incautiously. The leg buckled and she fell, barely managing to avoid dropping or falling on the baby. Jarred, it began to cry. The little girls leaned down to help their mother up.

Suddenly the woman screamed, "No! Not the children!"

A burst of phased plasma turned them all into torches. There was a hideous scream of escaping steam. Then two Centauri soldiers moved into view. One lifted his face screen, revealing an aristocratic Centauri face wearing a look of deep loathing. He spat on the burning corpses contemptuously.

Whoever was taking the recording withdrew at that point and G'Kar, looking drained, turned off the reader and rested his face in his hands.

"I don't know if I can bear to look at that again," he said.

Na'Toth, looking pale around the eyes, nodded silently.

G'Kar looked up at her. "Is it real?"

"Of course! How . . ." Her voice trailed off.

"Even if it is, the Centauri will say we made this up. I'd like to think it was actors and special effects," the Ambassador said wistfully. "I'd hate to think . . ." He shrugged. "Well, of course such things are happening, they did before and they will continue to happen as long as we are at war. But to see it and be able to do nothing but talk . . ."

"It's painful," Na'Toth agreed. "But it will make an impression on our allies. And so we must use it."

G'Kar barked a laugh. "Yes," he sneered, "it will make them dislike the Centauri. They may even say so out loud. But it will not make them join us in the fight against Centauri aggression. They don't want to die in our war."

"Who knows what might motivate them," Na'Toth said. "They're aliens. But we have to try to engage their interest." She took a deep and shaky breath. "It's our only hope." She offered him the second crystal.

He took it and put it down on his desk.

"I don't want to see this more than once," he said quickly. "I see no point in polluting my mind with pain when I need to think clearly. How are you coming on those statistics?"

"I've nearly finished with them," Na'Toth said. She offered him another crystal. "I've been working out an historical perspective. I thought you might like to review it."

"Good," he said and took it. "I wish I didn't have the feeling I was staring into the sun," he said wearily. "We need peace, or at least an extended cease-fire, or we're . . ." He closed his lips tightly and stared into the air before him. "If only we could inspire *one* other race to throw in with us."

"Will there be anything else, Ambassador?" Na'Toth asked after a moment.

"Yes, get me reservations for two at Chez Soir."

Na'Toth's glare would have ignited Semana's hair if she'd been present. The Narn woman turned on her heel and marched furiously out of G'Kar's office, her outrage all unnoticed by the Ambassador, who continued working on his speech.

Garibaldi tossed Ivanova's mystery crystal from hand to hand, pondering its possible contents.

Whoever did the first one was an artist, he thought. The tech he'd given it to had yet to find the flaws that would mark it a fake.

"Give me time," she'd said. "If it's fake, then somewhere it'll show." *If it's fake*. If it wasn't it would just about kill Ivanova.

Who could be doing this? the Chief wondered. In order to know what would bother her, the perpetrator should be someone who knew her. *And knows her pretty well. Susan doesn't open up about her family to just anyone.*

It would also have to be someone with access to personnel records, which were sealed. As well as someone who had the technical skills to cobble together something like this. *That would seem to argue for someone of fairly high rank who doesn't actually work with Ivanova, since those skills aren't exactly critical in C and C. Or . . .* He tossed the crystal one more time. *Someone of very low rank and high skills who's decided to hate her.*

It bothered him that there had been no demands, no gloating messages. Of course, that might be what was on the crystal. He plugged it into the reader.

A dark-haired head bobbed along in front of the camera. The head turned, revealing Vanya Ivanova's irritated face.

"Back off!" he whispered fiercely. "Why do you have to walk on my heels?"

"It's safer this way," the accented voice answered.

"How do you figure that?"

"If we're walking into an ambush, they're less likely to shoot while we're so close together."

Ivanova, looking startled, stared. Then laughed bitterly. "Maybe next time," he said. "I'm starting to think I deserve to be shot."

They moved cautiously down corridors dimmed for night running without speaking for a while. It appeared they were on a large warship from the corridor designation numbers and the general configuration of doorways and ducts.

Battlecruiser, Garibaldi thought. The depth of the bracing on the airtight doors was too shallow for a dreadnought's scantlings.

They ducked aside to avoid a passing crewman and the camera pointed down at feet clad in Earthforce boots and legs cased in Earthforce blues. So whoever accompanied Ivanova was human or Centauri passing for human; otherwise the uniform would be no disguise.

They encountered no one else as they moved forward, indicating that the ship was docked and possessed only a skeleton crew. Finally they reached a door with a keypad lock and a retinal scan.

Vanya punched in the code and then held a holographic shell before his right eye. The shell bore the retinal image of one of those who had legitimate access to the munitions shed. After a tense moment the lock went green and Vanya pushed open the door, the camera following. Vanya led the way to a weapons locker and pulled out a massive PPG cannon that looked as though it would need two to carry it. Ivanova placed it on top of a low-standing pile of boxes.

"That's it," he said.

A satchel appeared and human-seeming hands dug into it, taking out a boxy-looking item.

"What the hell is that?" Ivanova demanded.

"It's a resonator. It will evaluate the structure of this weapon. What do you think it is?"

"It looks like a bomb."

There was laughter. Its contemptuous edge brought color to Ivanova's pale cheeks.

"I don't think so. I'm not on a suicide mission. If it's any comfort to you, my friend, I'm in industrial espionage. I'm not in league with the enemy."

"And I'm not your friend." Vanya's eyes glittered with trapped rage.

There was silence for a moment, and the camera moved closer to Vanya, who stood his ground. But a flicker of his eyes revealed his uneasiness.

"No. You are not my friend," the voice whispered. "But as long as our association lasts, Vanya Ivanova, you had better hope that I think of myself as *your* friend. If I ever change my mind about that your usefulness will end. And so will your life. Whether I decide to let Earthforce take it for treason, or whether I take it myself will be the only detail left." The camera moved closer and the cameraman's shadow fell on Vanya's defiant face. "Is that clear?"

"Yes."

"Then go and stand watch and let me work. The sooner I start the sooner we'll be able to go."

Ivanova glared for a moment, then moved off through the racks.

The hands reached into the satchel again and pulled out an activator. Fingers flickered over the control pad, keying it into the fuse control circuits of the racked warheads. Then it was attached to the boxy instrument Vanya had objected to.

The camera showed feet climbing on top of the boxes where Ivanova had laid the weapon to be evaluated and hands tucking the bundle on top of one of the lockers. Then the satchel was picked up and the camera showed movement towards the door.

"Hold it," Vanya said. "Where's that thing you had?"

"In here." A hand shook the satchel at Ivanova. "Let's go."

Vanya stood in front of the door, his head lowered in challenge like a bull's.

"Show me," he said.

There was a "tsk!", then a hand plunged into the satchel and pulled out a duplicate of the bundle left behind.

"Satisfied? Now may we go? Or would you rather stay and be caught?"

Vanya turned and led the way out of the ship. No one appeared to stop them, no one even crossed their path. As they left the lock, the camera turned to show the glowing letters that identified the ship. The EFS *Kropotkin*.

Garibaldi rubbed his chin and stared unseeing at the frozen image of the battlecruiser's name. There was something about it that teased him.

"The *Kropotkin*," he murmured. It was familiar some-how, but the memory flittered away, elusive ... teasing ... gone.

"Computer," he said, "search for EFS *Kropotkin*. Is she still in service? If so where is she, and who's her captain?"

"EFS *Kropotkin* was destroyed in battle February fif-teenth, twenty-two forty-four. All hands were lost."

"Was there anything suspicious about the death of the *Kropotkin*?"

"Negative, the *Kropotkin* was overwhelmed by three Min-bari warships of superior capacity."

Garibaldi folded his hands before him and propped his chin on his middle and forefingers. *This is weird*, he thought. *The bomb never had a chance to go off.* Had the ship coin-cidentally blown up in the Minbari's faces? *What are the odds on that happening?* Infinitely unlikely, he decided.

"Had the *Kropotkin* ever been the victim of espionage?"

"No such activity was ever reported."

An eerie suspicion began to settle on him like a mantle of cold air.

"Commander Ivanova's brother, Vanya, died in battle. What was the name of his ship?"

"Vanya Ivanova was assigned to the EFS *Kropotkin* at the time of his death."

Oh.

"How did Vanya Ivanova happen to be assigned to that particular ship?" Garibaldi asked.

"He had made numerous requests to be assigned to active duty, and was assigned to the *Kropotkin* at his own request."

So what does that mean? Did he suspect there might be sabotage in the works? Did he just want to escape the spy master? He drummed his fingers on the desk. *Suddenly I'm treating this recording like it's real.* The thing to do was find somebody in the know who might be aware of something odd in the *Kropotkin*'s death. Trouble was, he didn't have those kind of connections.

But Sheridan did.

CHAPTER 11

THE breathing apparatus the Primes Phina and Olorasin wore appeared quite elaborate. The eyepieces were so dark as to be opaque to any but the wearer, and tiny puffs of steam were emitted occasionally, accompanied by a huffing-gasping sound that tended to make listeners catch their breath if they listened too long. Additionally, the two Primes were swathed in modified encounter suits and thick six-fingered gloves.

The masks were really nothing more than a filter that supplied them a slightly purified version of the common air supply. But they were an excellent disguise, allowing the two T'llin to walk boldly among the other aliens on Babylon 5.

Olorasin stared in wonder at the sheer overwhelming *size* of the station. Gazing through the windows of the tram that traveled along the spine of the station, she moved from side to side, to the amusement of other passengers, exclaiming over parks and gardens and buildings as though she'd never seen such things before.

Within the station Olorasin admired the way the grand mall gave way to the huge corridors, then branched into smaller pathways as veins gave way to capillaries within a living body. She walked beside the walls to examine the construction of the bulkheads, and read every precautionary sign with the appreciation most people reserved for very good poetry.

"This place," she whispered to her brother, "is a miracle!

That such a thing can exist at all lifts my spirits like the moment of first light.''

Phina looked grimly at his sister, imagining the excited face behind the mask. His spirits were not uplifted at all. He felt insignificant inside this great, rumbling construct. Like a microbe. Not a feeling he was especially fond of.

"I prefer being on a planet," he muttered. "It feels safer, somehow."

Olorasin smiled at her brother's typically negative response. She had been the firstborn of them and in perfect accordance with tradition looked on the brighter side of things. While he, coming after her as night follows day, always saw the dark.

"You cannot be speaking of our planet when you say that," she murmured sweetly, tweaking him.

Phina's shoulders slumped and she regretted her teasing.

"No," he said solemnly. "I suppose not."

"Phina," she said gently, touching his arm to comfort him. "We will find help here."

He looked down at her and after a moment nodded slowly. "Yes," he agreed. "One way or another."

Olorasin frowned. "But my way will be tried first."

Silently, he nodded again.

The Drazi and Packmoran Ambassadors would not see them. Their assistants expressed regret, but said quite firmly that they had nothing to discuss. "We are merely a trading mission," the Packmoran had said, his facial tentacles twitching nervously. "All that I can do is relay your greetings and your request to officials on Packmora. We wish you success in your quest for peace." And the meeting was over.

"I suppose," Olorasin said thoughtfully, "that we could expect little more from the nonaligned worlds. The very name implies a shyness of commitment."

Phina snorted, creating a ferocious little geyser of steam from his mask. "You know what I think," he said. ·

"I do. And will not listen to you on the subject until we have exhausted all of our options."

Phina sighed and smiled fondly at his sister as she strode down the corridor. *Ever the optimist,* he thought. But sometimes, in the face of all logic, Olorasin achieved her goals. And so he allowed her her way on this matter, as she had agreed to follow his plans should she fail. *When she fails, for there is no doubt about it.*

Phina would be pleased if his sister received the aid she sought, but knew that she wouldn't find it. Not here, nor anywhere. She sought the aid of the powerful, offering no reward more tangible than the dubious pleasure of knowing that they had done a noble thing. He could almost feel sorry for her. But she *would* cling to hope where there was none.

Olorasin was entering the Minbari Ambassador's office and he lengthened his strides to catch up to her.

"I am Lennier," the young male Minbari was saying as he entered. "I am the Ambassador's assistant. May I be of assistance?"

"We need to see the Ambassador herself," Olorasin insisted. "Our mission is very important."

"Regrettably, you have no appointment," Lennier said gently.

"Of course we don't," Olorasin snapped in exasperation. "We are fugitives from an oppressive regime. Persons in our situation don't make appointments. It's too dangerous!"

Lennier considered this for a moment.

"I must concede that you have a point. But naturally I require more information before introducing you to the Ambassador. Refugees are often given to intemperate actions and . . ."

"And you wouldn't wish to waste the Ambassador's time on a pair of savage sandal-makers with mayhem on their minds," Phina said.

Lennier studied the tall masked form for a beat.

"Precisely," he admitted.

Olorasin swept the mask from her face.

"I am the Prime Olorasin of T'll, this is the Prime Phina my brother. Our way to this station has been long and dangerous. Naturally we carry nothing in the way of letters or documents that might implicate those who have aided us. We *are* who we say we are. And we speak for the highest authorities on our planet. I insist that you inform Ambassador Delenn that we are here. Allow her to make the decision whether she wishes to see us or not."

Lennier paused, then bowed and left them.

"Cover your face, sister. This is a public place and anyone might enter."

Olorasin sighed and replaced the mask. She'd just finished adjusting her hood when Lennier returned, gesturing them into the inner office.

Both of the T'llin stopped short at their first sight of the Ambassador; they turned in unison to stare accusingly at Lennier.

With an almost undetectable sigh, Delenn announced, "I am Delenn, the Minbari Ambassador. You wished to see me?"

The two T'llin moved forward slowly, apparently wonderstruck by this most un-Minbari-looking woman. Then, as though simultaneously coming to some decision, they swept their hands towards her, palms out from the center of their chests. They took off their masks and studied her, their immobile, alien faces giving nothing away.

"Ambassador Delenn, we thank you for the gift of your time," one of them said. "I am the Prime Olorasin, this is my brother, the Prime Phina. We have come here today to ask for Minbari aid in our fight to be free of Narn domination."

Well, Delenn thought, *that is direct. And to the point. If more species did business this way life would be much simpler.* But a brutally frank request fairly begged for an equally blunt response, and every superrefined Minbari sensibility in her recoiled at the prospect.

"What would you have of us?" Delenn asked, delaying the inevitable.

"At the very least, that the Minbari recognize us as a free and independent species. Then you could insist that the Narn also recognize us as such and treat us accordingly." Olorasin blinked, a sign of agitation that she suppressed immediately, though she guessed that the Minbari wouldn't understand its significance.

"Since the Narn war with the Centauri began, their exploitation of our planet has been stepped up radically. They are poisoning our atmosphere so heedlessly that thousands are dying. Water is precious on T'll, yet they pollute it without a thought and our mineral resources are virtually stolen from us for a pittance, while our people are forced to labor as slaves in mines and factories. When one is too exhausted or sick to work he is thrown out into the wastelands to die of thirst or hunger." Olorasin's voice began to tremble. "Please, we need an ally. If the Narn know they are being watched, perhaps they will mitigate their behavior somewhat."

Behind her Phina shifted impatiently. *If we're going to beg, sister, let us beg for something big. Like a Minbari warship, fully armed with a trained crew eager to flay every Narn they meet.*

Delenn was visibly distressed by Olorasin's recital of Narn atrocities, turning her face away and raising one delicate hand in a warding gesture. When Olorasin was finished with her recital, Delenn stood with her hands clasped on her bosom, her face pale.

Why did I allow this person to torment me like this when I knew what my answer would be? she asked herself. Guilt, her heart responded, and shame.

"I am sorry for the evil that your people have suffered," she said aloud. "But our policy is well known. The Minbari are neutral in this conflict."

The two T'llin stared at her with their disconcertingly black eyes. Then they covered their faces with their masks, and making the graceful gesture that had preceded their plea, they left without another word.

When the door had closed behind them Lennier turned to the ambassador with an unreadable expression on his face.

"I am ashamed," she said.

"You gave them a hearing when others would not," Lennier observed.

"I gave them hope when I knew there was none to be had. Some would call that cruel."

Lennier crossed the room to stand beside her. "You have heard them," he said. "And I know that if there is anything that you can do, it will be done. That is all they asked."

Delenn smiled gratefully. "I shall try to live up to your generous opinion of me," she said.

"You always do."

Olorasin moved down the corridor with such blinding speed that Phina could barely keep up.

"Stop!" he said at last. "Or I shall collapse."

His sister stopped instantly, turned and walked over to the wall. She stared at it for a while as he stood beside her, catching his breath. Then she turned to him.

"Isn't it wonderful how everyone sympathizes with us and wishes us well?"

He laughed bitterly. "Sister, if wishes were PPGs there wouldn't be a Narn left alive." He clasped her upper arm and turned her gently towards himself. "Even you must concede that we are on our own. But on our own we can do nothing of any significance. You must let me make my offer to the Centauri. Surely you can see that now?"

"No," she said stubbornly. "I do not. Nor do I know what could make me see it. The Centauri have an evil reputation for laying claim to whole civilizations with less cause than you want to give them. I honestly don't see any advantage in choosing them over the Narn."

"I'm well aware of their methods, sister." Phina leaned closer. "But after the war both of these imperial races will be exhausted and we'll be able to hold our own against either of them."

"Phina, it is so unlike you to be insanely optimistic. The diplomatic approach is slow and frustrating but ultimately, I firmly believe, it will be more certain than going to war on behalf of the Centauri."

Light flashed across the dark surface of his mask as Phina shook his head violently.

"And you accuse me of insane optimism. I would welcome a peaceful solution, sister. But it isn't going to happen."

Olorasin moved closer to him and grasped a fold of his encounter suit.

"Look at what happened between the humans and the Minbari," she insisted. "A single act of violence almost resulted in the annihilation of the human race. We must not allow ourselves to forget that the Narn are much more powerful than we are. Just as the Minbari are more powerful than the humans."

Phina subsided, defeated by this unanswerable observation. Yet within himself he felt time and lives slipping inexorably away as events beyond their control moved forward with the gathering speed of an avalanche. And he resolved to contact the Centauri Ambassador at the earliest opportunity. Without consulting his sister.

"At the very least," he insisted, "you must admit that speaking directly to the humans is an error in judgment. They could easily arrest us and turn us over to the Narn Ambassador."

Olorasin turned and began walking down the corridor.

"No, I don't believe that they would do that. In any case, every avenue must be explored. I didn't come this far just to give up. I could have done that on T'll."

"Do you really expect a different answer from this human?"

"No," she admitted. "But then, diplomatic methods often work very slowly."

"Are you aware that to all appearances," Phina said dryly, "this time diplomatic methods aren't working at all?"

Olorasin didn't answer him. She simply continued walking, back set in rigid determination.

"I'm afraid that all I can do is relay your request and the reasons for it to my superiors," Sheridan said. "I can guarantee you nothing." *Which is exactly what you're going to get.* "It's highly irregular for me to see you at all. Technically, I should arrest you and have you deported as illegal entrants."

Technically, it had been highly irregular for him to grant the request for safe conduct that he'd received anonymously. Of course, if he hadn't granted it, he'd never have seen hide nor hair of these two, at least not until Garibaldi ran them to ground. It was always better to have a personal grasp of a potential opponent, though.

Choosing to aid the T'llin would undoubtedly be seen by the Narn as siding with the Centauri. Which could result in humanity being dragged back into war. *The wounds are still pretty deep and painful from the last one*, he thought. *It would be damned hard to motivate Earth to fight another.*

His face and voice betrayed his sympathy for the T'llin if they knew how to read his furrowed brow and the sadness in his blue eyes. But sympathy would save no T'llin lives, and he bitterly regretted his helplessness.

"Thank you for coming," he said, rising and offering them his hand.

They paused for a moment, puzzled by the gesture, and then imitated it by holding their hands out as well. Sheridan smiled and grasped them one at a time, giving each a quick shake, visibly startling them.

"How . . . friendly," Olorasin said in a falling-away voice.

"What a curiously intimate gesture," Phina observed disapprovingly.

Damn! I keep forgetting. It's bad policy to touch aliens. There were health reasons as well as social ones, but he'd felt so disconcerted by his inability to help them in any way that he'd forgotten himself.

"I beg your pardon," Sheridan said. "It's a human custom. I intended it as a gesture of respect." *Will I ever get this diplomacy thing down?* he wondered. *Before I start an intergalactic war over offering someone a stick of gum or sneezing at the wrong time.*

"Thank you for your time," Olorasin said.

The T'llin rose and put on their masks.

"Thank you for coming," Sheridan said. "And the best of luck to you."

Two masked faces stared at him for a moment, then both T'llin nodded and left.

Sheridan sat for a moment in thought. Then tapped his link. "Get me Garibaldi," he said.

I don't believe this! Londo thought with smoldering irritation. He had come to this tiny, out-of-the-way saloon to avoid the glad-handing of every Centauri he met, as well as the accusing or threatening glares of the Narn and their friends. *But who is in the booth behind me? G'Kar himself!* And talking loud enough to be heard three booths away, let alone when they were back-to-back. *Apparently the fool is unaware that the privacy shield in that booth is malfunctioning.* Well, since G'Kar couldn't be ignored, *in the manner of loudmouthed clods everywhere,* he might as well listen.

". . . a short-term loan," G'Kar was saying, somewhat diffidently.

"How much and how short?"

Londo started at the voice. *Cray!* he thought in astonishment. Sometimes, in his less solvent days, he'd found it necessary to resort to obtaining a loan from the thoroughly disreputable Mr. Lucius Cray. *Odd. G'Kar isn't given to gambling.* Which had been the usual reason requiring Londo to avail himself of Cray's services.

His particular vice is women. But since the war I haven't

seen him with . . . Ahhhh, yes, of course. The lovely Semana MacBride. She and G'Kar had fairly glued themselves together at the unveiling.

"Five hundred thousand? Are you crazy?" Cray's voice wasn't that loud, but its intensity cut through Londo's thoughts like a laser.

Five hundred thousand credits? Londo thought in astonishment. *What in the cosmos does he want to buy her?* Based on the behavior he'd seen, Semana hadn't looked all that hard to seduce.

"For a hundred and twenty standard days," G'Kar said.

"That's a lot of credits, Ambassador. It'll take some time to get it together. And I'll want collateral."

"Collateral?" G'Kar's voice was a study in disbelief. He sounded too shocked to be insulted, as yet, by this blow to his honor.

"No offense, Mr. Ambassador, but I'm a businessman. Y'know? I have a responsibility to my partners. So what have you got for me?"

"Uh . . . My personal transport? I paid eight hundred thousand for it."

"Oh, yeah. I've seen it. Nice piece of machinery. What else?"

"I'm sure your associates would consider an item worth three hundred thousand more than the loan sufficient . . . collateral," G'Kar spoke the last word as though it might soil his lips.

"No, sorry. See, it's used. Y'always take a loss on used." There was a pause. Finally, Cray said, "So, what ya got?"

"I have a statue by Cesea valued at a hundred thousand. If that is insufficient I'll go elsewhere."

"You got a deal. Meet me here in two days with the papers for your transport and the statue and you'll get your five hundred thou. It's been a pleasure doing business with you, sir."

"Thank you," G'Kar drawled, sounding substantially less happy than the loan shark.

He left his booth, glancing into Londo's on his way out. But apparently the privacy shield on the Centauri's booth was fully operational, for the Narn reacted not at all.

Whatever are you up to? Londo wondered. His instincts told him this had to do with the Earth woman. *I must give myself the pleasure of calling upon the lovely lady,* he promised himself. *I should so hate to feel left out of anything.*

"Sir?"

Sheridan looked up, grateful to be called from his dark thoughts. Since the T'llin's visit he'd been brooding about responsibility and duty and how, sometimes, one seemed to prevent him from doing the other.

"Come in, Garibaldi. What is it?" He straightened his chair and turned it to face the Security Chief, clasping his hands before him on the desk. "How are the arrangements going?"

"Very well, Sir. We'll be ready when the delegations arrive." The Chief walked slowly across the office and swung a chair over to face the Captain's desk.

"Four days," Sheridan said warningly, as though reminding him.

"We're ready." Garibaldi seated himself.

The Captain looked at him askance. "Ready? Or as ready as we can be?"

"Both," the Security Chief said. "Our people are in peak condition, and as far as is humanly possible we've prepared for every contingency."

Sheridan leaned back with a sigh and clasped his hands over his lean stomach. "There's already been a complication."

Garibaldi raised an eyebrow and cocked his head. "Besides the T'llin leaders showing up, you mean, Sir?"

"The President's niece is studying journalism and will be attending the conference. She's to be allowed free access to everything, while being guarded as unobtrusively as possible at all times," Sheridan said.

Garibaldi nodded. "The usual do-the-impossible thing," he said. "Sure."

The Captain grinned. "I knew I could count on you."

"Absolutely. And if I have any free time before the conference I'll be happy to paint a mural of the Last Supper on the outside of the station."

"Better not," Sheridan advised with a laugh. "Too topical. So what can I do for you? Or is this a social visit?"

"Actually, Sir, I'm here because I've got questions that you may be able to help me answer." The Chief paused and chewed his lip, then flashed a look at Sheridan. "But I'm afraid I'm not at liberty to answer any questions that mine might engender."

Sheridan raised his brows. "Personal project?" he asked.

"You might say, Sir."

The Captain made a moue. "Sure, shoot."

"Is it possible to distinguish battle damage from sabotage? Say there was a bomb on board a ship meeting hostile fire and it went off. Say around twenty-two forty-four to forty-five. Could you tell?"

Sheridan was already shaking his head.

"No. Because at that time a near miss with, say, a Minbari antimatter bomb could set up a neutrino flux that prematurely detonated the fission trigger in a fusion warhead. Lost a fair number of ships that way before we corrected that fault."

Garibaldi frowned, then shrugged. "Oh well. I just wondered."

"Was there a particular ship you had in mind?" Sheridan asked, intrigued. It had been an unexpected question. The Chief's wars were fought on a much smaller scale.

"The *Kropotkin*."

Sheridan opened his mouth to say, "Ivanova's brother's ship," then shut it. Personal, the Chief had said. If Susan wanted him to know about it she'd mention it herself. He shook his head.

"The *Kropotkin* met up with three Minbari heavy cruisers

while she was all alone. Sabotage would have been superfluous given the circumstances.''

The Captain looked as if he was going to burst from frustrated curiosity. Garibaldi decided to take pity on him and leave.

"That's kinda what I thought," he said, rising. "But it's not really my area of expertise. Thanks." He walked to the door and paused, then turned to face the Captain briefly. "I'll fill you in as soon as I can," he promised.

Sheridan laughed. "I'd appreciate that," he said.

"Retting, this report is inadequate," Ivanova said crisply. "I do read these things, you know. They're what I base *my* reports on. And I refuse to have my work look sloppy because yours is." She handed the notepad back to the blushing sergeant. "I'll expect a revised, updated, and *completed* version of this on my desk tomorrow morning."

With a muttered "Yessir," Retting vanished like smoke.

Susan grimaced. She'd been right; days when she overslept never did go right for her. She fell behind on every project with no hope of catching up. It made her clumsy and ill-tempered. *Witness poor Retting's dressing-down.* From the carefully averted eyes in C and C she guessed her rep had gone from Iron Lady to Iron Bitch. *Oh well, at least I'll start getting decent reports. For a while. And having the Commander in a bad mood should put everybody on their toes.*

She scanned the traffic board, as had become her habit since Larkin's arrival. A powered-down Centauri freighter was just sitting in the middle of an approach lane, apparently drifting.

"Larkin!" she snapped, furious at his inattention. "What is that Centauri doing out there?"

"Sorry, Commander," he said in a high, tight voice. "She developed a glitch in one of her steering jets and their main gyro went down. They swore they'd have both on-line in under ten minutes, so rather than send a tug I gave them a green on that. They've seven minutes remaining. I've redirected other traffic and set up a warning.''

Oh. "Very good, Larkin. But you're also supposed to send a message to my board.''

"Yessir.'' The message appeared.

Not bad for two minutes' work, Ivanova thought. *Maybe you'll work out after all.* "Thank you, Larkin,'' she said aloud.

"You're welcome, Sir,'' he said in a curiously dead tone. Ivanova raised one brow and glanced over her shoulder. *That was bold.* She'd marked Larkin down for the self-effacing type. *But then,* she thought regretfully, *when I'm in a bad mood, so's everybody else.*

Larkin's heart burned within him and every muscle in his body had stiffened with his fury. He drew his breath in several great, tearing gulps and he could almost hear his teeth crack as he clenched his jaw.

How dare she? How could she humiliate me like that? Knowing that no one here, not even her perfect self, could have handled that any better. She knows she's wrong. But does she apologize? Oh no. Can't do that. Who'd respect her afterward? Gotta look good at all times, don't we, darlin'? Especially after dumping on everybody within reach.

His internal tirade had soothed his temper somewhat. It was hard not to smile as he thought, *That little valentine I left on your doorstep must have really gotten to you, sweetheart. Didn't it?* If she thought that was something . . . *Oh, baby, wait for the next one.*

"My dear Ms. MacBride.'' Londo swept down on Semana where she sat at a café table. "May I join you for just a moment?'' Assuming the request was a mere formality, he seated himself, rewarding her with a smile.

"Actually, Ambassador, I am expecting someone.'' Semana looked embarrassed and her voice was warm and tinged with regret.

"Ah, well, I can't stay but a moment," he said, as though, despite his own wishes, it was the best he could do for her. "I wanted to discuss a matter of business with you."

Semana raised a well-pruned brow and slowly drew a tiny calendar-comp from her purse. "Shall we make an appointment?"

"Dinner?" he asked.

She considered him for a moment, then consulted her calendar. "Tsk!" she cocked her head prettily. "Tonight I have an appointment. But I'm free from seven to eight. I could join you for cocktails." She looked at him inquiringly.

"By all means," Londo said graciously. "I simply cannot wait. Perhaps after our discussion you'll find room in your calendar for dinner with me. The casino?" he suggested.

"I look forward to it," she said and offered him her hand.

He brought it to his lips as though it were an exceedingly rare and delicate flower and kissed her fingertips lightly, his eyes never leaving hers.

"Tonight," he murmured, and he was gone.

Semana allowed herself a grin; after all, that could be mistaken for pleasure. But she suppressed the torrent of laughter bubbling within, which could never be mistaken for anything but purest amusement.

What was that? she thought merrily. *There's one boy who's been watching too many bad vids from Earth.* Tonight! indeed. Her dark eyes snapped with laughter. *I wonder what he wants?*

It sure wasn't what that soulful gaze at parting hinted. His purpose seemed much too direct to be mistaken for wooing. *Particularly by a Centauri.* They conquered women just as ruthlessly as they did planets, but with far more finesse.

Maybe she should have spoken to him. It wasn't like she was busy. She pursed her lips. *Nah. The worst thing you can do with the Centauri is make things convenient for them.* So, cocktails at seven, Narn at eight.

CHAPTER 12

SEMANA was very demure tonight. If a shapely young woman in a tight red dress can be called such a name. It covered her from neck to ankles, flaring out just past the knees, and the sleeves were full length also. She'd pulled her hair back into a sleek knot at the back of her neck. Her aim had been to appear alluring yet businesslike.

Judging by the looks she'd been getting from some of the casino's patrons, she had the alluring part down all right.

"Dear lady, I am so sorry! I hope you haven't been here long." Londo swept her hand to his lips and sat opposite her. "I am devastated to think that I have kept you waiting."

Hah! Semana thought. *The very thought gives you a little tingle.*

"Oh, not at all, Ambassador, you're not late, I was early." She rewarded his gallantry with a warm smile.

Londo turned and signaled for the bartender.

Well, he thought smugly, *it seems you were very eager to talk to me for a lady with such a busy schedule.*

"Will you allow me to buy you another?" he asked.

"Yes, please." Semana pushed aside her half-finished drink.

When the drinks came she sipped hers with relish, as though Londo's paying for it made it infinitely more delicious than her own had been.

They exchanged obligatory bits of small talk; how was she enjoying Babylon 5, you must be sure to do this, quite a change from Centauri Prime, how were preparations for the conference going?

Finally, Semana asked, "So, Mr. Ambassador . . ."

"Londo, please." He touched her hand.

What is it with this guy, some kind of hand fetish? Is this a Centauri thing?

"Londo," she murmured. "What did you want to speak to me about?" She gave him a level look to indicate that all the fluffy stuff was over.

Ah, humans, Londo thought wistfully, *so eager to rush to the finish. They seem utterly unaware of the pleasures of the process. Do they not understand that the hunt is usually so much better than the kill?* Though how that could be he couldn't imagine; to a Centauri the concept was obvious.

"I heard," he said, holding his glass up to admire the light through the rich purple of the wine, "that you had something quite unique for sale."

"Oh?" Semana tried to look merely curious instead of surprised. *Welladay! Someone's got a big mouth,* she thought. How had he found out? And just what did he know? *Certainly he didn't get it from G'Kar,* she thought. The Narn's sharp-nosed assistant? *Couldn't be. From all reports she's as fanatical as her boss.* She looked at the Centauri Ambassador with new respect. *You must have one hell of a network of spies.*

"Yes," Londo said casually. "And I'm informed that the price is quite high. Somewhere in the range of five hundred thousand credits."

Semana widened her eyes and smiled slowly, as though her face knew before she did just what she was going to say. *Well, why not?* she asked herself. *It'll make the play a little more interesting and it'll cover my bets.* She sat up straight, her decision made.

"It's already under discussion with a buyer," Semana told him primly. "And the price is quite a bit higher than the figure you've named."

Londo blinked.

Cheapskate! she thought. A blink usually meant the mark thought the price too high.

But his eyes slowly kindled with interest. *More than five hundred thousand credits! The last time I heard a price that high was when I bought the Eye from that weasel Reno. What is the woman selling? The Emperor's crown?* His breath caught in his throat. *No, no! That's too incredible.* He laughed aloud at the thought.

Semana cocked her head.

"Mind sharing the joke?" She took a sip of her drink.

"I was just thinking you must be selling the Centauri royal regalia for that price."

Semana spluttered and coughed, having swallowed the wrong way. *What is this guy? Psychic?* She stared at him in astonishment, her eyes streaming.

"What an extraordinary thought," she wheezed.

Londo stared at her. *She couldn't mean . . .* He looked away and then quickly back at the human. *It's impossible! After all the trouble I went through to get it for them. How could they lose it? They could never keep such a loss secret.*

Actually, they probably could. *Would.* Heads would roll if such a thing became known—literally. Or perhaps the outraged public would revive the old custom of strapping the miscreant across a cannon. It was so outrageous a thought . . .

"Do you mean to tell me that you actually *have* the—"

Semana placed her fingertips on his mouth to silence him and leaned close.

"This is a little public," she whispered.

Londo's eyes widened and he stared at her for a moment.

"No!" he said. He was getting that feeling again, that he was running through his life and falling behind all the while.

Semana said neither yes nor no. She merely lowered her eyes and shrugged slightly.

He reached for her.

"Don't!" she snapped and her eyes were anything but playful.

"I must see it," he demanded.

She checked her timepiece.

"Well, not tonight. I have an appointment. I'll call your office tomorrow if my client hasn't met my price by tonight."

"I insist!" Londo said.

For the first time Semana saw what an impressive individual Londo could be, as the good-natured lech was eclipsed by the powerful political personality.

Go ahead, for all the good it will do you. She stood. "Thank you for the drink, Ambassador. One way or the other, I'll call you tomorrow.

She was surprised and a little shaken by the whole encounter, but felt the bubbling adrenaline rush of excitement singing through her veins. *No doubt about it,* she thought with a secret smile, *high stakes is the way I like it.*

Londo watched her walk away; tiny beads of perspiration sparkled on his forehead, growing colder as he realized that G'Kar just might be able to meet her price. *No, wait,* he thought. *Cray said it would take a couple of days to get the credits together.* He relaxed marginally. *So there's still a chance.* There was also an opportunity to call Centauri Prime to feel out his contacts regarding the Eye. Too bad Lord Kiro wasn't still alive. He would certainly have known if anything had happened to it.

Why am I giving this ridiculous story such credence? he wondered. *It is not possible for Semana MacBride to have possession of the greatest and best-protected treasures of the Centauri people.* He shook his head. *It's impossible.*

And yet . . .

Na'Toth found G'Kar already seated at a table in Chez Soir. She slipped into the seat reserved for Semana MacBride and glared at the Ambassador.

"What is it?" he asked with mild concern. "Why are you looking at me like that?"

"I've seen the Earther . . ."

"Human, Na'Toth. Please. We've discussed this before
. . . no derogatory terms for the species."

"MacBride was having a drink with the Centauri Ambassador," Na'Toth snapped. "He seemed angry with her towards the end of their discussion."

G'Kar smiled. "No doubt she told him that he'd been outbid. Londo wouldn't like that." He was fairly lit from within, his eyes gleaming with the pleasure he felt over stealing a march on the Centauri. "How I shall enjoy flaunting my success in his smug face."

Na'Toth's face went very still and her fingers gripped the table's edge convulsively.

"Out . . . bid?" she asked.

"Yes. It will take a couple of days to actually take the credits in hand, but I've done it."

She leaned towards him, her eyes wide.

"You mean the government actually forwarded the funds for this . . . this fantasy?"

G'Kar leaned his elbow wearily on the table and sighed. "It isn't a fantasy, Na'Toth. I've seen it."

"Did you touch it, did you hold it in your hands?" his aide demanded.

"No. Semana wouldn't let me, she said that even a light touch could leave traces that might lead the authorities to me should they recover it before I took possession. She hasn't touched it herself," he said defensively.

"It's a hologram," Na'Toth said in disgust. "How can you fall for this nonsense?"

"I'm not an idiot, Na'Toth," G'Kar said with exaggerated patience. "I know what a hologram looks like. They distort at certain angles. This item not only didn't distort, it shifted when I moved the box."

"Then it's a fake."

"I appreciate your determination to prevent my making a mistake," he said through clenched teeth. "But if it is a fake it is a superb fake. And in any case, all the proof that I need lies in Mollari's patent interest in the item."

Na'Toth lowered her head and looked away, her expression sullen despite her best efforts to keep her face a blank. *And I brought him word of the Centauri's meeting with her.* She couldn't have cut her own throat more neatly if she'd tried. *To think that I should aid that woman!*

"You must admit it lends credence to her claims," G'Kar said kindly.

Na'Toth looked up, red eyes blazing. "I wouldn't believe that woman if she told me Londo was a Centauri!"

"Well, what do you think he is, then?" Semana asked, her voice rich with amusement. "A Narn spy under incredibly deep cover? Because, Na'Toth, Londo is a Centauri."

"Excuse me, Ms. MacBride," Na'Toth said, stiffly getting to her feet. "I must be going. I have work to do."

G'Kar had risen at the sound of Semana's voice and he watched Na'Toth leave with a wry expression. Then he turned to the human and smiled.

"Good evening, Semana. Won't you be seated?" He took her arm and guided her to her chair. "I have good news."

Semana leaned her elbows on the table and cocked her head at him inquiringly.

"I shall have the total amount by the end of the week."

"By the end of the week?" She frowned. "Just exactly how long are we talking here?"

"I'll have it all in five days."

She shook her head.

"No good. I'm leaving in four." She fixed him with a steady gaze, then sighed and looked away. "I'm sorry," she said. "I wish I'd never told you about it. It was unfair of me."

"I can get it!" he insisted. "I can get all of the credits you asked for. Surely it's a sum worth waiting for?"

"No. I'm under a time constraint, I can't afford to get stuck here when they shut down traffic for the conference. Four days or forget it." Her face softened. "I hate to put you through this," she said, reaching out to touch his gloved hand. "But you must understand, I have to be in a certain place at a certain time with the credits or . . . my associates could get the wrong idea. And someone could get hurt.'' She laughed nervously. ''Namely me. It has to be four days.'' Her eyes were earnest. ''Sooner if possible.''

G'Kar squeezed his hands into fists. He knew that she wouldn't accept a lesser amount. Perhaps he should get the government involved in this.

''I'll do what I can,'' he said grimly.

Phina moved quietly down the blue-gray length of the sound-proofed corridor, trying to look as unobtrusive as possible. Thus far, perhaps because of the hour—too late to go out and too early to come home—he'd met no one.

I thought there would be guards patrolling this wing, he thought. *Of course, that could be ideal for a clever assassin. They could enter the area openly armed, anonymously dressed, and with tacit permission to go where they chose.* Or maybe the ambassadors felt that having guards would make a prison of their homes.

There were security cams, but they were far less obtrusive. *And there are fewer of those than I'd expected too.* Phina grinned. Doubtless the residents were shy of having their every visitor recorded. As for himself, all they would show was an alien in an encounter suit. Hardly a rare occurrence in this part of the station.

I'll have to take this mask off, he thought, *when I reach the Centauri Ambassador's door.* Otherwise Mollari would never let him in. *And who could blame him. The Centauri is hardly the most popular being on the station.*

He put up a gloved hand to adjust his mask and the nozzle of his steam emission hose dropped off. Phina caught it on its third bounce and hurried to an area clear of security devices. There he huddled close to the wall and, taking off his mask, proceeded, clumsily due to his gloves, to screw the nozzle back on. He dropped the tiny fixture again and, cursing, crouched to catch it.

As he stood he realized that he wasn't alone. Looking up,

Phina found himself facing a Narn woman. She'd taken a defensive stance, and held a knife in her hand, balanced for throwing.

Phina flung up his own hand. "No!" he cried.

As he moved Na'Toth threw, putting all the strength of her well-trained wrist and arm behind it. She struck him in the main heart in the center of his chest.

The T'llin cried out in pain and staggered backward, attempting to run.

No, he thought, *this can't happen. I can't die!*

Phina fell to the floor, blood pouring around his clenched fingers. Already, he could feel his limbs going cold. He crawled towards the far end of the corridor where he'd come in, leaving a wide swath of dark blood behind him.

Na'Toth followed him warily, another knife in her hand. With every effort he made, the T'llin on the floor before her grunted.

Die! she thought. *For the love of all, die! And get it over with.* The skin of her scalp crawled. The being on the floor was dead, he just refused to stop moving. "Die!" she whispered.

Olorasin! Phina stopped crawling, too weary to move, to fight the trembling in his cold hands. *Sister, I am sorry.* He began to weep, grieving for the grief he was causing her with his death. *How can you forgive me when I am leaving you alone?*

The light grew dim, and flashes of white began to obscure his vision. The wound barely hurt now, it had softened from an icy burning to a distant ache. The growing wetness beneath him terrified and disgusted him, and he wanted to roll away from it, but couldn't move. *I'm sorry, Olorasin, I'm so . . . sorry.*

Na'Toth stood trembling over the body. Feeling too hot, and feeling glad and ashamed at the same time. Glad to be alive and unharmed. Ashamed because she knew now that he'd had no weapon. But after two attacks on her by T'llin she'd reacted instinctively when confronted by one in a place where he'd no right to be.

Why else would he be here but to do harm? she asked herself. And yet, he'd run. Na'Toth shook her head without taking her eyes off the body. *Because he'd already done his mischief and that's why he had no weapon,* she reasoned slowly.

Shock, she realized, was slowing things down, distancing her emotions. She also heard the sound of running feet for the first time as two Earthforce security guards came pounding down the corridor.

"He's dead," she told them and dropped the knife she'd been holding. "I'm Na'Toth, the Narn Ambassador's attaché."

Garibaldi arrived as soon as he could in response to Kobayashi's call. Fortunately, he saw as he strode towards the small group of Narn and humans, none of the residents of this corridor, mostly high-powered people like ambassadors, had happened on the incident.

"What's happened?" he asked the Sergeant. Not that he needed to. There was Na'Toth glaring at him and at her feet was a dead T'llin, the whole thing as plain as a diagram. The scent of blood was heavy in the corridor, despite the automatic attempts of climate control to increase the circulation. It smelled heavier than human blood, more metallic and harsh, and it looked thicker.

Dry-climate adaptation, Garibaldi thought, then put the irrelevant flicker out of his mind.

"This," Na'Toth hissed, stabbing a finger down at the corpse, "is a known terrorist. He is wanted by the Narn Regime for crimes against the state. How did he get onto Babylon 5?"

"I don't know, Na'Toth," he said, walking over to her. "I just got here and this is going to take some investigation. What's his name?"

"He is the Prime Phina, leader of the Razye Tesh. A group dedicated to the violent overthrow of the Narn Regime on T'll. What *do* you suppose he was doing here?" Na'Toth asked pointedly.

"He appears to have been unarmed, Sir," Kobayashi said. There was no inflection in the Sergeant's voice, but the comment itself was an indictment.

"What would you have had me do?" the Narn shouted defensively. "I come upon a known terrorist practically on Ambassador G'Kar's doorstep, two days after being physically attacked by T'llin for the *second* time, and I'm not supposed to react? Should I have invited him to the casino for a drink?"

Garibaldi pursed his lips and just looked at her, until with a "tcha" sound she looked angrily away.

"I didn't say that. The Sergeant didn't say that. But I do wish you hadn't killed him."

Na'Toth's head swung back and she glared at him for a moment, visibly trembling.

"So do I," she said. "Because he was here for a reason and now we don't know what it was. My first thought was and is a bomb. And although my advice and requests are generally ignored by you, I *urge* you to commence searching for one. You should evacuate . . ."

"I know," Garibaldi said with understanding.

He nodded at Kobayashi, who got on her link to call the squad trained in sweeping for bombs. They'd never been needed before, but the group knew their job, and if there was danger they'd find it in minutes.

"He swept his hand up," Na'Toth said after a moment. "I thought I saw something in it and I only had a knife, so I threw." She took a deep breath. "But it was only his glove, and this." She nudged the nozzle with her booted foot.

Garibaldi looked down at the bulky hands and knew what she meant. T'llin had three-fingered hands, the glove had six. In the heat of the moment it would have looked as if he was bringing up something with a muzzle. For a moment he pitied Na'Toth almost as much as he did the dead T'llin.

"Stupid sand-bug," Na'Toth snarled in sudden fury, and she kicked the T'llin's leg.

"Hey!" Garibaldi snapped, grabbing her arm and pulling her away from the body. "That was uncalled for."

"Oh, you humans are such a fine people!" Na'Toth sneered. "You *never* do anything *uncalled for.*"

"Well, at least we don't go around claim-jumping whole planets."

"Oh, really?" she said, stepping closer aggressively. "Then what's all this I keep hearing about the Free Mars movement?"

"What is going on here?" G'Kar roared.

He'd left his disappointing dinner with Semana early in order to see if he could speed the delivery of the promised credits. And had found himself riding the lift with the bomb squad. He'd followed in their wake, curious and disturbed, until they came upon a trail of blood. Horrified, he'd followed more slowly. Only to come upon a dead body lying ignored on the floor while his aide engaged in an obnoxious political discussion with the Security Chief.

Garibaldi and Na'Toth looked guilty, and broke apart like kids caught in a clinch.

G'Kar stopped beside them, looking from one to the other. Then he turned to look at the corpse on the floor.

"That's Phina!" he exclaimed. Turning, he glared at Garibaldi. "What's he doing here?"

"Your aide killed him."

"Really?" G'Kar said in pleased surprise. He patted her shoulder. "Well done, Na'Toth."

Na'Toth ducked her head in embarrassment and clenched her fists on either side of her chest, bowing slightly in acknowledgment of his praise.

"What I meant," G'Kar said, turning back to Garibaldi, "is, *what* is he doing *here*?"

"We don't know, Ambassador," the Chief said tonelessly. "Because hc's dead."

G'Kar narrowed his eyes. "Is that humor, Mr. Garibaldi? I don't find it amusing if it is. A known terrorist lies dead at your feet, stopped, purely by chance, from doing who knows what evil, and you make jokes? I don't appreciate your sense of humor, sir."

Most people don't, Garibaldi thought. *But in this case I'm innocent.*

"I'm not trying to be funny, Mr. Ambassador." He jammed his hands into his pockets and turned slightly towards the body. "I'm merely stating the facts. We really haven't had time to come up with any information as yet."

"Are you implying some blame?" G'Kar asked, looking sideways at the Security Chief.

"Actually, no," Garibaldi said, looking at Na'Toth. "Under the circumstances I don't see how your aide could have reacted any differently. I regret that he wasn't wounded instead of killed. But then, I'm sure you both feel the same way."

The two Narn looked at him, apparently rendered speechless.

"What is going on here?" Londo roared.

G'Kar stiffened and Na'Toth squirmed in apparent disgust.

"Nothing to worry about, Ambassador," Garibaldi assured him. "It's all over."

The Centauri strode up to the Security Chief, ignoring the two Narn as though they didn't exist.

"A being is killed practically on my doorstep . . ."

G'Kar and Na'Toth exchanged quick glances.

". . . and you tell me not to worry? You expect more of me than I can give, Mr. Garibaldi. Murder in the vicinity of one's home is very difficult to ignore."

"There was no *murder*," G'Kar said with contempt. "My aide was attacked and she defended herself."

"Is that what she said?" Londo asked, looking at the Security Chief. Then he glanced overhead. "I see there are no security cams here. What a pity."

G'Kar stepped closer to Mollari.

"What are you implying?" he demanded with smooth menace.

"I am implying that in circumstances like these it is always better to have more evidence rather than less." Londo spread his hands. "What possible objection could there be to such an innocuous remark?"

"Speaking of evidence," Garibaldi said, "it's easier to preserve if there are fewer people around."

"Of course," the Centauri said graciously. "I shall be happy to retire. I have an appointment to discuss objets d'art with a beautiful young lady tomorrow. I want to be fresh and alert."

G'Kar swelled visibly.

"If you're talking about who I think you are, Londo," Garibaldi warned him, "I'd advise you to be *very* alert. She has a shady reputation."

"Thank you for your concern, Mr. Garibaldi. But in this case, pleasure is so intertwined with business that even if what she is offering is not genuine, I won't feel cheated."

G'Kar threw a glare at the departing Centauri's back.

"All clear, Sir," the head of the bomb squad announced.

"Do you need us for anything else?" G'Kar asked, turning back to the Chief.

Garibaldi had been watching the subtle interchange between the three aliens and thought he knew the source of this new antagonism between them.

"Not you too, G'Kar. You can't believe a word that woman says. She's a thief and a con artist."

"Do you need us for anything else, Chief Garibaldi?" G'Kar said with heavy emphasis.

Garibaldi tightened his lips. *There is none so blind,* he thought. *Good luck, Ambassador. With MacBride on your trail, you're gonna need. it.*

"No. Not really. We need a statement from Na'Toth, but I can get that tomorrow. And there'll be a hearing with the Ombuds. But that's about it. Just don't leave the station." *Well, actually we couldn't hold her, even if I did think it was murder rather than self-defense.* "If you don't mind."

Diplomatic immunity was a problem for cops anywhere, but on Babylon 5 it was a nightmare. Every second being seemed to have it, for starters; and far too many of them came from societies where . . . *armed self-help,* he decided . . . was standard procedure.

"I'll be here," Na'Toth said stoutly.

"I must tell you that I consider this evening's events to be largely your fault, Garibaldi." G'Kar narrowed his eyes at the human's almost comically startled expression. "You have allowed a steady buildup of these illegal refugees. A whole community was in place to welcome this infamous terrorist and to aid him in doing who knows what damage! All through your willful neglect." He leaned closer to the Chief and said softly, "They are a threat not only to the Narn on this station, Garibaldi, but to Babylon 5 itself. The Regime shall hear of this," he snarled. Then, glaring, G'Kar drew himself up to his full height to look down his nose at the Security Chief. "Perhaps this peace conference should be indefinitely postponed."

Garibaldi just looked at him. *Don't pull this garbage on me, G'Kar. It's the Narn who lose out if the peace conference is canceled.* Of course, the Ambassador did have a point about allowing the T'llin presence on B5 to grow unchecked. *I may have been a little remiss there,* he thought guiltily.

"Good night, Mr. Garibaldi," G'Kar said, taking his aide's arm and walking down the corridor towards his quarters.

CHAPTER 13

REFRESHED from a good night's sleep—for a change—and on time, Ivanova approached her desk in a far better frame of mind. She wasn't due to take over in C and C for a half an hour, and she sorted through the data crystals in her in basket, looking for Retting's revised report.

Ah, there you are. She plugged it into the reader and pulled her chair forward.

Her foot struck something and there was a tiny *click*. Ivanova froze, but nothing happened. She leaned over in her chair until she could see under the desk. In front of her right foot was a plain white plate with a data crystal on it. The crystal was lying on its side, apparently knocked over when she'd nudged it with her foot.

Oh no. Her abdominal muscles tightened and an icy spasm shot through her. *Earthforce!* she thought desperately, grasping at the first clue they'd had to calm herself. *It must be someone in the military.* Had to be. Access to the offices and C and C were severely restricted. *So that narrows it down to just about everybody I know and work with,* she thought sourly.

"Garibaldi," she said into her link, her voice weary.

"On my way, Susan."

"My office this time."

"Great. I can use a change of scene." There was a pause. "I didn't even know you used your office."

"I use it in secret," she snarled. "I like to keep my sub-ordinates guessing."

"Be there ASAP," Garibaldi assured her.

"Ivanova out."

She leaned back in her chair and studied the crystal by her feet. *Someone I know,* she mused. Her thoughts strayed in-evitably to Larkin. *But is that because he's the most logical suspect, or because I don't like him?* She grimaced. Both probably. He'd improved since their talk, but she still didn't feel safe turning her back on him. *Maybe that distrust is carrying over into this,* she reasoned.

Susan shook her head. It didn't make sense. In some ways, Larkin was the logical suspect. He was new and weird, and his records, despite a glowing service report, left her with the impression that he was a bad bargain from a gypsy trader.

But he couldn't know about Vanya. Her records were sealed to him and she certainly hadn't poured out her heart to the man. To a great extent she'd kept herself to herself even with her best friends. *I certainly wouldn't discuss my family with a subordinate. And if I did, it sure wouldn't be with Ilias Larkin.*

"Well, it's not outside the door." Garibaldi's voice made her jump.

"No," she said, shifting her chair. "It's under here."

Hands in his pockets, the Chief leaned sideways as he peeked under the desk.

"Maybe we're dealing with somebody very short," he said. "Why on the floor when he could have put it on the desk?"

"Because inconsistency is the hobgoblin of great big minds," she snapped. "How the hell should I know."

Garibaldi raised his brows at her and she looked away.

"Sorry," she mumbled.

"Well, this narrows it down a bit," he said. "It must be somebody in Earthforce. Not that I'm fond of the idea." *Actually, though, it could be someone with an accurate copy of an Earthforce uniform. After all, if they could override the security codes on Ivanova's files then I don't suppose finding the ID needed to get in here would present an insurmountable problem.* He glanced at Susan's miserable face. *Not that I'll mention that possibility to Ivanova.*

He gave a cursory scan of the plate and data crystal, then leaned in and picked them up.

"I keep expecting them to explode," Susan said.

"So do I. That's why I keep checking." He pocketed the crystal.

"Any progress on the others?" she asked.

"Not yet," Garibaldi admitted reluctantly. He'd been growing increasingly uneasy about that.

"Don't worry," his tech had told him. "It's smoother than most, but it's a fake, I'm positive." When he'd asked her why, she said, "It's too scripted. No way do people talk this smoothly, no um, er, uh's anywhere. It's all perfect give-and-take, the kind of thing you wish you'd said, but didn't think of at the time. Y'know what I mean?"

Yeah. He knew what she meant. He'd felt it too, right from the start. But he couldn't *prove* it. And that's what he needed to do, for Ivanova's peace of mind if nothing else.

"Was the second one as bad as I thought it was going to be?" Susan asked.

"Yup."

Maybe it's true, she thought. *Maybe you can't find any flaws because it really happened.*

She held out her hand.

"I want to see this one," she said.

Garibaldi shook his head. "No you don't. Don't put this filth inside your head, Susan. This is the product of a sadistic little mind. You don't want to suffer for his pleasure."

"I can't hide from it," Susan said grimly. "It makes me feel like a coward." She looked at him levelly, refusing to lower her hand. At last, he relented and placed the crystal on her palm.

"Mind if I stay while you watch it?" he asked.

"Mind? I'd have tackled you if you tried to leave." She

took a deep breath and plugged the crystal into its slot. "Well, here goes."

The Psi-Corps logo appeared on the reader and Ivanova's jaw dropped.

"*Psi-Corp's?*" Garibaldi exclaimed. "This guy expects us to believe he can penetrate *Psi-Corp's?*"

The screen cleared to show the face of an elderly man initiating a communication. At the bottom of the screen the dataline showed who he was calling: time, date, and a name, Dr. Levin Okakura, appeared.

"That's my father!" Susan gasped, jerking her chin towards the face on the screen. She pointed at the doctor's name on the dataline below. "The man he's calling—Dr. Okakura—was our Psi-Corps family counselor."

"Dr. Ivanova," a voice said, presumably Dr. Okakura. "How may I help you?"

"I'm calling about my wife," her father said. His face was grim and his eyes old before their time. "This can't go on. The last shots she took . . . my God, Doctor, she can barely move, let alone think! Surely she's being given too much?"

There was the sound of data crystals clicking together, while Ivanova's father wore the expression of someone forcing himself to wait for confirmation.

A sigh from the unseen Psi-Corps counselor, then: "Based on the last tests she took, the dosage is appropriate. She's in no physical danger if that's what's worrying you, sir."

"What's worrying me is that I've seen *dogs* with a higher intellectual capacity!" Dr. Ivanova's face was flushed with anger and his eyes sparked with rage. "It's as though my wife had died and her corpse refused to stop breathing! And she knows it and she's miserable. How long can this go on?"

There was a pause while Ivanova's father glared out of the screen, breathing hard.

"Indefinitely," Dr. Okakura admitted. "But you know, this isn't necessary. If your wife will agree to join Psi-Corps and accept training she can be cleared of the drugs with no ill effects in under a month.''

Dr. Ivanova closed his eyes, shaking his head wearily.

"She'll never do that,'' he said. "The children . . .''

"If you'll excuse me for interrupting, Dr. Ivanova, your offspring are not children anymore. Your son is about to graduate and he's thinking of entering the military, while your daughter will be leaving for college shortly. So if this sacrifice is for their benefit, it's needless. Their lives are moving on and so are they. The situation has changed. I think you need to reevaluate your responses to it.''

Dr. Ivanova looked as if he'd been struck with a two-by-four. "You're right,'' he murmured. "But if she joins Psi-Corps she'll have to leave me.''

"Tsk. Don't be selfish, Doctor. In a manner of speaking she already has left you, and she'll continue to drift, just out of reach, as long as she takes the psi-suppressing drugs. In any case, it's not true that she'll have to leave you for longer than her training will take. We're not inhuman, you know. We have civilian branches that permit us to assign our people just about everywhere. Would you be willing to relocate if it didn't signify a major disruption of your work?''

A hopeful light had come into Dr. Ivanova's pale blue eyes.

"Yes,'' he said. "Yes, I'd be willing to relocate.'' Then something seemed to occur to him and it was like watching a fire being doused with water. "But my daughter, Susan,'' he sighed. "She hates Psi-Corps with a passion.''

"I know.''

"What do you mean, you know?'' Dr. Ivanova looked suspiciously out of the screen.

A slight laugh. "Nothing devious, I assure you. Your privacy hasn't been compromised. But typically at least one member of the family, and usually more, hates us. They place full blame for what's happened to their mother, sister, brother, on Psi-Corps. *We're* not to blame. We didn't write the laws, we didn't select the genes that made their loved one telepathic. We only exist to educate, to counsel, and to enact the law. I shudder to think what would happen to the talented if we weren't here to protect them. More to the point," Dr. Okakura said earnestly, "why should your daughter's opinions matter more than your wife's well-being?"

"Because," Dr. Ivanova said, running a hand through his graying hair, "Susan and her mother are very close. And if my wife joins Psi-Corps Susan will despise her and she'll never speak to either of us again. It would destroy my wife. I'm not sure she'd want to make such a—to use your word—sacrifice."

"Hmmm. Is Susan really that implacable?"

Dr. Ivanova smiled, and there was affection in it. He looked down. "Well, yes. She's very strong-minded and her stubbornness has grown as she has. I think my wife would rather die than lose Susan's good opinion."

There was a pause.

"We can arrange that," Dr. Okakura said.

"What?" Dr. Ivanova's expression was alarmed and confused.

"In extreme cases, like this one, we've arranged for it to look like a family member has died. Then the member— your daughter, in this instance—will be able to retain unsullied their affection and respect for their relative. While, in this case, your wife is able to go ahead and live a full life."

"That's outrageous!"

"No it's not, really. As I said, you're dealing with an extreme situation. Such circumstances require extreme measures. While your children were young and needed her, it made sense for your wife to choose the suppressant alternative. But why should she be alone and suffering the consequences of that selection? You've told me that she's despondent. I've examined her, and I concur. I feel that she could be at risk if she's left on her own, with no children to justify her diminished capacity."

Susan's father looked out of the screen with tortured eyes, like a man contemplating a deal with the devil.

"To put it another way. Your daughter may find herself facing this situation for real if you don't interfere now."

"You think it's that serious?" Dr. Ivanova frowned, and his voice was distressed.

"Yes. Your wife is bordering on suicidal, Doctor." Okakura's voice was warm with sympathy, tinged with deep regret. "Leave her on her own for a few months and I'm almost positive that's what will happen. You're her legal guardian, you have a duty to return her to her full capacity. She no longer can make that choice without your help."

"I need to think." Susan's father looked desperate, and tired.

"You've had twenty years to think, Doctor. You know you don't like what you've got. You don't like the present alternatives. This really is your only choice. In fact, it does less harm than any other," the counselor coaxed. "You called me today for help. It turns out that I can give it. Please, let us help you and your wife."

"How?" Dr. Ivanova asked warily.

"I should meet with you personally to discuss the details," Okakura said briskly. "My secretary will make an appointment for you. You won't regret it, Doctor, I give you my word." Dr. Okakura's voice rang with certainty.

Fragments of emotion wafted across Dr. Ivanova's tired features: doubt, shame, guilt, hope, determination.

"All right. We can at least discuss it. Thank you, Doctor, for being so frank."

"It would have been irresponsible of me not to have been. Good-bye, Doctor."

With a final, bleak look, Dr. Ivanova said, "Good-bye."

There was an addendum. The date of Susan's mother's death, and the date she entered Psi-Corps.

Susan covered her face with her hands. "She's alive! My God! She's alive?"

"No." Garibaldi shook her arm. "This is no more true than the ones that say your brother was a spy. This one might promise a happier ending, but that doesn't make it real." He gave her arm another shake. "Are you listening to me, Susan?"

"But this is so like Psi-Corps! You know it is." Her eyes were wounded.

He nodded slowly, his eyes thoughtful. "Yeah, it is. But what's it doing here? I refuse to believe someone successfully infiltrated *Psi-Corps*, for God's sake, for the sole purpose of making your life miserable."

"Maybe my mother sent it," Ivanova suggested. "Maybe she wants me to know."

"Like she wanted you to know your brother was spying for the Centauri or the Minbari or whoever? Why would she do that, Susan?" He looked at her gravely, watching her tear the hope out of her heart. *I'm going to kill the bastard who did this,* he thought, knowing he wouldn't.

"I'm going to kill whoever's doing this," Susan said through clenched teeth. "I was only upset before, but now I'm really pissed off!" She struck the desk with her fist, hard enough to make the data crystals on it dance, then turned blazing eyes on the Security Chief. "And I think I've got a likely suspect."

Their links chirruped.

"Yes," they barked simultaneously.

"Ivanova, Garibaldi, my office, now," Captain Sheridan said crisply, then he was gone.

"Why is it the one time you snarl into your link, it's the Captain?" Garibaldi asked.

When they entered Sheridan's office they found him seated behind his desk, tapping a data crystal on its brushed steel surface. Blue eyes impaled them as they took their places before him.

"Why didn't you call me when this happened?" Sheridan

asked the Security Chief. "I thought I'd made my wishes clear when we last spoke about this sort of thing."

"Well, Sir, it was fairly late . . ."

"I'm on duty twenty-four hours a day, Garibaldi and you know it."

Okay, wrong tack. How do I tell him it never occurred to me.

"It never occurred to me to drag you over to the scene, when all I could tell you is what's in that report. I still can't add much. There's no official record of any T'llin entering the station, including one named Phina—I presume one of the two you mentioned. All we have is Na'Toth's word about what happened. Based on her recent experiences and the extreme hostility between the two races, I can't condemn her reaction."

"Or condone it, I hope." Sheridan was genuinely angry and it showed in the tightness of his jaw, the steadiness of his gaze. "I will say this one more time, Garibaldi, and one time only. I want to be informed when an incident of this type occurs. I don't want to find an incomplete report waiting on my desk in the morning. I want to know *at the time!* Are we clear?"

"Yes, Sir."

"Are you sure?"

"Yes, Sir."

There was a pause while the two men stared at each other.

"Excuse me, Sir." Sheridan shifted his gaze to Ivanova. "What are you talking about?"

"Garibaldi, if you would do the honors," Sheridan invited.

"Na'Toth killed a T'llin she found wandering around in the corridors outside the Ambassadorial quarters."

"I thought you said they'd disappeared," Susan said, puzzled.

"I did. I haven't seen any of them for several days. Nor have any of my informants. They're definitely not in Down Below, that much I can vouch for."

"I wanted you both here when I call G'Kar." Sheridan smiled briefly. "Both as witnesses and as moral support." He initiated the call to the Narn Ambassador's office.

G'Kar looked out of the screen gravely, his manner subdued and professional.

"Good morning, Captain Sheridan. I've been expecting your call. Have you any additional information for us?"

"Regrettably, no, Ambassador. In fact, I was wondering if you had any new information for us?"

G'Kar's eyes sparked and his face hardened. "Yesss," he said in a rumbling growl, like the warning of an angry cat. "I do have some information for you. I am not happy with the way Garibaldi has been handling this situation. This is three times my aide has had a run-in with a T'llin. And what is that Earth phrase? Ah yes, once is accident, twice is happenstance, three times is enemy action." G'Kar paused, his gathering rage plain in his face. "Which is what I've been telling you all along!" he bellowed. He sat forward, glaring at the three humans. With an effort the Ambassador seemed to calm himself. Sitting back, he regained his usual urbane manner.

"Perhaps the fault has been mine," G'Kar suggested, closing his eyes wearily. "Perhaps I've failed to make my desires clear in this matter, to tell you what I want." He opened red eyes in a cold, level stare. "What I want, Captain Sheridan, is to have every one of these T'llin arrested and confined preparatory to being deported to Narn space. I do not want *one* of them running free on this station while the conference is going on. I assure you, Captain, they have no other purpose here than to cause damage of one sort or another. And I advise you most strongly, for the sake of the station as well as the peace conference, to bring these people under control. They are terrorists, and mad terrorists at that." He paused, and gripped a gloved hand in a tight fist.

"I'll give you forty-eight hours, Captain Sheridan," G'Kar said through clenched teeth. "And then I shall advise that this meeting between the Narn and the Centauri be called off.''

G'Kar disconnected without waiting to hear what the humans might have to say.

Sheridan raised his brows at Garibaldi and Ivanova.

''I think you know what Earth would have to say if this conference were scuttled because we didn't cooperate with the Narn Ambassador.''

Ivanova looked grim and Garibaldi blew out his breath. ''The only one I can lay my hands on is the T'llin in Medlab's morgue,'' Garibaldi said. ''Until last night, I was thinking they'd quit the station.''

''I doubt that,'' Sheridan said, looking contemplative. ''They've nowhere to go but home.'' He shot a glance at the Security Chief from under his brows. ''And if they found T'll appealing they wouldn't be here in the first place. I can't believe that just two days ago the Prime Phina was in this office backing his sister's plea for political recognition by Earth.''

Ivanova leaned forward. ''What?'' she asked in a strangled voice. ''Sir.''

''Two T'llin came to visit me, and I've heard, the other ambassadors to plead for any kind of aid we could offer them against the Narn.''

''What did you tell them?'' Ivanova asked, a slight frown marring the smoothness of her high forehead.

''The usual,'' Sheridan said sourly. ''Thank you for coming, I'll relay your messages, nothing I can do personally but wish you well. It just about made me sick. The Narn have been giving those people a bad time.''

''I don't know much about them,'' Ivanova said. ''But from what I've heard, a bad time is putting it mildly.'' She grimaced. ''Kinda sheds a new light on the Narn situation.''

''Which may explain G'Kar's determination to have them all rounded up and thrown off the station. In Narn custody, of course.'' Garibaldi clicked his tongue. ''The press is going to be all over this station by tomorrow night and the T'llin would make a classic human interest story. Sort of.''

"A story that would definitely sway Earth's opinion against the Narn. Not that I think anyone will ever actually cheer the Centauri's behavior, but it would make the Narn's misfortunes seem deserved." Sheridan leaned forward. "Find them, put them in protective custody. We can work out the details later. Susan, I need for you to check out the shipping aspects of this. Garibaldi tells me there's no record of any T'llin entering the station at any time. But someone has to know how they did it. See what you can turn up."

"Yes, Sir." She rose and Garibaldi stood beside her. "Is there anything else, Sir?"

"No. Good luck, and''—he trained a steely eye on Garibaldi—"keep me informed."

Olorasin paced nervously, back and forth in the strait confines of the room. Usually, cramped quarters didn't bother one of her race; since before recorded history began, they had lived underground during T'll's fierce day. But now she wanted to get *out*, to run, to *do*. Since she'd awakened and found her brother gone her anxiety had increased until she literally couldn't be still. Only by an effort of will had she kept herself, so far, from raging at his followers for letting him stray into the station by himself.

He hadn't left until she was asleep, and no one admitted to seeing him leave their hiding place, so how long his absence had been no one knew. Since she'd wakened it had been five hours. And she paced. Turning, she went to the window between her quarters and those of the others.

"Open," she said and the glass went from opaque to clear.

They looked so tired, so anxious, these refugees. Even the children were subdued. Olorasin took a deep breath.

Still, this is a good place. I'm proud of my people for thinking of it. Safe, clean, private, they've done well. Despite the crowded conditions. She shuddered. *It's far better than Down Below.*

As she looked out, Segrea and Haelstrac, the local leaders of the Razye Tesh, came in through the back door. They'd exchanged their ragged robes for the mock encounter suits Olorasin and Phina had worn when calling on the ambassadors. Olorasin recognized them by their disparate sizes as much as anything else.

They looked up to see her watching them from the office window and stopped in their tracks. Segrea tore off his mask and the sheer mad grief in his black eyes froze her heart.

"Open," Olorasin said to the door. But she held herself back, refusing to charge into the common room to demand explanations. She backed away from them, allowing them to enter. "Close," she said and the window became opaque and the door shut behind the two Razye Tesh.

They stood together silently, while a heaviness descended on them, as though the air had grown too old to breathe.

"Tell me," Olorasin said at last, hoping in her hearts that it was only bad and not the very worst that could happen.

"The Prime Phina," Segrea ground out in a voice like stones being crushed, "has been murdered by the Narn Ambassador's aide."

The world flowed away from her, a physical sensation, as though she were being hoisted suddenly. Yet her body felt light, and devoid of feeling, as though it had dissolved into a mist and blown away. It was like being seized by some mystical force in a dream. Everything was suddenly very clear, every tiny detail shouted its importance, and her eyes fastened on the seal of Haelstrac's encounter suit as though it was a marvelous thing.

Olorasin felt her face go slack and her legs went weak. She sat with a suddenness that jarred her and made her jaw clop. She bit her tongue, a bitter pain that angered her a little, but remotely.

Segrea and Haelstrac lifted her to her feet and when she couldn't walk, Segrea carried her to the cot they'd furnished, laying her down gently.

"What's wrong with her?" Segrea asked. He'd expected

a vast outpouring of grief, cries, and ululations, the tearing of garments and even the rending of her blameless flesh. Not this. Not a collapse into vacuity. Segrea's hearts beat faster and his skin crawled with horror. He'd never seen anything like this.

Haelstrac looked bitterly down on the prostrate form on the cot.

"She's alone," Haelstrac said simply. "From the moment of conception her every heartbeat has been echoed by the Prime Phina's. Now there is only silence."

"Is she going to die?" Segrea demanded.

"I don't know. Such a thing as this has never been recorded." Haelstrac turned her face away. "She may well die. And if she does, then so will we."

"Tcha!" Segrea exclaimed, straightening. "Superstition! I looked for better from you."

"We're not discussing *my* superstition," Haelstrac snarled. "But that of T'll. Do you think any of us here are typical? To hide in the desert is our way, Segrea, not to flee the planet. But those at home, when they hear of this, will take it as a sign and they will lie down and die!" She turned away from her big friend and, shuffling over to the other cot, dropped down to sit with her face buried in her hands. "What are we going to do?" she sighed.

Segrea shifted his feet and frowned down at the fallen Prime. Sorrow ate at his middle like a slow fire. Haelstrac's words, "They will take it as a sign," echoed in his mind and he found himself tempted to believe that fate had spoken, condemning their enterprise.

No, he thought. *Too many have died, too many are suffering. We can't just abandon this. We can't give up.* They couldn't let the Narn win.

"The first thing we're going to do," he said dully, "is find out what they're going to do." He put on the concealing mask and pulled up the hood of the encounter suit. "Let's go." He began to shuffle to the door.

"Wait," Haelstrac said. "What do we do about her? And should we tell the others?"

Segrea stared at the closed door for a moment.

"Yes," he said at last. "We tell them. They'd find out sooner or later. Then we'll leave her in their care. They can all grieve as one. Come on," he said, reaching out his hand to her, "we'll do it together."

Na'Toth studied the Ambassador's stony face in trepidation. As yet he hadn't condemned her for killing the Prime. But she knew it had been an unfortunate mistake and she quailed within.

"Surely it's too late to cancel the peace conference now," she ventured. "That could do us irreparable harm."

"Yes," G'Kar said quietly. "An empty threat. Calling off the conference because the humans weren't dealing properly with a terrorist threat would be outbalanced by the reason for that terrorist threat. Human public opinion would be confused—that is, they would no longer view the situation between us and the Centauri in its proper, unambiguous light. Still"—he shifted in his chair and seemed to come alert—"the threat will carry weight with the Terrans. They don't know which way we'll jump. We are aliens after all."

Na'Toth couldn't help smiling slightly.

"The T'llin haven't been seen in days, Ambassador. Not one of them. And there's been no word of them from any of our sources."

"Which means we're not paying our sources enough credits," G'Kar said fastidiously. "Perhaps the death of a Prime will bring the T'llin out of their holes." He looked at Na'Toth out of the corner of his eye. "Or perhaps we should send you wandering around the station on some last-minute chores for the conference. That might bring them up to the surface too."

Na'Toth nodded. "Whenever you wish, G'Kar. I'm at your disposal."

What an almost perfect choice of words, G'Kar thought, then frowned at his own petulance. He knew he'd never waste a resource of Na'Toth's quality.

"Relax," he said aloud. "You'd be too much trouble to replace."

"Ah, Vir!"

Londo's enthusiastic greeting made Vir pull his head down into his shoulders like a turtle.

"Good morning, Ambassador," he said cautiously.

"Don't look so worried, my boy. I'm about to make you happy. I've got something I want you to research for the conference."

"Really?" Vir's face brightened and his heart opened with relief. "You're finally taking the conference seriously?"

"You've heard of last evening's unfortunate events, no doubt?" Londo sat on one of his elegant new chairs and crossed his legs.

"Yes, Ambassador. Na'Toth killed an alien."

"No, no." Londo shook his finger at Vir. "Not just an alien. A T'llin, and a Prime at that. T'll, you see, is one of the Narn colony worlds, and the native population doesn't seem to be enjoying their visitation."

He laughed delightedly, spreading his hands. "I don't know why I never thought of it before. One of our reasons for attacking the Narn is to stop them from depredating defenseless worlds. To prevent their unlimited cruelties towards non-Narn peoples. Eh? It's good, eh? So run along and put something together for me."

Vir felt his jaw dropping and with an effort of will clamped it back in place. *I'll never make it in politics,* he thought hopelessly. *I could never be that shameless.*

CHAPTER 14

"GOOD morning, Ambassador." Semana offered her hand with a graceful flourish, her smile coquettishly welcoming. "Thank you for meeting me on such short notice."

Londo swept the proffered hand to his lips without hesitation, and with every appearance of enjoyment.

"Truth to tell, dear lady," he said as he took his seat at the café table, "I anticipated hearing from you. I had some private information regarding your other client's resources that led me to believe the . . . item might still be available." He gave her a sharp look. "I'm correct, am I not?"

She nodded, smiling.

"Why else would we be meeting, Ambassador?"

"Ah, well," Londo rolled his eyes. "You might find me attractive, eh? Or, you might have some other piece of . . . um . . ."

"Art," Semana supplied sharply.

"Yesss, quite. Art, that you thought I might be interested in." His eyes turned cold, despite his smile. "I'm not. There's only one thing I'm interested in. And I would like to see it, if you would be so kind."

"Of course." Semana nodded, her eyes on the piece of fruit she was shredding. "But first"—she flicked her fingers and then wiped them on a napkin—"we should talk about the price." Her gaze met his like a stone striking sparks. "I don't want to get your hopes up if you lack the wherewithal to purchase the *item*." She hooked her arm over the back of her chair and crossed her long legs as she studied him.

Londo cocked a brow and dipped his head in acknowledgment.

"More than five hundred thousand, you said. How much more?" he asked with a quiet but undeniable menace.

"A million," Semana said calmly.

Mollari burst out laughing. "A *million*! You're mad!"

She shrugged delicately and straightened in her chair. "Well, you're right, of course. It's priceless." Her eyes bored into his. "But not to me. One million. Cheap at twice the price, and well you know it."

"Oh, ho ho," Londo shook his head at her, as though he believed her to be joking. "If it actually is the—"

"Do you want me to leave?" she asked, half rising.

Londo held up a placating hand. "Item," he finished. "Then yes, the price is reasonable. But I still have my doubts that it is authentic. When may I examine it?"

Semana sighed and gave the Ambassador an exasperated look.

"I'm only considering you as a potential buyer because my client is having difficulty coming up with the credits." She crossed her arms on the table before her and glared at Mollari. "You'll have two days, counting today, to come up with the funds. If you can't do it, then we're not going any further with this. This isn't an item I feel safe flashing around," she said, leaning back in her chair.

Londo leaned forward, closing the space between them, his eyes never leaving hers.

"Yes. I can get the credits, and within the time limit you've set. Now, may I see your merchandise?"

"But of course." Her smile was dazzling. "Let's go."

Londo gasped and he shook his head in wonder.

"It *is*," he whispered in awe. "You have the actual Eye!" He looked at her in wonder. "How did you get it?"

"I bought it. If you mean, how was it stolen, I have no

idea.'' She shrugged prettily. ''For all I know, the Centauri government sold it to raise money for the war.''

Actually, that sounds like them, Londo admitted to himself. When he'd contacted Centauri Prime and made hints about the Eye being missing, all he'd gotten were blank stares and rude questions about his drinking habits. Which was exactly what they'd do if they *had* managed to lose the Eye, of course. And there would be a very, very good copy on hand. He could imagine the justification: ''The Eye's effect is psychological. Our people need merely know it is there, and see what they think is the Eye, for the proper effect.''

It was exactly the argument he'd have used in their place.

But if the Eye was real, if they had sold it or lost it through incompetence, he suspected Mr. Morden would not be too pleased with their handling of his gift. But if he recovered it. . . . Londo's acquisition of the Eye had significantly increased his authority the first time. This time what might it do for him, both among his own people and among Mr. Morden's . . . associates?

He licked his lips and reached for the Eye.

''Ah ah!'' Semana's lean brown arm blocked him. ''It's protected by a unique security system. You'd lose a finger, or two if you were unlucky, if you actually attempted to pick it up.''

There was a ring of absolute sincerity in her voice that convinced him.

''How am I to determine that it is genuine?'' he demanded. ''You can't expect me to pay a million credits for something I haven't properly examined.''

''You may manipulate the box. But do not try to touch the Eye—either with your hands, or with an object. Believe me, you wouldn't like the results.'' She raised an elegant brow. ''Come now, Ambassador, it's not as though you were an expert in antiquities. What could holding it in your hands tell you that looking carefully at it can't?'' She picked up the box and placed it in his hands.

Londo looked down into the crimson-silk-padded box,

turning it this way and that. With every passing moment he became more and more convinced of its authenticity. Every mark he looked for was there, just as it had been when he'd seen it last year. He drew it closer and closer, fascinated by its ornate and sparkling surfaces.

"All right," Semana said, tugging it out of his hands. "That's enough." She snapped the lid shut and took it back over to the wall safe. *You clever little bastard,* she thought at Tiko. One of the things she'd learned very rapidly about her tiny associate was that it was able to exert a powerful fascination over its victims. Especially when it was hungry. And it was always hungry. Though she had to approve of its ambition. *I mean, going after something Londo's size,* she suppressed a chuckle. *Even I'm not that greedy.*

"I realize you're at a disadvantage," she said sympathetically, to the Centauri. "My client was able to hire independent experts to examine the piece and he was convinced by their reports. I could obtain copies of them for you, but," she smiled and shrugged, "we'd still be on square one. Namely, do you trust me?"

"No offense, dear lady, but with a million credits"—his mouth turned down—"I really don't know."

"Perhaps a scan?" she said. "You do have a standard unit with you, don't you?"

"But of course," Londo said. *And the fact that you suggest it makes it even more likely that this is genuine. Unbelievable!*

He took the unit from his pocket, flipped it open, and ran the wand over the box. *Unbelievable.* Exactly what he'd expected to see.

"Unbelievable," he murmured aloud. Then, hastily: "No offense."

"None taken," Semana said equably as she walked him to the door. "You have today and tomorrow to decide."

The Ambassador stopped and turned to her in appeal.

"Are you sure that you can't give me more time?"

"That's exactly what my client asked," she said. "The answer is no."

"But I need it *now*!" G'Kar's fist slammed the table in emphasis.

Cray looked icily at the Narn Ambassador and curled his lip.

"Don't shout at me, man. I said I'd get you the credits by the day after tomorrow and I will. It's the best I can do."

"If I can't get them by tomorrow I don't need them." G'Kar's red eyes glittered in the dim tavern light. "And I'm sure your associates wouldn't appreciate that at all."

"No, they wouldn't, but there's a five percent charge on the total for our trouble, so they'll take the shot like reasonable people."

G'Kar sat stunned for a moment.

"This is the first I've heard of such a fee."

"This is the first *I've* heard of you backin' out of our deal. I told ya how long it was gonna take me. If that wasn't good enough for ya, ya shouldna shaken my hand." Cray leaned back in the booth, looking petulant and just a little angry. "Remind me not to do business with you people again, okay?"

"I'll see what I can work out," G'Kar bit off after a moment's pause. He narrowed his eyes and studied the grubby-looking little human. "There's another matter I'd like to discuss with you."

"Don't bother." Cray held up both hands, palms out. "After this? I told you, I don't wanna do business with you."

"I'm looking for information about T'llin. Any T'llin and I'm willing to pay well."

"Yeah?" Cray looked away, then glancing out of the corner of his eye asked, "How much?"

"What's your usual fee for information," G'Kar asked smoothly.

"*Usually* I don't sell information. I'm an arranger."

"Well, if you can *arrange* for me to get some concrete information on the whereabouts of any T'llin I'll triple your usual fee."

"Yeah, well, you don't know how much that is," Cray challenged him, rather enjoying the exchange.

"It's two hundred credits," G'Kar snarled. Wildly extravagant, but he needed the information now.

Cray gaped.

"You'll pay me six hundred credits?" he wheezed. "I dunno . . . What are you gonna do to 'em?"

"What do you care?" G'Kar couldn't suppress a sneer; the wiry little human was such a pathetic specimen of his kind.

" 'At's why I'm not an informer," Cray explained. "I do care. Sumpin' bad happens, it bothers me."

I suspect it's a weak stomach rather than scruples, G'Kar thought sarcastically.

"I intend to turn them over to Station Security. They have associations with a terrorist fringe group. My expectation is that they have plans to damage the station in order to stop the peace conference."

"Oh," Cray said, looking thoughtful.

"One of their leaders was recently killed by a Narn," G'Kar pressed. "So I suspect they're in a bad mood."

"Oh. Yeah." Cray stared into space for a moment. "I might be able to help you," he said. "I think I know how to flush a few out into the open. Give me a few hours."

G'Kar laid a credit chit on the table.

"This is a down payment," he said softly. "You might say a goodwill token." He gave Cray a look that all but turned the little arranger's bowels to water. "Don't disappoint me."

The Ambassador slipped out of the booth and was gone.

Cray blew out his breath and panted a few times. Then he picked up the credit chit and slipped it into his reader. *Two hundred cool ones,* he thought with a grin. *Easy money.*

* * *

"Why, Chief Garibaldi. What brings you to my door?" Semana asked, ignoring the presence of the Centauri Ambassador.

"I have a warrant to search your quarters, Ms. MacBride, for stolen artifacts." Garibaldi smiled sweetly as he presented the document to Semana. Behind him the three security people he'd brought along and the Ambassador began to move forward.

"Just a moment," Semana said, steel in her lush voice, and they halted. "Before anyone runs over to my underwear drawer, I get to read this." She read the warrant, taking her time. She tapped the document. "This doesn't mention any Centauri officials, but"—she gestured towards Londo without looking at him—"you seem to have brought one."

Oops.

"The Ambassador claims to have seen a stolen Centauri artwork in your possession and wishes to be of assistance in identifying it," Garibaldi said somewhat uncomfortably. *That's what I get for trying to pass off a standard form on a pro like MacBride,* he scolded himself.

"Are you suggesting that I allow any volunteers you may have swept up on the way to examine my personal belongings?" Semana asked in astonishment. "Is it even legal for the complainant to help with the search?"

"Well, if you object—"

"I do."

"Then I'm sure the Ambassador won't mind meeting us back at Security Central," Garibaldi said, looking meaningfully at Londo.

"Absolutely not. Mr. Garibaldi, I regard it as my duty to take custody of this valuable Centauri artifact as soon as it is recovered." Londo looked into the Chief's frustrated glare and announced, "I insist."

"Then you won't mind waiting out here in the hallway, Ambassador. Because Ms. MacBride is correct, it wouldn't be legal for you to help in the search."

Semana made a sweeping gesture of welcome and Garibaldi and his three security people stepped into her quarters. With a glare at Londo she snarled, "Close." The door fell back into position, leaving Londo sputtering in the hallway.

"Now," Semana said, crossing her arms. "Just what is it you're looking for?"

Well, why not tell her? he asked himself. *If she's guilty, she knows anyway.*

"Londo said you had the Centauri Eye of Empire."

She narrowed her eyes, then let her lips turn up at the corners. "Yes, of course," she said. "I have the Narn Sacred Rock too. And the British Crown Jewels, don't you know."

One of the Security troopers smothered a chortle, then went ramrod stiff at Garibaldi's glare.

"I presume you have something," he said. "Londo isn't that kind of idiot."

"I have a *copy* of it," she snapped.

Semana walked over to the safe, and all three searchers stopped what they were doing to look from her to the Chief. Garibaldi signaled that they should continue.

Semana withdrew a small black box from the safe and handed it to him.

"Excuse me!" she snapped at a security woman who was lifting a bowl with a large yellow rose in it. "You're looking for an orb. It's round. Do you see something round hiding under that bowl?"

The Security woman took a quick sniff of the rose and, smiling, put it down.

Semana let out her breath slowly. *The fool woman will never know how close she came to rough rhino-surgery*, she thought.

Garibaldi had opened the box and was looking at a tiny jeweled sphere.

"What is this?" he asked.

"It's an exact copy, in miniature, of the Eye of Empire. It was made for a prince of the royal family in honor of his fifth birthday. Historians say it was the emperor's way of signifying his choice of heir. The poor kid was dead in a year. Which is the big problem with identifying exactly who you're going to leave the throne to when you're dealing with an unrelenting pack of weasels like the Centauri court.''

"That's a very biased remark," Garibaldi said in mild reproof.

"Well," she shrugged, crossing her arms again, "Mollari has given me reason to be prejudiced. I showed this to him and he expressed interest. But when we started to talk price, he called me a thief and warned me he had *friends*. I told him, very nicely, that he should think it over, but that I was leaving the day after tomorrow. And he marched off in a huff." She thrust a sheaf of documents at him.

Handing the box back to her, he started to look through them.

"You only paid fifteen thousand credits for this."

"Only!" she said in disbelief. "You must be making a very good salary when you can say *only* fifteen thousand credits."

"You're asking a million," Garibaldi pointed out.

"When I bought this, the Centauri art market had bottomed out. I admit it was a steal. Metaphorically speaking," she said hastily. "But you could get deals like this a couple of years ago. Now interest is starting to rise and it's whatever price the market will bear. If Londo doesn't want to pay a million, no one's holding a PPG to his head. But *this*"—she gestured at the searchers—"is an attempted shakedown and I resent it."

"Noted," Garibaldi said. Then he read the name of the auction house and the date and lot number of her purchase into his link for further research. Everything looked right, but she was slippery and it would probably pay to check.

The search took another half an hour and turned up nothing.

"I'm sorry to have taken up your time," Garibaldi told her in the open door of her quarters.

Leaning close to the Chief, she murmured, "What, no sympathy for the terrible emotional shock this has been?" Her dark eyes laughed up at him.

Frowning to prevent the smile he felt coming on, he said, "I'm sure it must be an awful experience for an *innocent* woman to endure."

"Well, none of us had much *choice* under the circumstances," she said aloud, pointedly ignoring Mollari. "Close," she snapped, and the door slid shut.

Garibaldi turned to Mollari and, pointing his forefinger, said, "I am not happy." Then he started off down the corridor, followed by the three security people.

"Don't you point your finger at me!" Londo shouted to the Chief's back. He hastened to catch up to Garibaldi. "Don't tell me you didn't find it! It's as big as a melon, you idiot."

Garibaldi stopped and leaned close to Londo.

"What she had was a copy of the Eye," he said softly. "About this big." He formed a circle with his thumb and forefinger. "And she owns that legally. There was nothing else in that room resembling the Eye of Empire. Now, I don't know what's going on here, Londo, but I'm feeling kind of embarrassed right now, and I am very, very busy arranging security for *your* peace conference. So I'd appreciate it if you didn't follow me down the hallway yelling about how dissatisfied you are." He turned and marched off, leaving the Centauri standing there with his mouth open.

"But I saw it," Londo said plaintively to himself. "I *saw* it. I *scanned* it and saw the readouts."

Leona Pelligrino stood nonplussed outside the closed door of the office space she'd rented to that nice Mr. Craighton. There'd been complaints, and her cold-blooded Minbari supervisor had sent her down to check things out.

But what would the neighbors find to complain about in an empty office.

The part of the office visible from the walkway was

empty: no chairs, no desks, no nothing. With an audible sigh, Leona slipped her master key-card into the slot and entered the office.

"Hello," she called cheerily. There was no answer, but a peculiar scent hung in the air. *Like cooking,* she thought. *Not good.*

She approached the panel that separated the front office from the rest of the property.

"Open," she said. The panel slipped aside to reveal a curtain. *Odd,* she thought. Leona swept the flimsy barrier aside and found herself confronting a roomful of aliens.

"Oh!" she said, startled by their universal attention and solid black eyes. Then she realized that they'd been camping out in the space behind the front office. "Oh!" she said again. "Oh, no. No, no. This isn't right. You can't stay here, it's against the rules!" All she could think of was: *He's going to fire me. That Minbari robot is going to blame this on me and he's going to fire me.*

"We have paid to be here," one of them said.

"This isn't a residential space," Leona said desperately. "You'll get a refund." *Minus any costs for damages,* she thought, but didn't say. "You'll have to be out of here by tomorrow," Leona said firmly.

One of them moved towards her and for the first time she realized how many of them there were.

"There've been complaints," she said and raw fear scraped in her voice. "That's why I came." She took a step backwards. "If one of your neighbors calls Security there'll be a huge fine, and, and they'll make you leave right away." A change came over their features; she thought it might be anger. Leona turned and fled.

"Close!" she said to the outer door and continued to move briskly down the walkway, prudently hugging its outer edge. She looked behind her. No one was following. *Oh, I am gonna be in such trouble,* she thought. Then she narrowed her eyes. *Wait'll I get my hands on that Craighton.*

* * *

Back in the office there was a stunned silence. None of the T'llin even moved for several moments. Then a female said, "We'd better pack."

"Yes," a male answered her. "The sooner we're out of here the better."

"What about the others?" someone asked.

"They'll be back before we're finished," the male answered after a moment's thought.

Slowly at first, and then more quickly, the refugees began to gather their ragged belongings together.

"What of the Prime?" one of the women asked.

"Leave her to rest," another answered thoughtfully. "The Razye Tesh have been protecting her. No doubt they will continue to do so."

There were nods all around at that, and the T'llin slowly went on with their packing.

Londo stood at a loss, watching the Security Chief and his minions march down the long corridor and enter the lift. Garibaldi gave him a very sour and disappointed look as the doors closed.

He paced back and forth for a while, thinking.

She couldn't have hidden it in her quarters, or they would have found it, he thought. But that didn't explain Garibaldi's attitude. After all, she could have found a safe hiding place, or she might even have a compatriot they knew nothing about. A simple failure to find the item wouldn't merit such hostility. *He behaved as though I'd done something unconscionable. Something worse than wasting his time. Which means,* he thought, staring at her closed door, *that she told him some slander, which Garibaldi found totally believable.*

Londo sniffed in irritation. *Humans!* he thought in disgust. *And their damned, naive, convoluted moral scruples.* Sometimes political necessity required sharp, or even dishonest dealing. *Can't he separate the exigencies of office from the person in that office?* He "tsked" and paced, cursing the forces that moved him beyond the common ken of Centauri and aliens alike.

He paused in his pacing outside Semana's door, staring in angry befuddlement at the blank surface. The door opened and Semana emerged in a cloud of provocative scent, marching past him without acknowledging his presence. Londo watched her walk down the corridor for a moment before rushing after her.

"You still have it, don't you?" he asked in panic. That explanation had only just occurred to him.

Semana walked on, ignoring him completely.

Women! Londo thought in exasperation. *Whether they're Centauri or human it makes no difference. If you're not groveling, they're not happy.*

"I'd like to apologize," he said, beginning to pant as he tried to keep up with Semana's long strides.

"Oh, I'm *sure* you would," she said, widening her eyes without looking at him. "For all the *good* it will do you."

"I'm still interested in buying it," he said, hoping the offer might calm her down, or at least slow her down.

"Right now, Mollari, I'd rather space that thing than sell it to you." She walked on.

That stopped him in his tracks. *She wouldn't*, he thought. "You wouldn't!" he gasped.

"That depends." Semana took another step and turned to look at him. "Would that bother you?"

"It would kill me!" he said, with great sincerity. "It is a Centauri treasure."

"Oh, you *tempt* me," she said with narrowed eyes. She turned and started walking again.

"Please," he said desperately, "give me another chance."

They'd reached the lift, and she signaled it.

"Another chance?" she said. "To do what? Entrap me?" Semana looked him over. "Are you still working for Security?" she asked. "Do you have some kind of recording device tucked about your tubby figure?"

"I beg your pardon!" Londo said, drawing himself up indignantly.

She laughed. "You wretched little weasel."

"You're being absurd. I have no recording devices and I'm not working for Earthforce Security!" *And I'm not tubby, either!* "In fact, Garibaldi was furious with me for accusing you. I don't know what explanation you gave him, but he accepted it completely."

The lift arrived and she stepped in. Turning, she placed a hand on his chest, preventing him from boarding.

Semana laughed again. "It's a real comment on your character, Mollari, that Garibaldi would accept *my* word over yours." Grinning, she stepped back and the doors closed.

Yes, Londo thought ruefully, *I suppose that it is.*

Segrea and Haelstrac glanced at each other and then back at the morose faces of the T'llin refugee community.

The blanket partitions had been taken down, and everyone's possessions were neatly rolled into portable bundles.

Just as well, Haelstrac thought unhappily, *that we didn't have time to accumulate more things than we could carry.* Still, this should have worked, her people should have been able to find safety and relative comfort in the secrecy of this hired space. She looked up at Segrea.

"Cray," he said quietly. But in a grating manner that held overtones of *will pay, will be mangled, will thank his deity for release when we push him out the air lock.*

She blinked once, then nodded her assent.

"Just a place of warmth and safty, that's all we wanted," said a tired-looking young mother, clutching her baby to her. "Was it so much to ask?"

"Apparently," Haelstrac muttered.

"What shall we do?" Miczyn asked plaintively.

"What we must," Segrea said. "We return to Down Below. As secretly as we can, in ones and twos to whatever places we can find. Security has been scouring Down Below for our presence for a week now, and found no trace of us. They probably think we've left the station."

"We're not idiots, Segrea," a youngster said. "The informants will be lined up at the comstations to turn us in. Unless we can pay them first."

"Or intimidate them," Segrea suggested with an evil grin. Then he shrugged his big shoulders. "We have no choice. But I've an idea, youngster; why don't you and some of your friends go scouting for out-of-the-way places for us. That will make it easier on the mothers and children." *And it will give you something useful to do, instead of posing and complaining.*

The young male nodded eagerly and with a gesture gathered up some of his age-mates and left the office sanctuary.

"What of the Prime?" Haelstrac asked the distraught Miczyn.

"She doesn't move, she doesn't speak, she neither eats nor drinks. I'm worried," he said and his eyes showed it.

Segrea shuddered and turned away.

"I leave her to you," he told Haelstrac. "I cannot deal with that."

Haelstrac nodded her understanding. *But how do I deal with it?* she wondered. How did anyone deal with a grief that seemed to have slain the soul of the Prime Olorasin?

Olorasin lay on her side, dimly aware of the comings and goings of others. They spoke to her, but their speech held no meaning. The words dropped one after the other into the abyss within, out of nothing and into nowhere without touching her.

She lay on her side, but felt nothing. Not the cheap blanket, nor the thin mattress resting on its rickety frame. She touched all of these things, but it didn't matter, the sensations were so unimportant as to not exist.

Within she felt hollowed out and the hollow was lined with frost. Sharp crystals of ice that froze the blood they drew with her every breath. She ached, and she was so cold. So cold.

CHAPTER 15

THERE was a note taped to the door of Midori Kobayashi's quarters. It was written on thick, rough-textured paper the color of rich cream, and was addressed to *Ambassador Delenn, and her Assistant Lennier.*

Delenn hesitated before she plucked it from the door and looked askance at Lennier, who merely waited calmly for her to open the envelope.

The note read:

Honored Guests,

Welcome to my humble lodgings. Please enter and refresh yourselves with contemplation of my poor garden. When you have had time to relax and all is prepared within I will come to greet you and we may begin.

If you should have questions, or wish to examine any object, please be assured that by tradition it is most polite to ask.

Midori Kobayashi

"Her garden?" Delenn asked, as though she thought she'd misread the word.

"So it says," Lennier agreed.

Delenn looked at her assistant, who stood politely with his hands folded before him, waiting for her decision.

"Open," Delenn commanded, and the portal swung aside. Within lay a space arranged like no other they had seen on the station. Ahead, and off to the side, was a small paper-walled hut; the hidden interior was lit by candles or lamps, for it glowed like a lantern. Beside the hut sat a bench, surrounded by plants of various height in harmonious gradations of green, their vicinity softly lit by a pair of lanterns with little peaked roofs. There was a small fountain in front of the bench, a simple pipe dripping water into a stone basin. The other wall of the paper-walled hut appeared blank at first, but a closer inspection revealed that part of the wall was apparently designed to slide off to the side, creating a door. The larger room that contained the little hut was in darkness.

Delenn hesitated. There was no sense of threat, but she was unnerved by the darkness. She opened her mouth to call out, then closed it, remembering their hostess's note. Delenn glanced at the patient form of Lennier, motionless in the semidarkness, and took a step forward.

With her movement a spotlight illuminated a plant, displayed on a pedestal.

"Oh," she whispered as she realized what it was and moved closer.

The plant was a tiny tree. Its gnarled trunk leaned in a way that suggested the harsh winds of some mountain slope. Tiny tufts of needles burst from the tips of its branches, gleaming with health and freshness. Its gray roots clung to the tortured contours of the rock it perched upon and moss clung to the base of the rock. The whole was planted in a beautiful brass bowl. But the effect was of looking out upon a mountain in early summer.

When she had looked her fill, Delenn moved on.

The next tree stood straight. Its silver trunk was planted in a bed of moss from which an occasional stone-boulder rose. The intricate twisted mass of its limbs bore a glorious wealth of golden leaves tinged with scarlet, some of which lay on the moss below like discarded jewels.

There were several others, each a wonder, each a perfect poem of a tree in miniature. The last was a tree with a gracefully leaning black trunk, like a dancer poised to burst into motion. The delicate branches bore a profusion of pink buds, each no larger than a teardrop. It was planted in a silver urn, the roots disappearing into a base of tiny white stones. It brought to mind the promise of early spring.

Delenn looked at Lennier, who smiled at her, and they moved over to the bench their hostess had provided to contemplate the still-lit trees on their pedestals. After a time, her eyes strayed to the fountain and she leaned forward and let the cool water rinse her hands. She noticed a towel beside the fountain and picked it up.

"Our hostess appreciates the desire to play with the water in a fountain," she said with a smile.

Lennier leaned past her and rinsed his hands as well, taking the towel from Delenn.

"I was hoping you would do that," he said.

After a while of sitting in the silence broken only by the voice of the falling water, contemplating Midori's wonderful trees, a peace descended on them, as though they sat in the seclusion of a real garden.

Without making a sound, Midori was suddenly beside them. She wore a close-fitting gown with wide flowing sleeves, of a glowing peach color decorated with printed flowers. It was bound with a wide brocade sash tied into the shape of a pillow in back. There was a white flower pinned onto her bound-up black hair.

Midori smiled gravely and bowed. Then she turned and walked away.

Delenn and Lennier looked at one another, then rose to follow. The door on the side of the lighted hut was open, but so low that they had to bend almost double to go through.

Within, in an alcove, was a simple flower arrangement. A branch of nethai, the Minbari wildrose, wearing its winter berries. A drop of water like a crystal bead clung to each one. At the base of the branch was a single Earth flower, a delicate frill of pink just bursting from its smooth green bud.

"Oh," Delenn said again, and shook her head. *However*

did she find such a thing as nethai? Minbari plants were rare outside of Minbar and her colony worlds. Her eyes feasted on this reminder of home.

The room they found themselves in was unadorned except for the floral arrangement and a scroll that hung behind it. The scroll was an ink painting of a small twisted tree half hidden by a veil of snow. Along the side of the scroll a series of beautiful letters, or perhaps words, had been drawn. Both of these held a place of honor. Three cushions had been placed on the floor around a carefully constructed fire pit.

A black iron kettle of obvious antiquity hung over a pile of glowing coals nearly hidden under a cone of ash. The only other objects visible were a small and very ugly container and a feather duster.

Delenn and Lennier took their places on the cushions and waited quietly. There was a doorway opposite them, curtained by pale, rough cloth. Midori entered from whatever space the curtain hid and, kneeling, bowed profoundly low to her guests. Then she went back through the curtain and returned with a tray of utensils.

She moved the kettle, and built up the fire, adding more ash and sprinkling it with incense she shook from its ugly holder.

Delenn's head came up in surprise as the delicate fragrance filled the room. *Again, nethai!* she thought. Rare, and very expensive and utterly undetectable to human senses.

"How lovely," she said, breaking the silence. "But you cannot enjoy it." It was almost a question.

Midori bowed slightly, smiling.

"It pleases me to give you pleasure," she said.

"Is this the way your quarters always look?" Delenn asked. It was somewhat worrying if it was, given the lack of furnishings.

"No." Midori smiled. "I have arranged things this way for the ceremony. My belongings are in temporary storage."

"You've gone to a great deal of trouble," Delenn remarked, wondering at the reason for it.

"It would have been impossible not to have gone to the trouble," Midori said enigmatically, shaking her head. "Besides, without difficulty there would have been no honor in the gift."

"Everything here is so pleasantly plain," Lennier said tentatively, "and done with such restraint." He indicated the little incense holder, garish in green and pink and white. "It makes me wonder if this object holds some special significance."

With a smile, Midori placed the little jar on a piece of silken cloth.

"My father brought this home one day all excited. 'Look!' he said, 'I got four for half the price of one!' And my brother and I looked at one another, because we couldn't believe anyone could make something so ugly, let alone buy it. But my father's delight in his bargain that nobody else wanted so charmed me that when I left home I asked him for one of these." She unfolded another square of silk and placed it before Lennier, then moved the jar onto it. "It represents my father's presence."

"I was wondering," Delenn said. "Are those words along the side of that painting? What do they say?"

"They say, 'To those who long only for flowers, fain would I show the full-blown spring which abides in the toiling buds of snow-covered hills.' The tree in the painting is the plum tree whose pure white blossoms symbolize character. I chose the painting and the winter branch with the budding blossom at its feet to symbolize that early spring is always cold and dangerous. But the warmth of summer is inevitable." Midori ducked her head shyly. "As is understanding between the Minbari and Earth." She paused for a moment. "Or vice versa. My mother painted it for me and it represents her presence. The vase holding the flowers was made by my aunt, who is a famous potter on Nippon, and it represents her presence."

Delenn and Lennier looked at one another.

What is she trying to tell us? Delenn wondered. Most of

the humans she knew were brashly straightforward. More like the Centauri sometimes than she was comfortable with. But here in this little room was a wealth of subtlety.

"Your kettle," the Minbari hazarded, "looks to be of great antiquity."

Midori actually bowed.

"It is," she said. "Regrettably it is too hot to examine closely. It was given to an ancestor five hundred years ago by his lord for a service he performed. We rarely use it, because it is so special to the family. It represents the presence of the whole of my family, past, present, and future."

Delenn frowned in puzzlement. "Is this usual?" she asked.

"No," Midori said, gently shaking her head. "If you will permit me to explain?"

"I would welcome an explanation," Delenn said with relief. She'd been wanting to ask since she'd been invited here.

"When I was a girl," Midori began, "and we were at war with each other, the Minbari fleet bore down on Nippon. We are few on my planet and our military was weak. No one expected that such an unimportant place would be a target. My father and mother and aunt were called up by the militia and flew out in our pathetic little ships to fight. But instead of engaging with our tiny armada, the Minbari surrendered and their great ships swept by us, leaving us unharmed."

She bowed profoundly low to Lennier and Delenn.

"I have always felt such gratitude for the sparing of those I love, for their continuing presence in my life." Her eyes were moist and grave. "I wish to honor you in this small way to express my deep thanks."

Midori rose and left the room, returning with a number of implements that she carefully arranged. Then she left again, to return a final time with still more.

Delenn and Lennier watched in silence as she performed the ceremony, each graceful gesture seeming to follow some simple yet infinitely refined script.

Delenn felt herself relaxing into a contemplative state such as she used to enjoy on Minbar when she was meditating in the academy's gardens. The cares and responsibilities, the aggravation of constantly dealing with fractious aliens, fell away as she watched Midori's white hands perform this ancient ritual of her people.

At last, Midori finished whisking the tea with her flower-shaped tea-whisk and placed the cup before Delenn. They bowed to one another.

Delenn sipped cautiously and smiled. It was good, slightly bitter and somehow soothing. She sipped again and bowed slightly to her hostess.

"This is wonderful," she said and felt rewarded when Midori smiled and bowed in return.

"It is," Lennier agreed, after sipping from his own cup. "It's very good."

They talked for a while and sipped the green tea, speaking of art and flowers and springtime. The time passed pleasantly and all too quickly.

When Delenn left Midori's quarters she felt lighter and younger, refreshed in her soul and vastly more confident that she had been right.

For just before they left, Midori had confessed, "If you hadn't transformed yourself, I don't know if I would have had the courage to approach you."

And then I would not have known the depth of the harmony we can share with the humans, Delenn thought.

A human went past them in the corridor, glaring rudely and muttering something Delenn did not choose to hear. She smiled, untroubled by the incident. For she had feasted on peace and beauty, and the fruit of that feasting was hope.

Susan had spent the last four hours of her off-duty time going over personnel records, looking for complaints of instability, insubordination, or any infractions that might indicate a personality disorder.

Not surprisingly, she hadn't found anything significant. *If you make it to Babylon 5, I guess you're pretty much tried and true.* She'd also gone looking for any sign of the training, or at least the artistic ability, that might make the creation of these flawless, but undoubtedly false, recordings possible. Again, so far, nothing significant.

She stretched her arms over her head and rotated her neck to ease the stiffening muscles. *God,* she thought, *I hope I find something soon. I think I'm going cross-eyed.* She took a sip of her now chilled coffee.

She'd kept Ilias Larkin's records for last. *I've got to be fair,* she'd told herself. *I'm so prejudiced against the guy that I've got to make a special effort not to condemn him out of hand.* Hence, the last several hours spent searching the files of about two hundred innocent people, starting with a sort of B-list of suspects and working her way through an increasingly unlikely roster.

Okay, she thought grimly, leaning forward again. *That's enough of being fair. Look out, Ilias, here I come.* She called up Larkin's too perfect record. *Nobody's got a perfect record,* Ivanova thought cynically. *Well, I do.* She grinned evilly. *So I should know what one looks like.* And there was something very off in the wording of Ilias Larkin's fitness reports.

I mean you either praise somebody all-out or not. His are the first I've ever seen that I'd describe as cautiously glowing.

In fact, now that she thought of it, why hadn't any of the people who, in writing anyway, thought so highly of him answered her calls?

"Computer," she said, "have there been any messages from"—she named the last three commanders whose names had appeared on Larkin's files—"for me?"

"No messages have been received from those sources," the computer responded.

That is so weird, Ivanova thought. It increased her suspicions, for why would they neglect to answer if they had nothing to hide?

"On what date did my messages to them go out?" she asked.

"There is no record of any messages addressed to those parties being sent out in the last six months."

What?

Susan called up her letters file and found the three she'd written. *So I did write them, at least.* The way things were going she'd had her doubts for a moment there. *Well, well, well. Somebody's been busy—hacking into my system and preventing them from being sent.* She set her jaw in fury. *I wonder who?*

Calling up a communications channel to Io Base, Ivanova asked to speak to Commander Trey Arkanos.

"Commander Arkanos," she said after introducing herself, "I'm calling you in regard to Ilias Larkin."

The commander's thin face twitched, but his eyes and expression remained mild.

"Oh?" he said cautiously.

"You wrote a glowing report on him," Ivanova offered, fishing like mad.

A very slight frown marred his high forehead.

"I wouldn't say *glowing*. It wasn't exactly negative, but his performance was certainly nothing terribly praiseworthy. How the hell did he ever end up on Babylon 5?"

"He made a request for transfer and his record indicated that he was superior at his job."

Arkanos's head was shaking before she was half finished speaking.

"His work, on his best day, was adequate. Most of the time he was almost more bother than he was worth. Half the mistakes made while he was under my command were the result of our looking over our shoulders at him. I was a nervous wreck. In fact," he said, looking thoughtful, "I seem to recall saying—officially—that he should be placed in another department entirely. When he was transferred out I assumed they'd taken my advice. So I didn't bother to follow up."

You didn't bother to follow up, Susan thought, sourly, *because you were so glad to get rid of him you never wanted to think of him again.* And frankly, having become the unlucky recipient of the incompetent and overly emotional Mr. Larkin, she was tempted to slam him right back to Io Base with a "Return to Sender" sticker glued to his butt.

Her thoughts must have been plain on her face, for Arkanos said defensively, "It wasn't just that he was a screwup. The guy didn't fit in. And there was a weird . . . he was weird and unpredictably moody. Nobody could deal with him. He didn't do anything really wrong. He just . . ."

". . . never did anything really right," Ivanova finished for him. "When you say *weird,*" she asked, "do you mean he was weird or that weird things happened to people around him?"

"He was weird." Arkanos's eyes tracked, flicking away and back tentatively. "What do you mean?"

Oh, ho! she thought. *What do I mean? Like you don't know.* The eyes always gave you away.

"Oh, strange incidents, things showing up on people's doorsteps or under their desks. Things like that."

He licked his lips and stared at her like a frightened dog watches the approaching boot.

"I don't think so. I can check if you like. What kind of things are we talking about?"

"Never mind. I'll speak to his other former senior officers. If it's warranted, I'll be back in touch with you. Thank you for your time," she said crisply, but with a smile.

The other two commanders on her list were unavailable. One was on extended leave; the other was in the infirmary, and there was no scheduled release date. She itched to ask why, but knew she'd get no answer. Still, Larkin's—she was sure now it was him—little tricks were very disturbing and highly sophisticated. Just the sort of thing to send one on extended leave or even to the infirmary. *And I bet I know which part of the infirmary.*

If Garibaldi hadn't been beside me when I viewed the first one, she wondered, *would I have asked for his help? Would I have told anyone?* She really didn't know. But she was grateful for his friendship. Being alone with the stuff she'd seen on those crystals would be a nightmare. She shuddered, then scooted her chair closer to the screen holding Larkin's data.

Look out, Larkin, she thought again, *here I come.*

"Ilias Larkin," she said to Garibaldi an hour later. "His hobby when he was a teenager was creating vids so sophisticated that he outclassed hundreds of adults in some very prestigious contests. Also, both his parents were in Psi-Corps. In fact, he was educated by the Corps until he was about twelve, even though he's got the psychic sensitivity of a rock."

Garibaldi shuddered.

"I don't think I'd like being the untalented kid in a Psi-Corps school. You know what kids are like."

Susan winced and raised her hand in a warding gesture.

"Please," she said. "I don't want to feel sorry for him."

"Well." He settled himself on the corner of her desk. "How do you want to handle this?"

"I think we should confront him," she said, her jaw firm. "If you're there it will lend an official air to things."

"Even though this whole thing is off the record." He grimaced. "It limits our options," Garibaldi reminded her. "So we confront him and he spills his guts. What do we do then?"

Susan leaned back in her chair and crossed her arms over her chest, looking thoughtfully into space. What did they do? She really didn't want to make the crystals he'd created public. They were too personal and too damning.

"Well," she said slowly, "if ever there was a guy who needed psych counseling it's Larkin."

"You can send him to counseling with your signature," the Chief pointed out. "You don't have to confront him."

He crossed his arms and looked down at her, not without sympathy, and waited.

"I want to see his eyes when I accuse him," she said. "I need that confirmation. All I've got now is—he's our best suspect. I want to know in my soul, beyond a shadow of a doubt, that he did this to me." Her blue eyes were hard.

"Okay," he said and stood. "Your office? First thing tomorrow morning?"

"I'll be there."

"Oh, hey, Ambassador, it's me."

Of course it's you, you worm-witted human, G'Kar thought as he looked at Cray. *Do you think I'm blind?*

"What do you want?" he said aloud to the human on the screen.

"I found what you're lookin' for," Cray told him. "You owe me four hundred, right?"

"If your information is good, yes." G'Kar's implacable expression was all the threat necessary.

"It's good, I swear," Cray said with a little laugh. "They been seen on Green twelve. Word is they're goin' back to Down Below."

"This is happening now?" G'Kar asked eagerly.

"Even as we speak, pal."

Ugh! I am not your pal! G'Kar thought with loathing. *I don't even like being your customer.*

"Where are my credits?" he asked sharply.

"I'm workin' on it," Cray snapped.

"Work harder. And faster."

G'Kar broke the connection and smiled. Then he called Garibaldi.

They'd left the Prime Olorasin for last, reasoning that in her present state she was better off resting in the quiet of the inner room. But when Security began arresting T'llin almost as fast as they arrived in Down Below, their plans changed.

"It's that human woman the people told us about," Segrea grumbled as he strode down the corridor. "She decided not to wait for us to vacate the premises."

"No," Haelstrac said, shaking her head as she ran to keep up with him. "If that were the case they'd have come to the office."

Segrea slowed down as he took that in. His partner was right. If Security knew the location of the office they'd be there now, yet there'd been no sign of them, nor report of their presence either.

"Cray," he said, approaching the office's back door. "Again. It must be." He dropped the key-card into the lock and the light changed to green.

When they entered the office the remaining refugees, mostly mothers, children, and the old, looked up anxiously.

"We've come for the Prime," Segrea told them, feeling vaguely ashamed. There was so little they could do to help themselves, and no room for them in the sanctuary the Razye Tesh had prepared against emergency.

They entered the darkened room where Olorasin was lying. Segrea lingered by the door as Haelstrac shook out the encounter suit the Prime had worn to her interviews with the Ambassadors.

She dragged the voluminous cloak over Olorasin's unresisting head and shoulders, then tried to tug it down farther.

"I could use your help," she said tartly to Segrea.

Reluctantly, he came over to them and lifted Olorasin's slender body. He noticed that her eyes were open and he dropped her with a sound of disgust. Haelstrac overbalanced and fell onto the cot with an "Unh!"

"What is the matter with you?" she asked irritably.

"She's not even a Prime anymore," Segrea said, his thin lips twisted with bitterness. "Why are we even bothering with her. Let Security take care of her. It's plain she needs medical attention."

Haelstrac drew herself up and glared at him.

"She will always be a Prime. A treasure to our people and a blessing. We bother with her because it is our duty. Now, help me," she said between clenched teeth.

He returned and lifted the limp form of their leader.

"She's useless like this," he complained.

Haelstrac sighed.

"This is grief," she said. "And shock. She'll come out of it in time. And then we shall see." Haelstrac walked over to the bench where the Prime's breathing mask lay, and paused, staring at the opaqued window before her as though she could see the forlorn people beyond.

"You know," she said thoughtfully, "the Primes made fairly convincing Minbari."

"Minbari don't go to Down Below," Segrea said. "It's a good thought, but it would never work. Besides, there are no Minbari children on the station."

With a sigh Haelstrac returned to Olorasin and fitted the mask over her face.

"Let's go, then," she said.

Something was over her face. It wasn't restrictive, didn't interfere with her breathing. But it displeased her. She took a deeper breath, and felt herself lifted to her feet by a pair of strong hands.

Her eyes stung as she was dragged into a brightly lit room from the darkness she'd been resting in. The lenses in her mask compensated, going almost black.

Olorasin blinked and saw her people looking anxiously at her. There were fewer of them than there should be. She frowned. She was being pulled away from them by a strong pair of hands. Startled, she kicked out and was released instantly. She tore off the mask and looked at one of Phina's people.

Segrea, she thought. Then, *Phina is dead.* Grief threatened to overwhelm her again, but she pushed it back. Something was wrong. Something else.

"What is it?" she demanded, her voice shaking. Olorasin frowned, displeased by her weakness. "What is happening?" Her voice was stronger this time.

Segrea and Haelstrac looked at one another.

"We cannot remain here," Segrea told her. "Our landlord demands we leave. We are removing you to a place prepared by the Razye Tesh for emergencies."

Olorasin blinked; her pride was affronted by the term *removing you.*

"This place," she said, "is open to all of us?"

"No, Prime. Only to the Razye Tesh and you." Segrea looked over her head, rather than at her. It shamed him, but he couldn't help but wonder why she lived and her far more useful brother had died.

"And what will happen to these people?" Olorasin asked, glaring up at the Razye Tesh warrior.

"At the request of the Narn, Prime, the humans are arresting every T'llin they can find," Haelstrac told her. A collective gasp broke from the refugees crowded around them. "We dare not let the filthy Narn get hold of you to murder you as well."

Olorasin took a slow, deep breath in shock. It felt as though a veil had been torn within her. Before she let out her breath a new soul stepped through the rent skin of the old one to see the world with new eyes. *We are alone,* she thought. *Every hand is raised against the T'llin and we shall have no help but that we give ourselves. Just as Phina said.*

"The Narn," she asked, and her voice was hard, "are they joining in this T'llin hunt?"

"Not at last report, Prime," Haelstrac said, her eyes beginning to gleam with hope.

"But I would expect it of them," Segrea rumbled, lowering his gaze to look speculatively at the remaining Prime.

Olorasin looked around her, at the anxious face that waited her orders.

"Mothers, children, and all civilians are to allow themselves to be captured by security." A murmur of consternation rose from them. "Listen to me," Olorasin said, holding up her hands for silence. "You will surely be safer in human custody than running free on the station for some Narn vigilante to hunt down and kill in self-defense."

"But for how long will we be safe?" an old male asked. "If we are being taken into custody at the Narn's request, then eventually we'll be turned over to them."

"Die now or later," a young mother said. "What sort of choice is that?"

"It's another day alive, for yourselves and your children," Olorasin snapped. "And it is our duty to live, if only to spite the Narn." She met their eyes, one by one. "Do as I have told you."

She put her mask back on.

"Take me to this sanctuary of yours," she said to Haelstrac. "And you"—the mask turned to Segrea—"tell the Razye Tesh, those who are willing to die may remain with me. Those who are not are to allow themselves to be captured with the others."

He stared down at her for a moment that hung like a threat between them. Then he bowed slightly and pulled on his mask. Behind it he was grinning like a death's-head.

CHAPTER 16

ILIAS had seen several famous faces since last night. It was very exciting. The newspeople were crowding into the station as fast as ships could arrive. Camera orbs zipped through crowds gathering the scenes that would precede broadcasts, or stayed stationary over small groups of humans or aliens for the inevitable man-in-the-street interviews.

When the summons had come this morning to report to Ivanova's office he'd begun fantasizing. *I could send a copy of one or two of the bitch's little gifts to Barbara Chang.* He'd always enjoyed watching her on the news when he was home. Barbara was so elegant, so exotic. *Imagine what she could make of the Commander of C and C being the sister of a spy and saboteur.* A rush of pure glee at the thought almost set him giggling. As it was, his maniacal grin won him a few strange looks from the people he passed.

He visualized Ivanova, her face red with shame, eyes filled with tears, being led out of Command and Control by hefty security people. "I'm innocent!" she kept insisting. But the Captain merely glared. And Kamal, who worked beside him and, Larkin suspected, reported on him, turned to Ilias and whispered, "Who'd have guessed it! She had a perfect record!"

He was feeling rather sprightly and in command of the situation when he knocked on the Commander's door.

"Come," her voice said from within.

His self-satisfied glow faded somewhat when he saw Garibaldi.

"Should I come back?" he asked politely.

"Sit," Ivanova ordered, pointing to the chair before her desk.

As soon as he was seated she rose and walked around him slowly, pacing back and forth behind his chair for a moment without saying anything.

Garibaldi just looked at him, his expression blandly pleasant. *This is Susan's show, it's up to her to run it,* he told himself. His job as he saw it was to be on hand in case of need. And maybe for a little moral support. *Even the invincible Ivanova needs a friend sometimes,* he thought.

Larkin turned to look over his shoulder at the Commander.

"Eyes front!" she snapped. She knew from her psych courses that she was engaging in intimidation techniques, but she didn't care. *He's tortured me enough that I think I'm entitled to get a little of my own back.*

"Yessir," Larkin said meekly and faced her desk. *What is this?* he wondered nervously. But he knew. They all eventually called him in to grill him. He couldn't help resenting the fact that it was invariably *him* that they all came to suspect. *Sure, I'm guilty,* he thought, *but that's beside the point. The point is they always have it in for me. The new guy, the misfit. It's always me that gets the blame.* He waited in silence, listening to her footsteps as she paced.

"Is there a problem, Sir?"

"Did I ask you to speak?" *He's awfully cool,* she thought, a tiny worry frown crinkling her brow. *What if I'm wrong about him?* But if it wasn't Larkin, then who was it? The only other people she knew that had access to personal information were Garibaldi and Sheridan, and she trusted them both.

"No, Sir."

"Then be silent." Larkin noticed Garibaldi's fixed, bland stare about the same time Ivanova did and shifted nervously.

"Sir?" he asked. "Is this about my performance? I'm sure I've improved."

Garibaldi looked at Susan and then he stood as well. She moved over to Larkin's side, just a little behind him.

"We've found out some very interesting things about you, Larkin." She leaned a little closer. "Trey Arkanos recommended that you be transferred out of C and C. But somehow, your records show him commending you. Can you explain that?"

"No, Sir."

"No, Sir," she repeated. *He could be telling the truth. It could be a transcription error.* But he *felt* guilty, despite his very convincing, innocent demeanor. *And there's a lot of evidence against this guy*, she reminded herself. "I also noticed that three information requests to your last three commanders were taken out of the queue. How did you manage that?"

"Sir?" He clenched his hands together in his lap and tried not to shake.

If ever there was a noncommittal answer, she thought sourly, *"Sir" has got to be it.* She was worried, he wasn't reacting the way she'd expected. Here he was being treated like a guilty man, confronted with some pretty strange circumstantial evidence, and while he looked nervous, he looked nowhere near cracking. *What if I'm wrong?*

"Look at me," she said, moving in front of Larkin. He looked up at her, his sallow face pale. "I understand you've quite a talent for making vids."

"You say that like you've heard I eat live children," Larkin said with a nervous laugh. "Yes, Sir," he said more solemnly when she narrowed her eyes in warning. "I used to when I was a kid. I haven't made one for years, though."

"Then why do you have a bag full of vid equipment among your belongings?" Garibaldi asked.

Larkin's head snapped up.

"How do you know that?" he asked, too astonished to remember that he was addressing the head of Security.

Garibaldi raised a brow and ducked his head.

"Excuse me?" he said.

Larkin blushed and licked his lips. "I've had the stuff for years, Sir. I keep thinking I'll use it again, but I never have. What's wrong with owning vid equipment?" he demanded. "Everybody owns something like that."

"Owning something like that and owning equipment with the sophistication of yours are two different things." Garibaldi moved to stand behind him. "Your parents are in Psi-Corps, aren't they?" he said suddenly.

Larkin froze. "Yessir," he said, his voice strangled.

"You see them often?"

"No, Sir. They're usually on assignment."

"You were kind of a disappointment to them," Ivanova said, crossing her arms.

"Weren't you?" Garibaldi asked.

Larkin sat still, his color rising, and his breathing changed to a harsh rasping.

"Why are you asking me these questions?" he demanded. "What are you accusing me of?"

"No one's accused you of anything," Ivanova said, feeling dirty suddenly.

"Then why are you asking about my parents?" he shouted. "Everybody knows how you feel about Psi-Corps. You're out to get me because my parents are—"

"I said, no one's accused you of anything!" Susan cut him off. *Talk about emotional.* Though to be honest she'd been counting on his instability to make him confess. *I guess emotional doesn't necessarily mean weak,* she thought.

"Oh? So you must want to know what it's like to live in a completely silent house because everybody else can talk mind to mind? Or do you want to know what it's like to be treated like the village idiot just because you've got no psi ability?" He snapped his fingers in inspiration. "Oh, I know! You want to know what kind of a nightmare it is to go to school with kids who think you're inferior and know *exactly* what you'd least like them to do to you." He flashed to his feet, fists balled up in front of his chest, his face a red knot of fury. "It's worse than hell!" he shouted. "It's pure, unrelenting, unending agony! Are you happy now? Are you satisfied?" *Bitch!* he thought. *Bitch! Bitch! Bitch! I'll kill—*

"*Hey!*" Garibaldi snapped. "Just who do you think you're talkin' to?"

"Sit down," Ivanova said coldly.

She moved around her desk and sat down just as Larkin did. Susan felt ashamed of herself; poking someone's open wounds was not her idea of reasonable behavior. She suddenly remembered one of her professors telling the class that the torturers of old had considered themselves to be honorable men engaged in an unpleasant but necessary task. *I was just trying to be fair!* she thought miserably. Yes, she'd wanted to make him confess, even, she had to admit, to make him suffer a little of the pain he'd inflicted. But she'd neither wanted nor expected him to come completely unglued like this.

"The reason I called you here, Larkin, is to inform you that I'm sending you for a psych evaluation. I'm relieving you of duty until further notice."

She fought down her newfound sympathy for the man before her. He'd had a tough time. This did not mean it was all right for him to cut bloody chunks out of her soul.

Larkin stared at the floor, feeling his heartbeat accelerate as his fury rose. *They went through my things!* he thought, feeling soiled. *They put their filthy hands all over my things!*

"Am I dismissed, Sir?" he asked in a choked voice.

"Yes," Susan said.

Larkin rose stiffly, like a man too bruised to move comfortably, and turned to go.

"I'll be watching you, Larkin," Garibaldi assured him.

"Thank you, Sir," Larkin said dully and walked through the doorway.

Susan pressed her hand to her forehead and smoothed away the frown lines.

"That was unpleasant," she said. *Talk about an understatement.*

"Well," Garibaldi shrugged, "you expected it to be. Didn't you?" He looked at her with raised brows. "After all, we behaved in a very intimidating manner, we asked a lot of personal questions. By the way, how come you never asked if he did it? I thought you wanted to know *positively* that he was guilty."

"Because," she sighed, "I suddenly felt like a bully. Actually worse than a bully. Up until that moment when we asked about his parents, I could honestly state that I'd handled Larkin with fairness and restraint. But now I feel like I've gone over the line." *And there's nothing worse than betraying your ethics for a perceived good.*

Garibaldi clicked his tongue.

"The psychs will sort him out. He'll probably tell them what he did to you," the Chief warned her.

"But that will be under medical seal, and not directly attached to my records." She looked sad for a moment, then she flicked her gaze to the Security Chief. "How did you know he had a bag of vid equipment?"

"I checked, and it wasn't listed on the manifest of personal goods he brought with him."

"There's a surprise," Ivanova sneered. "So you searched his quarters?"

"Nope. That was what we in the security profession call a shot in the dark."

"I thought I detected a hit," she said, looking grim.

"A very palpable hit," he agreed. "Unfortunately it didn't motivate him to confess."

"As you said, the psychs will sort him out." *But what if he didn't do it?* she wondered. Then—sometime soon—another crystal would show up. Better not to think about that. "Thank you for seeing me through this."

He gave her one of his little, pursed-lip smiles.

"What are friends for?" he asked.

* * *

Bitch! Ilias thought. *How dare they? How could they?* He walked swiftly, his breath coming fast and his eyes blazing. Had anyone met him, they'd have jumped out of his path like he was on fire. *Touched my things! Went through them, pawed, filthy, rotten . . . bitch!* Spittle flew as he breathed in and out through his clenched teeth. *I'll kill her! I'll kill . . .* his thoughts vectored into incoherence.

Larkin cast a baleful glare over his shoulder, in the general direction of Ivanova's office. And around the corner he'd just turned came a Security officer. He felt his heart jerk within him and he walked four steps before he remembered to breathe again.

Following me! Spying. Persecuting me. His disjointed thoughts matched the rapid cadence of his footsteps. *They're after me. This is it! They're coming to get me. I didn't want to believe it, but it's true!* Larkin turned another corner and slowed down. After fifteen steps he glanced over his shoulder again. The Security officer turned the corner.

He was a big, blond fellow, moving casually, apparently reading something as he ambled along. But he was armed, and this was the second turning he'd made at Larkin's heels.

Ilias had a PPG up his sleeve, held to his arm with a holster he'd cobbled together from a length of magnetic cable and a smart chip. He rotated his hand, then held it in the prescribed position. The PPG dropped into his palm.

One more corner, he promised himself. But if the Security man followed him . . . *Then he gets it.*

There she was. Sheridan tugged at his sleeves and plastered a welcoming smile on his face. *She looks exactly like the President.* Poor kid. Clark was a fairly good-looking man, but he would have made a homely woman and here was the living proof. Short brown hair, narrow brown eyes under level brows, a formidable nose and a wide, thin-lipped mouth.

"Hi," she said, swinging her hand up. "I'm Chancy Clark."

He took her hand and found his squeezed in a strong friendly grip. He also found himself thinking that she had a very engaging grin.

"Thank you for meeting me, Captain. It's appreciated, but unnecessary. I'm sure you must be extremely busy."

"Not at all," he, lied. "I just thought I'd escort you to your quarters and then, unless you're too tired, show you a little of the station. Maybe we could talk about exactly what you have in mind for your interviews."

She gave him a sidelong glance. "I wonder what they've told you. Well, I'd like to be able to go to as many press conferences as I can." She looked at him inquiringly.

"No problem," he assured her. "But you know about the lottery . . ."

"Which will determine whether I get a seat in the Narn or the Centauri press room. Yes, I know. Very clever that. Your idea?"

"Yes, actually." He gave her a genuine smile, for he found himself liking her. *The famous Clark charm,* he thought. "They said you wanted to interview as many of the ambassadors and conference delegates as we could manage to put you in touch with."

Chancy nodded vigorously.

"Absolutely. I've got to establish my reputation now," she said, "if I want to have a real job when I graduate. Instead of one of those cheap, exploit-you-to-death internships." She gave him a sidelong glance. "I wonder if you're thinking that I'm taking unfair advantage of my family connections."

"I . . . wouldn't say that," Sheridan said nervously. She'd pretty much put his thoughts in a nutshell and then cracked open the nut.

"Don't worry about it," she said cheerfully, giving him a nudge. "I've spent my whole life around the press and I learned one thing early on. They're sharks. Or perhaps that's a gross insult to sharks everywhere. There isn't one of them alive that wouldn't gleefully exploit the advantage I've got. And while they might praise me for not doing so, inside they'd be laughing. And it would guarantee that I would never be taken seriously, were I ever so brilliant. Don't ever feel sorry for them. They'd ruin your life for a ten-second sound bite. I've seen them do it.''

"Then . . . why do you want to be one of them?'' he asked.

She laughed.

"I don't want to be one of them,'' Chancy said, her eyes shining. "I want to do their job. See, with my connections I shouldn't have to stoop to anything tabloid—you know—low and disgusting. And if I handle myself right and respect my sources I'd be a valuable addition to any news-zine or paper that hires me.''

"What about vid?''

"Not with my looks, Captain. Which I've no desire to change.'' She was silent for a moment as they walked through the concourse. "And it will drive my uncle nuts,'' she said out of the side of her mouth. "There isn't a politician born since the invention of print who hasn't hated all journalists.''

He laughed out loud, caught off guard by her honesty.

"You've got a nice smile,'' she observed.

"Thank you,'' he said, blushing a little. Her nose wasn't the only formidable thing about Chancy Clark.

"So,'' she said, taking his arm. "What are my chances of getting those interviews?''

"Given your relationship to the President . . . I gather I'm allowed to mention it?''

"Absolutely!''

"The only problem should be trying to figure out how they'll try to exploit you.'' Sheridan smiled down at her. *Let 'em try,* he thought, feeling better about this situation by the minute.

"Who's that?" she said suddenly.

Lennier was talking to a Security woman. They bowed to one another and the woman moved off. Lennier saw the Captain and bowed to him as well.

"That's Lennier, the attaché to the Minbari Ambassador."

"He's cute! Introduce us!" Chancy's eyes were bright as she looked at Lennier.

He, apparently noting that Sheridan's attention hadn't wavered, had begun to move towards them.

"Cute?" Sheridan asked, startled. "He's Minbari." *And trust me, kid, they're not "cute."*

"If there's one thing I'm never wrong about, Captain, it's cute. And *that* is a major example of it. Look at him! He's adorable!"

Sheridan looked at her instead and his heart sank.

"Adorable?" he said in a faint voice.

All he could think of was the Admiral saying, "Don't let her do anything crazy." And here she was apparently about to attempt an affair with a Minbari. *On the one hand, I suppose it means the coming generation is looking forward to peaceful relations with the Minbari. So that's progress, I guess.* Of course, Chancy seemed to be a cutting-edge type of person. *On the other hand, why here, why now, why me?*

"Was there something you wanted, Captain?" Lennier asked politely.

Sheridan heard a soft sigh escape Chancy's lips. *This can't be happening.*

"Uh, no," he began to say.

"Are you busy right now?" Chancy asked eagerly.

Lennier looked at her in surprise.

"No, not at the moment." There was a questioning tone to his voice, though courtesy forbade him to ask why she was interested in his schedule.

"This is Chancy Clark . . ." Sheridan began.

"I'm President Clark's niece," she said, offering the startled Minbari her hand. "The Captain is terribly busy with arranging things for the conference and I was wondering, if you're free, if you would mind showing me the station in his place."

This was not a request, despite the phrasing. It was obvious that she expected to receive what she was asking for. And her utter confidence as she took Lennier's arm slew any objections the two men might raise like frost kills roses.

"I . . . would be honored," Lennier said with a bow and a quick glance at the Captain.

"Lovely," Chancy said, scaling back the atomic glare of her personality to a glow muted enough not to offend the Minbari. "Thank you, Captain Sheridan, for meeting me. It was so kind of you. I'll talk to you later about those arrangements," she assured him.

Sheridan shook his head as he watched her walk off arm in arm with a puzzled but fascinated Lennier. *The poor guy hasn't got a chance,* he thought. He'd never seen anyone so quickly obtain what they wanted. Clearly, Chancy Clark hadn't wasted the years spent among the movers and shakers of the Earth. *Of course,* he considered on second thought, *Lennier has occasionally shown himself to have unexpected depths.* Resources and strengths that you wouldn't suspect lingered under that gentle surface.

And he would need them.

Garibaldi was back in Security Central, trying to deal with the growing chaos as his people sullenly brought in more and more T'llin refugees.

Or maybe sulky *would be a better word to describe the attitude,* he thought. He couldn't really blame them. There were a lot worse criminals out there waiting to be caught.

The main squad room was a bedlam of noise. T'llin babies cried, T'llin mothers, their voices shrill with panic and outrage, shouted, elderly T'llin answered impertinent questions with icy dignity, and youthful T'llin glowered silently, somehow the loudest of the lot.

Babies in prison! Garibaldi thought in utter self-disgust.

Babies! But putting them in the charge of social services meant separating them from their frightened mothers. And despite rules saying that he should do just that ... *I can't, it would be inhuman.* The cells were clean. *It's not like I'm running a dungeon, for cryin' out loud.* And God knew the Narn wouldn't object. *They'd probably worry that the kids would crawl off and bludgeon some Narn to death with their rattles. Na'Toth, most likely. She's been catching all their action lately.*

A young T'llin mother marched up to Garibaldi and planted herself in front of him as if she intended to remain in his face for the duration. Then, shaking her tiny fists at him, she began a diatribe, while her three, big-eyed, obviously terrified children clung to her ragged robe. An elderly male followed in her wake and began interpreting.

"... black-hearted demon's spawn from the stars, no better than the Narn despots," the old T'llin said quietly, while the mother shrieked on.

Garibaldi was advising the elderly T'llin—who was ignoring him—when the call came in. *"Officer wounded, shots fired ..."* The location given, an ordinary enough residential area, was not someplace you'd expect someone to gun down a security officer.

Garibaldi just walked away from the shouting and the babies and the embarrassment, moving to a trot once out in the corridor.

"I was just walkin' down the corridor, just goin' home, minding my own business," the fallen Security man was telling Franklin, "when this guy in an Earthforce uniform just turns around and shoots me. Ahhh!" he shouted as Franklin positioned his wounded arm.

"Sorry," the Doctor told him, administering a painkiller. "You're going to be fine now. This will make you sleepy."

"How's he doing?" Garibaldi asked, coming up from behind and squatting down.

"He's okay," Franklin told him. "Nothing we can't fix with a little time and rest," he said as much for the patient as for Garibaldi's benefit.

Seeing a glazed look coming into the wounded man's eyes, Garibaldi leaned close to him and asked, "Can you describe the guy? Did you recognize him?"

"Seen 'im," the man on the stretcher said in a rasping voice. "Lives near here, I guess. Medium height, brown and brown, skinny . . . Earthforce . . ." he trailed off.

"I gave him a painkiller," Franklin said, "it has a sedative effect."

Garibaldi shook his head.

"Not a problem, I think we've got enough." He tapped his link. "What is Ilias Larkin's home address?" The link read back an address within a hundred feet of their location. *I just had to tell you I'd be watching you, didn't I?* Garibaldi thought. *Damn!*

He stood and, tapping the link again, put out an all-points bulletin for Ilias Larkin. Then, ignoring Franklin's curious look, he moved a little farther down the corridor and called Ivanova.

Larkin watched the tech go down the row of air locks checking the mechanisms. Or at least that's what it looked like. He compared the lock number with a list he had and ran a brief diagnostic.

Go away, Larkin thought with all his will. *Go to lunch, go take a break, go to hell, but get out of here!*

But the tech plodded on.

Ilias had checked each one of the air locks leading to the personal transports and only one had shown green, meaning one was prepped and ready for flight. He watched from his hiding place, fearful that the tech was looking for that transport. Perhaps to take it out.

Go away!

The tech had reached the lock that held Ilias's hope of escape and began his diagnostic.

"Hey, Hal."

The tech looked down the corridor. Larkin couldn't see who'd shouted from where he was hiding. *Don't let it be them,* he prayed. *Oh, please . . .*

"Aren't you done yet?"

"Just found it," the tech, Hal, answered.

"What the hell have you been doing?"

"There's thirty of these things on this deck! I like to do a thorough job," Hal said, his voice injured. "It's not as if they were used very often, or like you can do a visual on them."

He prodded the air lock with a stylus by way of illustration. It was a simple door, with a reinforced plastic window, set flush with the corridor. The air lock door within was even more basic, without even a porthole, built for a very unlikely emergency, just large enough to funnel evacuees into the escape transport pod beyond. It opened directly into the nacelle of the pod when one was docked, and the only way to tell that was from the lighted status display.

"The boss called a meeting, so let's go."

"But this—"

"Oh, c'mon, don't be such a pain. Nobody's scheduled to come down here for hours. The meeting'll be over in fifteen minutes."

Hal looked regretfully at the door he'd just begun working on. Then he sighed and pulled his instrument off the lock pad.

"Okay," he said and walked off.

Yes! Larkin thought. He watched Hal walk off and triumph filled his heart. Now all he had to do was override the lock code. *But I can do that in my sleep,* he thought confidently.

The first thing Ivanova did when she got Garibaldi's call was to head for the escape pods area. *If I were running,* she thought, *I'd want a Starfury, but Larkin has a civilian mind if ever I met one.* So to escape, she reasoned, he'd want a civilian ship; and not one of the ones departing from a normal dock. Something basic, something simple, something one person could send through the Babylon-5 jump gate.

The Security Chief had alerted the work crews down here about whom to look out for, but she wanted to be on-sight just in case he did show up.

This is my fault, she thought. *I knew he was unstable, but I just had to shake him up.* And now he'd exploded. Bad enough he'd shot a security man. But the crews down here were unarmed civilians, neither looking for nor equipped to handle the kind of trouble Larkin represented.

What she really wanted to do was evacuate this area and fill it with security personnel. *After all, he* has *to come here.* His only other option was Down Below and they'd eat him alive down there. But you couldn't shut down the station on the off chance that someone, somewhere might get hurt.

She looked around anxiously, wondering where to begin the search. Men and women streamed by her, apparently just released from a meeting where they were warned to look out for the fugitive and advised to call the boss if they saw anything unusual. Ivanova followed one at random.

"C'monnnn," Larkin growled at the lock pad. "Opennn." He was close, he could feel it, but the damn thing resisted him. He always thought of picking a lock as a kind of rape. Although at the moment, if his victim were alive he'd be beating her to within an inch of her life. *Ahhh! Gotcha!*

"Hey! You! Get away from there!" Hal shouted.

Ivanova sprinted up beside him, arriving just in time to watch the lock slide closed behind someone in an Earthforce uniform.

She and Hal ran to the lock, but Larkin had slid the failsafe bolt home and he laughed at them from behind the unbreakable door.

"There's nothing out there!" Hal shouted. "If he opens it, it'll be on hard vacuum!"

"The light's green," Ivanova said.

"It's broken. There's nothing outside."

Ivanova and Hal looked at each other in horror. Ivanova hit the com built into the lock's keypad. Fortunately, it worked.

"Larkin," she said frantically, "don't open the outer door. There's nothing outside!"

He turned from his work on the inside keypad to sneer at her.

"Oh, I think there is," he said. "I'm not as stupid as you all think I am."

"There's nothing there!" Hal shouted, nudging Ivanova aside. "There's a malfunctioning sensor that reads the presence of a transport pod even though there's nothing there."

Larkin gave him the raspberry and, chuckling to himself, went back to work.

"We're not lying, Ilias. I swear it on my commission," she said, desperately.

"The holiest thing you know," Larkin said, turning to them with wide eyes. "Isn't that blasphemy or something, Commander?"

"Larkin, believe me," Susan pleaded, "no one's going to hurt you." *He'll never believe that,* she thought. But she had to reach him somehow or he'd be dead in minutes. "Just give us a chance, please! I want to apologize, I was wrong, this is all my fault. Please give me a chance to make it up to you."

"That's right," he said, glaring at her. "This is your fault, every bit of it. Your picking and nagging and persecution. You deliberately humiliated me in front of everyone. You oosided with them against me every time. Not once did you cut me any slack, like you did them. I hate you," he finished, with such venom that it shut her up for a moment.

"Hah!" he said, happily. "Got it!" He turned to give her a smug grin. "Good-bye, Commander."

"NO!" she shouted, her voice echoed by Hal's.

Larkin turned the latch and disappeared.

Ivanova stared at the spot he'd last been. Nothing. Just the black of outer space. She tapped her link.

"Garibaldi," she said, and waited.

"Yes, Commander," he replied crisply, the way he did when he was focused.

"You can call off the search," she said slowly. "I know where Larkin is."

CHAPTER 17

You'd think, Sheridan thought, *that after this many months of riding herd on arrogant Centauri and angry Narn I'd be able to handle a roomful of mere reporters.* But instead the meeting with the newspeople verged on anarchy.

Everywhere he looked was a familiar face. Faces he'd seen smiling, looking grave, looking intelligent, looking interested. Faces as familiar as those of his staff. But they weren't smiling now, and despite the faces being familiar their behavior wasn't. *It's like watching a distant, but respected, group of relatives suddenly become possessed by toddler egos from hell.*

The words "my ratings" and "I demand!" had practically become a chant.

Sheridan made a thumbs-up gesture to the technician operating the sound system. "SHUT UP," his voice bellowed out loud enough to stun.

When he stopped speaking, everyone was frozen, staring at him with their mouths open.

"Thank you for your attention," Sheridan said. *And so willingly given,* he thought sarcastically. They were already beginning to mutter. *Y'know, it's really hard to watch a group of handsome, sophisticated people take a behavioral jaunt back to kindergarten.* "But we have a lot to discuss and we're going to have to take turns making our views known."

Which prompted every one of them to start talking again.

And naturally, none of them would shut up to allow anyone else to be heard.

Sheridan stood at the podium, looking down on them as they slowly turned towards one another and began the same arguments he'd just interrupted.

"Is this your idea of cooperation?" he asked in a normal tone of voice. By now the noise level was such that he literally couldn't hear himself speak.

The arguments had found their way back to the "my ratings," "I demand!" phase. *It's time,* he thought, *to make an executive decision.* The idea had been in the back of his mind for some time now. But he'd been reluctant to act on it for fear of being called unfair, or an enemy of the press. *But if they can't discuss the necessary arrangements in a civilized manner,* he thought, *then security considerations come first. And, unfortunately, they'll just have to live with that.*

Once more he ordered the sound control powered up to just below maximum.

"Due to security considerations the arrival of the delegates will be broadcast to an auditorium on Green twelve. You'll all receive handouts on the location and times later."

This announcement earned him a universal *"What?"* and, finally, the silence and attention he'd been asking for. *Too late, folks. I kinda like my idea, it'll make the reception of the delegates more . . . intimate.* He spotted Chancy Clark and she gave him a grin and a subtle thumbs-up.

The reporters were on their feet screaming in indignation. Sheridan heard the words "tyrant," "dictator," and "megalomaniac" thrown at him, killing what little sympathy he might have had.

"I'm sure you'll all appreciate that I have a million details to nail down in the next few hours," he said. "So, if you'll excuse me." *Or even if you don't.* "I'll leave you now. Thank you for your attention." *Such as it was.* "And I hope you'll all enjoy your stay on Babylon 5." *And then leave and never come back to annoy us again with your idiotic, prima-donna behavior.*

He descended from the podium and left by the side door to an angry chorus of "Captain Sheridan!" The Security personnel guarding him moved to block the angry mob from following.

Lennier was standing in the corridor outside the meeting room, looking as if he was waiting for someone.

"Lennier," Sheridan said in surprise. "Were you looking for me?"

Lennier offered a restrained bow, in the Minbari fashion.

"No, Captain Sheridan," he replied serenely. "I was waiting for Ms. Clark."

"Oh." Sheridan's brows went up. He'd thought that Lennier might have, well, dumped her by now. "She'll probably be coming out through the main doors," the Captain said.

"She said she'd be coming out here," Lennier replied. He looked at the Captain speculatively.

"What?" Sheridan asked.

Pursing his lips, Lennier moved closer to the human.

"I am finding Ms. Clark's behavior most intriguing," he confessed. "She seems extremely aggressive, yet almost alarmingly friendly. I've never yet encountered such behavior in your people." He paused, with that wide-eyed I-am-curious expression on his face that Sheridan had come to both respect and dread.

Oh, God. What's he going to ask this time?

"I have a sense of—how shall I put this—subtext in her behavior," the Minbari continued. "I was wondering . . ."

Oh, no. Here it comes. Sheridan struggled to keep the dread from showing.

". . . just what is Ms. Clark trying to tell me?" Lennier cocked his head, waiting politely.

"Ahhh. She likes you, Lennier." Sheridan made an uplifting gesture with both hands and Lennier imitated him.

"She is also quite likable," the Minbari said cautiously. "If a bit overwhelming. I do not mean to criticize," he added hastily.

"Not at all," Sheridan said with a nervous chuckle. "I find her a bit overwhelming myself."

"But now the subtext I was referring to seems to have entered your demeanor. In a different way, but there is a change in attitude. I'm concerned that I am in danger of causing offense. Please, I would appreciate whatever information you feel you can give me."

Poor Lennier, Sheridan thought, looking at the Minbari's worried face. *If I tell him he'll be downright shocked, I'd bet my commission on it. But if I don't he's liable to become involved in a serious misunderstanding with the President's niece.*

"She's trying to tell you that she really, *really* likes you," he said aloud. This time his hands were joined as he raised them up and down a few times. "She wants to be . . . close."

Lennier looked at the Captain's hands and then at the Captain.

"Really?" he asked. His expression was blank, but Sheridan could have sworn he looked a little pale.

The Captain shrugged. "She thinks you're cute."

Lennier's lips started to shape the word as the door opened.

"Wow!" Chancy said, taking the Minbari's arm. "What a madhouse. I thought I'd never get out of there." She smiled up at Lennier. "Thank you for waiting," she whispered. "Captain," she called as, with a smile of farewell, he started to turn away. "That was a good move."

"I'm glad you think so," he replied and began to turn away again.

"They'll go ballistic when they find out I'm going to be there," she said to his back.

He turned around slowly, his mouth slightly open.

"You are?" he managed at last.

"Absolutely!" She grinned impishly. "You know how the Centauri and the Narn are in regard to families. Something to do with having monarchies, I imagine," she said to Lennier. "They're going to find out I'm on the station when I do my interviews, and would be insulted that I wasn't at the reception. *They'll* never buy that fairness policy thing.'' She shrugged. ''Go figure.''

Sheridan laughed lightly. *She's right,* he thought, unnerved. But then, she'd been raised to think in diplomatic situationese. *You could stop a supernova more easily than this woman.* He looked at her with respect tinged with awe. *Was I this impressive when I was nineteen?* he wondered.

''I'll have you briefed,'' he said.

''Thank you, Captain. I'd appreciate it.'' And she rewarded him with a smile.

Sheridan remembered, as he walked away, something he'd once read. The very rich were careful to teach their children to treat underlings with respect. *And,* he thought, with a little spurt of annoyance, *Chancy Clark has learned her lessons well.*

Sheridan stopped reading Ivanova's report and leaned back in his chair, his hand over his eyes.

''Why didn't you tell me in the first place?'' he asked, looking at her where she stood with her hands clasped behind her back in a tidy parade rest. ''And sit down, for Pete's sake!''

Susan looked behind her and pulled a chair up. She sat stiffly, her hands clasped before her now, her eyes downcast, frowning slightly.

''I . . .'' she began.

''It was personal,'' Garibaldi said. ''And we dealt with it that way.''

''A man is dead,'' Sheridan answered him. ''A security man was shot.''

''But before that,'' Garibaldi said, ''it had all the earmarks of just being a particularly nasty piece of psychological sabotage. We're not psychic. We couldn't predict what he would do.''

''You're professionals.'' Sheridan glared at them both, leaning his arms on the desk before him. ''You have people under your command because you're *supposed* to be able to predict what they'll do.

Ivanova spread her hands. "I sent him to Franklin for an evaluation. The Doctor told me that he was emotional, but that there didn't seem to be anything in his makeup that would necessarily interfere with his ability to work." She rubbed her forehead. "I should have sent him for a psych evaluation, but I didn't want to put that kind of a mark on his record."

Sheridan leaned back again. "So instead you let him pull you into his sick little world with him."

Susan shook her head.

"I should have known better," she said bitterly. "But he was attacking my family." She bit her lip and then sighed. "And I reacted emotionally instead of rationally."

"Yes, you did." Sheridan looked at her severely, tapping his fingers on the arm of his chair. "But there's nothing in this report that will damage your record, Susan. You have a witness to the fact that you did your best to talk Larkin out of opening that hatch. And the Chief of Security will vouch for the fact that he did all the investigating."

"Well, that's not—" she began.

Sheridan raised a hand to stop her. "And in future," he said, "when you encounter an unstable compound you'll treat it with a little more respect."

"Yes, Sir."

"Dismissed."

Ivanova rose and saluted, and Sheridan, seated, returned her salute. She executed a neat pivot and walked away, back straight, eyes front.

"You were a little rough on her," Garibaldi said when she was gone. "Weren't you?"

Sheridan looked at the Security Chief for a moment. "She needed me to be," he said. "Now she can begin to forgive herself for making a mistake."

"Hey, he attacked her first," Garibaldi said, pointing at the Captain. "And he hit low."

"You spoke to him," Sheridan said. "Did he seem dangerous to you?"

Garibaldi reflected a moment, remembering Larkin sitting in Ivanova's office, looking nervous, outraged, alarmed, but never guilty. And certainly not threatening. More of a Milquetoast, actually. A classic wimp. *The worm that turned out to have a concealed weapon.*

"No," he replied. "He hid his feelings well. Probably something he learned dealing with the Psi-Corps kids." Garibaldi shuddered. "That must have been awful."

"Apparently they taught him how to inflict pain, as well," Sheridan observed. He looked up and nailed Garibaldi with a look. "I understand that you were trying to handle this as a friend. Which is why I'll tolerate the fact that I was left out of the loop on this. But next time, if there is a next time, handle it better."

"Yes, Sir," Garibaldi said, rising. He hesitated for a moment and then saluted.

Sheridan smiled and, standing, returned it.

The two men looked at one another for a beat. Then Garibaldi tapped his finger on the Captain's desk.

"Back to work," he said flippantly. "I have women and children to put in jail."

Sheridan grunted. "We'll think of something," he promised.

"I'll tell them that, Sir."

Sheridan frowned. It seemed to him that Garibaldi was getting all the good exit lines lately.

"I've been waiting for your report, Garibaldi," G'Kar said coldly. He wasn't feeling very friendly towards humans right now. And he didn't appreciate the Security Chief keeping him waiting until the last minute of the deadline to tell him what was going on. *It's not as if our request was out of line, considering the circumstances. If a terrorist had been killed not fifty feet from their president's door and the whole group could be rounded up easily, I doubt it would have been handled with such sullen reluctance.*

"Well, we wanted to be sure we'd gotten all of them before we contacted you," Garibaldi said grimly. "I'd hate to give you an all clear, only to find out we'd missed someone. We have seventy-eight people in custody, and they all say we've got everyone. Also, no one's seen or heard rumor of any others. So we feel pretty confident that the station's clear."

G'Kar smiled, but beneath the serene expression he was wilting in relief. The last thing he wanted to do was call off the peace conference. However good the reason. It would make him look bad back home. And . . . *We need this chance for peace. For a truce. Slender though it is.*

"I know this must be painful for you, Mr. Garibaldi," he said graciously. "You humans have such a love for the underdog, as you so quaintly put it. But I assure you, this particular underdog is mad. These people are barbarians capable of unparalleled viciousness. Your action has saved lives, Mr. Garibaldi, and my people thank you."

"Thank you, Ambassador," the Chief said flatly and disconnected.

"That's pleasant news," Na'Toth said with a smile. "It feels good to have security taking the matter seriously, at last."

"Yes, things feel more under control now." G'Kar checked the time and rose. "I have a lunch appointment," he said. "I should be back in an hour or two."

Na'Toth arched a brow and tilted her head to one side.

"If it's with Ms. MacBride, I'm afraid I canceled it," she said.

G'Kar stared at his assistant in speechless shock.

"What?" he said at last, completely unable to believe even Na'Toth would be so bold.

"She called to confirm your appointment and I told her that you wouldn't be able to . . . accommodate her," Na'Toth said as she sorted data crystals. "I knew that you couldn't possibly spare the time the minute I discovered that Da'Kal will be one of the delegates.''

"My *wife*!"

"Yes, sir. A nice surprise, isn't it?'' Na'Toth smiled at him, showing lots of teeth in a rather caustic smile.

"Yes, it is. So you can wipe that judgmental smirk off your face,'' he said with a glare. "I am delighted that I'll be seeing Da'Kal after all this time.''

"Well, naturally, I knew that you wouldn't want anyone mentioning your close association with an attractive alien woman.''

"When put in those terms," he protested, "it sounds sordid. But in reality my *association*, as you style it, is completely innocent. All I'm interested in is art.''

"Art!" Na'Toth leaned towards him, her eyes wide. "Ooooh. I see.''

"I've already told you,'' he said through clenched teeth, "Ms. MacBride has an item for sale that I would very much like to obtain.''

His assistant chuckled knowingly.

"Oh, I'm sure she has,'' Na'Toth said dryly.

"How dare you speak to me like that?'' G'Kar pounded his fist on the desk, really beginning to get angry.

"But I was only agreeing with you, Ambassador,'' Na-'Toth said with poisonous sweetness.

G'Kar made a disgusted sound and waved his arm at her in dismissal. Then he sat down and leaned back in his chair, a thoughtful frown on his face.

Na'Toth frowned as well. "Would you like me to deal with the lady for you?'' she asked.

"Yes,'' he snapped. "But unfortunately I don't think she'll consent to negotiate with you.'' G'Kar was obviously torn. He pounded a fist into the palm of his hand. "I *must* see her.''

"There's no time for this!'' Na'Toth said in exasperation. "You can't afford to put off anything that's on your desk. The delegates will be here tomorrow! And while your wife

is here, she will certainly expect you to be with her. Not
sneaking off to do who knows what with a highly suspect
... *art dealer!*"

"Na'Toth if you can't think of anything useful to say, I'd
appreciate it if you would just leave me alone to think,"
G'Kar said, his voice dangerously quiet.

Na'Toth clenched her fists at her sides and took a deep,
calming breath.

"I apologize," she said, bowing her head. "I spoke rashly
and out of turn."

G'Kar grimaced and flicked a finger dismissively.

"But I am concerned," she pressed on, despite his growing impatience. "Garibaldi told me that Semana MacBride
couldn't be trusted. He had no proof, just suspicion. But I've
learned to respect his feelings in these matters and so have
you."

Sulky, frustrated, and utterly unconvinced, G'Kar said,
"Perhaps you're right, Na'Toth." He fixed her with an in-
cendiary glare. "But in future, before you cancel my appointments, make sure I want them canceled."

Ivanova stood at her console working swiftly and efficiently,
with the fierce concentration that had helped promote her to
Commander.

But she was aware, at a deep level of her consciousness,
of the absence of pressure, pressure that Ilias Larkin's presence at the boards had always caused. There was a sense of
guilty relief in the air. Relief that no one would have to watch
Larkin's sky as well as their own to avoid the "almost ac-
cidents" his inattention was forever causing. And guilt over
the depth of that relief, considering his death.

The freighter *Orion's Belt* was arriving. She smiled. The
Belt was bringing an old shipmate with it, the sergeant she'd
served under on her first assignment. Zack had been in
charge of the battlecruiser's primary sensor arrays and was
a hard taskmaster, but a fair one. And if you were willing to
learn, which she had been, he'd go more than an extra mile

to teach you. Susan had been frankly awed by the skill and ingenuity he revealed when he opened his mind to her.

Susan also credited him with helping to mold her command style. She hoped there'd be time to see him.

She and the freighter exchanged formal greetings and technical information. Ivanova assigned them a berth and as she did a message scrolled across a screen that shouldn't have been able to receive it.

"Susie-Q—Gotta talk. Seriously important. Meet me at the Gate." And a small red flag flickered on the screen.

Susan blinked. If anyone could manage a secret message like this it was Zack. The red flag was an old symbol he'd devised for his people, meaning both trouble and a warning that it was security sensitive. She frowned.

Even though it was extraordinarily busy in C and C due to the coming conference and the temporary shutdown of traffic that would take place while the delegates were arriving, she knew that it would be worthwhile meeting with Zack to hear what he had to say. He might be working on a civilian freighter, but his instincts and his heart were still Earthforce.

When her board blinked confirmation that the freighter was securely docked she called upon her second to take over. Then she left C and C.

Zack was already pacing the dock when Ivanova arrived. Catching sight of each other they both saluted and then laughed. She strode over and gave him a warm hug.

"It's good to see you, Sarge," she said.

"Good to see you too, Commander." He looked her over and his face wore an expression of fatherly approval. "You look wonderful, Susan. Y'married yet?"

She blinked. *Why does everyone ask me that?* she wondered. Old friends and sometimes new ones inevitably came out with it. "Are you now or have you ever been married?" The older she got the more awkward she felt about it, as though she were failing to live up to expectations.

"Yes," she said with a wry smile. "I'm married to my career."

He laughed and put his arm around her shoulder, leading her off from the small group of crewmen who had congregated around the lock.

"Well, that's enough chitchat, I guess." He looked over his shoulder, gave her a little pat, and then lowered his arm.

She waited patiently, trusting that this meeting would be well worth the time she'd spared.

"I handle the *Belt*'s sensor array, among other things," he said, and she nodded. "And frankly it's a damned boring post. So I've tweaked the system quite a bit. It's not Earthforce quality . . . yet, but it's damned close."

Again, Susan nodded. This was pretty much what she'd expect from him. *I'm surprised Psi-Corps hasn't decided to study Zack,* she thought. *When it comes to sensors he's got a whole new kind of extrasensory perception.* He was the kind of technician who could make you believe machines were actually alive.

"So anyway, the reason I called you was, we came through Sector Red thirteen." He was watching her from the corner of his eye.

"So?" she asked.

"So there's a whole bunch of Centauri yachts out there. I mentioned it to the Captain and he says they're probably there to welcome their delegates to this peace conference they're holding here." Zack shrugged. "So I took a deeper look. Nice little ships, all the bells and whistles, leave it to the Centauri to know what real luxury is."

He shook his head and sighed. "But your average luxury yacht doesn't come with an armory of energy weapons and strap-on antiship missile pods. They had a nice eclectic mix, some PPG cannons, some Centauri stuff, some I've never even seen before. All fully operational, and all armed."

"Armed." Susan's eyes bugged. "They were sitting out there with their weapons hot?" she demanded.

"Yup. Figured you'd want to know since the Narn delegation have to use that gate too."

"Oh, God," Ivanova said, putting her hand to her forehead. "How many?" she asked.

"Nineteen," he said. "I counted a hundred and eight people aboard them. They didn't say anything. The Captain hailed 'em but they just stood mum. Sorta behavior that gets my back up." He cast Ivanova a look.

"Mine too," she said between clenched teeth. "Thanks, Zack." She gave him a quick hug. "I owe you one."

Zack laughed.

"Spank 'em for me, Susie-Q, that'll be plenty.

"I know nothing about it," Londo said, looking genuinely puzzled. "What welcoming committee?"

"Nineteen civilian yachts," Sheridan said, blue eyes fixed unwaveringly on Londo's image on the screen. "One hundred and eight—presumably—civilian crewmen and, I'm told, a very impressive array of weapons. *That* welcoming committee."

Londo sighed in annoyance. "Understand me, Captain Sheridan, if we wished to attack the Narn delegation we wouldn't hide behind a facade of dilettante vigilantes. We would engage them quite officially. And if we didn't want to talk we simply wouldn't show up at the conference."

Londo leaned forward and said emphatically, "I know nothing about these people. I urge you to go out and find out what they are up to." He leaned back again, his expression resentful. "Once you've done that, we'll both know how to proceed. End," and the BabCom logo filled the screen.

Sheridan took a deep breath and held it for a count of five, then let it out explosively.

"Susan, take Alpha Wing out to Red thirteen and get those people out of there." The Captain stopped short of saying *in any way possible,* but Ivanova could almost see the words crowding up behind his teeth.

Sheridan thought for a moment.

"Frankly, I don't care what their intentions are," he said, "but maybe we should take a cue from them and let Alpha provide an honor guard escort for the delegations. That ought to curb any troublemakers who come stumbling along." He sat down behind his desk, his anger apparent from the jumping of a little muscle in his jaw. "I'll want you here for the reception, though, so once you've gotten rid of those Centauri yahoos I want you to come back."

"Yes, Sir," she said.

He grinned suddenly. "If I have to wear dress uniform, everybody wears dress uniform."

Olorasin watched Segrea and another burly Razye Tesh frog-march a very reluctant Lucius Cray towards her. He looked around the cramped walls of the safe house with a look she recognized across all boundaries of species: fear. It was surprisingly pleasant to contemplate. The Narn who killed her brother should know fear. Much fear, before she died . . .

"I don't come down here, man," Cray was protesting. "Y'hear me? I *don't* come down here." As though it wasn't actually happening. Then he saw the still expression on her face, and his mouth shut with an audible snap. The pasty human complexion went even paler.

The three of them stopped in front of her and when Segrea released him, Cray dropped visibly.

"I don't do business in Down Below," he said again, straightening his ruffled clothing, his face resentful but his eyes worried.

"You do business where and when we tell you," Olorasin informed him in a voice as cold and indifferent as death. "You've been fooling yourself, Mr. Cray, if you believe we're some addled collection of innocents." She stepped closer to him. "We've been fighting the Narn for over twenty-five years, human. After that length of time you get so you can smell betrayal and follow the stink to its source."

"I don't know what you're talkin' about," Cray said stoutly. "I'm no fink!"

"Of course you are," Olorasin said quietly. She walked around him and stopped when she faced his back, then she leaned close and said over his shoulder, "I'm sure you were well paid for it too. One must think of one's self, after all. And who are we to you?" She continued walking until she was in front of him, but her back was to Cray.

"But, of course, we matter to ourselves," she said over her shoulder. Olorasin sighed. "Under circumstances like these it becomes necessary to set an example of just how badly we T'llin take betrayal."

"Hey! I didn't betray you, okay? I don't do stuff like that," he said, his voice rising uncontrollably. "It's bad business." Cray was sweating profusely, despite the typical chill in the air of Down Below.

Olorasin turned slowly to face him, an amused grin on her face. The sight of her tiny pointed teeth made Cray's Adam's apple bob.

"Didn't," he choked, barely a whisper.

"You're still underestimating us, Mr. Cray," Olorasin said. "It's very annoying. Do you think, given your position, that it's clever to annoy us?"

"I'm sorry," he said, near tears. "Sorry."

Olorasin looked as though she were tasting his reply, rolling the word thoughtfully around in her mouth.

"No," she said at last. "I find no help for my people in your sorrow. It changes nothing, aids no one." She shrugged. "It's no use even to you. Is it?"

Cray was by now a thoroughly frightened man, but he knew they wanted something. If they didn't his blood would already be on the floor.

"Let's deal," he said, voice shaking, but his eyes bold.

Olorasin grinned again.

"Very good," she said. "Very, very good."

"We need maps of the station's infrastructure," Segrea said. "And electronic override keys into secured areas."

"And something that will allow us to monitor Security communications and perhaps give us some computer access," Olorasin added.

"You don't want much," Cray said. "It'll cost you plenty to get stuff like that."

Olorasin laughed and the others grinned.

"Oh, no, no, no," she said. "You were well paid the last time and look what happened. We feel the key here is to get you to invest in our fortunes," Olorasin told him. "The more you invest, the greater your personal stake in our success, the less likely you are to sell us out. That's what we think."

Cray made a sound that was something like a derisive laugh. "Why would I do that?" he demanded.

"Because if you don't, I'll chew your black heart out of your chest," she said and lunged at him, snapping her sharp teeth shut just an inch short of his nose.

Cray sprung backward with a terrified shriek, only to be caught and pulled back by the two Razye Tesh at his side.

"We're not civilized," Olorasin said, crowding close. She grabbed two handfuls of his silk shirt and with a sharp yank ripped it open, exposing his thin, pale chest to the cold air. "Just ask the Narn," she whispered. "Now"—she placed her hand over his heart and licked her lips—"I sense a growing compulsion in you to contribute to our fight for freedom. Don't I?"

He nodded, his breath sobbing, and she nodded with him.

"Good," she said, pulling back. "Yssa will be your constant companion until we've accomplished our goal here." She indicated the big T'llin on his right. "Do yourself, and us, a favor and don't try to escape him. If we have to bring you here again I'll do what I promised. But I'll start at your toes."

She gave him a shove and Cray and Yssa moved off.

"We'll probably have to kill him," Segrea grumbled, just loud enough for her to hear.

"That will be up to Yssa," she answered. "Since he'll be the only one of us left alive to do it."

CHAPTER 18

ALPHA Wing arrived at Red thirteen in perfect arrowhead formation. A mailed fist ready to crush, *well, swat,* Ivanova thought, the Centauri menace. *Or mosquito, in this case.*

She looked down at her screens. Visual would have shown nothing—space was *big*—but the milspec scanners showed that the Wing confronted nineteen small ships arranged in a sort of ragged globe. Her computer pulled design specs and schematics out of its memory and rotated diagrams for her to inspect. Each one of them was a jewel of the ship designer's art, a fantasy of speed and grace, made more elegant by the fact that they had the sleek build of ships designed to transit plantetary atmospheres. Their elegant lines were marred, however, by the jury-rigged weapons platforms extruding from their gleaming surfaces.

Most of those things will break off and fly away if they attempt to fire them, Ivanova thought, *taking large chunks of the ship with them. Some will probably smash right through the hull with the recoil.* And *then* they'd spin off into infinity.

Ivanova was horrified. It seemed impossible that people this stupid were allowed off planet by themselves. Let alone that even the greediest black-market arms dealer would dare to sell them weapons.

I mean, the fear of meeting up with these bozos with their weapons hot would definitely keep me from cutting a deal—or sleeping at night. Of course money, which these people obviously had in abundance, was the greatest qualm soother in existence. *Maybe I'd sell them weapons, hang on to the instructions, and refuse to sell them ammunition. That'd make me feel safer.*

But then . . . fools, combined with determination and money, always found a way. She supposed it was a tribute to providence that they hadn't blown each other to bits while attaching them to their ships.

I wouldn't be surprised if they'd been fully armed while being welded to their yachts' hulls. Ivanova shook her head in disgust.

"Unidentified Centauri formation," she said crisply, "I am Earthforce Commander Ivanova from Babylon 5. I demand that you identify yourselves and explain your presence here with activated weapons."

While she waited for a reply Susan recorded their ship's markings, sending the information back through the gate in a message pod. Then she and Alpha Wing settled down to wait in ominous silence.

"Well, well, well," Sheridan said when Ivanova's information had yielded the yacht owner's identities. He keyed up Londo's quarters.

"Yes?" Londo said. Seeing Sheridan, he looked less than pleased. "What is it now, Captain? I have a great deal to do—as you might imagine—and can't be disturbed for every Centauri misdemeanor."

"One of the craft at Red thirteen is registered to a Sodev Mollari." Sheridan raised his eyebrows. "Is he a relative?"

The effect of the name on Londo was almost comical. Sheridan could have sworn that even the Ambassador's stiffened crest of hair sagged.

Londo collected himself with a weary sigh. "Unfortunately, yes. He's a cousin of mine, and a complete idiot. What is your human expression? Ah, yes. A 'loose cannon.' " *And a recurring nightmare,* his expression said. "No family is complete without one."

They'd been raised together and Sodev, a bully and a con-
niver, had made a career of tattling on Londo, stealing from
Londo, lying about Londo. Things hadn't improved in their
adulthood when Sodev had a rather public affair with Londo's youngest wife.

"If something unfortunate were to befall Sodev, the family
would grieve deeply for him. For about five, perhaps even
six minutes. Do what you have to do, Captain." *And I hope
whatever that is, it involves massive explosions.*

"He and his followers are most likely blowhards, trying
to impress the girls back home. But I can't guarantee that.
A shot across their bows should suffice. But who knows?
They might be feeling brave today.

"But as I said, do what you must. I don't want our delegates being greeted with a hail of charged plasma. Oh"—
Londo raised his finger—"if he gives you any trouble, tell
him that I said he was not going to embarrass the Empire
the same way he consistently humiliates the family. And then
give him one for me. Eh?" The Ambassador's face was quite
cheerful at the thought, and he was laughing when he broke
the connection.

Well, Sheridan thought charitably, *I guess every family has
at least one cousin like that.*

A pod came back from B5 in under an hour and broadcast
its message to Susan's Starfury.

"One of them's Sodev Mollari, the Ambassador's
cousin," Sheridan's voice told her. "And Londo gave us
carte blanche to do whatever we think necessary. Have fun,
Ivanova."

"Yes, Sir!" Ivanova said aloud. "Okay, Alpha Wing,
charge up your weapons. It's time to play a little cat and
mouse with the Centauri Citizens' Militia."

G'Kar entered the casino as nervously as a virgin meeting a
lover of dubious faithfulness. He spotted Semana immediately and moved briskly towards her. Beautiful as she was,

she had the capacity to stand out in any crowd. Tonight she was dressed quite plainly, in a garment that might have passed unnoticed were it not for the fact that her body-hugging coverall was the exact shade of her skin. For an instant it appeared she was wearing nothing but earrings and a necklace.

G'Kar was annoyed.

"Considering the *item* we're discussing," he said as he seated himself, giving her a meaningful glance, "I would have thought that a more conservative outfit, or perhaps a more private place . . ."

"No, no," Semana said with a good-humored smile. "If we come to an agreement, the *delivery* will take place in private. For . . . obvious reasons. But some negotiations are best conducted in the open. This way there'll be no undue curiosity, no one wondering what we're up to behind closed doors. Or if they do, this outfit establishes a likely reason." She shrugged deprecatingly. "So many of my clients demand absolute privacy, when secrecy is sometimes better maintained in public."

The Ambassador frowned slightly, shifting nervously in his chair. If he walked away from these negotiations with nothing to show for it, Semana's little security measure would backfire on him. He doubted if even the long-suffering Da'Kal would believe that he was courting Semana MacBride for the good of the Narn Empire. *Even I think it looks suspicious and I know what I'm trying to do.*

"You know the intensity of my interest," he said. "And you also know of my problem."

"Unfortunately," she drawled, "yes. I do. I hope you're not going to waste your time or mine by asking me to wait. I can't. That's final."

"I have obtained three quarters of your asking price," he said and tapped a credit chit on the tabletop.

You cheap bastard! she thought. *I am not going to be happy if I have to settle for that.* Semana hated it when a mark got the better of her. It was a matter of professional pride. She pouted.

"I can transmit the remainder to any bank account you choose to name," G'Kar was saying.

Oh, right, like I'm going to leave a trail for you to follow. She huffed out an impatient breath.

"I don't know," she said tersely, glancing around the room. "I've explained my problem to you." Her eyes met his. "My partners are not going to like taking less, or taking a chance that you'll come through with the rest. And I'll be honest, G'Kar, I'm unwilling to risk being seriously hurt for your benefit. I'd be better off to bring them the merchandise and tell them I couldn't make a deal. An item like that will always have a market somewhere." She recrossed her legs and looked away from him again.

So she almost jumped out of her skintight coverall when a hearty "Hello, Ambassador!" shattered their privacy. Semana turned to find herself looking up at Na'Toth, who had a wide and insincere smile plastered on her sharp features.

"And hello, Ms. MacBride. I'm afraid I'll have to drag the Ambassador away from you now. We've a lot of little deadlines to meet before tomorrow morning. His wife is coming, you know. There's so much to prepare."

Semana looked at G'Kar with heavy-lidded eyes.

"But I thought that was why people had assistants," she said, coolly. "So that they wouldn't have to handle all those little details themselves." Her attitude said as loud as words, *Get rid of her.*

But Na'Toth held the upper hand tonight.

"Off we go, Ambassador," she said, taking his upper arm and tugging. "I need your approval on a dozen different things."

"Not now, Na'Toth!" G'Kar whispered, his eyes trying to convey complex levels of meaning, most of them hostile.

"Yes, Ambassador," Na'Toth said in an utterly flat, firm voice. "I fear I'm on the verge of absolute panic. And I must insist that you come with me right now." *Before I start screaming.*

As though in a dream, not sure if he was being rescued or damned, G'Kar rose and went with her. He turned at the entrance of the casino to cast a last glance at Semana.

If looks were PPGs he'd have been dead on the floor.

Semana looked away with an impatient flick of her head. It was useless to be angry. She'd misread the Narn Ambassador from the first. He was comfortably well off, that had been easily ascertained. But of course she'd assumed that like most politicos he had access to large sums of semiofficial under-the-table monies.

Instead, the jerk has nothing. Not even friends apparently. *Cheap bastard!* she thought sullenly.

"What a crime," observed a richly accented voice.

She turned, one brow lifted mockingly. "A lovely lady all alone." Ambassador Mollari placed his hand on G'Kar's vacant chair. "May I join you?"

She gave him a slow, shrewd smile and gestured gracefully in agreement.

Segrea signaled and another Razye Tesh slipped silently across the corridor behind the security woman's back.

Odd, he thought sardonically, *how whenever we meet with Cray to pick up supplies, there's always a station security person nearby.* Two other thoughts crowded his mind. One, that Cray had some coded means of communication so subtle that Yssa, his T'llin guard, was unaware of it. Two, that perhaps he ought to take note of which security people were showing up and send Mr. Garibaldi an anonymous warning about their association with Cray.

No. Best not to call attention to Lucius until we're finished with him. Garibaldi was smart, and he'd react to having his people accused of being on the take as a personal insult. *The last thing I want is his attention fixed on this part of the station.*

Cray's betrayal had turned out to have unexpected bene-
fits. For one thing, it had brought out in the remaining Prime
a cold-blooded efficiency that even Phina at his most deadly
had never achieved.

That was the problem, Segrea admitted to himself. *He was
deadly but disorganized.* At some point it would have gotten
a lot of T'llin killed. If only the two Primes had been of one
mind, working together.

We'd have been invincible, Segrea thought.

Or at least, as invincible as an underarmed, planet-bound
people could be when facing a ruthless, space-faring race.

He signaled another of his people to cross the corridor.
His greatest fear now was a failure of will on the part of the
remaining Prime. He'd never understood Olorasin, nor did
he know what was driving her now. Lacking that understanding he was, not surprisingly, also lacking in trust.

"What is this stuff?" Segrea asked as his fellow Razye Tesh
unburdened themselves of the supplies they'd picked up from
Lucius Cray. This was another thing that bothered him. Phina
had filled him in on all of his plans, but Olorasin kept her
own counsel.

"This," the Prime picked up a tightly rolled piece of gray
material, "is memory plastic." She released the holding cord
and it sprang out into a long flat sheet, about two centimeters
thick. "It's used for insulation and is designed to be held
between the supporting ribs of the station's less visible areas.
Storerooms, for instance, or safe areas where people only go
if there's a hull breach." Olorasin looked at him expectantly.

Segrea sighed. "What is your plan, Prime? If anything
happens to you, one of us will have to implement it. And as
of now, all I know is that it involves insulation."

"It isn't my plan at all," she said, beginning to roll up
the thick sheet of plastic. "It's Phina's backup plan. He had
already arranged for quite a lot of its elements to be in place.
For us, the most difficult part will be entering Docking Bay

17 after the final sweep. If we manage that, all we have to
do is hibernate behind these in the safe area until we hear
the signal.''

"The signal?"

"Yes. If all goes as planned."

"You anticipate problems?" Segrea asked.

"Always," Olorasin said. "And I'm rarely disappointed."

Ivanova studied the silent little cluster of yachts and wondered what was going through the minds of the people
aboard them. Were they afraid? Or were they defiant?

She sighed. *Take the arrogance of the average Centauri,
multiply it by a massive personal fortune, add a dollop of
important family blood, and you've got a recipe for disaster
under any circumstances.* She hoped Londo really meant
what he'd said.

Flicking switches to *universal broadcast,* she started her
plan in motion.

"All right, Alpha Wing, command has given us a go. Prepare to commence plan C."

There was an overwhelming gasp of horror from Alpha
Wing.

"Sir!"

"Yes, Alpha Two?"

"Plan C?" Webber's voice was shrill with disbelief.
"Isn't that a little . . . drastic? They're only civilians!"

"They've given up their right to be treated as civilians,
Alpha Two. We have clearance from the Centauri government, they've given us cart blanche to do whatever we
want." Her voice was harsh and threatening; to the listening
Centauri she must have sounded like a bloodthirsty fanatic.
"And I'm declaring these people military targets. Dispersal
pattern four!"

Ivanova grinned as the Starfuries around her tumbled into
a star-shaped pattern that would afford maximum firing efficiency. The pilots added a few flashy spins and rapid place
exchanges, heart-stopping maneuvers designed to inspire

awe, and hopefully a healthy dose of fear in the watching Centauri yachtsmen.

"Pick your targets, people." Thirty-six targeting lasers found their mark. Even muted civilian-style sensors would pick up that threat and shrilly report it. "They have one minute to surrender. Then, if they're still in a weapons-ready condition . . ." Ivanova drew the pause out until even she couldn't stand the tension, then growled, "shoot to kill!"

She set her computer to broadcast a sixty-second countdown in Centauri. Then she and Alpha Wing waited, praying they wouldn't have to fire.

"*. . . yasech . . . yasas . . .* "

Six seconds, Susan thought, her heartbeat uncomfortably fast. There was sweat on her brow and upper lip too. *C'mon, you jerks! Give up! We'll blow you into atoms—you can't be so blindly arrogant that you don't know that.* She rubbed her thumb lightly over the firing stud, nerves thrumming. *Give up!*

"*. . . yasan . . .*"

Three. Oh, God. Susan licked her lips.

"It occurs to me," a bored Centauri voice drawled, "that certain factions could willfully misinterpret our intentions, as well as our actions here today. In light of that thought, I believe it best that we be on our way."

Not so fast, buddy!

"Your weapons are still armed," Ivanova snarled. "Stand down immediately or we will commence firing."

Instantly, almost as one, the sensors showed the Centauri weapons as disarmed.

"Your next jump point should be in Green Sector," Ivanova told them. "I hope we won't be meeting you there as well. Pleasant journey, ladies and gentlemen."

Without responding, the humbled little militia pulled itself into a ragged formation and plunged into the jump gate's vortex.

There was silence for a moment, then first one pilot and then another began to chuckle. It grew and grew until the whole wing was laughing uproariously, celebrating the fact that they hadn't had to kill anyone.

"Oh, no!" Susan mimicked in a high-pitched voice. "Not plan C! Anything but plan C!" She grinned at the renewed shrieks of laughter. "Alpha Two, you should have been an actor."

"You were pretty impressive yourself, Commander."

Who says I was acting?

"Well, I've got to head back. The Captain wants the whole family on hand to greet our guests. You folks keep this gate clear of riffraff and provide escort, half and half to the Centauri and Narn delegations when they arrive. Webber," she said to Alpha Two, "you're in command."

Ivanova headed into the jump gate to the sound of Webber ordering the Wing into a less threatening configuration.

"Ahhhh ha-ha-ha!"

The braying laugh brought the two security people guarding the doors to Docking Bay 17 to full alert.

A crowd of eight young Centauri men in stained brocade frock coats stumbled towards them. They were obviously drunk and in that uncertain, half-happy, half-angry mood where anything can happen.

"Look! Look!" the tallest of them said, an expression of mock horror on his homely features. "It's Earthforce Security! I'm sooo scared!" He turned to his friends, his eyes bugging out, and they all burst out laughing.

The two Security people looked at one another in resignation. No matter where you went, somehow the drunks could always find you.

"This is a secured area," one of them said, resignedly. "You'll have to move along, folks." He took a couple of steps forward, holding out his arms in a shooing motion.

The tall Centauri drew himself up, a haughty expression supplanting his drunken smirk.

"I," he said, advancing on the guard, "am not a folk! *I* am related by marriage to the royal family!" He stopped directly in front of the offending guard, put his hands on his hips, and belched loudly.

His friends burst into laughter again and stumbled towards him, slapping him on the back and congratulating him on the fine ending to his speech. Some of them congratulated the guard as well.

"You'll have to move along," the Security man said again, loudly and firmly.

His partner moved over to the group who were urging the first guard to come with them for a drink.

"C'mon, break it up, here. You fellows will have to leave."

"Fellows!" they roared and surrounded him too.

Before they could react, the two guards found themselves being dragged down the corridor by the merry crowd, their arms immobilized at their sides.

"Let go!" the first Security man bellowed.

"Stop this!" the other said, struggling to get at his link and, failing that, his PPG.

Howls of derision greeted their orders and the Centauri gripped them more tightly still, picking up the pace until they rounded the corner and were halfway to the lift.

At their deserted post a T'llin technician attached the lock-pick device Cray had supplied to the door's keypad and went to work.

"It's ready now," he said softly.

Olorasin stepped up to the lock and paused thoughtfully.

"*La're tessana* T'll," she said into the speaker, and the tech went back to work.

"Let T'll be free," Haelstrac said with a tight smile. "It pleases the ear, Prime."

The door opened and Olorasin and the Razye Tesh slipped through. They wore cheaply made mock-ups of Earthforce Security uniforms, complete with riot helmets bearing darkened face masks.

The echoing hull of the deserted docking bay was as ready for a diplomatic ceremony as human ingenuity could make it. Pale blue bunting, bearing the B5 logo, had been hung behind the low, carpeted platform placed dead center and against one wall. Both delegations would leave the docking tubes at opposite ends of the bay to meet there. It bore a podium with a row of chairs behind it and was bracketed by a small garden of green plants. Several rows of folding chairs faced the platform.

"Go," Olorasin said to the Razye Tesh, pointing to the safe area. "Prepare yourselves. Segrea, Haelstrac, with me, I need your expertise."

She led them to a bare wall. Olorasin ran her fingers over the metal; even through four thick walls and several feet of cushioning air it bore the chill of space.

"Here," she said and carefully peeled back what looked like a very small bump in the wall.

"It's a timer!" Segrea said and squatted beside the Prime. "How did it get there?"

Olorasin shook her head once.

"I don't know. Phina arranged it. There's a shaped charge behind there, enough to blow a small hole right through the hull. Can one of you set the timer?"

Haelstrac allowed herself a tiny smile and went to her knees beside the miniature timing device. She opened a small purse on her belt and withdrew a tool kit. From it she took an instrument with a metal prong not more than a millimeter in thickness.

"When do you want it to go off?" she asked.

Garibaldi looked around in disgust. His cells were full of nursing mothers, distinguished old people, fervent peace workers, and kids. Hardly a group capable of much in the way of barbarity.

Heck, they make me feel like Attila the Hun. He checked the time. Less than three hours to the arrival of the peace delegations.

"This doesn't smell right," he said aloud.

"Chief?" Ensign Torres asked, her brow wrinkled.

"The Narn said this guy Phina was a terrorist. A leader. Seems to me there should have been somebody here waiting to be led. You see anybody like that in there?" He indicated the holding area with a jerk of his head. "You could lead this bunch to a shearing station to have their wool removed, but to a fight?"

Torres looked puzzled.

Garibaldi shook his head and turned away. He had the unshakable feeling that someone wanted these prisoners to be taken . . . possibly for safekeeping. *Which means that someone else is out there, and probably up to no good.*

He tapped his link.

"Garibaldi to Captain Sheridan."

"What is it, Chief?" the Captain's voice sounded harassed.

"I may be late for the reception, Captain. I have some people to question. I'll try to make it, but no promises."

There was an ominous pause.

"Just who is so important that they can't wait for a couple of hours?" Sheridan asked.

"I've got a bad feeling about these T'llin," the Chief confessed. "They're so . . . innocent! If Phina was a terrorist, where are his minions? Because they're not in Security Central."

"That T'llin that Na'Toth killed," Sheridan said slowly, "he had a woman companion named Olorasin. Is she among your catch?"

"Torres, is there an Olorasin among the prisoners?"

A few moments later Garibaldi said, "No, Sir. She's among the missing."

"Then I think you're right. We may have a problem. Take as long as you need, Chief, but find her."

The three T'llin stared at Garibaldi, the boy and his mother blinked rapidly, the old man acting as interpreter did not.

Well, I don't need to be an expert in T'llin body language to know they're all terrified, Garibaldi thought. If the mother held her son any tighter the kid's bones were going to pop through his skin. *It feels like they're holding their breath, waiting.* And he knew that he'd never get them to trust him in the short time he had left.

The mother said something rapidly in a liquid language that soothed the ear, despite the quaver of fear in her voice.

"She says," the old T'llin told him, "that the Prime Olorasin has left the station to seek help elsewhere."

Which is exactly what the last dozen have said. Obviously it was a rehearsed statement. But hearing it over and over was fanning his fears. *There are terrorists loose on the station*—he checked the time—*and the delegations will be here in less than an hour and a half.* He chewed his upper lip.

His instincts put them in Down Below. *For the time being at least.* But his staff couldn't easily be called away from the direct preparations for the conference.

"Ensign Wang," he said into his link.

"Yes, Sir?"

"I want you to take two of your people and go over Bay 17 again. Check for explosives, look for odd occurrences, or people out of place. Has anybody shown up that shouldn't be there?"

"We had a couple of reporters come by and try to browbeat their way inside," Wang told him. "And Sherman and Kline got dragged down the hall last night by a band of drunken Centauri."

"What?" *Why didn't anyone tell me this? Do they think we're playing games here?*

"They had them picked up for disturbing the peace. They could still be locked up," Wang suggested.

"Right, out," Garibaldi said tersely. *Not bloody likely,* he thought. No matter what the Centauri were arrested for, they rarely spent more than a few hours in jail.

Sure enough, when he checked, they were gone. The names they'd given were the Centauri equivalent of John Doe or Smith or Jones. He made a disgusted sound; one of the new kids had taken their information and then had allowed them to make their calls.

I don't suppose it ever occurred to him to call me, Garibaldi thought. He gritted his teeth. It wasn't a mistake the boy would be making twice.

The Chief looked around the office. The place had a skeleton staff of experienced people and a half dozen of his new trainees. With a regretful sigh he pulled Kobayashi and three of the newbees and made them put on armor, then headed for Down Below in person.

Londo moved down the corridor like a thundercloud. He was dressed in his very best semiformal brocade afternoon coat and gray silk vest. His stock was precisely tied and his jewels and decorations perfectly displayed. Despite this sartorial perfection, usually pure pleasure, his expression would have soured milk.

Vir, panting his way down the corridor some distance behind the Ambassador, wanted to ask him to slow down, but given Londo's mood, he didn't dare.

"Oh, Ambassador," Semana gushed, rushing up to him. "I'm so sorry. All this security, it took me forever to get here." *Of course, I only started out about ten minutes ago.*

Actually, she'd made incredibly good time and had to kick her heels in this little side corridor until Mollari came roaring along. *I thought you'd never get here.* "They all wanted to look in the box. It took some convincing to prevent them." She gave him an arch look. Then she offered him a square black box.

"Your property, Mr. Ambassador."

"Ah, dear lady," Londo said, beaming at her. He took the box into his hands reverently. "I'll admit, I was concerned about you," he said offhandedly.

She gave him an old-fashioned look and shook a good-natured finger at him.

"Now, don't you have something for me?" she asked.

"Yes, of course." He reached into his pocket and took out an envelope, which he reluctantly handed to her. "Before you go," he said quickly, "I suppose I should look inside." He smiled.

She shrugged prettily and stuffed the envelope into her pocket.

"Well, I'm going to trust you," she said.

"As you wish," he said, and for the first time took a good look at the box.

It was a perfectly sealed square, with no obvious method of opening it. He tried to slide the top off, then turned it over and over, faster and faster.

"What is this?" he demanded.

"It's got a trick catch," Semana explained. "That way no one could casually look inside and, well . . . you know."

"How do you open it?" Londo glowered at her. He was already running late, didn't the fool woman know that?

"It's touch sensitive. You push down on the top and push to the right, then you give a little twist." Nothing happened and Semana caught her lush lower lip in her teeth. "No, no, you push with your left hand, while with your right . . ."

"I have no time for this," Londo said, quickly losing patience. He was smiling, but conveying both nervousness and irritation.

"Here," she said, reaching out, "let me do it." Semana took the box and pushed and prodded and pulled at it. "Grrrrh," she said in frustration. "I'm sorry, but you've got me so nervous."

Londo put his hands over hers.

"It is all right. We'll open it later." He took the box from her and gave it to Vir. "Put this in my quarters, would you?"

Vir's mouth opened and shut a few times.

"Go," Londo said, and with a frown and a flick of his fingers sent him scuttling off.

Taking Semana's hand in his, Londo kissed it and said, "I'll be seeing you this evening at the reception, will I not?"

"Yes, Ambassador, I received your invitation this morning. Thank you."

"I must be going," Londo said with a strained smile and he hurried off. *I wouldn't be trusting you this far,* he thought, *if I didn't know that your name isn't on any ship's manifest.* Not to mention that from a half an hour before the delegates arrived, it would be five hours before any ships were scheduled to leave Babylon 5. *And I will certainly find time to open that damned box before then.* The woman was no fool; she'd know exactly what he would do to anyone who tried to cheat him.

Semana rushed down the little side-corridor and recovered her bag from the Security man who'd been watching it for her.

"Thanks, you've saved my life."

She gave him a light kiss and a wink, and rushed off to catch her transport, the last ship to leave before the delegates arrived, one with no scheduled passenger berths at all. Non-humans, of course, with an internal environment deadly to humans. The little life-bobble in the cargo hold had been arranged long before; one should always be thinking about one's exit.

I'm sure going to miss being Semana MacBride, she thought, jogging along. *But then, Maia St. Cyr will probably be fun too.*

CHAPTER 19

D OCKING Bay 17 was brightly lit and had been made surprisingly comfortable for such a utilitarian space. Ambassadors in all their richest panoply were clustered in little conversational groups, taking advantage of this opportunity to do a little business with some of their more elusive colleagues. Everyone, with the exception of Ambassador Kosh, was in attendance. But then, the Vorlon was a law unto himself.

I wonder what his absence means? Sheridan fretted. He didn't doubt for a minute that it had some significance. *But what? Does it mean the Narn-Centauri war isn't important to the Vorlon? Or that Kosh somehow knows the outcome and so doesn't need to attend?* Worrying about it was as useful as beating his head against the podium. *But I can't stop.*

He realized he was probably trying to distract himself. *I wish I could distract myself with something soothing.*

He glanced at Delenn, smiling serenely at the Drazi representative. Even when upset, the Minbari still had a sense of unshakable calm about her. He allowed himself a wry smile. Delenn was certainly distracting, if not exactly soothing.

An Earthforce Security woman went by him with a handheld chemo-sensor. He frowned.

"Didn't you already do that?" he asked quietly.

"Yes, Sir. But Chief Garibaldi just asked us to do another sweep."

Nice to know I'm not the only one with the willies.

"Carry on," Sheridan said.

"Yes, Sir." The young woman continued on her way.

Sheridan noticed that several other Security people were moving around the Bay, poking into corners, even checking out the hull breach shelter. He was pleased by Garibaldi's thoroughness.

If Olorasin is hiding out on the station with mayhem on her mind, I really do believe that the Chief will find her. It was nice to have at least one worry off his mind.

He glanced up as a camera ball zipped past him. He'd allowed four cameras in, from four different networks. The reporters had still been howling their protests at him as he walked from the lift to Bay 17 and the doors had slammed shut on their demands. Sheridan pictured them up in the auditorium on Green twelve, sticking pins into the heart of Sheridan dolls, or maybe lynching him in effigy.

Chancy Clark also had a camera with her. She claimed it was her personal log and swore that she had no intention of selling any part of today's recordings.

He believed her. And even if he didn't, she was the president's niece.

His link chirruped and he tapped it in response. "Yes?"

"Captain? The Centauri delegation is ready to begin."

"One moment." Sheridan looked to the opposite end of the Bay and caught the Security man's eye.

The man turned and spoke to someone out of sight.

The Captain's link chirruped again.

"Yes," Sheridan answered.

"Sir?" the Security man said. "The Narn delegation is ready."

Sheridan moved to the podium.

"Ladies and gentlemen, we are ready to begin," he said. There was a momentary increase in the volume of con-

versation as people broke apart and moved to their seats.
Delenn joined Sheridan on the platform, as did G'Kar and
Londo. Sheridan allowed everyone ample time to settle in,
then cleared his throat and began his brief remarks.

"We are gathered here today to greet two groups of men
and women who are dedicated to the greatest cause of all.
The cause of peace. Let us show them our high hopes and
our faith in their efforts," he said and began to applaud.

Ambassadors and their aides rose from their seats, applauding with him. The Narn and Centauri delegations swept
out of the docking tubes at either end of the platform. This
was the only facility on the station that would allow such an
entrance. Perhaps it had been planned for by a farseeing
architect who had visualized a meeting such as this. Unfortunately, it was also the one aspect of the ceremony he *hadn't*
been able to precisely choreograph in advance. Too many
stubborn diplomats, too little time. *Always some detail that
gets left out,* he thought. *Well, it can't be that important.*

The richly dressed Centauri moved slowly, as though listening to Mozart, while the Narn in their leather kilts came
on like soldiers on parade. Observing that their enemies were
moving faster, the Centauri increased their walking speed,
and so did the Narn. The two sides bore down on the welcoming committee like colliding storms, each obviously in-
tending to reach them first in order to make a statement. The
pace picked up from stately walk to quick-step, until both
delegations broke into an undignified jog, their august expressions lying about what their feet were doing.

Sheridan stopped applauding.

"Welcome," he said, stealing their thunder, "to Babylon
5, ladies and gentlemen. We're honored that you will be the
first to use this station in the way its builders intended. To
make peace—to find accord on neutral territory."

The two groups of peacemakers glowered at him, and just
about every Narn or Centauri lip was curled into a sneer.

"I want you to know that I and my staff will be at your
disposal throughout your stay here. *Anything* that we can do

to aid you in finding peace"—*such as beating your heads together*—"will be done . . ."

There was the sudden, vicious *snap!* of an explosion. Sheridan reacted instinctively, going to one knee as he turned towards the source of the sound, his hand reaching for a PPG that wasn't there. There was a high-pitched whistle of escaping air, which could be felt as a soft determined breeze across his cheek.

The crash doors slammed closed with a sound that lived up to their name and through the blaring of sirens and the flashing of warning lights a computer voice announced the obvious.

"There has been a hull breach in Docking Bay 17. This area has been sealed off for the security of the station. Please report immediately to the safe area indicated by the flashing yellow lights. When the breach has been sealed, the doors will unlock automatically." The message went on and on as the computer repeated it in several languages.

The crowd began a surge towards the doors into the station. It stopped when the bellowed announcement and flashing lights made it plain that they were inoperative. Ambassadorial dignity was entirely forgotten in a mad scramble for the safe area.

"It's a small breach, ladies and gentlemen. We're in no immediate danger," Sheridan shouted above the babble of growing panic. "Please proceed in an orderly manner, there's plenty of room."

We'll be packed in like sardines, he thought. *But we should all fit.*

Very briefly, the Captain considered remaining behind in the Docking Bay. He didn't relish spending the next couple of hours jammed into a room with the two warring factions blaring accusations at each other. But the steady rush of escaping air forced him to be sensible. He sighed, and wished there were some way to get all the other ambassadors between the Narn and Centauri in a sort of living cushion.

But in the scraggle of sentients rushing for the safe area,

base political considerations had given way to the much more important issue of personal survival. Only the thin outline of gray Earthforce uniforms on the outskirts of the terrified crowd showed that anyone was trying to keep their wits about them.

Within the safe area the T'llin in their ragged disguises stood ready. At the words "hull breach" they'd wakened from their hibernetic trance, pushing away the thick sheets of plastic that had hidden them from the security sweeps.

It's fortunate, Olorasin thought groggily, *that our prisoners won't be here for a moment or two.* She couldn't be the only one who was slow to wake. Though it was very fortunate that the T'llin metabolism could be slowed to the point where routine scans could detect no life. She hoped the others were recovering from hibernation more quickly than she.

But of course it was impossible to tell, since their faces were invisible behind the darkened face shields. *Only fifteen of us,* she thought, looking at her followers standing very still around the edges of the large room, each gripping their PPG. *But it will be more than enough.* Because fortunately they were dealing almost exclusively with cowards and the Earthforce personnel—who were *not*—would be paralyzed by concern for the diplomats.

The door opened and frightened aliens burst into the room. Those who were first to enter began to panic anew as the flood of newcomers continued unabated, pushing them to the back walls.

Busy herding the crowd, and trying to keep them reasonably calm, none of the Earthforce personnel even noticed the bogus gray uniforms around the perimeter of the room. The crowd itself paid them no attention, assuming they were Earthforce and belonged there.

"Plenty of room!" Ivanova kept shouting, though the people at the back would have disputed that. "Stop shoving!" she snapped, grabbing a Centauri sleeve and giving his arm a shake. "There's room for everybody."

She and Sheridan were the last in, pulling the door closed together and sealing it shut, locking the damn cameras out. Ivanova had actually batted one away as it tried to zoom in.

"I don't think we need to have this situation broadcast," she said in Sheridan's ear. "Do you?"

He shook his head. "For some people this isn't going to be their finest hour," he agreed. "I see no reason for the entire universe to know that."

And I am going to have a long talk with Chief Garibaldi.

Sheridan winced at the volume as people pushed and shoved and shrieked in outrage or panic. Ivanova gave him a sympathetic look. *Babylon is right,* he thought.

He raised his arms and started to speak. "Ladies and gentlemen," he shouted.

And felt the cold muzzle of a PPG pressed to the base of his neck.

"You are all my prisoners," Olorasin shouted.

No one, with the exception of Sheridan, paid the slightest attention. Even Ivanova, standing right next to him, continued looking the other way. The noise level in the contained metal space was frightful. And growing more so as the people, packed in cheek by jowl, with barely enough room to turn around in, sought their Aides, or friends, or to get as far away as possible from the person next to them.

Furious, Olorasin pulled the PPG from Sheridan's neck and fired into the air above their heads. The Razye Tesh followed suit, the crisp discharges blinding in the dim light. The crowd screamed with one mighty voice. A sound so overpowering that everyone fell silent in shock, finally able to hear Olorasin's outraged bellow of "Silence!"

"You are all my prisoners!" she repeated.

Sheridan saw Ivanova's hand moving towards her weapon, and made a small emphatic gesture. *No.* Not while diplomatic hostages were at risk. He moved his lips in a word she would understand: *Garibaldi.*

Her look of intense frustration was a wordless explanation. They were cut off from the station's communications net.

Figures, Sheridan thought. The T'llin obviously wanted privacy—and they'd obviously planned this very carefully. There were going to be some hard questions asked about how they'd managed to conceal fifteen terrorists in the safe area, at that.

His trained eyes scanned the T'llin in their shoddy imitation Earthforce uniforms. They held PPGs . . . and one of them had an obvious switch in his hand, and a bulge on his chest.

"*Uh oh,*" he muttered, flicking his eyes. Ivanova glanced the same way.

Deadman switch, her lips shaped soundlessly. A bomb or grenade, set to go off if the switch was released . . . as, for example, would happen if the T'llin holding it was shot. That put a different complexion on things. What would happen to the hostages if that bomb went off didn't bear thinking about.

The crowd had shrunk in on itself, trying to pull away from the menace along the walls.

"You!" Olorasin said to a Centauri. "And you!" she said to a Narn. "You claim you came here to talk peace. You lie! You came her to give justifications for war." Olorasin grabbed Sheridan's hair. "Well, I'm going to give you more than something to talk about. I'm going to give you enough war to choke on!"

"They're gone," the old drunk said. "Gone, gone, gone." He held out a dirty hand for a bribe.

Garibaldi just looked at it. "You oughta wash that," he said.

The old man glared, his jaw thrust out pugnaciously.

"I'm talkin' to ya, ain't I? I'm tellin' ya, ain't I?" He shook his cupped hand again.

"You haven't told me anything I can't see for myself, Parker. I'm not giving you credits for that."

Parker narrowed his eyes shrewdly and chewed his lower

lip. "They had a place over in Brown section. Wouldn't let nobody near it. There was a lot of comin' and goin' the last three, four days. Now they've up and left. Nobody seen 'em go, nobody knows nothin'."

Garibaldi looked at him.

"It's true!" Parker exclaimed. "I can show ya where they was. But they ain't there now." He held up his hand hopefully.

"Show us," the Chief said with a jerk of his head.

Parker glared and made a disgusted sound, then he shuffled off, the five Security people in tow.

"Sir?" Midori said, moving to the Chief's side. "What does it mean that no one's seen them?"

"It means they've either left the station or they have a plan and they're acting on it even as we speak."

Garibaldi's link chirruped and he tapped it, answering, "Garibaldi."

"Sir, there's been a hull breach in DB-17. Preliminary sensor readings indicate the impact came from inside the hull."

The Chief stopped short. *Well, now we know they haven't left B5.*

"How serious is it?" he asked.

"Based on the amount of air lost, Sir, I'd estimate that the hole is less than four centimeters at the point of impact. Probably considerably smaller at the station's outer skin."

"Put me in touch with the head of the repair crew assigned to DB-17," Garibaldi said, moving towards the lift at a jog.

A woman's voice said, "Cahill."

"This is Chief Garibaldi," he said. "What's the situation up there?"

"Our instruments are telling us that it's a small hole. The breach is located in a well-braced area, so the station's in no danger," Cahill told him. "We're suiting up to go outside now."

"You're not there yet?"

"Hey, give us a break, Chief. It just happened."

"Keep me informed," he snapped and broke the connection. Then he called up C and C again. "Garibaldi, here. Any word from the people inside Docking Bay 17," he asked.

"No, Sir. Indicators show that the communications apparatus in the safe area has been disabled."

"Disabled? Not just out of commission?" Frustration was running neck and neck with genuine fear now. Virtually everyone he valued was locked in that safe area.

"Yes, Sir. And apparently the Captain and Commander Ivanova deliberately prevented any of the network's cameras from following them inside."

Great! Thanks a lot, guys.

"And no one's using their link? Right?"

"No, Sir. Not a peep."

"All right, patch me through to Security Central." They left the lift heading for the tram that would bring them to the general area of DB-17, which was over three miles away.

"Security Central."

"Torres, we've got a probable hostage situation in Docking Bay 17. I want you and the rest of the hostage squad up there stat. I'm on my way now." Garibaldi tapped his link to break contact, tapped it again. "Cahill," he demanded.

"Cahill, here." Her voice sounded small and far away.

"You're outside?" he asked, recognizing the sound of a suit-mike.

"Yes," she answered, sounding exasperated. "We're outside and we're moving on it. We should be finished in an hour or so."

"Is there any way to get into DB-17 before you're finished?" he asked.

"Absolutely not, Chief. The doors will open automatically when the hole is sealed and the air pressure rises to minimum acceptable levels. Until then that bay is locked up."

Damn! It was a sensible precaution and he knew it. But it had never been designed with a situation like this in mind.

Because without question DB-17 was where the missing terrorists were.

"Override it."

"Yessir . . . oops."

"What is *that* supposed to mean?" he barked.

Actually, I know what oops means. It means "I screwed up."

"Sir, there's an internal block on the doors. Someone's put a software loop between them and the central system. We can't override."

"Young woman!" a tall Centauri exclaimed, pushing his way towards Olorasin. "I can understand your wishing to harm the Narn. They are your enemies . . ."

"Stop!" Olorasin snapped, training her PPG on him. "One more step and I'll splatter your brains all over this *distinguished* company."

She raised her voice. "These PPGs are not the only weapon here! We have a bomb powerful enough to kill everyone in the room, and we will use it rather than relinquish control of the situation!" She pointed to the T'llin spaced around the edge of the little room, each surrounded by a bubble of space provided by the fear of the weapon leveled at the crowd. "All Earthforce personnel, turn over your weapons immediately!"

The uniformed Security people looked to Sheridan. He nodded tightly. A T'llin pushed through the crowd to collect them.

Offended and a little frightened, the Centauri delegate stood still.

"I—I don't understand," he spluttered. "We are both enemies of the Narn. That should make us friends," he smiled encouragingly and raised his hands towards her as though tentatively offering a comradely embrace.

"As far as I'm concerned, you are as much our enemies as the Narn. And I despise you just as much as I do them."

"But why?" Londo asked in amazement. "What have we ever done to you?"

"You created *them*!"

The Centauri delegate and Londo glanced at one another uncertainly.

"Without *your* influence, if they ever had reached my world, would they be as they are now? Would they be conquerors? Would they be as cruel?" Olorasin shook her head, her black eyes flaring. "You're not innocent. You trained them, you helped to arm them and you warped them into the vicious monsters they've become. Whenever they murder a T'llin some of the blood stains you!"

Haelstrac reached out and pulled the link from Sheridan's hand, adding it to those in the sack he carried.

"And what about Earth?" Sheridan asked. "What about the Minbari and the nonaligned worlds? We've got nothing to do with this conflict.

"Oh you, with your best wishes, with your sympathy." Olorasin jammed the PPG up under his jaw. "When you see a murder being committed and all you offer is, 'Oh, too bad, I would help if I weren't afraid of getting hurt,' how do you think the victim feels? Don't you think they loathe you as much as they hate their murderer?"

She yanked his hair, pulling him closer. "Well, let me tell you, Captain Sheridan, they do. I came to Babylon 5 to ask, to reason, to plead, to *beg*. I came with evidence of how my people were being destroyed." She tapped the PPG against Sheridan's temple. "Nobody listened to me. But you'll listen to *this,* won't you."

"Surely you don't mean to kill us all?" Sheridan asked. "What can you gain from that except more hatred? You'll make T'll the enemy of every world represented here."

She laughed bitterly. "I see you still believe in the power of public opinion," she sneered. "But you see, it doesn't matter what people think. It matters what they do. The Centauri taught the Narn," Olorasin explained. "And the Narn are teaching us. Though I believe we're learning more quickly than they did."

When he arrived at DB-17 Garibaldi found a throng of bellowing reporters and network cameras whizzing every which way.

The harassed Security people assigned to guard the doors had given up being polite a while back and were now doing their best to avoid being crushed by the excited crowd.

When the reporters saw the Security Chief they stampeded towards him, only to crash into a surprisingly unyielding wall of determined young security people, who'd snapped into position around him like experienced professionals.

Well done, kids, Garibaldi thought, both surprised and pleased. He just stared silently at the reporters for what seemed like ten minutes before they began to realize that he had no intention of speaking until they shut up. Even then it took a while, and not everyone cooperated.

"You know what we know," the Security Chief told them. *More, actually, since you saw it on vid and I didn't.* "There's been a small hull breach. We have repair teams on it and expect that everything will be taken care of inside of two hours. This is a minor mishap and no one has been reported hurt." *In fact no one has reported, which scares the shit out of me.* "You have to leave this area. You will all be kept informed. As soon as we know something, so will you."

"What are you hiding from us?" a woman shouted and a chorus of "Yeah" supported her.

"We're not hiding anything. You saw the accident, and your cameras are still inside. When the door of the safe area opens you'll be right on the scene."

"Captain Sheridan and Commander Ivanova deliberately kept the cameras from entering the safe area," a famous reporter said aggressively. "Do you have any comment on their behavior?"

"Only that I'm sure they did it out of consideration for the ambassadors' feelings. Not everyone likes being photographed when they're in a frightening situation. In fact, some people really object to it." *Which, if you had the sensitivity of a blunt instrument, you would know.* But then they wouldn't be reporters. "And you must remember that many species find our human curiosity to be very offensive." *Any other stupid questions?*

"If there's nothing going on," a woman asked shrewdly, "then how do you explain your presence here with armored troops?"

"We were told that you people were on the verge of rioting," Garibaldi informed her. "And it didn't look far short of that when we arrived." They didn't like that from the looks on their faces. "You'll have to leave," he said again, firmly. "The same security considerations that kept you out of here in the first place still apply. Anyone who is found in this area within the next twenty minutes will be asked to leave the station."

They went absolutely still for at least two seconds.

"You can't do that," one of them shouted.

"Yes, we can," Garibaldi assured them. "Now this interview is over and the clock is running. I suggest you return to Green twelve, so you'll be ready when the delegates emerge from the safe area. If you have further questions, you'll have to hold them for the press conference."

"Then there is going to be a press conference?" a woman yelled.

"Absolutely," Garibaldi said. *And I won't have to be there, thank God!*

The hostage squad arrived and Garibaldi signed to them: move them out.

"This way, please, ladies and gentlemen," Torres shouted cordially. "To the lifts, please."

Gloved hands holding shock sticks waved them on their way and slowly, reluctantly, the disgruntled reporters turned to go.

Midori and the rest of Garibaldi's trainees, without being told, moved up in the rear, preventing any strays from lingering.

"Chang," the Chief said. When the young man turned, he said, "I want you and your squad to stay at the elevators, turn back anyone who isn't in an Earthforce uniform."

"Yes, Sir!" Chang's face brightened at what was probably his first command.

An hour and a half later a frustrated Garibaldi was still kicking his heels outside the crash doors of Docking Bay 17.

His link chirruped. "Yes," he said anxiously.

"Mr. Garibaldi," Cahill said, "we've completed our repairs. Air pressure should be back to normal in the bay in about five minutes."

"Finally," Garibaldi muttered. "Thank, you, Cahill," he said more loudly. "Good job."

"Yeah, finally."

Oops. She was gone before he could say anything else. *Just as well, I'm not at my most tactful right now.*

He waited for seven minutes and nothing happened.

He tapped his link to get C and C.

"How's the air pressure in Docking Bay 17," he asked.

"Back to normal, Sir."

"Then why haven't the doors opened?"

"It appears that whoever it was installed that software loop in the lock has overriden the pressure sensor as well, Sir."

Garibaldi glanced at the guards, who shrugged and shook their heads.

"Can you release it?" he asked.

There was a pause.

"It's not responding to standard codes, Sir." The voice sounded very unhappy. "Apparently it was designed to go into effect when the crash doors came down."

"Great." *They covered every eventuality,* Garibaldi thought with grudging respect. "How long will it take you to crack the new one?" He could almost hear the gulp.

"I . . . don't know, Sir. It takes a while, sometimes. Sometimes only a few minutes."

Suppressing an unworthy desire to tear the technician's head off, he said, "Do your best. Let me know when you've got something. Out."

Garibaldi stared at the stubbornly closed crash door, thinking hard. All of the T'llin he'd yet encountered had been exceptionally decent and law-abiding people. That gave him some hope. On the other hand, G'Kar had called Phina and his followers terrorists, which implied that not all of them came from the same mold. *Which brings me back to where I started. Either there's nothing going on but a whole lot of talking, or everybody's dead.* Which was a thought he refused to contemplate. *Either way, the T'llin have the whip hand for a change.*

He smacked his hand against the doors. If only he could *do* something!

Then a thought struck him. He pointed at Kobayashi and three others, indicating they should follow him.

"Cahill," he said into his link.

"Yeah, Chief?" She sounded tired, or maybe she just didn't want to talk to him.

"Don't get too far from your suit, Cahill, or your crew either. You're going out again. Only this time I'm coming with you."

There was dead silence in the safe area as everyone contemplated their situation.

"What exactly do you want?" Sheridan asked. *Keep them talking,* he thought. That's what the experts said. Getting them to talk to you reminded them that you were a person too.

"I *want* the Narn to leave T'll, never to return. I want there to be no reprisals against my people for what we're doing here. I would like justice for every murdered T'llin. But I'm not a complete fool, to expect what will never be."

"Then why don't you make your demands," Ivanova

asked. "You have our links. Tell them what you want the Narn to do."

"Yes," Sheridan agreed. "Get the process started."

Olorasin laughed. "What would be the point? The Narn would agree and then when you are all released they'd take back their word and there'd be reprisals against my people. And you would do nothing. Why go through all that? We all know what the outcome would be."

"No, you don't," Sheridan insisted. "You have to at least give us a chance."

"If you'll recall," Olorasin said coolly, "I already did."

Sheridan expected the Centauri to speak up, to make promises, but like everyone else they maintained an uneasy silence.

They sure don't like being on the receiving end of things, the Captain thought, looking at the Centauri's glum faces.

Finally, G'Kar could no longer stand the silence. "You can't actually expect the Narn to leave your planet!" he said. "We've invested millions on your world. We've set up—"

"Invested! *Invested?*" Olorasin leaned towards him as though she hadn't heard him properly. "Is that what you call it? When the Centauri strip-mined *your* world it was a crime. When you do it to us it's an *investment*?"

"Your own First approved," the Narn delegation leader said.

"Our First no more speaks for us than your Leader did when the Centauri had you under their heel. And you know that!" Olorasin held her hand out to him in appeal. "*Look* at what you have done! *Listen* to what you are saying!" She pointed at the Centauri. "If you do you'll hear their voices, you'll see their deeds, but it is you who are following their methods. It's as though you were still their slaves!"

"Young lady!" Londo expostulated. "I do not mind being accused of things we have done, but we Centauri are innocent of ever having caused any T'llin the slightest harm. Our ships have never visited your world. Our armies have never fought yours, we have never exploited your resources, or interfered in any way in your politics. Surely you don't imagine that we have conspired with the Narn?''

Olorasin took a deep breath and let it out slowly.

"You are being deliberately obtuse," she said, her black eyes full of rage. "But though the revelation may go no farther than this room, before this day is out, at least one Narn or Centauri will acknowledge the wrong you have done."

Delenn moved forward and the PPG in Olorasin's hand instantly aimed at her heart.

"You do not seriously expect the Narn to vacate your world, Olorasin, do you?" she asked gently. "Even if you kill all of us."

"Of course not," Olorasin said sarcastically. "Think of the millions they've invested. What are a few lives against that?"

Delenn took another small step towards her. "The Centauri inflict pain on the Narn and they in their turn inflict pain on the T'llin. And you," Delenn curled her delicate hand towards her own breast, "inflict pain on us. If what you are doing is right, then how are their actions wrong? Is it always wrong to kill, or is it always right?"

"This isn't a philosophical debate," Segrea rumbled. "*This* is reality."

"The same reality that T'll labors under every day. No one here is innocent," Olorasin said bitterly, her voice rising. "My brother is murdered and Earthforce arrests the T'llin." She closed her eyes and visibly composed herself. "To answer your question, murder is always wrong. But defending your life is not."

"If you wish to save lives," Delenn said, raising her hands in a pleading gesture, "then you must give this up. You know the Narn will strike at T'll for this. You *know* this!"

"My planet is being destroyed by the Narn and you tell me that the Minbari are *neutral* in this conflict," Olorasin said, mimicking Delenn's accent. "What luxury," she sneered, "to be able to dismiss the rest of the universe so easily. But don't you see, Ambassador, that doing nothing, while you pretend it's because we're all so far beneath you, is the same as helping the Narn? So doing nothing, in this case, makes you their ally."

"No. We are not," Delenn said firmly. But she was shaken, because in essence, the T'llin had a point.

"Yes, you are," Olorasin hissed.

"Look," Sheridan said reasonably. "Openly criticizing the Narn for their behavior towards your people at this time could be considered by them as a hostile act. A way of siding with the Centauri. Earth and Minbar are still licking their wounds from our war with each other. Our people are not willing to risk being dragged into another. Give us a chance to talk to them quietly . . ."

Olorasin smacked him with the PPG, her teeth clenched and her eyes wild. Then she did it again, opening a cut on his brow. He winced, but said nothing more, staring at her.

"We are snuffed out, life by life, and you shake your heads behind the Narn's backs and you whisper so they won't hear you, 'We're so sorry, best of luck.' My brother was murdered by them. And *you*," she stabbed a finger at Sheridan, "did not even question them. You arrested *us*! To appease them. They'll ask you to kill us next, and you'll do it. After all, you wish to avoid appearing prejudiced in favor of the Centauri, so what else could you do?"

She paused, breathing hard and looked at their faces, seeing Narn fury, Centauri disdain, Minbari reserve, and human shame.

"I ask you, ladies and gentlemen, what will it take to make you risk offending them?" She studied them a moment longer. "I'll tell you what it will take. It will take being touched directly. Sharing the threat *we* live under daily. The disruption of your orderly lives, the interruption of your important business. This is what it will take."

"You're wrong," Sheridan said, wiping the blood from his brow. "You won't change anything by killing us. Except to get more of your own people killed. When the Narn retaliate, and they will, innocent people will pay for what you've done. Don't you see? You won't just be killing us."

"Perhaps," Olorasin said tiredly, "that would be merciful. Disappointed hope can be a painful thing, Captain. I know."

"The truth is," the Captain said, "you're not interested in peace, Olorasin. You're interested in revenge."

She cocked her head. "And I should be interested in peace, shouldn't I? Because, according to you, if there were peace between the Narn and Centauri, then Earth would be free to express its opinion. And then, of course, the Narn would have to leave us alone. Isn't that right?"

A little muscle jumped in Sheridan's jaw. "It would be a start," he said.

Olorasin turned and addressed the crowd.

"This will be your last day of life, ladies and gentlemen. And therefore, your last chance to do something noble."

She concentrated her gaze on the Narn and the Centauri.

"Why don't you make peace between yourselves?" she asked them. "If you won't do it because it's right, then do it because it will be a great joke on your people. You won't be around to worry about the results, so why not?"

The peace delegates looked around uncertainly, frightened and embarrassed at once.

"Go on," Sheridan urged them. *Humor her. Stall for time.* The message was none the less urgent for being unspoken. "She has a point. If it's the last thing you ever do, something utterly devoid of self-interest is a good choice."

"Why not?" Londo said. "At the very least it will take our minds off the situation." He gave a slight smile and inclined his eyes slightly upward—to the hull, where he knew quite well that Garibaldi would be doing *something*.

The Centauri lead delegate glared at the T'llin. "Very well," he said at last. "Where is my secretary?"

Not to be outdone in insouciance, the Narn delegation began to pull itself together as well.

Before long, the two sides were lined up belly to belly, with peace in the universe the very last thing on their minds.

CHAPTER 20

GARIBALDI tried to hold himself in place within the huge plastic bag that Cahill and her people had attached to the station's skin. Every time he or one of his team bumped into it, one of the techs would turn and snarl that they were going to detach it if they didn't stay still; Midori usually murmured a small apology. Her elfin face was set, hard as a marble statue behind the faceplate of her suit.

The work crew's greater experience with EVA showed in their deft and confident movements; they made the Chief feel like a hippopotamus in a wallow.

"We're through," Cahill said.

The drifting plastic sack slowly stiffened into a bubble as it filled with air. This would allow them to remove their bulky suits when they got inside and move about freely. It would also prevent the alarms from going off again, warning anyone in the safe area that a rescue was being attempted.

Garibaldi thrashed his way to the opening, trying not to notice the disdainful expression on Cahill's face. *So I'm not an artist in zero G. I'm the Security Chief, okay? It's an inside job for the most part.*

"Don't seal this up until you've got an all clear," he said.

"That seems like a good idea," Cahill agreed in a voice so flat it could only be sarcastic. "Feet first, Chief."

"I knew that," he said, struggling to bring his legs forward against the pressure in his suit.

Cahill and one of her crew gave each other a look, then

they each took one of the Chief's arms and spun him into position as though he were nothing more than a bulky tool.

"Thanks," Garibaldi grunted and dropped down the hole.

Fortunately it was no more than a six-foot drop, because the station's gravity grabbed him immediately. *So headfirst would have been a problem,* Garibaldi thought as he scuttled for cover behind the podium. He cautiously looked around.

No one. The docking bay was empty.

He popped off his helmet and was struggling out of his suit when a series of electronic *zzztt*s startled him and he dropped the floor behind the podium, only to find himself eyeball to lens with one of the network's camera balls.

Damn! I forgot all about them. He had a mental image of the reporters charging up to DB-17 to break down the crash door using the Security guards outside as battering rams.

"You are still forbidden to enter the area around Docking Bay 17," he whispered to the camera. "And if any of these things gets in the way I will not be responsible for damages. So keep them *out* of my face."

The cameras obediently lifted, to hover approximately six feet off the floor.

"Thank you," he said tersely. Then he tapped his link. "Okay, team. All clear, everybody's still in the safe area."

One by one, Midori, and the rest of the hostage team dropped through the hole, into the docking bay. They quickly divested themselves of their bulky suits and fell into position, advancing cautiously on the safe area.

Olorasin had quickly discouraged both Narn and Centauri from posturing, or braying meaningless accusations at one another by the simple expedient of whapping any offenders on the head with her tiny hand. The lead Centauri delegate's crest of hair was seriously dented on one side, and the Narn leader looked as if he was ready to go ballistic.

"What do you want?" she asked the Centauri. "And what will you accept?" she asked the Narn.

"The Narn are a threat to our peace and security," Londo

said. "They have never made a secret of the fact that as soon as they felt strong enough they intended to make war on us."

"We have cause," G'Kar insisted. "And you have never made a secret of your enmity."

"So we made a preemptive strike," Londo shouted. "What choice did you leave us?"

"The Ambassador has a point," Olorasin observed. "Who but a fool would wait for a declared enemy to become equal in strength? Wouldn't you do the same in their situation?"

The Narn looked around and saw agreement on every face. "*We* are the injured party, here!" G'Kar declared. "It is *our* innocent civilians who have been butchered! Our people who have been enslaved!"

"I know the feeling," Olorasin said dryly. "What guarantees can you offer to the Centauri to make them stop?"

"What will they offer us?" the Narn delegation leader demanded at the top of his voice.

Segrea smacked him with the hand holding the deadman switch. Everyone in the room who had understood what it was winced. T'llin smiled broadly at their reactions.

"Thank you," Olorasin said with a smile, "my hand was beginning to hurt. Remember, you're here to make peace," she said to the fuming Narn.

"We will not give back any of the territory that we have *re*taken," Londo said firmly.

"Then you might at least return our people to us," G'Kar demanded.

"And you might give us some financial consideration for the installations we had in place," the Narn delegation leader added.

Londo and the Centauri leader looked at one another.

"Perhaps," Londo said slowly. "If you could obtain transportation for the displaced persons from some neutral party . . ."

Well, that's progress, Sheridan thought. It was a shame that the circumstances prevented it from meaning anything. He glanced at Olorasin and if he were knowledgeable about her race he would have sworn the expression on her face was something like envy.

As the hours ticked away, everyone became more and more interested in the progressing negotiations, murmuring approval or displeasure as the tide of reasonability flowed from one side to the other. The delegations seemed as swept up in the process as if the negotiations had been genuine . . . all except Na'Toth. Instinct turned Ivanova's head sharply, as she suddenly realized the Narn woman had been drifting backwards through the crowd—backwards towards the T'llin guards, now as absorbed in the diplomatic give-and-take as the rest of the safe-room's occupants.

Blindingly swift, Na'Toth grabbed the PPG hand of the T'llin behind her and yanked, hard, while driving her elbow into the T'llin's throat. His hand opened as he gagged helplessly and she snatched the weapon up, turning to fire at Olorasin who fired first, with devastating accuracy.

Na'Toth was flung backwards, into the arms of the other hostages. Her deadweight dragged her slowly to the floor as G'Kar and Dr. Franklin fought their way to her side.

"Move back as far as you can, people," Sheridan shouted over the exclamations of the others. "Give her some air."

"I hesitate to seem selfish," Segrea said, taking hold of Franklin's collar. "But my T'llin brother is choking to death." The big Razye Tesh swung the doctor around. "If you would be so kind as to help him, I would be most grateful," he said mildly, shoving Franklin towards the fallen T'llin.

"Be silent!" Olorasin bellowed. Except for a few whimpers and some muffled sobbing, she was obeyed.

The Prime pushed her way through to the wounded Narn. G'Kar was supporting her against his knee, Na'Toth's head in the crook of his arm.

"Can you hear me?" he asked urgently, his eyes on the smoking wound in her shoulder.

Na'Toth's eyes opened and she found herself looking up into the face of Olorasin.

"You are the one who killed my brother," the Prime said. Olorasin felt very strange, as though she were only observing what was happening, instead of being a part of it. She felt nothing for the terribly wounded Narn on the floor, nor for the obvious distress of the Ambassador, who held her.

"He was where he had no right to be," Na'Toth said, her voice taut with pain. "He threatened the Ambassador. It is my duty to defend him."

"My brother was unarmed," Olorasin told her. "Everyone knows this."

"I thought he was." Na'Toth winced and gritted her teeth with agony. "His gloves," she said, tears streaming down her cheeks, "they fooled me."

"And if he had been wearing no gloves at all," the Prime asked her, "would you still have thrown your knife at him?"

Na'Toth looked at her and her eyes slowly focused until they were hot with rage. "Yes!" she hissed through clenched teeth.

"So it was no mistake," Olorasin said as she raised the PPG, "when you killed him."

Garibaldi finished setting the charges that would blow the lock on the safe area door. *Thank God these doors don't open upward,* he thought. *Now there'd be a terrific position to be in when you're facing armed terrorists.* He imagined himself saying, "Now hang on a sec, and just look peacefully at our feet while the door rises, then we take care of this, okay?"

The Chief shuddered. *That's the trouble with these terrorists, no sense of humor.*

When he finished, Garibaldi fell back against the wall, where his people had arranged themselves in the best cover pattern conceivable for five operatives charging an incredibly crowded room—held by an unknown number of assailants.

The charge went off with a sharp *snap!* and the smell of burning plastic. Released from the sabotaged locks, the door panels snapped inward into the recesses on either side.

* * *

"You *wanted* to kill my brother," Olorasin said in wondering tones. It was obvious that the Narn would do it again if offered the chance. The Prime was sickened by a cold wave of disgust so profound it was almost physical.

The hand holding the PPG snapped up.

"But I don't want to kill you," she said. Olorasin looked around the room, at her own people, who looked confused and angry, at their frightened prisoners. "Any of you." *Is this mercy, or weakness?* she wondered, and sighed. "It's over," the Prime said. "Give them back their weapons." She handed her PPG to Sheridan.

"No!" Segrea shouted, leveling his PPG at the Prime. His other hand held the deadman switch aloft. "I will not allow it. This is our one chance to strike at the heart of Narn! How can you throw it away like this?"

"What are you going to do, Segrea?" Olorasin asked calmly.

"If you won't fight for us you are useless!" the big T'llin said. "But if you die here, everyone will believe the Narn killed you, just as they did Phina. You will be more use to us as a martyr than as a mewling traitor."

A PPG was thrust up into the soft underpart of his jaw.

"I love you dearly, Segrea," Haelstrac told him. "But I will not let you live to commit the Narn's crimes for them. There's nothing good in your idea, my friend." She reached out and took the PPG from his hand. "Eventually, there has to be a limit to revenge," she said softly.

Turning, she gave the two PPGs to Ivanova.

There was the sound of a small explosion and the leaves of the door slammed open with a grinding sound. Five Earthforce personnel burst into the room, PPGs leveled. At Garibaldi's gesture they fanned out, moving through the gap between crowd and wall where the terrorists were standing. Singularly irresolute terrorists, he thought; their PPGs wavered and then went up in surrender.

"Nobody move!" Garibaldi shouted. "Hands up!"

Everyone just looked at him.

Did'ja ever get that feeling that your surprise has fallen flat? he asked himself, with a horrible feeling of anticlimax. Then he saw the big T'llin with the deadman switch. The alien's face changed, and it was a change Garibaldi had seen before—the calmness of someone who had decided to die.

"No!" he shouted, beginning a charge that he knew would be far too late.

Midori was much closer. Her leap struck the T'llin with the full weight of her body, and she plastered herself to him as they went down, wrapping arms and legs around his torso. The sound of the explosion was loud but horribly muffled. Blood and bits of tissue spattered those closest—but not the white-hot fragments of crystal synthetic that would have sprayed into the crowd if the grenade had not been trapped between two bodies.

"Clear, clear, let me through!" Garibaldi shouted. Then he muttered quietly, *"Damn."* Franklin was kneeling beside her—what was left of her—and several of his people were calling for medics on their links, but it was obvious that not much could be done.

"Okay," Garibaldi said aloud. Quickly assessing the situation, he picked out the T'llin. "You, you, you, drop your weapons, up against the wall!"

"At least when you arrest us this time," Olorasin said to the Captain, "we're actually guilty of some significant wrongdoing."

The crowd was growing loud again and the Ambassadors, their aides, and some of the peace delegates were drifting towards the door.

"Uh." Garibaldi caught Olorasin's sleeve as she moved to join the rest of her people. "There's a code locking the crash doors outside," he said.

"Oh, of course." The Prime spoke a liquid phrase that Garibaldi recorded on his link.

"C and C," Garibaldi said into his link.

"Yes, Sir."

"This recording should open the doors on DB-17." He sent it to the tech.

"Yes, Sir," C and C told him. "That's done it."

"Great." Through the thinning crowd he saw Na'Toth on the floor and someone trying to give her first aid with nothing but a handkerchief. "Get that medical team up here, stat. Garibaldi out."

A dozen more Security people had arrived, and were passing the civilians through the doorway, looking for any T'llin trying to slip by.

Garibaldi made his way over to the Captain.

"What took you so long?" Sheridan asked grimly.

Garibaldi shook his head. "We did our best," he said. He glanced at Midori's body being carried out on a stretcher, a thin-film blanket hiding the terrible mass of her crushed torso. "Some of us did our *very* best."

The head of the Narn delegation brushed by Garibaldi to confront the Captain.

"I demand that these prisoners be turned over to the Narn for disposal," he snarled.

"I'm afraid that's not possible," Sheridan said calmly. "As this incident occurred on Babylon 5 it's in our jurisdiction. They'll be judged by the Ombuds. Assuming they come to trial at all."

"What do you mean? They would have killed us!" the Narn bellowed.

"No!" Sheridan shouted back. "At the last, they couldn't do that. *You* would have killed us in their position. *They* were too civilized. But after they've been in Narn hands for two hundred years, *then* maybe they'll be able to slaughter a room full of innocent people to make a point. Then maybe all of them will be like *him.*" He pointed to Segrea's body, staring with empty blood-flecked eyes at the ceiling.

"How dare . . ."

"I'll give you some advice, Sir. Let them go; let the whole planet go. If you keep persecuting these people they'll be a dagger at your back in this war. And the opening wedge the Centauri will use to crack Narn space wide open. Give them their freedom and they'll most likely remain neutral. Keep them enslaved and you risk everything. Is it worth it?'' Sheridan asked.

The delegation leader appeared too furious to even consider the question. But some of his fellows looked thoughtful, and that gave Sheridan some hope.

''You might also be interested to know that I plan to recommend the Prime Olorasin be given asylum,'' the Captain said.

''And what's the point of that?'' the Narn sneered. ''Without another already recognized species to second such a recommendation it means nothing.''

''Ah, but what you don't know,'' Delenn said, ''is that the Centauri have been contemplating such an action for some time now.'' She looked to the Centauri delegation with a gentle smile.

The Centauri delegation leader looked as if he'd swallowed a whole pineapple, sideways and with the leaves still on it. He shot a glare at Londo, who was wearing his best professional diplomat's face.

''You have, haven't you?'' Sheridan insisted.

The delegation leader drew himself up to his considerable height and opened his mouth.

''Yes,'' Londo said shortly. ''We have.'' Which won him another glare.

Before the Narn leader could do more than begin to bluster, Delenn turned to him and said, ''I think the Minbari may also be willing to unbend sufficiently as to recommend the Prime be given asylum.''

On that soft note, the discussion was effectively ended and the Narn knew it. He bowed sharply to the Captain and Delenn and rejoined G'Kar, who had remained with Na'Toth.

''Well, then,'' Londo said, clapping his hands together and rubbing them. ''Perhaps we should get out of the Security people's way. If you ladies and gentlemen would care to join me in my quarters for a restorative drink?'' He gestured and the Centauri delegation began to move off. "I have just acquired the most fascinating item," he said loud enough for G'Kar to hear.

The Narn Ambassador's head came up in shock.

"My esteemed colleague, Ambassador G'Kar, was most interested in it. But apparently lost his nerve while bidding on the item."

The Centauri moved off in a chorus of appreciative chuckles.

G'Kar and the Narn delegates followed Na'Toth's stretcher out, breathing heavily and clenching their fists.

Garibaldi cocked an eyebrow at the Captain.

"So much for the peace in the peace conference."

Sheridan sighed. "Yup. I suspect things will stay pretty much the same," he agreed.

"Oh, I would not say that," Delenn said, looking up at them. "The Narn on T'll will now be operating under the glare of publicity. Even now, that will make some difference."

"Oh, I can pretty much guarantee that there will be a lot of publicity," Chancy said, coming up to them. Her camera hovered over her. "And I've got every word the delegations said on record. So they might even feel obliged to stick to some of what they resolved today."

"That may be a little too much to ask," Ivanova said with a smile. "But maybe the T'llin, at least, have cause for hope."

"I think so," Delenn agreed, thoughtfully. "No one approves of what the Narn are doing there. I think that they will at least moderate their behavior . . . a little. They are a young species and fiercely proud. They are not fond of public humiliation."

"And who knows," Sheridan said, his brow furrowed, "maybe they learned something about themselves today that will prevent them from creating another T'll."

"It would be nice to think that peace has gained some

ground today,'' Ivanova said with a sigh. ''Unfortunately I doubt it.''

''Yes,'' Chancy agreed. ''This hasn't been a total waste of time at all.''

They all looked at her.

''Bye,'' she said cheerfully and left the safe area, her camera following like a devoted puppy.

I wonder what she meant by that? Sheridan wondered. He caught Garibaldi's eye and knew the Chief was thinking the same thing.

''Well,'' Garibaldi said. ''I've got some more T'llin prisoners to process. So if you'll excuse me, I've got to go to work.''

''More?'' Delenn asked.

''There are some in protective custody,'' Sheridan told her.

''We must discuss this,'' she said.

''Yes. Let's,'' he agreed and offered her his arm.

After a moment's hesitation, she took it, and as they walked away, Sheridan began to tell her the whole story.

''Behold!'' Londo said gaily as he pried off the top of the box. *Now I can safely brag.* Just for this select audience. Nothing would ever come out in public, but those in the know—people of real importance—would understand what he had done for the Republic . . .

Once the top was off the four sides fell flat, revealing . . .

''What is that?'' the delegation leader asked.

''It's a cake,'' Londo said. He was amazed that he could talk, because his face felt paralyzed. *I have paid a million credits for a cake,* he thought. *I will kill her slowly!*

''A *cake*?'' the leader repeated. ''Is this the item that the Narn was bidding on?''

''No, no. I only said that to 'jerk G'Kar's chain,' as the humans say. The item in question was not worth the asking price.'' *What have I done?*

"A cake in the shape of the Eye of Empire?" a venerable old Dame exclaimed. "I think that's in rather poor taste, Londo," she said severely.

But she would know *that I will kill her,* he thought. The carefully timed handover, with no second to spare . . . and it was impossible that she be able to get off Babylon 5, but there must be some means. And he would have to make up the cost of the Eye . . .

"I . . ." *Have lost virtually my entire fortune!* Londo thought. "I have been among humans for too long," he explained weakly. "They are irreverent creatures. And this is one of their customs. They make cakes in the form of important landmarks, or even portraits of their friends, and they eat them. They think it is all very jolly, but I can see now that it *is* in bad taste. Here," he said, picking it up. "I'll remove it."

Londo picked it up and hurried to his bathing area, sliding the door closed behind him. He put the thing down on the counter and stared at it, whimpering softly.

Then with a sudden rush of fury he smashed his fist down onto it, and saw a folded note among the ruins. He picked it up slowly and unfolded it.

Hi, Baby,
    I've left the station, so don't bother looking for me. If you'd been nice to me I'd have left you a little something worth at least half what you gave me. I picked it up cheap, so I thought, why not?
    But you were a fink instead, so this is your punishment. Always remember, Londo, it's impossible to flimflam an honest man. Not that I can vouch for that since I've never met one. And neither will you if you stay in politics.
    So take your lumps and stay as sweet as you are, sugar.
    Thanks for the credits.

                                        Kiss, kiss,
                                        Semana.

Londo lowered his hand and stared into space, wondering if it was worth a million credits to avoid the "I told you so" look that Garibaldi was sure to give him.

He folded the note and put it in his pocket. Then scraped the remains of the cake into the disposal and wiped his hand with a towel.

I can't think about this today, he thought with a sigh. *I'll consider it tomorrow. After all—as my mother used to say— tomorrow is another day.*

Commander Susan Ivanova raised her glass and chinked it gently against Garibaldi's.

"To Midori," she said.

"A credit to the uniform," Garibaldi said.

They drank, she sipping the hot *sake,* he his water, and set their cups down. There was a ring of empty tables around them; the gloomy quiet of the bar suited their mood.

"I don't envy you, having to write to her parents," she said.

Garibaldi grimaced. "No. Although . . . it's odd, but Ambassador Delenn said *she* wanted to write them. Something about an obligation."

Ivanova shook her head and sighed. "It's been a hell of a week. I had a series of revelations about my family that never happened, the peace conference came up with a peace that won't even be *mentioned,* much less implemented, and three people are dead."

"A nutcase, a terrorist, and a damned fine Earthforce sergeant," Garibaldi said. "She did her very best."

"Nobody can do more," Ivanova said.

Almost simultaneously, their links chirped. They met each other's eyes and smiled.

"No rest for the wicked," Garibaldi said.

"Or the rest of us," Ivanova replied.